'A wonderful writer. These stori
so skilfully balanced and interv
to pick out the pattern it is a .... of delight'

Hilary Mantel

'Morrissy bewitches the reader with an immaculate yet irreverent turn of phrase, her imagination slanted at a rare angle'

Daily Mail

'All human life is there in Prosperity Drive... Morrissy is not without humour, sometimes offering laugh-out-loud observations. But the undercurrent throughout brings to mind Thoreau's line about most men (and women) living lives of quiet desperation. Her style, her intense moments of close clinical dissection, reminds me a little of John Banville. But she shows more compassion for her cast of characters, perhaps not unlike Alice Munro... It's a magnificent read'

Irish Independent

'One of the best Irish books you'll read this year'

Sunday Business Post

'Story by story Morrissy stitches together a hundred tiny plots, moving backwards and forwards across 60 years, and outwards to Italy, America, Australia and Vietnam... Morrissy proves herself a steady observer of the bleakness of everyday life, as well as when bleakness becomes catastrophe'

Observer

'Makes for exquisite reading... We are left with the urge to go back and read the book again as so many layers of meaning and possible interpretations co-exist inside the tome... Morrissy succeeds in creating a deeply moving work here, one that remains in the mind and the heart'

Headstuff

'Mary Morrissy ranks among the very best...how she writes!'

Fay Weldon

'A master of language, she is also a keen observer of human nature... I simply loved these stories for their diversity... Sheer perfection throughout... She has the same forensic eye for detail; the same analytical touch, and sleight of language, allied with a quite astonishing ability to get inside her characters' minds'

Irish Examiner

'One of Ireland's finest writers'

Penelope Fitzgerald

MARY MORRISSY

Mary Morrissy has published three novels – *Mother of Pearl*, *The Pretender* and *The Rising of Bella Casey* – and a collection of short stories, *A Lazy Eye* (1993). She has won a Hennessy Award and a Lannan Literary Foundation Award and currently teaches at University College Cork.

www.marymorrissy.com

ALSO BY MARY MORRISSY

A Lazy Eye
Mother of Pearl
The Pretender
The Rising of Bella Casey

MARY MORRISSY

Prosperity Drive

VINTAGE

1 3 5 7 9 10 8 6 4 2

Vintage
20 Vauxhall Bridge Road,
London SW1V 2SA

Vintage is part of the Penguin Random House
group of companies whose addresses can be found at
global.penguinrandomhouse.com

First published in Vintage in 2017
First published in hardback by Jonathan Cape in 2016

A CIP catalogue record for this book
is available from the British Library

ISBN 9781784700577

Printed and bound in Great Britain by Clays Ltd, St Ives plc

Penguin Random House is committed to a sustainable future
for our business, our readers and our planet. This book is made
from Forest Stewardship Council® certified paper.

for Colbert

CONTENTS

THE SCREAM

She is lying at the top of the stairs, her shoulder crushed against the newel post, her hands clawing for the banister. Her hair is fanned about her. It is too long; she would never have let it grow this much, though Norah – or is it the nurse, the foreign girl? – keeps it clean. The shampoo they use smells of nettles; she gets whiffs of it now as if she were lying in a field. She cannot remember the last time she had colour in her hair, though once she would have been particular about such things. Was it weeks ago, or months? Time has bloated and clogged. These days, oddly, it is only when she has fallen that she comes to her senses. It brings her to know mostly the unpalatable. Just now, for example, a flight below – down to the return, then down again – sitting at the kitchen table is her daughter watching a small portable TV while she lies here, stricken.

A microwave with pictures is how Norah has described it. It is one of the new things that has been added to the house.

'So you can have the big TV upstairs,' Norah had said, 'all to yourself.'

The ground floor of her own house is a mystery to her now, like upstairs might be to a child frightened of the dark. It is so long since she's been in the kitchen that she has to work to imagine it. In her mind's eye she sees it flooded with a gauzy early morning light coming in through the French window Victor had installed forty years ago when the walls smelled of lime and the house had a bald, ripening air; as did their lives.

Norah is at the table, a pale full moon of melamine on a tubular pod – unless it has been changed too – eating a meal. She can hear the lonely scrape of cutlery. Norah had brought dinner upstairs to her on a tray earlier and had fed her, spoon by spoon, though she hadn't much interest. Appetite evades her these days. In the end Norah had whipped the dish away. Or was that the nurse? Sometimes she gets them mixed up.

She may be confused about some things, but just now, Edel Elworthy – that is her name, she is sure of that – knows that as she lies here, her daughter has turned up the volume on the TV. She can hear the unctuous urgency of a hair advertisement – gloss and sheen and self-worth all rolled into one voice of honey – and she knows that Norah is deliberately ignoring her.

It isn't as if Norah doesn't know she's fallen. When Edel falls, she finds herself making whimpering sounds; they seem to just come out of her as if the child in her is talking. Which is the opposite to what she feels. Because when she's stretched like this, incapable and dependent, everything else about her situation is for once, clear; luminously so. It's one of the reasons she tries to get out of bed, against Norah's wishes and the strict command of the nurse. Because once she's upright she feels a clarifying rush in her head just as the power drains from her legs. It's a sensation like flying, but sickening like vertigo. And there's an exhilaration in it too, a nauseous euphoria. She's not aware of even wanting to be vertical until she's out of bed on mottled legs that seem so gelid and blue they can't be hers. And then before she crashes, there's another sensation, a monstrous feeling like the discovery of a squalid secret. And then she goes down.

She imagines what she must look like to Norah, or the nurse, or whoever might be looking down at her. Everyone has an arm's length view, people trying to keep their distance. Her hair wild and ragged like an ancient wizard's, her mouth open – it must be, she's making noises – her body gnarled and frozen in this arch and petrified pose. She thinks of a poster one of the girls used to have tacked on to the wall of their bedroom when they were teenagers. She can't remember if it was Trish or Norah. (Even before this calamity their combined adolescence had blurred into a general fug of secretive passions and obstinate grievance.) It was a picture of a creature painted in a wavery, sick kind of way; it must have been Trish, she was the arty one. Edel couldn't even tell if it was meant to be human. It had big hollows for eyes, its paws clasped in horror to its cheeks and its mouth open emitting the soundless howl of a nightmare. Maybe that's what people do now when they see her, hold their hands up in horror and scream silently? Or is that creature her? Though she *is* making sounds and drooling on her quilted breast, and Norah knows and still won't come.

Between her and Norah is the cupboard under the stairs. She can hear Norah rummaging in there sometimes. Well, it is where the Hoover is kept as well as the iron and board, a box with shoe polish and rags, tins of gumption and cartons of detergent giving its normal musty smell a purged overtone. One of the first things Norah did when she moved back in was to get a light installed in there with a 100-watt bulb, though Edel is sure that 60 watts is all the fixture can take.

'So that we can see what's in there,' Norah explained.

Edel knows what's in there. Boxes of old Christmas decorations, tangled threads of fairy lights, Victor's dressing gown packed in tissue paper because she couldn't bear to part with it. Her own wedding veil – for one of the girls, she had thought. Something borrowed. Or something old. But Norah didn't want it and Trish showed no inclination to walk down the aisle. There is Victor's toolbox – he was handy, she'll give him that – still with its trays of nails and washers, its accordion floors packed with chisels and screwdrivers and tins of 3-in-One oil. There are brooms and mops and dustpans, her gardening shoes, spare bulbs, some defunct lampshades – quite sound but out of fashion now. It's not chaotic; well, it wasn't the last time Edel was in there. No, it was always orderly. But it is the only place in the house where useless things are still kept – too good to throw out, but not old or precious enough to be of value.

Usually, as soon as Edel hits the floor, Norah is up to rescue her. She rarely even gets to the top of the stairs, but lately, Edel notices, her response has become slower. It is as if she knows Edel is deliberately defying her. And once Edel is lying down again she can't explain, not when Norah has manoeuvred her back into bed with a firmness of touch that seems, somehow, more impersonal than the nurse's. Not when Norah is looming over her. Edel doesn't have the words in her head then for the sensation of clarity that comes over her when she is upright.

She thinks she understands why lately Norah has refused to come running. Payback. When the girls were babies and woke in the night and she was an exhausted young mother, she would often lie in bed just listening. She would be wide awake but resistant to the drowsy peeved wails of Norah or Trish. Often it was Victor who, just shortly abed from the night shift, would nudge her in the ribs and say: 'Edel, it's Norah.'

Victor always knew which one of them was calling. She'd tell herself that it was only laziness that kept her horizontal, or the hope that it was one of those cries that might die away rather than rev up into something more hostile and aggrieved, but she knows, too, there was sadism in her refusal. Let them cry for a bit, she would think, why don't I just let them cry.

If Norah would come now, Edel might be able to say what she gets up to say every time she makes one of her escape attempts. She would say to Norah – thirty-seven last birthday, she thinks – remember when you were a little girl? A few times she has managed to blurt out these words but Norah has only hushed her. Then she leans down and with great effort – Edel is not heavy but she's a dead weight – puts her arms under Edel's shoulders and lifts her with that brusque tenderness Edel has come to know as her elder daughter's signature touch.

'Try not to talk,' Norah always says.

And Edel surrenders, saying to herself, not to worry, Norah knows, she knows already.

Victor said she was too hard on the girls. Her word carried weight – a sharp smack on the bottom or across the back of the legs. It was how children were brought up in those days. And it was how Victor had been raised. His mother, revered for her sanctimonious indulgence and his father, stern and forbidding, who used his belt when it was necessary. He wasn't cruel, Victor used to say, he was efficient. It pained his father to punish them and so it was done in silence. Children were meant to be subdued, Victor would say, we were dealt with, not talked to. His father thought most people – particularly women – talked too much. Yack, yack, yack, he would mime when he came across Edel and her mother-in-law trading stories about Victor. This was in the early days of her marriage and Edel liked to discuss Victor with anyone who'd listen. His mother was a natural ally in this. Victor was her favourite and she talked of her eldest son as if she was similarly smitten. After a while, Edel felt they were like a pair of teenagers nursing a crush that could only be deliciously speculated about but never requited. Victor's father, emphysemic and tethered to his tank of air, said listening to them made him breathless. When the children came, Edel was pleased to see how good a father Victor was and how much he wanted to help. If the girls misbehave, he would say to her, I'll talk to them. So though it was Edel who would send them under the stairs for

5

serious wrongdoing – tantrums, smacking one another, giving cheek – it was Victor who dealt with them. He talked to them in the velvet darkness.

She'd only opened the door a fraction. It was a partial view, she kept telling herself, years afterwards. A sliver. She'd sent Norah in there for backchat. Norah was six and had acquired a stubborn lower lip and a fascination with the word 'no' since starting school. She was Edel's firstborn, a blackberry of a child, with her dark brown eyes and almost black hair and her ripe cheeks and her little breathy voice with its appealing hoarseness. That day – it was a humid summer's day, hot and broodily grey after days of rain as the sun tried to burn away the cloud – Norah had run into the garden and sunk up to her ankles in the newly rotovated earth. Victor was only then getting round to the garden. For the first six years they were in the house, the garden was a wilderness, choked with weeds and scutch grass growing up around the builders' debris. Now Victor had taken it in hand and it was a churned-up mess, a ploughed field rather than the manicured lawn and privet hedges Edel had in mind. These things take time, Victor had said. But the earth had been turned in April; now it was June and no progress had been made. New shoots of grass were already growing in the overturned clods.

Norah had a high-tide mark of mud on her legs and was refusing to change her socks and sandals. Trish had just woken from her nap and was being grizzly about her food. When Edel told Norah a second time, instead of ignoring her, Norah simply said no. Then she stamped her foot and, for good measure, said no again. Edel caught Norah by a dimpled arm and with Trish straddled awkwardly across her hip, busily making a sodden pulp of a rusk in her fist, Edel opened the door under the stairs and propelled Norah inside. She was rougher than she had intended to be, but she was furious. Norah always seemed to play up when Edel had her hands

6

full, as if she sensed Edel's fluster. Edel swiftly locked the door and breathed a sigh of relief with her back to it. Norah beat on the door with her fists and started to bawl. Tears of injustice and complaint and, of course, then Trish chimed in. Victor's head appeared over the banisters. Freshly out of bed and in the middle of shaving, his face was awash with lather.

'Jesus, Edel, what the hell is going on?'

She felt tears sprout in her own eyes.

'It's Norah,' she wailed like a wronged child, 'she just will not do as she is told.'

Victor sighed.

'Let me finish this,' he said above the din, 'and I'll talk to her.'

She went back into the kitchen, set Trish down unceremoniously on the high chair, and wiped the child's face clean of the mealy mess. Then she took two or three deep breaths. She hated Victor to see her like this as if she were unable to manage her own children. As if she needed some kind of supervision. She stepped out into the yard, a small apron of concrete beyond the kitchen door bounded on one side by two outhouses – one a lavatory, the other a coal bunker. Thanks to Victor, this was what they were reduced to for a place for the children to play. It was a real sun trap, though, and the next-door neighbour's roses hung over the wall and dropped their petals on the Elworthys' side. Unlike Edel, Miss Larchet had plenty of time to cultivate her garden. The petals gave the place an exotic air. Edel imagined a lover scattering them for her. The sun broke free of the gunmetal clouds. She thought she would sit out in the gratifying sun for a bit, until she had calmed down. It was a chore moving the high chair out and finding a shady spot so that Trish would not be scorched in the early afternoon heat. Having dispensed with the rusk, Trish had decided she wanted a drink so Edel had to retreat into the kitchen to make up a bottle. All was quiet within, she noticed, and she relented on her hardness of heart against

Norah and decided to fetch her out and interest her in doing something with the fragrant petals strewn in the yard.

Before she had opened the door she heard the low murmur of talk within. She inched it open a fraction. It was Norah she saw first, astride her father's knee. He was down on his hunkers. She had one arm resting on Victor's bare shoulder – he was still in his vest, his newly ironed shirt was hanging in the kitchen – the other one entwined around his neck. Norah was wearing that nice, smocked sundress that had come in a parcel from America with the little cap sleeve slightly off the shoulder and her head was turned at an angle that Edel could only describe to herself afterwards as seductive, her shoulder cocked like a model posing for a calendar. Her little leg was dangling – she seemed to have shed the sandals and socks – and her small, plump foot was cupped lovingly – that was the only word she could use – in Victor's hand. And then one of them, Edel didn't know which one, maybe Victor with his fist, slammed the door shut on her. She backed off, feeling as if she'd been struck. The low murmur resumed inside. She hurried back through the kitchen and stood in the small yard among the fallen petals trying to quell the quick pulse of alarm racing through her. Trish had fallen asleep at a comical angle, one arm flung over the side of the high chair, the other bunched at her heart in a fistful of terry-towelling bib. She didn't know how long she had stood there when Victor came to the back door.

'There, see,' he said, 'everything's quiet now. I've told her she's got to stay in there for another ten minutes.'

Edel turned slowly. Victor was busily buttoning up his shirt; she could see the crease lines on the sleeves that she had left with the iron.

'You've got to talk to her, Edel, that's what does the trick,' he said, giving her a look she couldn't decipher.

She suddenly felt adrift in her own world, as if her under-standing had slipped its moorings. Victor spoke to her as if in rebuke but the expression on his face, where had she seen that before? After making love, that's when; just after he had relieved himself. That's how it always seemed to Edel, as if relief was the most explicit proof of Victor's affections. As long as she saw that look of rueful satisfaction, Edel was happy. It was enough.

With Victor gone, the house returned to a squeamish silence. Edel went to fetch Norah. Victor had not locked the door but Norah had stayed inside in the gloom, sitting on an upturned orange box, still barefoot and crooning to herself, which stopped as soon as Edel opened the door. Norah looked up. Her face was rapt, blissful. It startled Edel. Norah's socks like grubby slugs were on the floor, as were her sandals, the buckles still tied as if they had been torn off in a hurry. Edel quelled her irritation – she was forever telling Norah that she would ruin her shoes if she didn't open the buckles. But it wasn't Norah she was irritated with, but Victor; he'd obviously encouraged her.

'Well,' Edel said, 'don't you want to come out? Trish and I are in the garden.'

'No,' Norah said simply, without the usual jib of her mouth.

The air inside the room was stuffy and rank. And Norah, despite her persistent negatives, was placid now, appeased, her 'no' dreamy and abstracted. No amount of *her* talk, Edel realised, could produce this kind of calm.

She blamed it on the day, two children made stroppy by the thundery heat, her own fearfulness about Vic as she called him when they were alone or in bed. It returned him to the perilously good-looking man she'd fallen in love with. She worried about his night-time life, the shifts at the newspaper. Putting the paper to bed. Even that had an illicit air as if his very work were about conquest. But she was lucky; not every wife knew for sure where her husband was at night. Afterwards, though, she watched Norah. No, she watched

9

them together. The tip and tig in the garden when finally he put grass down, the Sundays in the paddling pool, the bedtime stories when Victor was around to tell them. She manoeuvred him out of bath-times. Only in the car did she relax. There Victor had strict rules; he became his father behind the wheel. In the back even *their* children were subdued, Edel noticed. But she never saw that look on Norah's face again. Though perhaps – and this tormented her more – Norah had learned to hide it.

Four years later, Victor was diagnosed. He couldn't bear to be touched. The chemo had given him thrush in his mouth. But often in the afternoons she would find the pair of them snuggled up on the sofa together, Victor, bald and bloated, spooning up to Norah in another dark room. The light gave him headaches, he said. Norah had filled out, turning to puppy fat that had dampened down all her fiery little-girlness. Clothed in her protective shell of flesh she seemed more childlike than the sassy, nay-saying six-year-old. There's so little time, Victor would say, a dumb terror flickering across his distorted features, as he cupped the children's heads or threaded their fine hair through his fingers. It was the only time he acknowledged the truth – mostly he just toughed it out – so how could Edel refuse him? But towards the end, she had sent Trish away. Irene Devoy had offered to take her on holiday to Courtown with her boys.

'Better,' she told Irene, 'that Trish isn't around all this sickness . . .'

Suddenly, it is all flurry. Norah bounds up the stairs, elbows her way under Edel's shoulders so that she is propped now on Norah's lap. The effort has winded Norah and so they sit there like some afflicted representation of the Pietà, Edel thinks. Norah rubs the papery skin of her legs, which are bare and goose-pimpled. Her slippers seem to have got lost in the fall and Norah tries to work some feeling back into her frigid feet.

Remember, Edel begins, remember, but the sound she makes is a gurgle. Norah strokes her hair.

Remember, Edel tries again.

'Mother,' Norah half-croons, half-sighs, a tender reprimand. 'Mother.'

Edel feels herself lapsing, sinking.

Remember . . .

Gone now the beautiful clarity.

Remember, remember, remember what?

THE GENDER OF CARS

Fat Norah Elworthy sits on the bonnet of the family car. It is a black Austin, portly, round-bottomed and it sits brooding in the garage. It has not been moved for months, not since her father died. A stepladder is lodged near the passenger door, leaning up against the wall. By the boot, several bulging bags of coal nuzzle. The old fridge, white and enormous, has been wedged up against the front bumper, its open door emitting a polar yawn. A green hose coiled loosely around a nail on an overhead beam drips lazily down, grazing the car's roof. It's as if these items know the failing power of the car, as they move in to colonise new territory.

Norah sits splay-legged so that her calves bulge out on the glossy surface. She leans back against the windscreen, clutching the edges to steady herself, trying to ape the sinuous drape of a starlet at a motor show. But it is too awkward a pose and after a few minutes she straightens up and sits cross-legged instead. Her father would have a fit if he could see this. The car was his pride and joy, washed and tended to like a baby, the leather interior polished, the dashboard dusted. Clambering up on it was expressly forbidden. Even inside the car, she and Trish were not allowed to put their feet on the seats for fear their shoe buckles would scrape the leather.

It is hot and airless inside the dark garage. A broiling summer's day has driven Norah inside to seek shade, and solace, oddly. The beloved car is like a temple, some male essence of her father enshrined in it. And its days are numbered. It is going to be sold. Norah's mother does not drive and as she says matter-of-factly – talking to herself though in the children's presence – no point in letting it rust away in the garage.

Norah supposes her mother needs the money. At eleven she has a hazy idea of adult finances but without a bread-winner – this is how her mother refers to her father in company as if he had been engaged in some kind of floury lottery – belts will have to be tightened. Whatever that means. Well, it means selling the car, for one. Her mother puts an ad in the paper. One careful owner, it says. Her father had traded in his Zodiac to buy the Austin A40. He used to talk about the sherbet-coloured predecessor as if she were a brassy blonde. (Cars and boats are always she, her father used to say.) The Zodiac was apparently sporty-looking with flashy fins and banquette seats. A young man's plaything, her mother had said, not a family car.

Men with hats have been calling round to look it over: a neighbour cranks it up and reverses it out into the driveway for these occasions. These men walk up and down, frowning at the rusting foreparts. They rap their knuckles on the exterior and kick the tyres. They tut-tut when the engine is slow to start.

'The battery,' her mother offers in a helpless kind of voice.

Norah detects an unseemly kind of courtship in this, as if the selling of the car is a ploy to acquire a new father for them. She is having none of it. She is autocratic about their loss. She will not stand to listen to her mother talk fondly of the past. Mrs Devoy, their honey-haired neighbour, encourages her mother's nostalgia. Norah has come across them in the kitchen, nursing cups of instant coffee, while her mother softens and grows tearful. Norah shoots her mother a warning glance, and if that doesn't work, she leaves the room abruptly. Her mother's grief is too threatening. Norah feels it is her duty to guard against disintegration.

But selling the car is another thing. It is too irreverent, too pragmatic. As long as Norah knows that the car sits there, albeit fading to a dusty pallor, its oiled working parts slowly deteriorating, its battery going dead, some process is still going on. Decay, reduction. She wants to watch that, she wants to see her father fade away, to lose his authority, his power. She wants to see the ephemera of the house already encroaching on the car to take over, to bury it completely. Her father's vanity, eclipsed.

He was a printer. He worked the night shift at the *Press*, disappearing after a mid-afternoon dinner and not returning until the small hours. On the days he wasn't working he would examine the newspaper forensically, not reading it but hunting down widows and orphans. These were stray singular words, or sometimes pairs, left stranded on the top or bottom of columns. A complete no-no, he would say. Who let this through, he would demand, smacking the offending page with the back of his hand. It grieved him, this absence of symmetry. After he died, the *Press* ran a brief obituary. He leaves a wife and two daughters, it read.

One of the men in hats finally comes up trumps. He and her mother haggle on the driveway. Gone now the flirtatious tone of distress.

'My late husband was very mechanically minded. The engine is clean as a whistle. And, as you can see, not a mark on the bodywork,' she says proudly. 'He was devoted to it.'

Devoted to *her*, Norah wants to say.

She cannot believe the car is actually going to be sold. She thought her mother's air of plaintive ineptitude would make the men in hats think she was trying to sell them a pup. But no, this large bald man (he has taken his hat off and it sits territorially on the roof of the car) is now patting his chest pocket in search of a pen to write out a cheque. Norah, standing at the other side of the car, wants to raise her hand

14

and say stop in a commanding tone that will make the adults pause, and obey. But though she can stem the slow tide of her mother's mourning with an angry glare, she cannot battle against the calculated transactions of survival.

'Come inside, won't you?' her mother says to the man.

Norah loiters outside as the man follows her mother into the house. When they are out of sight, she fishes out a coin from her pocket and digs it into the Austin's paintwork. She draws a line from the front passenger door backwards, a searing, silent protest. Spite fuels her, or is it revenge? Whatever it is, it is deeply satisfying. When the man emerges, she is sitting on the garden wall, legs swinging. She smiles sweetly and waves as he reverses the Austin out on to the road. He drives off unaware of the damage she has done on his blind side.

Norah Elworthy, seventeen, is going out on her first date. She is slimmer now, her puppy fat having fallen away. She thinks, of course, that her thighs are too big, and wishes she could fit into a size 12 and a B cup. She has just stopped being a schoolgirl. The intervening years have been unremarkable. They have passed in a blur of brisk normality, a normality Norah's mother considers a triumph. Your father would have been proud of the way we've managed, her mother says, generously including both Norah and Trish in the achievement. There is still an air of financial hazard, unspecified but ever present. The absence of a breadwinner, Norah has learned, does not mean that they've gone hungry. But there is a constant impoverishment of confidence. Nothing is ever as solid again. This is what not having a father means.

What has changed is that Norah would now welcome the chance to share in her mother's ruminative wistfulness that once seemed so dangerous. She would like to be the companion in the kitchen talking about the fleeting and seemingly unnecessary presence that their managing has reduced her father to. But it is too late for that. Having fended off the bereaved companionship her mother offered, she is left only with a field of combat.

'What do we know about this boy?' her mother asks, standing by the bedroom door as Norah wrestles into a pair of jeans.

'Nothing,' Norah replies. 'That's the whole point.' Then she relents. 'I told you I met him at the bicycle shop.'

He mended her puncture then asked her out.

'A bicycle mechanic, that's all we need,' her mother says, sighing.

'I'm not marrying him, Mother,' Norah says, 'we're just going out.'

She feels a fluttering anticipation. She could soon be engaged in a romance, a hazy notion of chaste kisses and hand-holding.

'He has a car,' she adds, as proof of his suitability.

His name is Dave. At twenty-one, he is enormously older than her. He is small, dapper-looking with a little goatee beard and moustache and he is wearing a suit and tie, which he straightens as he sits into his squat, low-slung Mini, catching his reflection in the wing mirror. Norah feels scruffy and more knowing than she is. She regrets not having worn a dress.

'Why don't we go for a drive first?' he says as she gets in beside him.

It is the dirtiest car she has ever been in. Motor magazines with lurid covers, maps and pieces of paper wash up on the floor. In the dish-like dashboard a bruised apple sits, some leaking pens, a half-eaten sandwich, a blackened cloth, a silvery spanner. There is an oily smell and something else, something rancid like milk gone off. But he seems hardly to notice so she stifles her disgust.

'Nice car,' she says.

'Oh, it's just a runaround.'

She's just a runaround, Norah corrects him in her head.

'I don't know much about cars,' she says and immediately regrets it. She has successfully stubbed out the conversation. He drives rakishly, too fast she thinks, but she is glad that he is taking charge. She concentrates on the exterior, the neon-lit suburbs giving way to overgrown country lanes.

'I know just the spot,' he says, 'you can see the whole city spread out, the lights and the harbour. A lovers' lane,' he adds, looking at her and smiling slyly.

The word lovers frightens her.

They are climbing now into the foothills that overlook the city. Through the gaps in the hedges she can see the intricate embroidery of lights as if sewn on to the inky sky. He takes a sudden left turn and drives in an extravagant arc on to a gravelled open space. They come to a piercing halt at a metal barrier and he switches the engine off. The keyring jangles nervously in the ignition. They sit for several minutes in the busy darkness. She is about to admire the view when he shifts, reaching his arm across and dragging her towards him.

'Come here,' he says.

He crushes his bristly mouth on hers while he fumbles with his fly.

'Here,' he commands, 'take this.'

He forces her free hand down on his penis, wrapping her fingers expertly round it and thrusting with his own hand. He has stopped kissing her now and she gazes at the moon face of the speedometer while he works away fiercely. The spanner on the dash glints dully. Within minutes he has come. Her fingers are a mess of clammy ooze.

'I've been waiting for that all week,' he says, sighing luxuriantly.

He gazes ahead as if the twinkling panorama was what he'd been missing. Her hand still rests on his thigh. She is afraid to move it. He rummages in his pocket and produces a hand-kerchief which he uses to wipe himself off, then hands it to her. She finds herself saying thank you. He zips up and then puts the car into reverse and with a great screech of wheels he spins it around and roars back out on to the road again.

He tries small talk on the way back. How many in her family, what she's going to do next, his job at the bike shop. What he really wants to be is a car mechanic and run a garage of his own.

'What about a drink?' he asks.

Norah knows she cannot face that, not after this brute business between them.

'No,' she says, 'I think you should drop me home. My mother will worry.'

Shamefully, she is back in Prosperity Drive by nine o'clock. As she gets out of the car she grabs the spanner from its nest of litter on the dashboard.

'Going to put a spanner in the works?' he jokes.

She walks around to his side of the car. He rolls down the window – is he expecting a kiss? – and sticks his head out companionably then withdraws it quickly as Norah lifts the spanner and smashes the wing mirror in one deft swipe.

'Hey!' he says.

His reflection is splintered into a malevolent spider's web.

'Cars,' she yells at him. 'Cars are *she*!'

LOT'S WIFE

The YMCA was like coming home, in a weird unwanted way. Well, he *was* a Catholic, and a man, and if you counted thirty-eight as young (habitual covering-up can make your life *seem* long) then he qualified on all counts. They started him small with **Polliwogs** (*Get your child acquainted with the pool, introduce them to front paddlestroke and wetball*). He couldn't believe his luck. Angels with water wings. Little legs cycling chubbily in the blue, fat digits clutching his shoulders. All glorious trust for him – Gabe Vance. Mister Vance to the kiddies. The Y insists on it, Yelena Markova had told him with a Brighton Beach twang. Miss this, Miss that, she sneered. He was disappointed she hadn't a trace of the treacly Slavic accent her name suggested. She was a fiercely angular woman – no, girl, he would have said – with a cruel mouth and bleached tresses. How did she maintain them, he wondered; as a veteran he knew what a lethal cocktail pool chlorine and hair colour was. Back home he used to teach Seniors' Sessions. The old birds' hair turned copper and ochre and all class of strange lurid hues because of the chemical mix. He recalls with a shiver their lumpy bodies squeezed into Lycra, bulging arms, gnarled hands threaded with blue-rinse veins. Bunions shiny as tubers and knees flapping like elephants' ears. He remembers mostly the banality of decay.

He'd opted for the elderly at a time when he was still struggling with his . . . predilections. When he still believed; believed in a cure, that is. When he had thought that staying out of the way of temptation could save him and avoidance might banish his worst cravings. But the withdrawal symptoms had been agony; not being in contact with children every day had made him distraught and reckless. That time at the Municipal Baths – long after he'd left the seminary – he'd almost been ruined sneaking into the female changing rooms. A convent school had rented the pool out. He'd hidden in an empty cubicle dragging a CLEANING IN PROGRESS sign across its mouth and pulled the curtains to. His feet had given him away. His size tens under the jellyfish hem of the curtain. A fat girl, plump and juicy, her towel wrapped like a tube around her, sneaked up on him and poked her head slyly through the crack in the curtains he was using to peer out. Fish eyes met. She let out a piercing shriek and dropped the towel, revealing her ample puppy-fat thighs, her chillingly bare pubes. It was worth it, well, almost.

'There's a man in there,' she yelled, pointing a finger while he shrank into a corner of his dank, wet little room. 'Miss Malone, there's a . . .'

There was a kerfuffle, the flurry of little girls' wet feet slapping on tile – he was surrounded by babble, a tableau of pink, offended-looking damp flesh and gaping chatter. He squared his shoulders, straightened his tracksuit bottoms and yanked the curtains from their moorings with a decisive whiplash. The metal rings screamed as if they'd been molested; a whistle blew. Miss Malone strode in – a ramrod-straight greyhound of a woman with steely hair. Spare and lean.

'What, sir, are you doing in here?'

The Sir threw him off. Last time he'd heard Sir was at school – Yes Sir, No Sir, three bags full Sir. *Mister Vance, Sir* – rich with polite irony and armed with a cane – *bend over*.

'Maintenance,' he said. 'Curtains.' He gestured emptily to the still shivering rings and added Ma'am to match her Sir.

20

'Can't you see there are children here?' she demanded, placing a protective manacle on the shoulder of the one who'd caught him out. Oh yes, he wanted to say.

'Very sorry, Ma'am,' he answered, backing away, stumbling into the foot-bath, fumes of disinfectant reaching his nostrils while he fumbled blindly behind him for the door to the pool. The girls tittered. How quickly he had turned from bogeyman to figure of fun.

'I've a good mind, young man . . .' Miss Malone began and he thought, I must stop her.

'The manager told me the pool was free. I'm very sorry, Ma'am. Please don't tell the manager or else I'll lose . . .'

'Very well,' she interrupted. He knew she was the type who could not bear abjection. 'On your way.'

That was when he knew that abstinence was not the answer.

All behind him now. New life, new country, fresh start. Here at the Y on 21st Street, Yelena Markova by his side and a classful of bobbing **Guppies** in the pool. *Leave the flotation devices behind! Learn to synchronise basic strokes!* The Y likes to exhort, some old evangelism still at work, even with seven-year-olds. About the age he was when he got his first inkling. You're kidding, his American friends say, the ones he trusts enough to tell. He's wary, obviously. You knew at seven? It is the age of reason, he starts, then starts again. Well, I was being groomed. That's the way it was, even in the Sixties. His Uncle Pascal was a missionary priest in Africa. He appeared first (completely without warning, his mother muttered, and no cake in the house) on a summer's evening, a beautiful balmy St John's Eve, when the days only barely surrender to darkness.

'It's like Finland here,' Uncle Pascal had said, as if he were a tourist in his own place. 'Land of the midnight sun.'

He was very geographical in his references. As if his head were a globe, Gabriel's mother said afterwards, noting his receding hairline, resentful of his name-dropping. 'Finland, how are you!'

Uncle Pascal was unlike any priest Gabriel had come across before. He was burly and tanned with freckled hairy forearms, an open-necked shirt you might play golf in, and no sign of a dog collar. And he had a dream, a pipe dream.

'We're thousands of miles from water where I am.' A village in the Sudan. 'And I was thinking, what we need is pipes, man. If we could import the piping and lay it down, then we could bring the mountain to Mohammed, so to speak.'

He paced, gesturing with one hand, whiskey tumbler in the other. To Gabriel's ears it sounded like business, not religion. Pascal's plan was to beg sufficient lengths of pipe from factories in Ireland and export them to his desiccated African mission.

'That's a hell of a lot of piping,' Gabriel's father said.

'Granted,' Uncle Pascal conceded, 'but it's a damn sight easier than trying to irrigate with natural resources. My God, man, there hasn't been rainfall there in three years!'

As if to mock him, the eaves dripped. Outside was all green blur and drench; balmy St John's Eve giving way to the deluge.

'What do you think, Gabriel?'

Gabriel, agog at this paunchy man, his red face like impossible plumage, said nothing.

'I don't suppose,' Pascal said to his father but flashing a beady eye on Gabriel, 'that this fella has a vocation?'

And that's how it started. Afterwards, Gabriel was never sure. Was it for the piping, or for him, Uncle Pascal had come?

Minnows are his favourites. Darting in quick spurts across the pool. Flashes of brilliance, nipples erect – theirs and his. *Can breathe on side and swim back crawl.* Advanced beginners, in other words, though the Y is intent on this euphemistic ranking system. But why fish? Why cold-blooded invertebrates when these creatures are all warm flesh and soft surfaces and mouths like damp rosebuds? They're leggier now, their feet no longer plump cushions of flesh. But when he holds them in the water or catches them under the armpits, the wet slap of their suits excites him. Luckily, the water covers it; covers a multitude.

Swimming made him feel clean. All that purging, the showers before and after, the baptismal plunging in, the transubstantiation of a new element. It saved him from bullying at school. He was small and wiry, a late bloomer, and he'd had some success. Relay medals at schoolboy meets, mostly. He was never going to be a champion. His stroke was workmanlike, not stylish. He had no acceleration. Anyway, he didn't like the competition – all that thrashing about, the turbulence, swallowing great green mouthfuls of chlorinated water. No, he preferred an empty pool, watery sun-scribble on the ceiling, an empty lane ahead. That was his primal instinct – to be wet and alone.

Fish can dive from a kneeling position. His heart sinks each time the water parts to receive, unaided, the sleek spears of their beautiful bodies. It means he can no longer touch the trembling small of their backs or count the knobs of their spines arched like an eternal question mark.

'Ready?'

He delights when, at the last moment, flustered, they lift their heads or lose their concentration and are consumed in the torrid explosion of a belly flop. Failure endears. Success means they move on.

As he has. He's not Gay, or Gabriel or the priest in the family any more, but Gabe, standard dependable bloke. Regular guy. He can't opt for total denial, of course. There's the accent, though there are only a few words left now that have remained uncontaminated. The flat A in bath, car, and father. If anyone asks him does he miss home, he says no immediately without hesitation. Because what is home now? Not the jagged outlines of a small island on a map, or the fusty seminary with the nineteenth-century beams still reputed to be infected with TB. Not even the house he grew up in, now no longer in the family. When he thinks of Prosperity Drive, it's the hollowed-out scoop of dried earth under the swing in the back garden he remembers. Cracks in the dried mud like fault lines, parched as Uncle Pascal's desert, carved out by the foot-dragging of years. This was the place you had to return to when the flying was done. A whole new generation must have been launched from that old green chipped frame by now. Girls, he hopes. And when he's asked about Ireland, what comes to mind is the sheep field, though he doesn't talk of what happened there.

The sheep field was an overgrown plot at the end of Prosperity Drive, officially out of bounds. Why it was so called Gabriel didn't know; he'd never seen any sheep there. It was a piece of scrub, high with reeds and scutch grass and middens of dumped clay and builders' rubble sprouting with loosestrife and valerian and sometimes poppies. The thrill of the place was that you could get lost in it. He was lost there that summer's day lying on his stomach in a scratchy hollow resting on his elbows and gazing up at the sky muddled with cloud when he heard a rustle behind him. Alarmed, he rolled over and stared up at a figure turned to silhouette because it stood between him and the sun. When his eyes adjusted he saw it was a woman, a woman he vaguely knew. People called her Aggie. She was his mother's age and known to be odd. Harmless, they said, simple. Most of the time she sat in the window of an abandoned shop in the village on a kitchen chair staring out at the passers-by, as if she was the last item of stock as yet unsold. (By the time he left school the shop had become a Chinese takeaway and who knew what became of Aggie?) Her hair, the colour of faded heather and cropped like a man's, stood on end, her pale eyes popped, there were gaps between her teeth and her face was dirty. Boys he knew said Aggie wore no knickers.

Gabriel had never seen her outside and that was what gave him the biggest fright. To see her here, standing over him, with her soiled gabardine coat and her bare legs stuck into a pair of unlaced shoes.

'What are you doing?' she asked. She had a flat, phlegmy voice. That was a surprise – one of the other rumours about Aggie was that she was a deaf mute. The fact that she could speak made him afraid.

'Nothing,' he said.

'Were you swimming?' she asked, though it wasn't like a question. There was no rise and fall to her voice, no hint of animation.

'But there's no water,' he said. It was true what they said of her, she was a sandwich short of a picnic.

'There doesn't have to be water,' Aggie said. 'Turn over and I'll show you.'

He hesitated.

'Go on,' she said. He rolled back on to his stomach and she lay on top of him. He felt winded by the weight of her and smothered by her rancid stink. That was why he didn't cry out. But he wasn't sure he would have, even if he could. This was the very reason children were warned not to go into the sheep field. Strangers might nab you. But no one mentioned women. Aggie's arms circled in arcs at the corner of his vision as if she were doing the front crawl. He turned his head away.

'That's right,' she whispered in his ear, 'breathe to the side.'

Her fingernails grazed the spears of dry grass flattened beneath them. He saw how filthy they were. He could feel the nylon stuff of whatever she was wearing underneath her coat against the back of his legs and something else – soft, damp, tufty – pressed against his buttocks. She swam a full length, after which she was exhausted. Gabriel found he had bitten his lip and associated the blood with whatever had been going on. For several minutes they lay there, so still that Gabriel wondered if she were dead. But then she stood up and fixed herself; he could hear her. He was about to raise his head and look behind him but she said no, commandingly.

'Remember,' she said, 'Lot's wife.'

So he lay there, hectic and flushed, with a damp patch on the front of his shorts, until the sun went down and he was cramped and hungry.

'What have you been doing?' his mother demanded crossly, pointing to the dried blood on his lip.

But he couldn't say, except that it had been pleasurable, Aggie's rank body up against him, pressing down on him and producing a sensation he knew only as perilous ecstasy. It never went any further with Aggie, though he returned every day that summer, and so did she.

Flying Fish (*50 yards front and back crawl, breast and dolphin kick*) can evade him; they can swim away. Anyway, they're already beginning to lose their allure. Buds of breasts, down on their upper lips – and below – and an idea of themselves not tied up with trying to please him. He can still mentor them pool-side, though.

'Stretch your arms, fingers steepled, bend at the waist – like so, here.'

He places a hand gently on their shivering rumps or on their rubbery caps – their heads sheathed in condoms – and sometimes, with the merest tip, he can help launch them into mid-air, into that extravagant distance between bank and water.

On holidays from the seminary he would give the girls on Prosperity Drive rides on his black bike. They called him Father and liked to wear his bicycle clips as bracelets. He lifted them on to the crossbar, then sitting behind them – it was like spooning – they would take off in the direction of the cancer hospital. The other forbidden territory of his youth. He had a regular lap – through the wrought-iron gates, up the drive lined with chestnuts as far as the Chemo block and round by the kiosk. This was a pagoda-shaped little hut, like a house in a fairy tale, set in a swathe of rose beds, a folly left by the previous owners. St Jude's had once been a Big House owned by a Quaker crowd in trade. They'd called it Prosperity House. The upwardly mobile handle was all that was left of the place. (That was the trouble with home, bits and pieces of the scattered past always nosing their way in.) He would wonder as he pedalled these girls around if it had fucked them up growing up so close to the house of death. It had done something to him: made him doomy, prone to darkness.

The girls used to love those cycle trips. Those Elworthy kids, especially. They had it strict at home, and no father. They were mad for it. Then there was that little spitfire with the red hair, Ruth, was it? Names escape him. She was a screamer. When they built up speed she practically yodelled. When the wind blew through that mane of hers, he would catch strands of it between his lips. Invariably, it tasted of salt.

Sharks: Well, they speak for themselves. Teeth bared and ready to devour you. They've turned into frogmen with goggles – even the girls – muscles hardening for the adult class they will soon join. Muscles repel him. He keeps himself in shape – well, he has to – but he doesn't want to touch a version of himself. All those breasts and bulges, the uncertain voices, the ungainly exuberance. Even if he wanted to, he couldn't go near them. They'd whiff it off you, the yearning, the desperation.

It was boys just like these who had been his downfall at the seminary; they had made advances and when he'd . . . no, let's draw a veil over that, shall we?

'The fact is, Gay,' Father Dowdall, the director of vocations said, all unctuous candour, 'you just don't have it.'

As if being in the priesthood was a talent contest and he lacked star quality.

In retrospect, he was relieved. The burden Uncle Pascal had placed on him a lifetime ago had finally been lifted. And it was something to tell his parents.

'*They* didn't want me.'

His mother looked forward to the prospect of grandchildren. His father, benignly gaga in a nursing home, was too far gone to pass any comment. Lilian, his sister, was frank in her relief.

'Thank Jesus you've left those bloody druids. Weirdos every one.'

He'd wondered who he'd been trying to please all these years.

But it wasn't that simple. The seminary had cultivated in him a vision of himself, avuncular in soutane, pacing the schoolyard, gathering the children to him with a benedictory hand. A kindly figure, someone they could look up to. It seemed impossibly messianic to him now, a thin, vague dream, as naïve as Uncle Pascal's pipe-laying, though not half so extravagant. But he found he missed it, the promise of salvation, the costume of trust.

Coaching had been a practical solution. How else could he have earned a crust – a failed priest, fit for nothing? He's imparting something valuable, useful. Survival, life-saving skills. Salvation in another guise. Look, he's not a pervert. He's not hurting anyone. He doesn't scour porn sites, he has never so much as kissed a child. Once or twice there may have been an accidental brush of their lips on his cheek, but he has never, *ever* initiated anything. That's not what it's about. It's about trust – his; and innocence, theirs. His solitary pleasure, their unknowingness; just like with Aggie that summer in the sheep field.

GRACEFULLY, NOT TOO FAST

FIAEVI SJ XLI HSK!

This is how the world appears to the illiterate

Ruth stands under the legend she has just written on the blackboard. It is an Infants classroom so even though there are only five adults in the room it seems crowded because their outsized limbs are squeezed between the yellow tubular arms of the child-sized chairs or squashed under the low tables. There are drawings pasted on to the walls, abstract splotches or keenly symmetrical houses. In the Play Corner there is a raised sandpit where upturned buckets, saucily showing off their crenellated bottoms, jostle with jauntily anchored spades. Above the coat hooks, which line three walls of the room, the letters of the alphabet are drawn on large white cards with an accompanying illustration. A is for apple, B is for book.

Ruth could have had the pick of any of the rooms in the school but Senior Infants is a deliberate choice. It reduces her students. They don't *fit* here; they are too big. Depending on their own experience, they will either be swamped by nostalgia or – and this is Ruth's hope – will relive some of the terror of the infant's first day of school, the bawling distress, the inexplicable abandonment.

It is a winter's evening. A hangover of slush is banked on the sills of the high schoolhouse windows, spookily irradiated by the sulphurous glow of the street lights. It is wintry within too. The ancient radiators are tepid and everyone, including Ruth, is wearing an overcoat. Next door there's the busy homeliness of Experimenting with Watercolours, festive clinking of brushes in jars clouded with spools of Prussian Blue and Burnt Sienna; in Room 2B the plaintive chorus of Basic Italian – *c'è una banca qui vicino?* But here it is silent, and uncomfortable.

Ruth surveys her latest group. She prides herself on being able to read them. There is a young man, about nineteen or so Ruth surmises, unfortunate carroty hair partnered with a pale, pocked face. (Jasper Carrott, she thinks, but only as a mnemonic device.) A plump woman with a sculpted chestnut-tint perm, clip-on earrings like bulbous saucers and a soft, weak chin, sits at the very front, her hands clasped together like a Victorian songstress. Beside her is a fresh-faced woman in her thirties, a mother of young children, Ruth guesses, armed with a notebook. Her ash-blond hair is cropped for practicality's sake, but is stylish, nonethless. There is the ghost of a package holiday tan on her face. A placid, moon-faced girl with fair ropy plaits (like a figure on a Swiss barometer) peering over granny glasses sits tentatively in the middle row three seats back. She will be zealous and shy, Ruth decides, probably a reader at Mass, a frequent volunteer at the offertory procession. An elderly man sits at the back of the class. He has the ravaged looks of a drinker. Beneath the false bloom of those ruddy cheeks lurks a pasty-faced, malnourished invalid suffering from a terminal loss of appetite, she suspects. He has thinning hair half-heartedly spread over his pate and the unkempt air of a widower or a late divorcee; he has not been touched for a long time. This is Ruth's raw material, the blind leading the unlettered.

Ruth Denieffe was a bit of a prodigy. (In retrospect that sounded like a qualification but out of the mouths of maiden aunts it had been coolly admiring. *A bit of a prodigy.*) She was sent to the College of Music for piano lessons when she was seven. At eight she was attending singing lessons. By the age of ten she had performed on the radio. Hers was a precocious talent. Her father was immensely proud of her. When she looked back on those early years she remembered little joy in performing; but she savoured his quiet, enormous pride in her. It was his form of love. At great expense she was sent to Mr Jozsef Polgar for singing lessons. She remembered the first time her mother led her up the overhung path to his house. The garden was kept rather than cherished. (It was a time before garden centres.) The house was in what was later to be dubbed the Jewish quarter, when the school at the corner of Mr Polgar's street was converted into loft-like apartments and the dingy little bakery became a place of pilgrimage for atheists to buy pastries on a Sunday morning. But back then it was merely a huddle of worthy red-brick streets backing on to the canal. A sign on Mr Polgar's gate showed a line drawing of a fierce-looking Alsatian and a sign which read BEWARE OF THE DOG.

'Oooh,' Ruth's mother said. 'I hope he's tied up.'

She was terrified of dogs. Once, on her way to the shops, she had stood for a whole hour at their gate on Prosperity Drive, paralysed with fear, because the Fortunes' dachshund, Queen Maeve, had ambushed her. The silly little sausage dog was stationed at the kerb within a few feet of her and kept up a barrage of barking. Ruth had come home from school and found her mother clutching her shopping basket, white-knuckled, pleading weakly with the dog to go away. Ruth had sent Queen Maeve running with one well-aimed swipe of her foot.

The heavy, brown front door was opened by Mr Polgar's mother, although Ruth's mother mistook her for a housekeeper. She was a knotty little woman, red-handed as if she had been interrupted in the middle of bleaching. Her grey hair was scraped into a bun. She wore a navy housecoat, sprigged with white.

'Yes please?'

'We've come for my daughter's lesson,' her mother said tentatively.

'And what is your name?'

'Mrs Denieffe, Mrs Alice Denieffe.'

Mrs Polgar looked at her stonily.

'I arranged it on the phone,' Ruth's mother went on, 'with the professor.'

Ruth blushed. The professor bit was aimed at putting this woman in her place, which her mother thought was below stairs. It was a tone she used when she was trying to be masterful but it came out prickly and aggrieved.

'Please to come in,' Mrs Polgar said. 'My son will see you.'

Now it was Ruth's mother's turn to blush. Oh, she mouthed to Ruth behind Mrs Polgar's back. They stepped into a russet-tiled hallway. Mrs Polgar showed them into the front parlour. This was a brown room, nicotine-coloured wallpaper, a large foxed mirror over the mantel, a brass bucket housing an unruly fern eclipsing the empty fire grate. A couple of respectable but lumpy-looking armchairs crouched together around the hearthrug defying occupation. Ranged around the wainscoted walls were several other upright chairs, refugees from a dining-room suite upholstered in worn but well-polished leather, but equally forbidding. The door was closed on Ruth and her mother and they were left alone.

'It's like a doctor's waiting room,' Ruth's mother whispered, 'except there aren't even magazines.'

Several minutes passed. Mrs Polgar reappeared.

'You can ascend now,' she said.

They followed her up the carpeted stairs, a red fleur-de-lis pattern, to a return and then up another flight. Straight ahead of them a door stood ajar. Mrs Polgar gestured to them to enter. Ruth's mother, expecting her to follow, marched in boldly, then turned around only to find the door being closed behind them as Mrs Polgar melted away into the varnished landing.

This was an airier room than the one below, with two sash windows looking out on to the street, and pale leaf-patterned wallpaper. A baby grand piano dominated the centre of the room. Along the wall by the door was a glass cabinet stuffed with sheet music and loitering by one of the windows a couple of music stands, slightly askew like windswept women holding on to their hats. Weak flames sputtered in the high-built fireplace. Mr Polgar, who had been sitting at the piano, bowed between the jaws of the opened lid, stood up stiffly and made his way laboriously across the room, fingering the hip curve of the piano as he inched his way forward. He was a tall, thin man, balding on top but with tufts of tawny hair curling around his ears. The late evening sunlight formed a halo effect around his head, giving him an angelic air as he approached. He was dressed formally like a bank clerk, in a three-piece suit, pinstriped, carefully pressed. He did not meet their gaze, his eyes demurely down-turned, intent on the floor, it seemed. It was only when he drew level with them, and stretched out his hand with an odd jerky movement, that he opened them. They were phlegm-coloured, milkily ghoulish. Ruth's mother gasped.

'My mother didn't tell you, then,' he said, smiling faintly, as his fingers juggled with air trying to find her hands. 'That I'm blind.'

When he found her hands, he clasped both of them in his like a priest offering condolences.

'And where is little Ruth?' he asked, freeing a hand and threading his fingers through the air in search of her head. Ruth's mother hurriedly pushed her into position.

'Ah there,' he said, smiling again. 'So, young lady, let's hear you sing.'

He took her by the hand and they moved at Mr Polgar's stately pace back to the yawning piano. It turned out he did have a dog, not a harnessed guide dog – nor the ruthless

Alsatian the sign on the gate suggested – but a small Scottie which sat on his lap during the lesson. When he made for the piano, it scuttled away and sank into a basket by the fireplace.

'Meet Mimi,' Mr Polgar said that first day. 'She sits in on all my lessons. If she doesn't like what she hears, she howls. It's Mimi who decides whether you stay or go.'

Ruth's mother stood, gloves in hand, watching their procession uncertainly.

'That will be all, Mrs Denieffe,' Mr Polgar said when he and Ruth had reached the piano and he had eased himself down on to the padded stool. 'We'll call you when we're done.'

Suddenly, as if on some unspoken cue, Mrs Polgar materialised at the door and ushered Ruth's mother out.

'Well?' Ruth's mother demanded afterwards when they were safely out on the street. She had spent the half-hour lesson standing in the unwelcoming front parlour, afraid to sit down.

'Without even so much as the offer of a cup of tea,' she added. 'Must be that they're foreigners.'

The waiting had sharpened her air of grievance.

'Well?'

'Oh, we just did some scales, and arpeggios.'

'And?'

'He said I'd a strong voice, but my range needs work.'

'Motivation,' Ruth says loudly. It is the first word she speaks and it sounds – as it is intended to – like a reprimand. 'Why are we here?'

Ruth already knows the answers. Guilt masquerading as a social conscience, a love of books, a social activity that gets you out in the evenings, do-gooding.

'Why indeed,' smirking Jasper Carrott says under his breath.

'I just can't imagine what it would be like not being able to read,' offers the Swiss *Mädchen*.

'Anyone else?' Ruth asks.

'Books have been such a comfort to me . . .' the permed matron declares. 'Mrs Longworth,' she adds helpfully, 'Mrs Daphne Longworth.' She turns awkwardly in her chair to appeal to the other students in the class. 'Especially since my husband passed away. And I always wanted to do charity work . . .'

'Well, Mrs Longworth,' Ruth interrupts. 'Let me remind you that literacy is not a matter of charity; it's a right.'

After the first couple of weeks her mother stopped coming with her – it was only a short bus ride away – and so the singing class became for Ruth a time apart, a little oasis away from her mother's twitchy unease, her deep undertow of unworthiness. Ruth treasured the cloistered quietness of those journeys to Mr Polgar's and the joyless discipline of the lesson itself. It was hard work and Mr Polgar was not very patient.

'No, no, no,' he would cry, banging down his hands on the keys in the middle of a song. 'Flat, flat, flat. Can't you hear it?'

When he shouted like that, Mrs Polgar would wind her head around the door.

'Is all in order?' she would ask, looking gimlet-eyed at Ruth as if it was she who was causing the commotion.

Mr Polgar usually ignored the interruption.

'It's like this. Bah bah bah, bah – bah.' He hummed rather tunelessly himself, Ruth thought. She would watch him when he was in a rage like this, his bleached pupils turned searchingly heavenward. She wondered what he saw when his eyes were open. Was it the same darkness as she saw with her eyes closed? Or was it different? But she didn't ask. Since that first day with her mother, no mention of Mr Polgar's blindness had been made. After a while she simply forgot about it. And yet, and yet it made a difference. Expressions would flit across his face, irritation a lot of the time, a dark cloud of impatience settling on his brow, but other emotions too that she found harder to read. A sort of rapture if he were pleased, a secretive kind of joy. And of course, his blindness protected *her*. She could pull faces whenever she liked. Frequently, when he made her go over a particular phrase again and again, she would stick her tongue out at him.

Her timing was poor and he would make her sing unaccompanied, using the metronome. She would watch him fumbling with the menacing pendulum – how she hated it, ticking back and forth, back and forth, full of leaden reproach – and she would deliberately shift position knowing that this confused him. Suddenly he would look up and with a strange kind of lostness ask: 'Where are you? Where have you gone?'

Mimi hated the metronome too. She would dive off Mr Polgar's lap and burrow into her basket, yowling painfully. Frequently she made such a racket that he would turn the metronome off and Mimi would scramble back on to his lap. It was the only time Ruth liked Mimi. She was envious of the little mutt who nestled on Mr Polgar's knees. He fondled her, stroking her thick wiry coat. Sometimes he would bury his face in her coat and make growling doggy sounds and Ruth would look away, embarrassed. That was the thing about blind people: everything about them was visible.

Ruth desperately wanted to please him, because, she supposed, he was so hard to please. His foreign name (refugees, I'd say, her father had said, from the war), his air of suffering and his blindness gave him a kind of unapproachable nobility which unnerved her. It was not that she didn't know how to wheedle affection. When her father came in from work in the evenings she would climb aboard his sprawled but tense limbs as he slumped in the armchair in front of the television. She would drape her arms slyly around him and cradle her head against the rough skin of his neck. Beneath his shirt she could hear the steady thump of his heart. And she would wait for his jaded indifference to give way, for him to throw one arm lazily across her knees and prop her elbow up with the other and snuggle into the hollow of the armchair until both of them were snoozily comfortable. Meanwhile, stretched out on the carpet watching TV, Barry and John would greet him with a casual 'Hi, Dad' before turning their attention back to the screen.

'Boys,' he would say as he sank into the slovenly cushions.

She envied and admired this easy, male shorthand. She had to work harder, she knew. But she couldn't cajole Mr Polgar so easily. The only way with him was to be the best little singer she could be. Early on she had some success – highly commended for her rendition of 'Where'er You Walk' at the Feis (under-tens), a spot on the radio programme *Young People at the Microphone*, singing 'The Harp that Once'. But it wasn't enough. Ruth always worried that Mr Polgar had brighter pupils than her, more ambitious, more musical, prettier. Though why should pretty make a difference? He couldn't see, after all.

The more musical, more ambitious, and prettier pupil did exist, though. She materialised one spring evening.

'Come in, come in, Ruth,' Mr Polgar said, somehow sensing her hesitation when she entered the music room and found the interloper standing by the piano. A stunned twilight threw faint shadows on the busy wallpaper. 'I want you to meet another one of my star pupils. This is Bridget. Shake hands, you two.'

Neither of them made a move. Bridget Byrnes was very pretty, taller than Ruth by a head, with glossy dark hair and eyes that seemed jet black. But she was wearing a tacky-looking school uniform. The skirt dipped at the front and there was a piece of the hem hanging. The collar of her shirt was dingy and frayed; her tie was not real, but one of those fake ones on a piece of elastic. And there was a funny smell from her. A smell of dampness as if her clothes had not been properly aired or she had bathed in cold water. Her fingernails were bitten and not very clean. Ruth knew that look from the tinker women who called to the door with their broad ravaged faces and creased palms, leathery women with swaddled children. But she wasn't sure if the look came from being a tinker or just being poor. The girl smiled bashfully, showing a crooked set of teeth.

'Howr'ya,' she said.

'Now, I thought,' Mr Polgar said, 'that it would be good to get my two brightest pupils together for a spot of duets. Wouldn't that be fun? Two voices better than one, and all that!'

He obviously doesn't know, Ruth thought. He has no idea how poor she is. Ruth's experience of poor people was limited. Sometimes it seemed that *they* were poor; when it came to the singing lessons they certainly were. Her father indulged in jocular grumbling about the cost of indulging 'notions' – and Mr Polgar fell into this category. But then when they passed beggars on the street, it was undeniable that they, the Denieffes, were better off. Ruth's mother would pull her roughly by the arm if she even so much as halted at an outstretched hand, or listened to the pious lament of their woes. She said it was wrong to give them anything because it only encouraged them. They would only use it for drink, anyway. Poverty was something to be feared: not for what the poor in their rage might do to you but for its perilous proximity. As if it might be infectious.

Ruth suspected that this girl had got here under false pretences. That she had duped Mr Polgar in some way. That she had taken advantage because he was blind. Ruth, however, had been brought up to be polite so she said hello in an icy bright voice.

Every second week, Bridget came to Ruth's lesson and they practised together. She had a clear, high voice which relegated Ruth to singing harmony.

'Your strength, Ruth,' Mr Polgar said, though Ruth saw it differently. She was the background, the plodding undertone to Bridget's soprano. Ruth was going to piano lessons at the College of Music so she could read notation but Bridget relied on her ear. She spoke about music in a totally different way.

'That bit in the middle, where it goes up, like going upstairs,' she would say in her flat, hard accent, so at odds with her singing voice.

'The bridge,' Ruth would offer.

'There's a watery piece towards the end, like the bath tap dripping.'

The run of semi-quavers, Ruth thought.

'Well,' Bridget added, 'that's just like our bath tap. Drips something rotten and there's a big green stain on the bath from it.'

So, Ruth thought, they do have running water.

'She's so instinctive,' Mr Polgar would say admiringly of Bridget, 'such a feel for the music, and perfect pitch with it.'

He often talked about her to Ruth. At first, she was quite flattered. It gave her a pre-eminence; it was *some* kind of recognition.

'I know you won't mind sharing your class with Bridget. It's just she hasn't had all the advantages you've had. I know what it's like to struggle for your talent. When my parents came to this country they were outcasts . . . much like Bridget.'

Ruth wondered if the Polgars had been like the Frank family, locked up in an attic. But she couldn't fit Bridget into this picture. Bridget hunted? On the run?

She didn't tell her parents about sharing her classes. She suspected they wouldn't approve. Her mother would only go round to Mr Polgar's and protest vociferously, helplessly. Her father would say they weren't a registered charity. She knew, too, that being compliant about Bridget's presence was one way to please Mr Polgar. Maybe the joint lessons wouldn't last, maybe they'd just enter a few competitions and then it would be over. In the meantime, she was pleasant, if offhand, with Bridget. She noted assiduously any further signs of impoverishment, and there were plenty. Bridget never had her own sheet music, for one, nor did she have a music case, whereas Ruth considered her slim leather wallet with the chrome handle proof of the seriousness of her vocation. Bridget didn't press for friendship either. She seemed nervous to Ruth, or was it shifty? Her crooked smile was placatory and sometimes when Mr Polgar was losing his rag – as Bridget called it – she would throw her eyes to heaven in a comradely fashion. But Ruth treated such overtures with disdain. It was alright for her to pull faces right under Mr Polgar's nose, but the two of them doing it would have smacked of collaboration. And betrayal.

For Bridget singing seemed effortless. She never had to look at the music, she just took a deep breath and out it came, pitch-perfect, sweet, tuneful, whereas Ruth, stuck with the more sombre line, felt she had to struggle to be heard. Sometimes she was distracted by the beauty of the melody line, though in truth it was Bridget's voice that distracted her, so clear, so uncluttered, as if it was the most natural thing in the world to open your mouth and just . . . sing. It wasn't natural for Ruth; it was practice, it was work.

Jasper Carrott puts up his hand.

'If, as you say, (Ruth bristles) literacy is a right, then aren't we doing the state's job for them? I mean, these people have been let down by the education system. Aren't we just applying plasters here?'

'That's as may be,' she replies. 'But we're not here to discuss the rights and wrongs of the system, Malachy.' She has scanned the register and decided that he must be Malachy Forde. If she doesn't get to know his name she might end up calling him Jasper to his face.

'But we must look at the bigger picture, surely?'

'Go to the cinema,' she says, 'if you're after the big picture.' There is a nervous ripple of laughter. Jasper's pallid face colours.

'I was just saying . . . there are implications.'

'We're here to be effective teachers, to be of use. You won't find much interest among your pupils in discussing the how and whys of their illiteracy. We're not here to nurse their grievances, we're here to do a job of work. They want to be able to read and write. End of story.'

There's always one, Ruth thinks, a show-off, a waffler.

Mr Polgar entered them for the Junior Duets at the Feis – girls, singing pairs, under-twelves. He sprang this on them after several months of classes together. 'The Ash Grove' was the set song. He had the sheet music ready and after their warm-up scales he handed them a copy each. Normally he would give them a new piece at the end of the class and tell them to throw their eye over it for next week. A curious turn of phrase for a blind man. So this was a departure. He played through the piece twice, humming along in his grating voice. Ruth watched Bridget. She seemed fidgety; distracted, somehow.

'Got it?'

The girls nodded in unison. An old habit. Anyway, there were some silences Mr Polgar could read.

'Ruth, why don't you start, you can sight-read. Bridget, you'll pick it up, as we go along. Key of G.'

Ruth launched forth. *By yonder green valley where streamlets me-an-der* . . . She muddled through it to the end.

'Good, now let's try it together. You take the tune this time, Bridget; Ruth, you try the seconds line.'

Bridget held the tune, of course. But after the first couple of words she resorted to singing la-las.

'Lovely,' Mr Polgar said. 'This time, Bridget, let's have the words as well.'

Ruth, standing beside Bridget, noticed her hand first. It was trembling. She was holding the sheet in front of her with one hand, while with the finger of the other hand she was tracing the shapes of the letters as if they were in Braille, as if by running her fingers over them they would come to life.

'Them's hard words, aren't they?' she said quietly.

'A bit arcane, I'll grant you,' Mr Polgar said. 'And by the way, note how it is to be sung, Bridget. What does it say above the clef?'

Bridget was a clenched ball of concentration.

'What does it say?' Mr Polgar repeated.

Bridget shook her head sadly.

She can't read, Ruth realised. It's not that she can't read music. *She can't read.* Ruth felt a weak swell of triumph. She glanced over at Bridget and caught her eye. There was panic there, a terrible naked fear, a pleading for help. Cover for me, the look said; help, the look said.

'Girls?' Mr Polgar asked.

Silence.

Ruth and Bridget were locked in that glance, fear meeting refusal. Neither could break it.

'Girls?' Mr Polgar repeated in that lost voice of his as if he weren't sure if they were still there.

Neither of them moved.

'Bridget?'

If he had said Ruth's name, she might have relented. She might have volunteered the words that could have saved Bridget. Four little words. But no, it was Bridget, it would always be Bridget first. So it was really Mr Polgar who had decided.

'I seem to remember asking a question, Bridget,' Mr Polgar said in that sarcastic tone he used when he was uncomfortable. 'Or is nobody bothering with the blind old teacher?'

He tinkered idly at the keys, playing the opening phrase of the melody.

'What on earth's the matter, Bridget? What's the problem here?'

Bridget snuffled noisily, but that was nothing unusual. She seemed to suffer from a permanently running nose.

'Ruth, we seem to have lost Miss Byrnes for the present. Why don't you try it?'

Ruth sang as she never had before, strong and clear, the words perfectly enunciated. She closed her eyes so she wouldn't have to see Bridget standing there, vanquished. When she opened them again, Bridget had disappeared. She had fled, closing the door silently behind her. Mr Polgar didn't even realise she was gone.

'Lovely,' Mr Polgar purred at the end. 'Maybe we'll give you the melody line this time. And why don't you inform Miss Byrnes how this piece should be sung?'

'Gracefully,' Ruth read to the empty room, 'not too fast.'

Ruth pads between the aisles passing out pieces of paper. On each sheet is the musical notation of 'Three Blind Mice'.

'To understand the plight of those who cannot read, we must first of all know what it *feels* like,' she says, putting on her reading glasses. 'Now, Miss Furlong, isn't it?'

'Marianne,' the Swiss barometer girl says pleasantly.

'Well, Marianne, you'll notice some musical notation on the sheet in front of you. I'd like you to sing the piece of music. It's quite a well-known tune, you probably sang it on your mother's knee, so you shouldn't have any difficulty.'

Marianne paws the paper timidly. There is an uneasy silence in the class coupled with relief that it is she who has been put on the spot.

'I don't read music, actually,' Marianne says smoothly with a self-deprecating look. 'You'll have to ask someone else.'

'But I'm asking you, Marianne.'

'I told you, I don't read music.'

'Come on, Marianne, you must make an attempt.'

'But how can I?'

43

'Everybody's waiting, Miss Furlong.' Ruth takes off her glasses slowly and sets them down deliberately on the table in front of her.

'You mustn't badger me like this. I told you I can't read music. Ask someone else.'

'But I want *you* to do it.'

'But I can't . . .' Marianne begins, her voice rising to a wail.

'Exactly, Miss Furlong, my point exactly. Now, how does *that* feel?'

Bridget did not return. Mr Polgar was baffled.

'I thought I was giving her an opportunity here. She has a real talent. I wanted her to make use of that, to better herself.'

He had taken to confiding in Ruth. He would reach for her hand, looking for consolation, reassurance. He was like a man scorned in love. Even Mimi was getting short shrift, pushed impatiently off his lap and sulking now in her basket. Mr Polgar rubbed Ruth's fingers thoughtfully. He seemed to need her to make sense of it.

'Have you any idea?'

Ruth shrugged, then remembered that Mr Polgar couldn't see shrugs.

'Maybe her parents couldn't afford it?'

'It wasn't a case of money,' he said sharply. 'It was never a matter of money.'

The mother of two asks a question. Her name is Jean Fleming.

'What should we use for materials? I've got primers at home from my own kids but that'd be insulting, wouldn't it? I wouldn't like to be faced with those Dick can run books at my age. Didn't much care for them even when I was four.'

Ruth smiles. She likes this woman; she *gets* it.

'All that business about Mummy in the kitchen making endless sandwiches. And all Daddy seemed to do was wash the car.'

A titter runs through the classroom.

'I'm glad you raised that,' Ruth says. 'Every pupil is different and often you'll have to adapt to their needs, which can be quite specific. It means making up your materials as you go along. Word games, picture cards and the like. You can use the labels on household goods, cereal packets, cans. Everyday stuff.'

'How do they manage?' Jean muses, as if she's thinking aloud, as if she and Ruth are friends chatting over a cup of coffee, trading confidences. Her forehead creases quizzically. 'How do they get by? They must be terrified, afraid all the time of being discovered. Always covering up, covering their tracks. I don't think I've ever met anyone who couldn't read. But then, how would I know?'

'I remember the first person I met who couldn't read.' Ruth discovers herself talking, taking up Jean's reflective tone. *Stop, stop.* 'I remember her name, even, Bridget, Bridget Byrnes . . .' Ruth falters, remembering the advice she always gives her trainee tutors. People don't want to hear how much you love reading, what prompted you to get involved, my first illiterate and all that. This is about them, not you.

'Now where were we?'

It was a sin of omission, a lesser offence. If she had told Mr Polgar that Bridget couldn't read, what difference would it have made? She had protected Bridget from exposure by saying nothing. She wondered idly how Bridget had managed to hide it for so long. Someone at home must have been able to read. She must have memorised the words between classes. Sooner or later, though, Bridget would have been unmasked. Better that Mr Polgar thought her ungrateful than for him to know her secret. The shame of that! This way Bridget's secret was quite safe, stowed away in Ruth's hard, competitive little heart.

All it bought her, in the end, was time. Another year of solo lessons unencumbered by Bridget's better voice, more instinctive feel for the music, her bloody perfect pitch. She remembered the day she arrived for what was to be her last class. She had just turned twelve and Mrs Polgar steered her into the front parlour instead of guiding her upstairs, which was unusual. Mr Polgar came down presently. He had Mimi in his arms.

'Why don't we sit here for a while, Ruth?' he said.

She got to sit – finally – on one of the big armchairs. He perched on the edge of the other one, fondling Mimi's ears.

'I've been thinking,' he said. The expression on his face was candidly sorrowful, but his glassy eyes seemed blankly evasive. 'About your lessons. And your voice.'

'My voice?'

Mimi leapt off his lap and scampered away, pushing the door open with her nose. Ruth could hear her nails clicking on the tiled hallway outside.

'Well, you see, often at your age the voice changes, modulates because of . . .'

Because of breasts and periods was what he wanted to say, she suspected, but couldn't.

'And sometimes it's best not to train the voice during puberty, to let it develop in its own way. Then in a couple of years, if you're still interested we can work with what will be a fine, mature voice, I hope.'

The room was dark, shadowy. It was winter, the clocks had just been put back. The lights should be turned on, she thought, but the mood was gloomily in tune with Mr Polgar's mortifying verdict. Somehow, she thought, somehow he has found out.

'But it's been fun, hasn't it?' He said this with a false brightness, the brightness he used to jolly things along.

He was absolutely wrong about that, she thought vehemently. The singing classes had been a lot of things for Ruth Denieffe. But fun, never.

*   *   *

46

The piano lessons petered out too, though she managed to get as far as Grade 5 before, three years later, she simply gave up. It wasn't that she lost interest; it was Mrs Bradley who changed. Towards the end, Mrs Bradley – stout, whiskered, irritable – seemed content to let her play on, faults and all. Once she would have stood over Ruth; drumming time on the lid of the upright, stopping Ruth so often that in an hour-long lesson she would never get through a piece from beginning to end. But latterly she had taken to sitting by the window looking out dreamily over the roofs of the city. She seemed sunk in a kind of trance so that Ruth would have to cough loudly when she had finished to attract her attention. Ruth could read the signs, indifference as a prelude to rejection.

Meanwhile all around them music flourished – the brash din of the college orchestra, the smooth and fluid bow of some bright young violinist, the urgent arpeggios of a soprano yearning towards cadence.

'Well,' Ruth says, gathering together her papers. 'I hope I haven't put you off completely.' She's taking bets with herself that Miss Furlong and Mrs Longworth will not be back next week. It's better this way, to weed out the faint-hearted at the start before they can do any harm.

The students heave themselves out of their miniature traps, and file out. The drinker at the back is the last to leave. Perry is his name. Robert Anthony Perry. The furnishing of a full name gives him away, its titular pretension, its striving self-importance. Anthony is probably his Confirmation name. He pauses at the desk smiling in a gamey way; an old reflex, Ruth imagines, drawing on some ancient source of shabby charm. After-class approaches like this are usually a form of special pleading, a false frankness. Between you and me, the hanger-on is saying, I'm different, not part of the common herd. I'm worthy of your individual attention.

'So what does it mean, then?' He gestures towards the motto on the blackboard.

Ruth has forgotten about it; usually she asks the class to guess at the end, to lighten things up a bit, but something has distracted her with this group.

'Oh that,' she says distractedly, hoping to put Mr Perry off. Jean Fleming saves her. She bounces back into the classroom having left her gloves behind.

'Oh, by the way, I meant to ask,' Jean says on her way out. 'Are you the same Miss Denieffe who used to teach at St Ignatius's? My niece went there and spoke so highly of you.'

Jean Fleming is lying. With merciless adolescent judgement, Marie used to call Miss Denieffe a total bitch. Jean's sister Molly, hushing her daughter, would concede that Miss Denieffe had a reputation for standing no nonsense; she could face down a class of unruly boys with the set of her shoulders and the fix of her stare.

'You should see her, Jean,' she used to say, 'she's *tiny*, five foot nothing, mop-top ginger hair like Shirley Temple, or one of those other child stars.'

She was a great loss to the school when she went, Molly said. Played the piano for all the school operettas and would gladly do Beatles numbers and ragtime during the intervals at concerts and open days though she wasn't even the music teacher. No one was surprised, though, when she moved into Adult Ed; she was always a bit of a crusader, Molly said.

'Yes,' Ruth says, 'that's me.'

'Still tickling the ivories, then?' Jean asks brightly.

Ruth is suddenly furious. Furious about the years of practice, the tantalising promise of perfection, all that cruel vocational energy expended. For what? For this – *tickling the ivories*. Mr Perry is still standing there. He shuffles his feet conspicuously.

'Oh, I'm sorry,' Jean says, 'I interrupted you.'

'No,' he says, switching his gelid attention to Jean, 'I was just asking Miss Denieffe about this.' He points again at the blackboard.

'Yes, what does that mean? I was wondering too, but to tell you the truth, I was a bit afraid to ask.' Jean laughs nervously.

Ruth pushes past both of them. She hits the light switch as she reaches the door, plunging them both into darkness.

DIASPORA

Mo Dark is coming out of the Gents toilet in the terminal when he sees her. He's left Keith looking after his trolley. Can't be too careful these days. Security would nab it in a nano-second and blow it up. He's tucking his shirt into the draw-string waist of his shorts when she walks across his field of vision. Is it her? Or has he been smoking too much? The terminal is almost deserted. Through the huge plate-glass windows there's a golden spear of light on the horizon that will become sunrise. Torpedoes of maroon clouds cruise the blanched sky like a Sunday painter's vision of the Day of Judgement. Pathetic fallacy, he thinks.

She's wearing a floral sundress and some silky kind of jacket the colour of mushrooms that breezes behind her as she hurries along. That was always her mode. Quick impatience. She looks prosperous; yes, that's the word. Large pouchy handbag slung over her shoulder, and one of those wheelie bin cases on a stick. Her hair seems to be a different colour. It's long now, copper tinted and rippling behind her like an ad for shampoo. The last time he saw her she'd had it short, a close shave growing out. (She was going for the Sinead O'Connor look.) But despite her best efforts – the shaggy jumpers, the bolt in her ear – Trish could never have been anything other than pretty. Rinsed grey eyes, those pert delectable breasts. They're still in evidence, he notices. A memory of her comes to him, in her school uniform. Navy blue tunic, designed to shroud sexuality, the regulation shirt and skewed tie, dishev-elled white knee socks. Those socks really did it. Phew! Did the nuns not realise how girls of a certain age just – *sprouted* – out of that prison gear? The memory of Trish, rather than her presence 20 feet away, arouses him. Jesus! Stirring of the loins. Early morning job. Down, boy, down. Pathetic phallus, more like.

God, she's going to miss her flight. She can't believe it. Well, no, she can. Trish has missed dozens of flights. All that security business! She clings to a time before terror when you could just rock up with an hour to spare before a European flight and step aboard. The world may have changed, but Trish, in this one mulish aberration from her usual efficiency, baulks at the new demands. Cosmetic miniatures banished to see-through baggies, the pulling-off of coats, the shedding of shoes. Ridiculous! She's lost count of the number of tweezers she's forfeited, the bargain-sized shampoo containers she's been forced to abandon. It's a futile kind of defiance but she constantly runs the gauntlet, the last adrenalin rush left to the modern-day traveller. She halts under the board with its fluttering eyelids of information. Rome. Go to gate, it flashes furiously.

Hi there, he practises. Hi there. Trying to sound casual. He reaches for films – of all the gin joints in all the world . . . no, maybe not. Should he say *Hola*? Trouble is, he's out of practice. Not used to talking to people. In any language. He talks to Keith and Manny but that's not the same. Real people, he means. Anyway, talking to Trish Elworthy, with the distance of years yawning between them, would be immediately freighted with the need to explain. Explain *this*.

She was his first love, his childhood sweetheart. The vocabulary of the distant past sounds archaic to his ears. Childhood. Sweetheart. This is the foreign language for him now. And then there's how he looks. Living like he does changes how you look, or how you appear to other people. Like being disfigured or emaciated by illness. Would she even recognise him? Would he *want* her to recognise him? Would he want her to peer at him and say questioningly, Mo? Mo Dark?

She rummages in her bag, hunting for her mobile phone.

'An interview?' Gianni said, disbelieving, when she told him about the trip, and in the next breath, 'you're leaving me, aren't you?'

'Madonna!' she'd exploded. (It had taken her years to get the hang of pious cursing in Italian.) 'This is not about you! If I get this I could be a director of a school, my own boss.' When she said it, it sounded like ambition, something she's been studiously avoiding for years.

'Your Spanish isn't good enough,' Gianni said.

'That's what you used to say about my Italian,' she replied hotly.

But he has hit the nail on the head. She *is* trying to get away from him. Nothing he did; it's her, her sneaking propensity for betrayal. (Recently, she filled in one of those online personality questionnaires – who's your favourite biblical character? St Peter, she answered. Her ringtone is a crowing cock.) Gianni's phone goes to message.

'Leaving Malaga now, should be in Perugia by evening,' she informs the silence as a bing-bong sounds and her flight is announced. Last call.

What to call him. That was always the trouble; people were never sure about him. Never sure who he was. The confusion started at school. First day. They were late – they were always late. His mother could never achieve the oiled management of the nuclear family. Mo saw it capitalised: the Nuclear Family, efficient, deadly. Neet heaved the heavy door open. It had a heraldic escutcheon brassily marked PULL. They stepped into a tantrum of noise, a miniature world of protest. Letterbox mouths, brimming eyes, anger-pocked faces, the about-to-be abandoned. Neet handed him over at the door of Low Babies. The teacher, standing at the desk, was a faded-looking woman in an Indian smock with ash-blond hair and denim eyes. Twenty pasty faces stared back at him. That was the first time he noticed. Noticed the difference.

'Is this little Maurice?' the teacher asked sweetly, bending down and peering intently at him.

'We call him Mo,' Neet said helplessly.

He was picked on, of course. Where did he live? Sesame Street? There were older boys who wouldn't let him play ball, who told him to feck off back to where he came from – which they imagined was Africa, since all nig-nogs came from Africa. But look, if they hadn't fixed on his skin colour they'd have found something else. A big nose, freckles, glasses. The girls took his hand and led him around the playground like a pet. They allowed him to turn rope and in time he could skip for Ireland.

The roped-off alleyways leading to the X-ray machines look like a stage set for some glitzy red-carpet event. Bloody place is deserted but still you have to wind your way through the maze. Trish halts at the mouth of the security area and fingers her jacket – is that considered a coat? She's wearing sandals, but they have wedges – could the goon in the uniform mistake her for a heel bomber? She decides to brazen it out. Why volunteer? She will only take off what she absolutely has to. She places her carry-on in the grey plastic tray and puts her phone beside it. As she waits to be beckoned through, she looks behind her. Across the butter-coloured distance she sees a figure coming out of the Gents toilet. Loud shirt, rumpled shorts. For some unaccountable reason she thinks of Mo. Mo Dark. (Burnt Sienna, that's the colour of your skin, she had said to him. I'm not a fucking paint chart, he had barked back.) That was Mo. Difficult, touchy.

'*Señorita?*'

The goon points to her shoes.

Back then, he counted himself lucky. He had two mothers, Neet and his nan. Nan lived with them and looked after him when Neet was out at work – in a grey office with a yucca plant in the Admin Block of St Jude's. Nan was a rosy grandmother, a ruddy crab apple of a woman, bright as a bead and his stoutest defender.

'He's a growing boy,' was her justification to Neet for any misbehaviour. Nan was obsessed with growth.

'Eat that up,' she'd command, 'or you won't grow up to be a big boy.'

Nan liked to ramble with the pushchair up and down the tree-lined avenue of St Jude's, skirting the Outpatients Department and coming back by the morgue. The expeditions with Nan were less about rambling than talking. She talked all the time even before Mo could answer back. Pushed ahead, skirting the arthritic roots of trees cracking through the paving slabs, Mo was fuelled by Nan's chatter.

'You're going to be a fine big lad, you're going to grow into a man, tall and strong like Victor Mature or Charlton Heston. You're going to be the biggest lad in this family, taller even than Pops Dark and he was no midget. You're going to go to the university, no reason why not. You could be a doctor, or a pilot . . .' (This was a concession on Nan's part. She knew how Mo loved the chalky vapour trails of planes in the high blue sky; he'd follow their crayoned streaks with his finger.) When he was with Nan, he felt like a pilot, swaddled in his little cockpit on wheels, propelled by Nan into his big future. Here's my future, Nan, he thinks, as a jet takes off, roaring behind plate glass.

*   *   *

In the sonic thunder, Trish bends to unbuckle her sandals and the world of Prosperity Drive comes swimming back. God, how she hated that place! Crossroads to nowhere. The avenue leading to St Jude's Hospital formed the upright, patches of green on either side with ancient oak trees, low clumps of whitethorn and forsythia, and wild clusters of snowdrops in the spring. Prosperity Drive was the cross-beam, bisecting the avenue. It was a later addition, an afterthought; a paved street of pebble-dashed houses petering out in two bland cul-de-sacs. The hospital dominated. Crushed-looking men paced the grounds in dressing gowns and slippers, their faces marked biblically where they'd had radiation treatment. There was the slow glide of hearses up and down the avenue. Not that when she was a kid Trish took much notice of that. St Jude's and its discreet morbidity was normal. She only knew it wasn't a normal hospital because when she fell off the swing in the Devoys' garden, she was taken to St Vincent's. Girls with broken arms did not go to St Jude's. It was for hopeless cases, she'd heard her mother say.

Mo lived in the hospital's gate lodge with his mother – Neet, he always called her just Neet. It made mother and son seem hip and matey, like a pair of blues musicians. Neet had a vaguely hippyish air with her ragged-hemmed gypsy skirts, porridge-coloured cardigans, her undernourished footwear. She had lived in Australia once, Mo had told Trish – was that where he'd come from, she'd wondered. Wherever Neet had been, she was a world away from Trish's mother in homely Fair Isle twinsets and stippled Crimplene hurrying off to her night-time job at the telephone exchange. Although she barely remembered it, Trish was nostalgic for that time of sweet domesticity when her father was still alive, a time she was permanently excluded from now. What she liked about Mo was a similar sense of deficit.

He asked Nan about his daddy.

'You're our little foundling,' she told him.

Here was the story Nan told him. He had been left on the doorstep of the gate lodge by his real mother, who had mistaken the cottage for the official face of the institution. She had placed him in a plastic carrier bag on the worn well of the doorstep and melted away into the summer's night. It was August, nine in the evening and Nan was inside the umber glow of the cottage when she heard him wail. She was in her dressing gown, a damp turban of towel around her head.

'I'd just washed my hair; it was dripping everywhere,' she said. 'Bloody cats, that's what I thought.'

Set on silencing the enraged love mewls of the neighbourhood tabbies she threw open the door and almost fell over the writhing package. Nan picked up the baby and crushed him to her damp breast. Beneath her fingers, she could feel the tiny pulse of his fontanelle. She wandered into the snail-littered garden.

'I don't know why. I don't know what I was looking for,' Nan said. 'Your poor mother was long gone.'

She planted a kiss on the baby's forehead. She called out Neet's name, lovelorn in the night. Neet pushed aside a net in an upstairs casement, lifted the metal hatch and leaned out into the stock-scented night.

'Look what the stork left!'

Sounds outlandish now. A fairy tale. Like something out of Thomas Hardy. (He'd seen *Far From the Madding Crowd* on TV one night with Neet.) But, look, he was five years old. And hey, it was the Sixties. Those things happened then. Around the same time, Nan had told him, another little boy, a toddler, was abandoned in the doorway of Woolworth's coming up to Christmas, a note pinned to his coat collar with a heartfelt plea for someone to look after him. Only difference was he was white. And *that* story was true.

The contents of her bag on the monitor are in sepia and as plain and unadorned as a child's drawing – all outline, no substance. The goon beckons to her magisterially. She looks over her shoulder towards the concourse, rattled by the thought, however unlikely, that once again she's turned her back on Mo Dark. The bloke's still standing there but she's further away now and she hasn't got her contacts in. Even if she could see clearly, she couldn't exactly abandon her shoes and her bag and run in bare feet after a stranger who looks like Mo Dark. That would make her look guilty. Guilty of something. She passes barefoot through the empty doorway.

Despite her tall tales, he was sure of Nan, sure of her uncomplicated love, in a way he wasn't of Neet. He saw himself and Neet as semi-detached, like a pair of movie Nazis – his mother helmeted at the controls, Mo dwarfed in the little sidecar. His was a life of female demarcation. Nan did the birthday parties, Neet the trips to the cinema, the camping trips. Nan did Hallowe'en. She made costumes, cowboys and pirates – eyepatches and fringed hats. The masks helped, the sleek shades of the Lone Ranger, the dripping plastic of the ghoul. His favourite, though, was the ghost. Shrouded in a white sheet with holes scorched out for the eyes, nobody could guess who he was.

Trish is thinking of the first time with Mo. She'd had an argument with her mother and had stormed off, heading for St Jude's. Down by the mortuary was a good spot for a sulk. The dead centre of St Jude's – a place the living avoided superstitiously. There was a funeral that day. She watched as the attendants opened up the double doors of the mortuary and slid a coffin surreptitiously off the trestles and on to the brassy tray of the hearse. They worked silently and stealthily as if even here, in the house of death, discretion was required. She stretched out on the grass and let the soughing of summer leaves crowd out the rerun of hostilities with her mother playing in her head. A shadow fell across her. How was it that even with your eyes closed, you could sense someone was there? When she opened her eyes to a silhouette against sun-glare, that someone was Mo Dark.

They had played together as kids. Sprawling soccer matches – more stoppages than play while the boys argued over fouls and penalties – complicated street games with chanting and finger-pointing, the lonely hiding and frantic seeking. But educational segregation and puberty had put paid to their childish ease. Now she was shy of him, locked in her convent blues while he swaggered about in ripped jeans, a sanctioned drop-out.

'Hi,' she said and he silently took that as an invitation. He lay down beside her on the grass. She sat up, pulling at her school pinafore where it had rumpled up underneath her. It was one of those drowsy summer afternoons, the riled bee-hum of a lawnmower somewhere in the distance, and the sway of leaves overhead, and suddenly – not even suddenly, lazily (that was the curse of adolescence – the awful tedium of it) Mo leaned over her and stroked her cheek. She remembered still the rapture of it, the silky feel of his hand on her skin, soothing after the aggravation with her mother, as if he was trying to quiet the clamour in her head. Then his lips were on hers and her swoony acquiescence gave way to enraged passion, as if some switch had been thrown. She was eating his face and clawing at his belt and they probably would have done it, there and then, if some busybody nurse hadn't come along.

'Mo?'

The nurse was a burly creature with butch hair, a corpulent body encased in white armour; her name tag read Audrey Challoner. She stood towering over them, flushed with indignation – and embarrassment – as they hurriedly tried to fix themselves. Mo rose up to sitting, cross-legged, trying to quell his erection. Trish fidgeted with the buttons on her shirt.

'Hi, Aud,' Mo said, shading his eyes against the glare. The nurse's? The sun's?

'Come on, Mo,' she said in that infuriatingly reasonable tone adults used to suggest candour rather than judgement. 'Not here, okay? Just not here.'

She turned away without a backward glance, leaving Trish and Mo in a queasy backwash.

'Will she tell on you?' she asked Mo.

'Aud?' he queried. He knew most of the hospital staff by their first names. 'Nah,' he said lazily – as lazy as his first move.

Although nothing had really happened, there was no going back from the day of trespass in St Jude's. Sometimes Trish thought she and Mo were loyal to the transgression rather than to each other. Their trysts always followed the same pattern – fevered groping and lecherous disarray always teetering on the brink of the absolutely forbidden.

When her mother found out that she and Mo were an item – that's how she put it – she issued florid warnings.

'Remember Shan Mohangie,' she said. '*He* was from Africa, murdered his Irish girlfriend. A teenager, just like you. Worked in a restaurant, what was it called? The Green Rooster, that's it! Killed her in a jealous fit, and then chopped her into little pieces and put her in a pot!'

'This is Mo, Mum, Mo from St Jude's,' Trish said. Exasperated.

Looking back on it, Trish could see only the other fascinations about Mo. He was a sometime roadie for Wingless Stock, a vegetarian heavy metal band. He was nineteen and out in the world. And like her, he had no father. Except where hers was indisputably dead, his was just missing. She couldn't resist prying. Hadn't his mother ever talked about it, told him the story? He would shake his head. So she invented her own scenario – his father might have been a student, at the College of Surgeons, maybe? They had loads of foreign students. Africans, Indians. Who knew? Maybe your dad's still around, she pestered Mo, maybe we could track him down? She envied him this live connection somewhere out there, far away from the confines of Prosperity Drive. But Mo refused to co-operate.

'I'm Neet's son,' he said, 'isn't that enough for you?'

The trouble with Trish's questions was they made the silences between him and Neet manifest. Nan was gone by then; she'd been taken by a stroke that had left her lopsided and speechless. He was angry. Angry with Neet; angry that she didn't seem to miss Nan at all, barely mentioned her even, angry that she had let him drop out of school with barely a protest, angry that she had allowed him to move out. It was only across the yard, mind you, to an aluminium caravan like a piece of downed artillery parked at the gable of the house. It had lain idle for several years but Neet had helped him fix it up. Nevertheless, he had pinned a skull and crossbones on the door with a KEEP OUT signed scrawled underneath – meant, of course, for her. He'd turned it into a fetid hole, subverting the tight-lipped presses, the picture window with its scrawny nets and the fierce tidiness it was designed for. Everything in it was two-faced. The toilet hid behind what looked like a cupboard door, the banquette seats with the table wedged between them turned into a bed. And though he had opted to move, he had felt banished there as if Neet had sent him into exile. He still went into the house for his grub but, ridiculously, he felt Neet had turned him into a latchkey lodger.

'Lucky you!' Trish said enviously.

When he and Neet passed in the kitchen they only found things to quarrel about. There was just one area of truce. The movies. Neet loved the cinema and even when they became estranged they still trooped once a week to the local fleapit. His friends – with the exception of Trish who found it touching – jeered him for going out with his old lady, but he made the weekly pilgrimage to keep faith with Neet. He owed her that much. The deal was that he would pick the film one week, and she the next. Thanks to Neet he got to see a lot of period dramas and some awful French turkeys. What he hated was the subtitles. He felt as if he was being duped. There always seemed too many words on screen for what was being said, sound clogged up with too much explanation. The exact opposite of his life with Neet, where there wasn't enough.

An alarm goes off, a red light flashes. Her watch. She reverses, throws it into a plastic tray and tries again. Again the buzzer goes off. A female guard steps forward, thick heavy hair crowded on her shoulder like a burden, with the eyes of a stricken Madonna. She forces Trish to extend her arms like a child playing aeroplanes. With a seamstress's finesse she runs her fingertips down Trish's hips and thighs. She nods, gives her the all-clear. Trish steps to the side to retrieve her jacket, her shoes, the watch. When she's reassembled, put back together again, she turns to check. Is he still there?

Trish! He could still call out; it's not too late. But he finds himself locked in a paroxysm of indecision. Look, she's in a hurry. Must be the Rome flight she's aiming for. (He knows the schedules by heart.) 6.55, connecting in Madrid. Stirrings of curiosity now. What's she doing in Rome? But if he had questions about her and the years that have intervened – he feels suddenly archival – then she, too, would have questions and he's not sure he would be able to explain. Explain how he got here. He's tried Munich, Düsseldorf, Bremerhaven. But Malaga is the most comfortable; the weather is kinder. Keith raves about Paris. Not the airport ('Charles de Gaulle is poxy! That hub system, all about crowd control!') but the city, where you can get three square meals a day. Early morning breakfast at the convent in Picpus, lunch in Belleville, an evening meal with the monks on Rue Pascal. But Mo never got in on that circuit. Anyway, Paris is brutal in the winter and he's mistaken

61

for a Berber. Funny that – here he's seen as vaguely white. In Paris he felt like a tramp. Here, he's permanently in transit; he could be just about to get back on the carousel of life. One ticket away from normality. And it's sheltered, he's under cover. He collects plastic bottles in the morning, scavenged from the litter bins, and takes them to the supermarket on the ground floor of the terminal, which gives cash back. He hoovers up food left on the café tables when passengers' flights are called. The security guards know him and mostly turn a blind eye. Last month someone nicked his trolley and it was a parking attendant who located it in the underground car park and returned it to him. Who the hell would want to steal his trolley? Sad fucks. He pictures it now with the plastic bags swinging from the handles and his bed roll bent over inside, lolling like a sludgy tongue. His life is a small, smelly trove locked up in a wire basket on wheels.

She could try a wave, on the off-chance it is Mo. Just like she did the last time she saw him. A sad little wave because she was seventeen and she didn't have the words to say I'm scared. She wasn't scared of the big adventure, the delicious and longed-for escape from Prosperity Drive, the tantalising whiff of freedom. No, she was scared of cool, knowing Mo Dark with the absent father and the quicksilvery temper and the brooding silences, scared of all his unknowns. But she couldn't say that, out of a sort of politeness. Because he wasn't white. It would only hurt him, she told herself, covering up for her cowardice. And because she couldn't speak, she did the cruellest thing of all. She said nothing.

They were going to run away to London when she'd finished her Leaving Cert. They had it all planned, the mailboat to Holyhead, then the train to Euston. They'd find a squat – he had muso friends there and an address in Kilburn. They would live together where no one would know them. No parents, Mo said emphatically. Trish imagined them as a plucky,

62

mixed-race Romeo and Juliet without the bad ending. Mo would get work as a roadie or a sound man, maybe even join a band himself – he played bass guitar – and, somehow, though they had never discussed this, Trish's life would begin in some way too.

They had travelled through the early morning – two bus journeys – to be at the pier at seven in the morning. She'd rehearsed what she was going to say but she couldn't get started.

'It'll be alright,' Mo kept saying as if he suspected what her tense silence was about.

He was comforting her because, unlike him, Trish was running away. He'd told Neet he was leaving, whereas Trish had just left a note for her mother. She didn't say anything at the terminal as they queued to go through the barrier. He let go of her hand to fish out the tickets and she simply fell out of step with him. She held back. The crowd surged between them and suddenly he was on one side, and she was on the other. She watched as his army surplus knapsack jogged ahead and waited for him to realise she wasn't with him. He was probably still talking to her, not realising. Then he turned around. The crowd streamed either side of him. She watched as his face registered bafflement, then hurt and resignation. The three stages of grief in a couple of minutes.

Probably wasn't her, anyway. And if it was, serve her right. It would be sweet revenge for him to turn his back on her. Fifteen years ago the positions were reversed. He was the one left standing at the terminal, the black hatch of the ferry yawning behind him while she stood at the visitors' side of the gate shaking her head.

'Come on,' he'd shouted, 'Trish? Trish!'

And her only answer was to wave, or not even a wave, a kind of falling gesture with her hand as she turned away and trailed off across the forecourt, through the glassy doors and into the pearly morning, while he, like some lost child, kept on calling her name. Trish, Trish, Trish, until one of the porters came up to him and said, 'Come on, sonny, are you embarking or not?'

And that's when he saw how it was, how it would be. Trish's essential caution and her respectably dead father versus Mo with his uncertain skin colour, his illegitimacy and a flaky mother. They might have grown up on the same street but they were worlds apart. Just as they are now, him on one side of the barrier, and her on the other.

Trish had never heard from him again. She took to avoiding his mother, crossing the avenue if she saw Neet coming, afraid she would attack, like some enraged lioness. But Neet never said a word to her. Did she even know that Trish had been planning to run away to London with Mo? He was so close with information, he might never have mentioned it. Or her.

There's a guy, Keith has told him about, a prof at some university in the UK who's doing a study of airport people. An anthropologist.

'What's that?' Mo had to ask.

'A zoologist for people,' Keith said. 'Gave me a hundred quid for info about airport vagrants. That's what they call us.'

Mo likes the sound of it because it makes him, *this*, sound transitory, a rite of passage, not a destination. Unlike London where he did have a fixed address and an occupation. He made a life there, for a while. Or a living. Squatting, picking up work with bands here and there, drawing the dole, but there was a lot of down time. Literally. He smoked his way through a lot of dope. Had a full season of self-pity. Disbelieving at first, then bitterly resigned. He'd composed vengeful letters in his head to Trish, rehearsed phone conversations he couldn't afford to have long-distance. And what was he going to say?

'You are the girl who broke my heart!'

64

At the time he thought it a killer line.

He moved into a basement flat in Clapham for a bit. A scene of industrial clutter. Stacks of speakers, cables snaking underfoot, the strewn innards of amps which he rented out piecemeal. Pale monsters, emissaries from Mo's night-time world, would march through the garden at noon forcing him out of bed, staggering under the weight of Bose speakers with gaping beaks, colliding sometimes with the becalmed sheets on the whirligig line put out by the woman who lived in the upstairs flat. Somewhere along the way, work drifted out of his existence and his existence *became* his work.

No, not true. It was a dark winter's evening in the flat in London – what might have been the love nest he would have shared with Trish – when it struck him. He hadn't done a gig in weeks; the rain had seeped in under the front door of the flat so the basement hallway was awash. He'd had to put towels up against the crumbling sash windows to keep the moisture at bay and he thought – only love would keep you hopeful in this grief-stricken climate.

She walks the corridor of glass towards the gate, her heart as heavy as that morning she left Mo. It's half a lifetime ago, well half her lifetime anyway, but the pangs of betrayal are as sharp as when it happened. She's not reminded very often, except when there's a man around. But then, there's often a man around. She can't turn back now, anyway. A planeload of travellers sitting on the tarmac would curse her from a height. The public address system would name and shame her. Airport security would hunt her down. And if she were to go back, what exactly would she say to Mo Dark? I'm sorry would seem a bit lame after all these years.

Maybe she could sympathise with him on the death of his mother; Neet had died a couple of years ago. Breast cancer apparently – died in St Jude's. The irony of it. It must have hit Mo hard. A mortal blow. But then, hadn't Trish already delivered that? She chastises herself. Look, Mo Dark is probably heading up some indie record label in Los Angeles by now, has destroyed his septum snorting too much coke and is on his third wife. (While you're a lowly TEFL teacher who's just made a mess of an interview that might have allowed you *your* chance of escape.) That bloke you've just seen, he's not the director of a record label, is he? Not dressed like that, so it can't be Mo. And if you turn back and the bloke isn't Mo, then you'll look really stupid and you'll have missed your flight into the bargain.

She hurries determinedly towards the gate. But something just won't let go. A thread of plaintive possibility niggles at her. She halts on the moving travelator. Sun-glare blinds her. She turns around and begins to run, the wheels of her case on the ridges making the sound of an aggravated buzzard. She crashes into one person, then another. She finds herself thwarted by the travelator's momentum like she is trying to push the giant hands of time backwards. She turns back and faces forward; she will go to the end of this section, then she'll turn back. Yes, that's what she'll do; she *can* put this right. She can go back to the fork in the road.

Mo is slouching back to his trolley when he thinks he hears her call. He doesn't believe it at first; thinks it's the dope. It's true what they say: you *do* hear voices in your head. He hears Neet's mostly, now that she's dead. Poor Neet, who demanded so little from him. Was she like all the rest, keeping her expectations low to avoid disappointment? No, it was more than that, it was as if she expected him to turn out as he had and welcomed it, as her punishment. Because of what *she'd* done, merely by having him. The impossible equation: a single mother, a brown baby, the 1960s, Ireland. Long after Trish, he'd tried asking straight out about his father, but even on her deathbed Neet wouldn't relent.

'I've been your mother and your father, that's all you need to know.'

Like a bad line from *Chinatown*.

He's standing over a trolley full of plastic bags, and what's that – a bed roll? What have I done, she thinks, I've missed my flight for a complete stranger. Not just that, a hobo, for God's sake. Fuelled by some mad notion that she can undo everything. And then he turns around.

'Mo?'

Her voice comes out of a dream to him. The dream of the past. That time Neet had taken the stabilisers off his bike on the avenue. One minute she was running along behind him, laboured breathing in his ear, her hand on the saddle. He could feel the wind rushing by him making his cheeks smart.

'Don't let go,' he roared into the wind. He was picking up speed. He felt the heady exhilaration of being in flight. Then her voice from a long way back.

'You're on your own, Mo, there's a good boy, you're doing it on your own!'

He wobbled, veered crazily and fell off.

You're on your own, Mo.

'Mo? Mo Dark?' the voice demands. 'Is that you, Mo?'

Is it? Is *this* really him?

He turns to answer.

MISS IRELAND

The maid stuck her head in the gas oven one Sunday afternoon in the Devoy house, 27 Prosperity Drive, but not
before she had fed and changed the baby – Fergal, it was –
and put him down for his nap. The family was out visiting
Nana Devoy, as they always did after second Mass, and the
maid had timed it, or so Betty Fortune had heard, so the
deed would be done before they got back and before Fergal
woke again. She had put soaking towels in the gap between
the kitchen door and the floor so that the fumes would not
escape into the rest of the house and left a scrawled note
pinned to the kitchen door saying DANGER – KEEP OUT. There
was a deadly precision to the arrangement, a precision Irene
Devoy had never noticed in the girl before, though she didn't
voice this, not wanting to speak ill of the dead. She wanted
everything about the terrible scandal that had been visited
upon her household to be proper because what Irene felt
deep in her heart about the suicide of the maid was selfish
relief.

Liam had suggested the maid. She can deal with the baby,
the night feeds, and help out with the chores etc., etc., Liam
had said. Etcetera was a phrase he used a lot, and it covered
a multitude. But Irene couldn't complain. Liam was a good
provider. With a new baby in the house, he was worried about
Irene losing her beauty sleep, as he called it; that was why
Quinny was hired in the first place.

Of course she wasn't Quinny when she came. She was Marguerite Quinn, recommended by a colleague of Liam's in Public Works. She was a country girl, as all these maids were, and on first sight, Irene's heart took a dive. She expected someone mousy and cowed, but Quinny was a big girl, big-boned that is, with breasts and curves sheathed in a black Bri-Nylon polo, a skirt in houndstooth check tight around the beam end, and black stockings with, Irene noticed, a ladder stopped above the knee with nail polish. She wore kitten heels. She had long auburn hair, long enough to sit on – which delighted the boys – and brown eyes, large and placid. And she had a beauty spot, pasted high on her pale cheekbone. The only way in which she satisfied Irene's expectations was in her accent, flat and tinkerish. She called Irene Missus.

'Where have you been working before this?' Irene asked her.

'Worked for a lord in the County Meath, Missus. In a castle. With a moat and all. But I was let go.'

'Oh.' Irene felt a tiny tremor of alarm. She waited for an explanation but the girl offered none.

'Well, we don't have a castle here,' Irene said, laughing nervously as she showed Quinny the box room in the back that they'd cleared for her and the baby. With the cot in there it looked poky and the sun went in just at that moment, so it took on a dingy air. Irene was about to apologise. Then she thought better of it. This was a maid, for God's sake.

'Now, come and meet the boys.'

Rory was seven and Owen coming up for three, and it was he who lispily christened her Quinny. Marguerite was too exotically long and syllabled for him, and since every name he'd mastered had a long e at the end and sounded diminutive – Daddy, Mummy, Rory – Marguerite became Quinny. Irene rather liked it. It had the ring of a family retainer, as if Quinny was comfort-ably old, someone they'd inherited from the generation before. Until people clapped eyes on her, that is. Once they did, she was back to being the maid. The young one, the pretty one. The postman, who'd been to America, called her Red.

Before she came, Irene had nursed visions of being munificent with the maid, being the lady of the house, firm but fair. But once Quinny arrived in the flesh, a whole new set of ambitions attached themselves to her. She imagined schooling Quinny in housewifery and, in some hidden part of her, maybe even becoming like a mother to her, or if not a mother a helpful older sister. (Irene felt her singularity in a male household.) But Quinny's manner did not allow any of Irene's vague fantasies to be enacted. There was something feral about her, Irene thought, like a hibernating animal that was only barely house-trained. Not that there was anything to complain about in Quinny's work. She did the night feeds without complaint, she got Rory up and out to school in the mornings, and gave Owen his breakfast. She would even bring Irene a cup of tea in bed where she was allowed to lie on for the first time in years. Quinny's attitude to work, though, was graceless. She had a kind of phlegmatic loathing for the tasks Irene herself hated – cleaning the bathroom, ironing the sheets. She handled Fergal with a brusque expertise. (Irene remembered how tentative she'd been as a first-time mother with Rory and she was sure, as a baby, he had sensed that, somehow.) Irene couldn't identify the source of her unease about Quinny except perhaps that in a very short time her boys became more attached to Quinny than they were to her.

Rory's face would fall when he came in from school on Wednesdays forgetting it was Quinny's day off. Owen would trail up to her room and sit on her bed waiting for her to come home. Or if she was doing the ironing – in the dining room with the radio tuned to Luxembourg – he would sit at her feet and play with the rolled-up socks. Irene would watch her to see what it was that Quinny did differently. She ignored the boys benignly, Irene discovered, let them talk and chatter.

She didn't lead their conversations, she followed them. She was like a bigger, duller child.

When the children were in bed, Irene would urge Quinny to join Liam and her in the sitting room to watch TV, thinking that this might make her more malleable.

'No thanks, Missus,' she would say, 'I'll stay in the kitchen, if you don't mind.' Or she would go to her room, Irene guiltily seeing her chaste single bed pushed up against the cot, the scarred bedside locker they'd bought second-hand, the curtained-off alcove in place of a proper wardrobe.

'We've fallen on our feet there,' Liam said, very pleased with himself.

They had, Irene had to admit.

But still, she wanted more from Quinny, or more of her.

She tried being friendly, gently prodding the maid with the kind of questions that allowed the possibility of another life outside the confines of Prosperity Drive. Have you friends in the city, do you go to the pictures, or, this said blushingly, do you have a boyfriend? That, Irene suspected, was the rock all maids perished on. No, Missus, Quinny would say. But Irene couldn't believe that. Not of a girl with false eyelashes and a beauty spot. There *had* to be a romance. Irene's own young life had been shaped by such certainties, her life before Liam, and what's more they had been made flesh. As Irene Cardiff, she had once been Miss Ireland. (The inner picture of herself, if she closed her eyes, was wearing the Connolly ball gown with the black velvet bodice, the petalled waistline, and those full skirts of pleated linen gauze, and the two runners-up, like a pair of comely handmaidens, settling the winning sash on her hips; her crowning moment.) People took note of her luminous green eyes and white even teeth, her clear complexion and oatmeal hair, her still pert figure – despite three babies. She could see it in their gaze; she was used to frank admiration. What they didn't know was that she had once been a beauty queen. It wasn't that she was ashamed of it. She'd represented her country, after all (and reached the final sixteen at Miss World in London). But among her neighbours, wives of clerkly types, legal people, engineers, the Miss World contest would have been regarded as common and shoddy, she was sure. It would lower the tone, that's what they would think. So when she chatted to Betty Fortune, or Edel Elworthy, and especially Miss Larchet, she mentioned she had been an air hostess before her marriage, but never the beauty queen business. Air hostess was a job, a glamorous occupation; beauty queen was a state of mind. They'd think her a ninny.

Her marriage to Liam Devoy had won her a sense of achieved seriousness. His grandfather had done something in 1916, and Liam was part of the organising committee for the fiftieth anniversary celebrations of the Rising. That's who she was in the eyes of neighbours, the capable pretty wife of an up-and-coming civil servant with a serious pedigree. If they knew about Miss World, they'd look at her differently. They'd regard her carefully tended blondness, her discreet make-up (she never went out of the house without what Liam called her 'warpaint'), and her stylish clothes as some kind of striving after a station in life to which she was not entitled.

Even if Quinny would not allow herself to be mothered, Irene thought there was one area where she could help. The girl's attempts at fashion were ham-fisted, to say the least – that houndstooth skirt was positively slutty – and though Irene was touched by Quinny's cheap scents, her false eyelashes, even the beauty spot, they all seemed like a girl playing dress-up. In this, Irene felt, hers was precisely the kind of expertise Quinny needed.

'Don't you think something with a slightly longer hemline would be more flattering?' she suggested one Wednesday afternoon as Quinny headed out in a red pencil skirt halfway up her thigh. Irene had Owen on her hip. Quinny looked at her with an expression between wounded offence and outright hostility.

'It's just,' Irene went on, 'that for a girl of your build, something a bit longer might be . . .'

'It's my afternoon off, Missus,' Quinny said mulishly.

'Of course,' Irene said, 'it's none of my business. It's just I have an eye for these things. I used to . . .' She was going to tell Quinny about being Miss Ireland, thinking *she* might be impressed with it. 'And you know it's my experience that young men prefer a little bit of mystery.'

'What young men?' Quinny asked. Irene could hear the bridling tone, as if she had accused Quinny of something.

'A pretty girl like you,' Irene said, 'there *must* be a young man . . .' How many times had Irene herself heard that line. Flirty, wheedling.

'Is that all, Missus?' Quinny interrupted; quite rudely, Irene thought. 'I'll be off, so.'

'How do *you* find her?' she asked Liam though she already knew the answer. For him, Quinny was a problem solved. He didn't trouble himself about the maid's social life.

'What do you mean?' he asked. 'She's perfectly hard-working, does her job, the children love her. What's the problem?'

'I don't know,' Irene admitted. Then, suddenly fierce, 'So why did she leave the job in the big house in Meath. Close to home and all.'

'Close to *the* home, you mean?'

'She came from a home? You didn't tell me that.'

'What difference does it make?'

Irene couldn't have said why, but it did make a difference. There was something shameful about those homes where children were left, if only by the deaths of their unfortunate parents. On one of the red-brick avenues near the church there was a place called the Cottage Home, and though she didn't know much about it because it was Protestant, Irene always hurried past it (particularly when she had the boys in tow) as if the building itself, like a house in a fairy tale, might reach out and devour them. The face of the home was austere. Grey unpainted plaster; long, thin windows set in deep embrasures, which gave them a hooded look; gravel out front where a garden should have been. But the most forbidding thing about the Cottage Home was that there was never any sign of life there. No evidence at all, in fact, of children.

The fact that Quinny was an orphan quelled Irene's uneasiness for a while. The girl simply wasn't used to a good family; or any family at all, for that matter. That was it. That *must* be it. But then she began to worry if Quinny was damaged goods, in some way. Should they have looked for references for her? When they'd hired her, word-of-mouth had seemed recommendation enough, particularly when it was from Enda Dowd, the Assistant Secretary in Liam's Department.

'Ask him,' Irene urged Liam, 'why it was she left the job in the castle.'

'Lord God, Irene, would you leave it be? You're only making a problem where there isn't one.'

But then there was. It was a stupid thing, really, but afterwards Irene was sorry she hadn't acted.

That day the children were in the playroom in the extension which had been built on to the back of the house by the previous owners, an elderly couple, who had used it to grow plants. It was no more than a glass lean-to, but some day when the boys were grown, Irene determined, she would deck it out with bamboo blinds and cane furniture and turn it into a sunroom. But for now it was for the kids, a place for them to let off steam when it was raining, as it was that day. The Fortune twins had come over to play. Kitty and Liv were a few years older than Rory, and Irene had always thought them a civilising influence. Also, she wanted her boys to mix with little girls; soon enough they would be packed off to boarding school, as Liam had been, where the female of the species would be reduced to Matron and Nurse.

It was a Wednesday, and Irene was feeding Fergal in the kitchen. Quinny was about to leave for her afternoon off. It had, she'd noticed, gone awfully quiet in the playroom and she asked Quinny if she'd mind checking on the children before she went. The only entrance to the playroom was from the garden, so Quinny went outside. What Irene heard next was Quinny screaming. She thought there'd been some kind of accident, and she rushed out, her heart thumping, with Fergal in her arms still sucking greedily on his bottle. Thank God, she was thinking, Quinny is still here.

But there was no accident. Quinny was standing just inside the open doorway of the playroom, gripping the door handle.

'It's a sacrilege, a sacrilege, do you hear. Do you understand?' she was shouting.

Beyond her, Irene could see Rory and one of the Fortune twins draped comically in a pair of red velveteen curtains she'd recently taken down because they were past their best. Owen was kneeling in front of them, swathed in a bed sheet. Irene found herself stifling a smile – the female influence of the Fortune twins was obviously making itself felt.

'What is it?' she asked, stepping into the frozen scene, still expecting to see blood.

'Your boy,' Quinny said accusingly, 'your boy has committed a sacrilege.' There was a catch of grief in her voice.

'We were playing Mass,' Rory rushed to defend himself. 'I'm Canon Burke, Liv's Father Dolan, Owen is the altar boy, and Kitty is the audience.'

'Congregation,' Irene found herself saying.

'It's still a sacrilege, Missus,' Quinny said, gulping noisily, 'making a mockery of the Holy Sacrament.' Her breath was coming high and fast, her cheeks were flushed.

Irene handed the baby over to Kitty, the more capable of the twins, and put her arm around Quinny, who was heaving dry tears. Hyperventilation. She'd seen it a couple of times with nervous flyers in her time.

'Take a deep breath, there's a good girl,' she said as the children looked on, aghast. What a strange reversal this was, she thought, being in the position of comforting Quinny.

'I'm sure the children meant no harm by it.'

'It's a mortal sin,' Quinny said.

'They're only children . . .' Irene said.

'It doesn't matter,' Quinny said, 'it's still a mortal sin.'

'I'm sure the boys didn't mean any harm by it, did you, boys?' She couldn't presume to speak for the Fortunes.

'Those twins put them up to it,' Quinny said.

'Rory will make a good confession about it and that'll be the end of it,' Irene said decisively. 'Isn't that so?'

Rory nodded gravely.

'They were using Tom Thumbs as the Sacred Host,' Quinny persisted.

Irene saw the offending bag of sweets sitting on a kitchen plate on the floor. They were Rory's, and Irene was rather touched that he had offered his personal hoard up for the sake of verisimilitude.

'Maybe Kitty and Liv should run along home now,' Irene said. She was tiring of trying to console Quinny, who seemed so adamant in her refusal. Kitty handed Fergal back.

The twins looked relieved to be out of the line of fire.

'Now,' Irene said to Quinny, 'why don't we make you a nice cup of tea and we can all calm down.'

Rory, she could see, was quite shocked at this strange behaviour of Quinny's. Owen was simply confused.

'You go and put the kettle on, Quinny,' she said, figuring that, as with an upset child, distraction was the best policy.

But Quinny just stood there. 'Are you going to sack me, Missus?'

And that's when Irene should have said yes.

* * *

'Well, it's hardly a hanging offence,' Liam said when she told him about it. 'And at least it proves she's pious.'

But, Irene wanted to say, what I saw was not piety but terror. Quinny had been more terrified than the children were, terrified of them and what they had done. As if she expected instant retribution. She was a religious girl – Irene had seen the holy water bottle in her room, the missal. She went to early Mass every Sunday, but there was nothing to account for *this* kind of zeal. Irene found herself examining her own conscience. She was a believer, of course, but she didn't go in for craw-thumping. She prayed spasmodically, but more out of desperation than routine. Hurried imprecations to stem panic, bargains offered in return for specific favours. She began to see how childish and lazy her faith was. How lax and deficient she must seem to someone of Quinny's fanatical heart. She felt herself already judged in Quinny's eyes for not punishing Rory. She would have to do something, or be seen to do something. Cravenly, she followed Quinny's lead and blamed the Fortune twins for the whole business.

'I've told Kitty and Liv's mother that it might be better if they didn't come over for a while,' Irene told Quinny, even though she realised she was engaging in appeasement. Appeasing Quinny.

What she said to Betty Fortune was quite different.

'The maid,' she said, adopting an air of helpless fatalism, 'seems to have taken some kind of set against your girls.'

And that seemed to be the end of it.

The episode had its consequences; it made Rory wary of Quinny. He was nervous by disposition, and Irene knew he feared another outburst, particularly since the first one had been aimed at him. But Owen's devotion remained. If anything, it grew. He wanted only Quinny to bathe him, or to read him his bedtime story. Irene wondered if this was her younger son's attempt at appeasement. Or was it the other way around? Since the sacrilege incident, Quinny had taken to favouring Owen, as if he were her primary responsibility. 'How's my little Oweny?' she would croon and his little face would light up. He'd clamber up on her, and she would nuzzle him and whisper to him. Irene began to feel gently elbowed out. In the afternoons, Quinny would take Owen into her bed for his nap, and Owen wouldn't settle anywhere else. Irene found herself knocking tentatively at Quinny's door when nap time was up.

'If Owen sleeps too much during the day, he'll be awake half the night,' she would entreat.

'Sure, I'll mind him, Missus – don't I always?' This directed at Owen, who looked up adoringly at Quinny. Like a depiction of the Virgin and Child, Irene thought. Irene felt panicky; could a child be killed with kindness? The balance of power had shifted, and she was afraid. Afraid of the maid.

In the meantime, though, there were the summer holidays. They rented a chalet in Courtown for the month of July. Irene took Quinny, and Liam came at the weekends, work allowing, so Irene's memories of that summer were all Quinny. At close quarters in the chalet, Irene realised how solitary the girl was. It came as a soft shock. Irene tried to compensate. When they went for treats, Irene would determinedly include her. Sticks of candyfloss, ice-cream cones, a matinée at the cinema even though there were only cartoons showing. When they went to the carnival, she doled out small change to Quinny as if she were an honorary child, though she was nineteen and Irene feared she might be offended. But she didn't seem to be. At the Spin the Wheel, Quinny won a pink bunny rabbit, which she presented to Owen, although it would have been more suitable for the baby, Irene thought. Owen was delighted. He hung on to that bunny for years. Refused to let Irene take it away, even to wash it, so that it became a grubby talisman of Quinny's that would not be banished. In the light of what happened, Irene felt she couldn't deny him.

The weather was glorious. So hot that the tar on the road to the beach melted and the children's feet stuck to it. She remembered having to stop Owen scraping the black stuff off with his fingers and eating it; he thought it was liquorice. There were long, lazy days of picnics and sandcastles and dips in the sea. Quinny was not equipped for the seaside, Irene noticed. She had no swimwear, and she seemed to have nothing even vaguely summery in her wardrobe. Her only concession to the heat was that she dispensed with stockings. Her legs looked pale and sorrowful stuck in her kitten heels and she didn't shave her legs, Irene saw, so there was quite a thicket growing there. Irene offered her one of her old bathing suits, though she thought it would be a bit of a squeeze for Quinny to get into it since she was much better endowed on top than Irene was. (Miss Pays-Bas had told her that was why Irene hadn't got into the top five in London. *Vulgar creature.*)

'It's alright, Missus,' Quinny said, 'I'm not much good with water. Can't swim.'

Irene felt sorry for her. While she and Owen paddled in the shallows and Rory bobbed in the breakers, Quinny sat miserably behind the candy-striped windbreak looking after Fergal. It made Irene feel like a girl again, larking about in the surf with the boys, while Quinny seemed more like the mother, sitting in the shade and watching their fun remotely. And Owen was returned to her. He could not resist the fun of the water, the one place Quinny couldn't follow him.

But with Quinny there was always the grit in the oyster. One afternoon when Irene had gone to the beach shop, Quinny had let Owen – it would be Owen, of course – bury his sandals. They were newly bought, the ones with the clover pattern and the blond soles. Quinny was always engaging in this kind of play with them, Irene thought crossly, not supervising them but sinking to their level. When she came back with a net of oranges for the children (no crisps and chocolate bars for her boys; she insisted on healthy snacks to protect their teeth), she interrupted their game, so it wasn't until they were getting ready to pack up and go that the absence of the sandals was discovered. Irene was furious.

'They can't have gone too deep,' Quinny said when they started their search. But an hour later, when Irene and the boys were reduced to dogs, scrabbling at the sand with their paws, her nonchalance had disappeared.

'Where did you last see them?' Irene demanded.

'I don't know,' Quinny said forlornly. 'That was the whole point of the game.'

They excavated until the sand all around their encampment was a field of coarse rubble. Owen used his spade and thought it all part of the silly game Quinny had started. Towards the end, Rory let out a victorious halloo when he unearthed one sandal. But that was nearly worse. What good was one? The light began to fail. The beach was deserted now, and they were steeped in a chilly salmon-coloured dusk. The children were getting shivery, the baby in Quinny's arms yelling to be fed, but Irene insisted they continue. She'd wanted to punish Quinny, but in the end the children had been made to suffer by the fruitless search. There'd be trouble, Irene knew. Liam couldn't stand the idea of waste. He wasn't tight-fisted, exactly, but he was frugal by nature so that she had to account for every penny of her housekeeping allowance. She was thriftier than he knew – she still had that Connolly gown and all her other beauty queen finery. In case, she told herself, in case she might find an occasion – some function to do with Liam's work, maybe – where she could wear them again. But, she suspected, those taffeta and satin dresses lovingly preserved in their plastic shrouds represented something different to Liam. For him, they spoke of an extravagant nature that might sprout again at any moment. The very things that had attracted him – her style, her poise – had become vices that must be reined in.

'The price of Owen's sandals will come out of your wages,' she said to Quinny as they trooped back home through the darkening dunes.

'Yes, Missus,' was all Quinny said.

The days at the beach were memorialised not in holiday snaps – because Irene was useless with the camera; that was Liam's domain – but by an unseen hand. On one of those long, lazy days a John Hinde postcard photographer had captured the scene. Two years later, when Irene had had the courage to return to Courtown, Owen spotted the card on the swivel rack in the beachside shop.

'Look, look,' he screamed, 'it's Quinny!'

Irene ignored him as he tugged at her sleeve. It was a scene that had been replayed again and again. The sight of any long-haired girl on the street could prompt him. He would run after her, calling out Quinny's name, Irene in resentful pursuit. She was weary of trying to explain to long-haired strangers why her son was clinging to them. The sightings on the street were always heartbreaking; he would be inconsolable for days, crushed by the enormity of his own expectation.

'Now, Owen, you know it can't be Quinny. Quinny is . . .' Irene didn't like to use the word.

'But she's here,' Owen insisted, waving the card at her. 'Look, look.'

He was getting so hysterical that she bent down to look at the card, and she saw that Owen was right. The photographer must have stood in the dunes at the curve of the beach – the view was a long one. The sky blared blue. Irene and her boys were reduced to heads bobbing in the frothy water, but Quinny's face was captured quite clearly in side view, and wearing Irene's straw sun hat. Some old sense of propriety flared in Irene.

'You're absolutely right, Owen,' she said, feeling her voice tremble. She bought the card to appease him and in the hope that it might provide solace. But part of her wished he had never seen it. While Owen was in the world, she realised, Quinny would have a hold over her.

Quinny took Owen on a morning in September; well not exactly took him, she was technically in charge of him. Irene didn't know how to explain this – Quinny went missing, and for several hours she had no idea where her son was (though she never told Liam this). Quinny was supposed to be taking Owen to the barber for his first big boy cut. Up to then, Irene had used the scissors on his baby curls, but she'd decided it was time. Time to let go. This was the first step on his journey to boarding school; Irene reckoned she'd better get used to it. In a year's time, Rory would be sent there.

They set off at eleven, Owen happily (a jaunt with Quinny!), and Irene expected them back within the hour. When lunchtime came and there was no sign of them, Irene began to fret. The barber's was only in the village, a ten-minute walk away. She considered putting Fergal in the pram and going in search of them, but Rory would be in from school for his lunch so she couldn't leave. When Rory arrived, she pretended nothing was amiss; she fed him and he went back to school. She put Fergal down for his nap – it was 2.30 now, and for the first time she gave in to panic. Where could they be? Had there been an accident? She thought of ringing Liam at the office, but she didn't. She didn't want to disturb him, and she didn't want to be accused of scaremongering, once more making a mountain out of a molehill where Quinny was concerned. Anyway, she felt vaguely implicated – why hadn't she brought Owen to the barber's herself and left Quinny with the baby? Wasn't it Fergal that Quinny was employed to mind, in the first place?

Rory came in from school and asked mildly where Owen and Quinny were.

'They're having a day in town,' Irene lied.

The lie emboldened her: this is what she would say to Liam. Already she was thinking ahead. This way it would appear as if the trip was sanctioned, instead of their toddler son being missing for the best part of the day and Irene having done nothing about it.

At six she heard the key in the door and rushed into the hallway, praying it wasn't Liam, because now she was more afraid of his censure than the fact that Owen was missing. A tousled-looking Owen appeared, holding Quinny's hand. He was filthy. There was grime on his face and chocolate stains around his mouth. His baby curls, she noticed, were still intact.

'Thank God,' she said, forgetting to be cross with Quinny. 'I was out of my mind with worry. Where have you been?'

'We went up the Pillar,' Owen declared proudly.

Irene looked at Quinny.

'Nelson's Pillar?'

She was expecting a rush of apology, some abject excuse for keeping the child out for seven hours, some explanation, but Quinny said nothing.

'I'll bring him up for his bath, Missus,' was all she said as if she was simply resuming duties.

She led Owen upstairs. (He kicked up a terrible fuss when Irene insisted on a bath, but with Quinny, he was always docile.) By the time Liam came home, a scrubbed and dressing-gowned Owen was having his tea with Rory, and everything was back to normal. Irene was relieved she didn't have to explain her neglectful part in the affair. But she was determined to get to the bottom of it. Tomorrow, she would tackle Quinny.

But she didn't. She interrogated Owen instead.

'We were on the bus,' he said. That was a novelty for him. 'On the upstairs.'

'And what about Nelson's Pillar?'

'It was dark,' he said, 'but Quinny held my hand.'

Irene had never been inside the Pillar. There were 168 steps that wound up in a spiral to a viewing platform at the top. Liam had wanted to take her during their courtship, but Irene hadn't liked the sound of it.

'You can see for miles from up there,' he had said.

But it was the enclosure Irene was afraid of, the seeping granite walls, the imprisonment of it.

'And what did you eat?' Irene asked, because Owen was fond of his food.

'Crips,' he answered.

'Crisps,' she corrected, though usually she found his lisp endearing.

He nodded.

'And chocolate?' Irene prompted, remembering his muddy mouth. 'And what else?'

His brow furrowed in concentration.

'Quinny has a little boy,' he volunteered.

'What do you mean?' Irene said, and she shook him.

'I'm her little boy,' Owen said and smiled cheesily. It was the closest Irene ever came to striking one of her children. She raised her hand, then let it fall.

Over the following weeks there were several more disappearances, though none as alarming as that first time. If Irene asked Quinny to run to the shops, she would always take Owen with her, and the errands took longer than they should have. She would take detours to the park (Owen loved the swings). They went to view the building site. Eight new houses were being built on to the end of Prosperity Drive. There were pyramids of gravel and sand on the road and the churning of cement mixers all day. She took him to the sheep field – Quinny seemed to know all the secret places in the neighbourhood – and into the grounds of St Jude's, the cancer hospital

84

at the end of the avenue. Owen came back from that expedition excitedly proclaiming he'd seen the bald children. Irene had ruled St Jude's out of bounds precisely because there were children there, sick and dying children whom she didn't want Rory or Owen exposed to.

'St Jude's is no place for him,' she said to Quinny. But what was meant as a reprimand came out feebly, and still Quinny made no apology.

'Nita asked us in,' she said. 'Isn't that right, Oweny?' *His name is not Oweny.*

Nita Dark lived in the gate lodge at the entrance to the hospital. Mother of a little coloured boy who was in Low Babies with Owen. Irene was not sure she approved but Owen and Mo were friends, so she couldn't exactly forbid the association. But she didn't want to encourage it either. The first day he'd come home from school, Owen had asked why Mo was a different colour.

'He's a baby from the missions,' Irene had lied, furious at having to defend Nita Dark's unsavoury morals. 'He's from Africa.'

Trust Quinny to pal up with Nita Dark, of all people.

'She's a brave woman,' Quinny said as if reading Irene's mind.

'Or foolish,' Irene said.

Quinny made a dissatisfied pout, like a child being corrected. Then she lifted Owen up and carried him off to give him his lunch. Irene felt wrong-footed. As always with Quinny, they never got to talk about the real trouble.

The day, *that* day, it was Liam who found her. He had Owen in his arms and as soon as he put the key in the front door he could smell the gas.

'Stay back,' he shouted at Irene and Rory, who were trailing in behind him. But in his panic he carried Owen into the kitchen so Owen *saw.*

'Holy Jesus!' Liam cried and shut the door on the sight.

'What is it?' Irene asked.

'Quinny is praying,' Owen said.

It made them notorious. The house where the maid had gassed herself. What could drive a girl to do such a thing? Irene saw that question in the eyes of her neighbours. An unwanted pregnancy. That's what they thought, Irene was sure, and they would look at her and wonder why she hadn't exerted her authority more firmly. How could she explain that was not it at all? With Quinny the worst had already happened, before she had ever darkened the Devoys' door. It was nothing I did, Irene wanted to say, but of course, this being Prosperity Drive, no one came out with any such accusations.

She and Liam went to the funeral in a country church near Kells, though Irene didn't want to.

'We have to,' Liam said, 'we were *in loco parentis.*'

'She was the maid, Liam, for God's sake.'

The maid who had tried to purloin her son and then did *this* to them! Brought disreputable death into their midst. Quinny couldn't even be buried in consecrated ground because of what she'd done. She was taken away after the funeral to God knows where.

Her parents were there, her father a rough-looking man unkempt with grief, her mother a version of what Quinny might have become. Fleshy, jowly with startling high-built black hair. Quinny also had two brothers, it turned out. Grown men, large, bewildered.

'I thought you said she was an orphan,' Irene hissed at Liam as they travelled gingerly up the aisle of the church to extend their condolences.

'I said a home,' Liam said crossly, Mr Etc. suddenly a stickler for distinctions, 'a mother and baby home. She gave the child up.'

'Oh,' Irene said, wondering why he hadn't told her before.

86

Chastened, she kept her head bowed beneath her black mantilla. She let Liam do the talking when they shook Quinny's mother's hand at the top of the church. This new knowledge should have helped, but it didn't. She had known nothing really of Quinny, nothing at all.

A lot of things happened that year. There was the Rising commemoration, which went off without a hitch and won Liam a promotion. The railway stations were renamed for the signatories of the Proclamation. The Pillar was blown up by hotheads who said Nelson shouldn't be lording it over them. Irene was secretly delighted; another place associated with Quinny reduced to ruin. At the end of the year, the new houses being built at the end of the street were finished. As a result, everyone on Prosperity Drive got a new house number. The Devoys lost Number 27 and inherited 10 instead. Quinny's associations were gradually dwindling.

But the dead maid remained lodged in Irene's mind. And in Owen's too, Irene was sure, though the running after strangers in the street did stop, and her name, so often invoked in the early days, also fell away. But some things stuck. Even years afterwards, and with another new baby in the house, Owen still called the nursery Quinny's room. Irene felt his loyalty to the dead maid as a constant rebuke, as if there was blame attached. When the time came for Owen to be sent off to boarding school, she quietly welcomed it. There had been scenes with Rory; tears, hers, her eyes red for days on end. The gap he left at the dinner table, his unslept-in bed in the boys' room, his favourite books in Owen's or Fergal's hands, wounded her, as if there'd been a death in the family. But with Owen, there was reprieve. Now there would be no more Quinny ambushes. If that's what it took to be finally shot of her, Irene thought, hardening her heart, then so be it.

'See,' Liam had said to her when she deposited Owen dry-eyed in the big dormitory. 'I told you it would get easier.'

Nearly three decades later, when Owen brought Kim home and announced he was marrying her, the ghost of Quinny rose again. Not that Kim looked in the slightest bit like Quinny, apart from her hair, long and silky and down to her waist. Otherwise, though, she was petite and sallow, a trained pharmacist. And oriental, for God's sake. One of those unfortunate boat people.

'You can be the daughter my mother never had,' Owen said to Kim in that half-mocking way he talked about her, in her presence. 'Isn't that right, Irene?' (He had long ago stopped calling her Mum.)

But Irene would not make that mistake again. Looking at her future daughter-in-law, she felt only a disowning surge of triumph. She worried how Liam would take to the prospect of little Vietnamese grandchildren in the Devoy family line but, unlike him, she could afford to be magnanimous; she was not seeking to gain a daughter, but to lose a son, this time for good.

CLAIMS AND REBATES

Afterwards, in the hotel, he dreamt he saw Norah rise from the bed beside him and go to the window. Or, at least, it was a transparent version of her, one that he could see right through. Yet, when he looked in the bed, her back-turned body was also there, all solid flesh. The wraith-like Norah at the window was like a film ghost; he even remarked upon it in the dream. But he was too terrified to call out in case he might alarm this frail version of her and she would be trapped for ever outside the body that was still lying beside him. Then he woke and found himself alone.

*　　*　　*

Her innocence had provoked him. No, it was stronger than that, it had offended him. She had no right to be out in the world parading her raw, sheltered bloom like that. He blamed it on her clothes. That black roll-neck sweater, a blue pinafore and a pair of tights too tan for the rest of her pale complexion. Her shoes, brand new, were pinching her. As soon as she was shown to her desk she slipped her feet out of them and he saw her flexing her instep, her toes squirming within their ochre prison. He looked away. Oh God, another modest, convent-educated child! He could see the home she came from, a half red-brick on a respectable cul-de-sac with a kitchen hatch, a melamine breakfast counter, exuberantly floral wallpaper in the bedrooms; the same kind of house he was now condemned to, full of worthy suburban striving and cast-iron respectability.

He had always preferred the girls from the country; their fumy loneliness (damp bedsits, laundry dried indoors) gave them an edge, a certain racy recklessness. He had had dalliances with several of them – none current. These were usually one-night stands, which, nevertheless, required some kind of courtship ritual – a trip to the cinema, an hour or two listening to mournful Janis Ian records beforehand and a great deal of reassurance afterwards that it wouldn't affect their jobs. In the throes he was Hugh, but afterwards they reverted to calling him Mr Grove. There might be some awkwardness in the office for a while, but it was more often on their side than his; he actually liked the post-coital air of tension and their pliant uncertainty. But he could not imagine someone like Norah Elworthy succumbing in this way; *she* would be hard work.

The Redundancies section was situated in a large ground-floor room of a five-storey block overlooking the canal. On sunny days, swaying leaf-dapple lent spattered visual relief to the office but the prevailing mood was a stunned grey. A military formation of dove-coloured filing cabinets split the room in two. On one side was Hugh's kingdom, Claims; on the other, Rebates. There were typing-pool rows of desks, the girls – they were mostly girls – all facing the one direction; facing him, in fact. It was not a popular section, not sexy in other words, though it fairly oozed with the pent-up frustration of twenty-seven girls finding themselves in the sparse company of seven men, who, like him, were for the most part years older. As a result, they did not stay long. They applied for Careers – with out-of-office trips to conventions in large hotels and visits in the mobile unit to schools, or Equal Opportunities, a newly opened section on the fifth floor with glossy brochures and a ministerial pet project, or if they were seriously ambitious they transferred out.

Claims was designated as the trenches of the Department. They were assiduous handmaidens to the depressing times. Every news bulletin heralded shortages, the oil crisis, a roll call of factory closures and lay-offs but it was they who attended to the minutiae of the wreckage. Their currency was thousands of manila folders fatly stuffed with sheaves of forms, the coffined remnants of lives returned to statistics. Their clients weren't people any more but redundancies, empty vessels making no noise. If an economic upswing ever came, which Hugh seriously doubted, he wondered how he and his 'team' would be deployed. (Personnel insisted on such terminology as if Hugh were managing a bunch of athletic champions, not a disparate and unhappy crowd of lowly clerks.) Hugh liked to think his girls liked him. He was not one of those section heads who stood by the attendance register with a stopwatch taking down the names of latecomers when the line was drawn in the book at 9.15 every morning. He had trouble himself rising and since he did only a rough approximation of a nine-to-five day, he could hardly impose strict punctuality on his staff. This apparent laxity made him popular with his girls and efficient in the eyes of the powers that be and it spared him the torturous procedure of having to listen to a catalogue of preposterous excuses related to their female complaints. It was 1976 and they felt emboldened to use their hormones as justification for every failing. That was fine by him; he just didn't want to hear about it.

Hugh was, just at the moment, sort of separated. Marriage, he had discovered much to his secret relief, was a revolving door. In the four years they'd been together, Elaine had thrown him out numerous times, but he had never believed it to be a permanent state. He felt a similar impermanence when he was back in her good books and living at home;

in fact, the uncertainty was the only thing that made marriage bearable.

Elaine had once been one of the girls in the office, which gave her an unfair advantage. She knew how he was; she had been one of his graduates. She'd been a blowsy overripe kind of girl with her large hair and a smutty laugh. She had flirted with him from the start while acting as if she didn't give a toss about him. If it was a strategy, Hugh had to concede now, it had worked. It was the first time he had seen tenacity decoupled from neediness and he couldn't resist. He was nearly thirty-five; it wasn't that he no longer wanted the freedom of the single life, he just didn't want to be a sad, ageing Lothario, mistaken for what the tabloids called a confirmed bachelor. A distinct danger, since he still lived with his mother.

Hugh had spent his childhood behind the perfume counter in Switzers where his mother worked; he adored it. He would take the bus into town after school, then sit on the tub-like stool the girls used to reach the higher shelves and do his homework perched at stocking level to the swish of satin slips. When they had a spare moment, the girls would help him. They had unexpected gifts – Sylvia could do tots in her head, Marie helped him with his comprehension. He loved their porcelain visages, these surrogate aunties. He'd never seen them less than perfect, although he had often witnessed his mother take her make-up off. She always waited till bedtime to revert to the pale and wan version of herself, bleached and blanched and somehow smaller than life. The girls on the Revlon counter – beauticians, they called themselves, a word too close to mortician for Hugh's liking – were like his own harem of painted paramours wearing white coats to make them look like pharmacists. Like dress-up tarts in a porn mag. When Miss Hyde, the floorwalker, did her rounds, the girls would push Hugh's head down and hide him among their skirts so that Dolly's secret would not be discovered. That was what Hugh was – his mother's secret. The time came, of course, when he graduated from the comforts of the Revlon counter and progressed into surly adolescence, but his attachment to perfume persisted. He didn't hold with eau de toilette or body spray; none of those light fragrances. No, he wanted cloying, heavy musk he could drown in. Norah Elworthy wore no perfume, he noticed. When he was close to her, she smelled of apples from her lunch. (Like the rest of them she was watching her weight.)

It was the small matter of Sive that had clinched the situation with Elaine. Regardless of the compensations of the perfume counter, fatherless Hugh didn't want a disowned child out in the universe. It wasn't even as if Elaine pleaded or begged. That was not her style. After months of uncomplicated fun (she had lasted way longer than anyone else) she simply broke the news and left a pregnant silence. So Elaine became the one for whom he surrendered his old life. Or tried to. Their first separation had occurred after Sive was born. He blamed it on the new baby and the terrible sleeplessness: the only brand of sleep deprivation Hugh had known before was the kind born of night-long drinking sprees or hectic dawn sex, but this tiredness was of a different tenor. Even when he did manage to sleep, it was a shallow, uneasy kind, not the deep, dumb, dreamless slumber of the over-sated. When he woke, Elaine would be pacing the floor with the small, angry creature that was his daughter latched to her shoulder like some physical disfigurement. Sive dictated everything, their sleeping, their waking, their very conversation; that is if Elaine had been capable of finishing a sentence without leaping up to answer the baby's call even when it was just a tiny whimper. The house was taken over by pastel mounds of miniature clothes, piles of nappies, rows of bottles and teats, vats of sterilising fluid. The amount of baggage one child involved appalled him. And whereas Elaine had transformed into a mother overnight – she was clothed in rolls of doting maternal flesh – Hugh was just a sleep-deprived, more irritable version of himself. Except in one thing. When he imagined this peeved baby growing up into a girl and being at the mercy of some bastard like him, it made him want to bolt . . . he took Angie from Reconciliation out on the town and found himself out on his ear.

In the intervening years he had spent as much time apart from Elaine as with her, but since Hugh Junior's birth, Elaine had become more intransigent and each temporary separation was longer than the one before. The September day that Norah Elworthy started in Claims, Hugh realised with a start that this time they had been apart for six months.

The girl was hopeless at calculation. Jesus, why did Personnel send him innumerates! She needed a lot of hand-holding – that must have been why Dan Gildea was constantly hovering about her, poking manfully on her adding machine. But he had to concede that she was good with the public, often distressed and irate ex-workers who already felt aggrieved before they picked up the phone. To them Norah Elworthy was sweetness itself: efficient, calm, soothing. She excelled at assuagement. She was the human face of Claims. (Jesus, he was beginning to sound like one of those slogan-spouting poofs from Personnel.) Was it something as simple as her voice that made him change his mind about her? Was it that she was sitting directly in his line of vision, so that he spent 40 hours a week gazing at her? It certainly wasn't her wardrobe, which still looked like the garb of a defrocked novice – skirts like lampshades, rubbed-looking sweaters, a rain mac the colour of mud. But she had the kind of blank clear face that belonged to someone to whom nothing had happened yet. Such clarity, the tame clothes, the chaste bob cut of her hair, the total unknowingness that she had breasts and, despite her beached quietude, a certain allure. He wanted to be the one to tear all of it away; he wanted to see her tested.

He started to take note of who she was friendly with. Well, it was important for him to know of alliances and loyalties in his team. There was Ellie Fox, a soft motherly woman ten years his senior who seemed to take Norah under her wing. She went for coffee with Maggie Joy, a flaky girl, bright but lazy, who came to work in denim skirts and tarty blouses, and she had long conversations with Martina Beale, a cool thirty-something with coltish limbs and hair the colour of tawny toast. Not forgetting Dan Gildea, of course, that weed from Rebates, whose lantern jaw and lank, foppish hair made him seem like a seedy predator. What on earth did she see in him? Once, Hugh had spied them sitting by the canal having sandwiches at lunchtime and they were often together in the canteen. This caused him some alarm. He couldn't say why. Dan was harmless. Hugh wasn't even sure which team he played for but he felt duty bound to take Norah aside and warn her off.

'Norah? A minute please,' he called after her as she was making for the door one Friday evening. The office didn't clear on a Friday, it was evacuated with fire drill speed once five o'clock struck. Half into her coat and struggling with the second sleeve, she approached his desk.

'Yes, Mr Grove,' she said.

'Call me Hugh,' he said. The Mister made him feel ancient.

'Hugh,' she said, trying it out tentatively.

'You know we don't encourage fraternising among the staff.' He found himself colouring at the outrageousness of the lie.

'Pardon?'

'I couldn't help noticing – you and Dan.' He cocked what he hoped was an ironic eyebrow at her.

'What do you mean?'

'Ah now, don't get up on your high horse, Norah.' Using her name like this was a peremptory weapon; it suggested both authority and informality.

'Dan and I are just friends.'

'Bet you that's not how Dan sees it.'

'I beg your pardon?'

'Have it your own way, but that fella's not to be trusted . . . he's a bit peculiar, bit of a track record, if you get my drift?'

It was her turn to colour. A virginal blush that inflamed her cheeks and animated her features in a way he had never seen before. Tears gathered in her wounded eyes. Oh God, not the waterworks! Hugh stood up and came out from behind the desk, hoping the move would bolster the avuncular candour he was aiming for.

'Look, Norah, all I'm saying is – be careful.'

The irony was not lost on him, warning this cautious, timid creature to take care. She was still wrestling with her coat so he helped her into it and she murmured thank you before scurrying away.

If anything had been developing between Norah and Dan, Hugh felt he had successfully nipped it in the bud. They still chatted but there were no more cosy tête-à-têtes by the canal (Hugh found himself eyeing the waterside benches surreptitiously) a fact which made him feel oddly relieved. He wasn't sure what his next move would be. Then out of the blue, in November, Elaine made her peace with him and he returned home determined, inasmuch as he could be determined, to make a go of it. He put all thoughts of Norah Elworthy out of his mind.

The Christmas party was always a minefield, particularly when he and Elaine were back together. The obvious imbalance in the sexes at the office – even with half the country girls already scattered to the provinces for the holidays – the no-spouse rule, the fact that everyone made an effort, were all reasons for Elaine to be touchy about it. Not to mention that Sive was conceived after such an event. The girls always got dolled up in sparkly dresses, applied foundation and mascara, however inexpertly (Hugh was a bit of an aficionado, after all) and got their hair done. Claims joined with Rebates for the annual do (Rebates having more men) so there was always the frisson of not so familiar faces to enliven the mix. They hired a function room in the Parliament Hotel which the Department paid for out of its entertainments budget and Hugh footed the bill for the cocktail sausages and the white bread sandwiches (always left uneaten and decapitated at the end of the night like women with their hats askew).

'I'm off,' he had called to Elaine at seven on the night of the party, trying to sound casual. He was standing in the hallway, the front door open, frosty air fingering into the house. Elaine was upstairs putting Hugh Junior to bed.

'Oh by the way,' he shouted up into the well of the stairs, 'I've booked a room at the Parliament, so don't expect me home.' It wasn't as if it was something he'd never done before. There was no response from above. 'You know what it's like trying to get a taxi in Christmas week.' At the other end of the hall he could see Sive finger-painting at the kitchen table.

'Close the door, Daddy,' she whined, 'I'm cold.'

He pushed the door to with his foot but he didn't close it. Elaine came down the stairs, her brow thundery.

'Who is it?' she asked resignedly.

'Don't start, Elaine. There isn't anyone. If you weren't so damned suspicious . . .'

'What?' she demanded crossly, folding her arms, 'you wouldn't stray? So now it's my fault?'

Oh God, he thought, this was exactly what he was trying to avoid.

'If you're that worried, why don't you ring me later?'

'And what would that prove?'

'Look, look!' Sive called out and held up two vermilion palms. She had climbed down from the kitchen table and was veering up the hallway, red paws aloft, aiming for Elaine's hips.

'No!' Elaine cried, turning her back on him as she tried to divert the child.

Holding Sive at arm's length, Elaine set her unceremoniously down on a stool beside the sink.

'Let's wash your handies before you hug Mummy.'

Hugh followed them into the kitchen. Mummy, he thought. How he hated that she called herself Mummy. She plunged Sive's hands into the waiting water, scrubbing them vigorously with a nail brush.

'You're hurting me,' Sive wailed but Elaine ignored her. Hugh watched as the water gradually stained.

'If you stay the night, don't bother coming home – ever!' She lifted Sive down and rubbed her hands dry with a towel. 'I mean it.'

'Ever!' Sive repeated triumphantly.

The Parliament had laid on a disco and the exultant boom greeted him at the door and made him feel energised and hopeful. Claims were gathered in an alcove when he arrived, festooned with party hats and boas of tinsel, and when he approached (always studiously late so they would have time to warm up and get a few drinks in) they all lifted their glasses and hollered in unison above the din. Such extravagant enthusiasm cheered him though he knew it shouldn't; they merely wanted to show him what a good time they were having, what fascinating, interesting specimens they were with a few vodkas on board, and that *this* – the glossy hairdos, the high heels – was who they really were, not the office drones Hugh saw every day.

Norah was there at the edge of the group as if she'd just arrived, with an untouched glass of beer in front of her. She, of all of them, looked most like her daily persona. Same hair, an unruly cluster untouched by chemicals, the impossibly clear skin, the unglossed lips. Not even remotely his type. She had, according to her own lights, dressed up: in a tiered gypsy skirt in stained-glass colours and a demure white blouse with (oh God, he thought) a sailor collar that looked luminous under the disco's strobe lights. The only concession was her shoes, a pair of black pumps with some silvery stuff running through them. Hugh found his heart turning; it was the strangest sensation and so long since he'd felt it that he didn't recognise it. He promptly sat down beside her.

'Move over in the bed there, Norah,' he said throwing a comradely arm over her shoulders. The rest of the gang, noting the gesture, responded – Maggie, sheathed in leather, wolf-whistled, Ellie in some frilly confection, twirled the stem of her Babycham glass and clapped her hands together ineffectually, Martina leapt up from the banquette seat and hallooed. That was the other part of the bargain here: not only did Hugh have to be a benign witness to their letting their hair down but he, too, had to be casually outrageous. They wanted him to misbehave. No, they expected it.

Norah's body stiffened as he touched her, her shoulder tightening as if her inner self was recoiling. Their thighs rubbed together. He could see the outline of hers under the flimsy stuff of her skirt. Now that he had his arm around her he felt he should keep it there out of a kind of politeness. If he pulled away it would look as if he were withdrawing favour. The lounge girl came at that stage to take his order, which gave him an excuse to move honourably. He fumbled in his hip pocket for his wallet.

'Another round for the table, love,' he said and the girls erupted once more.

Generally, he didn't dance. It wasn't that he couldn't. In fact, he fancied himself at the jive but most of these girls were schooled only in solipsistic shuffling and any attempts to match his expertise resulted in arm-twisting and awkward entanglements so he avoided it. It looked too much as if he was pushing them around. Anyway, it was too weighted to choose one of them over the others, so he usually sat the dancing out. As did Norah. By eleven they were the only two left, the table before them scattered with the debris of the night, watchtowers of half-empty glasses snagged with frothed beer and dejected lemons, an ashtray rubbled with butts, sodden party hats. The DJ made smooching innuendoes into the mike between numbers, the only time it was possible to hazard conversation, the music being too loud otherwise. And anyway, what would he say – I have a room upstairs, meet you there in ten minutes? When he looked at Norah, he felt he would have to explain what he meant.

'Come on, you two,' Maggie Joy roared, coming back to the ruined table for her drink.

She pumped Hugh playfully on the shoulder before being dragged back to the dance floor by Pete from Rebates. Otherwise, Hugh might have asked Maggie up; at least she would have been fun to dance with. He'd seen her in other years dancing pogo-style, graceless but energetic, fisting the air and hopping about like some beefy biker.

'Norah,' Maggie mouthed in encouragement, the music having started up again.

Norah looked at him meekly. Jesus, better to dance with her than be left stranded here with her looking like a wounded lamb and obviously counting the minutes until she could safely leave. She had already twice looked at her watch and he needed more time.

'How about it, Miss Elworthy?' he asked and held out his hand.

The dance floor, a circle of scarred wood in front of the DJ's table, was heaving. 'Dancing Queen' was just coming on and the assembled company could not decide if it was a slow number or not. Norah stood, hands hanging, so Hugh took the lead, holding her as if for a waltz. She was much shorter than he was and it was quite a stretch for her to reach his shoulder, so instead she clutched him awkwardly at the waist.

Her touch through his damp shirt – the place was stiflingly hot – was so tentative, so determinedly noncommittal that he could barely feel it but even so, or because of it, it made him blanch with desire. He dropped his leading hand and clasped her around the shoulders, drawing her in so that they were less moving to the music than swaying gently on the one spot. Locked like that, he was aware of every minute move of hers. The fluttering began in her shoulder blades as of something trapped, a tremor that spread to her arms even though they were wrapped around his waist and her head was buried in his chest. The girl was terrified, he realised; the only reason she had moulded her body to his was to suppress the tiny trembling. It should have been a turn-on but instead Hugh felt strenuously entrusted. It was, strangely, not a burden; he felt, rather, that he was steering a delicate cargo through the crowded room. The music throbbed, the crowd pulsed about him but so powerful was the feeling and his own sensations so surprisingly fragile that he and Norah danced the entire set like this. He felt like a life raft in a turbulent sea. Also he didn't know what he might say when it was over and, in truth, he wanted the sensation to last. Not just the quivering – who wouldn't fancy a quivering virgin at their mercy, he would joke with himself afterwards – but this unspoken intensity, all hers, which he had never been the object of and certainly had never experienced himself. He wanted to draw off it; he was greedy for it, so greedy that when the music stopped and all about them the dancers were clapping and then dispersing, they stood there, raft and survivor, until Dan Gildea tapped Norah on the shoulder and she awoke, it seemed, since the state they had entered into was close to an animated slumber, and pulled away from him.

'Are you alright?' Dan asked, but looking accusingly at Hugh. Jesus, maybe he was sleeping with her, Hugh thought. How else to explain the Caped Crusader pose? Hugh stepped back.

'Yes, I'm fine,' she said faintly, giving Hugh that look again, except it wasn't meekness, Hugh realised, it was something so naked and unguarded that he couldn't bear to look.

'Take her away, Dan,' Hugh said and stumbled off the dance floor, feeling in some obscure way that Norah had made a fool of him.

Early in the new year he made his move. The magazine was one of a stash he'd kept locked in the drawer of his desk, a hangover from his wilder days. Beasts and women, strictly top of the shelf fodder, dogs mostly, slavishly about the models' pubes or appearing to suckle at their breasts. It was crude stuff, in the sense that these models wearing only stilettos and pouting in fake ecstasy being licked off by dogs had never really worked for him, at least not in the way it was supposed to.

He slipped the magazine into a sheaf of folders and laid it on the side of Norah's desk during her lunch hour so she couldn't guess its provenance. He felt fuelled by a kind of savage reprisal as if she had openly and deliberately spurned him. He was right in her line of vision when she opened the buff folder. He waited. He expected shrieks, some dramatic gesture. He'd even imagined the magazine might make her throw up. He'd felt a bit queasy himself on first seeing these images. She looked up and around on discovering it but then she leafed deliberately through it before closing it. Opening her desk drawer she placed it quietly inside and continued on with her work. Not a flicker crossed her face; she did not raise her eyes; she did not bolt from the room. Boy, she was good, Hugh thought; she'd denied him a scene.

He'd imagined how it would go. He would catch her eye, enquire what was wrong and when she'd break down, he could be first the comforter and, if the circumstances demanded it, the avenging boss, declaring a witch-hunt against such filth.

But she had yielded absolutely nothing and he was the one who felt unmasked.

The first smell that assailed her when she blundered in was, inexplicably, wet dog. The heavy door of the pub swung closed behind her with a dry whinge, shutting out the sludge-grey day, the rain falling in large, spiteful drops, the sky a low frown, the air mistily dank. The place was blessedly deserted, a sanctuary, gloomy as a church. She threaded her way around the low lounge tables with their carefully arranged little stools set out on a square of livid carpet. They had a patient, expectant air. Unpeopled, they seemed ridiculously miniature, like nursery furniture. The only other patron sat at the bar with the intro-verted slump of a lone drinker. She deposited her things on one of the baby tables – her flapping umbrella, her damp briefcase, her sodden handbag – and made her way to the counter.

'What'll it be, love?' the barman asked, his fist muffled in a towel as he polished pint glasses. Business was slow. It was late afternoon, mid-winter. She blew on her hands ruddy from the cold. She'd intended only to have a coffee but the encounter with Louis had so shaken her that she changed her mind.

'A hot port,' she said.

It wasn't the first time she'd bumped into Louis since the split. It was a small city, after all, too bloody small. This time he had spotted her (she would have avoided him if she had seen him first) and must have had to run to catch up with her on the street, tapping her on the arm. She turned swiftly, thinking someone was trying to pick her pocket. When she saw it was him, a reflux of fondness rose in her throat that made her eyes smart. When, she wondered, do you get to the end of feeling? He was wearing his donkey jacket, the collar up around his ears to keep off the rain, hands thrust into the pockets. The scarf she'd given him last birthday was bundled about his chin. His hair was plastered over his crown and rivu-lets of rain were trickling down his face. She half expected him to stick his tongue out to catch them; that was the sort of clownish thing he did.

'Will you let me under your umbrella, Miss?' he asked.

It was a ridiculous transparent thing she'd bought hurriedly when the downpour started. Like walking around with a glazed version of St Peter's on her head. But there wasn't room for two beneath it. She peered at Louis through the speckled plastic.

'I can't talk to you like that,' he said. 'Take it down.'

She struggled to deflate it. Finally he took it and did it for her.

'How are you?' he asked.

'Fine, and you?'

'Oh, you know . . .' He'd shrugged and looked at her wryly.

It was as if they were back at the beginning again, feeling their way into intimacy. But it was the opposite. There was so little that could be said without falling into habitual ease that they had to resort to this stilted code. Or silence. Damp crowds parted for them. She fixed on the pooled pavement.

'Norah,' he said, always a prelude to some declaration. He extricated a hand and made to touch her cheek.

No, no, she would not let herself be seduced. Not by mere fondness, though there was nothing mere about it; it was hardier than desire, more contagious than lust. And then she saw he wasn't wearing his ring. She didn't even have to remark upon it; he knew she had noticed. It was as if she had caught him out in a lie.

'It's been six months,' he said, 'I didn't see the point any more.'

It was the same tone he might use with his students. Patient, entreating, reasonable. He clenched his hand into a fist and thrust it back into his pocket. This, she thought, is how you get to the end of feeling; other people do it for you. She turned on her heel and strode off, leaving him there, drenched on the street, calling after her.

'Miss?' The barman set her drink down on the bar.

The hunkered-down figure raised his head as she approached and she watched his features in the intricately scrolled mirrors behind the bar materialise into someone familiar, distantly familiar. My God, she thought, it's Hugh Grove. Or an older version of him. His over-long hair (he'd always been vain about his dark mane) was a salty grey, his face thinner than she remembered, shadows in the hollows of his cheeks, a downward drift to his features. Don't recognise me, she prayed.

'Norah Elworthy,' he said and swivelled around on the stool to face her. Too late. She looked at him directly in the hope that flinty defiance might ward him off.

'I'm right, amn't I?' he said, peering at her blearily though she couldn't be sure if that was due to the drink or the dimness of the interior. 'Norah Elworthy.'

Then he laughed. It was less a laugh than a lewd wheeze.

'Hugh,' she said evenly.

He patted the stool beside him.

'Come and join me,' he said.

She did as she was bid – old habits die hard, she thought grimly. Why did they make these damned stools so high, she thought, as she freed the trapped wings of her coat from underneath her.

'I'll get that, Dec,' Hugh said to the barman – of course, he would know the barman by name. 'And sling some brandy into it, for God's sake. Look at this woman, she's perished.' He fished in his pocket and passed over a note. The barman sidled off and the register rang merrily. Hugh looked at her sidelong.

'Of all the gin joints in all the world . . .' he started and laughed again. 'It must be ten years . . .'

'Twelve,' she said miserably, depressed by her own exactitude.

She caught a glimpse of herself in the mirrors behind the counter. She'd been to the hairdresser the day before and her hair still bore the stylist's taming hand. It had the helmety appearance that passed for adult grooming, though she always felt prim emerging from the salon and longed, perversely, for it to go back to its unruly self. The coat was a mulberry colour with a large collar; in the glass she looked like a buttoned-up cardinal. Then she checked herself. What am I doing, making an inventory of myself for the benefit of Hugh Grove.

'Cheers!' Hugh said.

Norah lifted her drink and they clinked.

'So, how the hell are you, Norah Elworthy?' And he laughed that combustive laugh as if he had swallowed flame.

She didn't answer. Once, she remembered, she had been painfully in love with Hugh Grove.

'Married, I see,' he went on, gazing at her ring finger. He cupped his hand over hers. Their wedding bands clacked. 'Me, too,' he added ruefully. 'Sort of.'

'Wasn't that always the way, Hugh?' she said, emboldened by the first surge of alcohol. This was the way she had longed to speak to him back then. Saucy, jaded.

'Well, you've changed,' he said, withdrawing his hand. 'Time was when you wouldn't have said boo to a goose.'

'I got over that,' she said.

They contemplated their drinks – his almost finished pint, her ruby balloon.

'Still in Claims?'

'Yeah.' He nodded and sighed. 'Not upwardly mobile like you, Miss Hotshot! You moved on pretty quick smart.'

'Well, there were reasons for that.'

After that Christmas she had applied for a transfer. Something had come up in Agriculture and she took it, swapping the jobless for the landed, serving her apprenticeship among headage payments and milk quotas. Hugh clapped his thighs and signalled to the barman.

'You'll have another?'

Without waiting for an answer he ordered again.

'So who's this husband of yours? Not Dan Gildea, I hope?'

'No,' she replied, 'as I recall, that was *verboten*. Isn't that what you said?'

'Oh God, you're not going to start quoting me back to myself, are you?'

The second order came and she tossed back the first quickly in the hope that she could briskly extricate herself from the encounter. It was getting on for five. If Louis were still at home, he would be waiting for her. He always cooked on a Thursday – hearty stews with cheap cuts, always too much for just the two of them.

'What does he do, then, your hubby?'

She sipped cautiously on the second drink. Steady, steady she told herself, but her cheeks were already aflame.

'He's a teacher,' she said.

She felt herself slipping back into the monosyllabic prison of her youth when this man had had the power to reduce her to silent confusion. She didn't want to go back there.

'And you? Where are you now?' he enquired, nodding towards the briefcase still slung with the rest of her stuff on the table behind them.

'Education,' she said.

'Well, you look like a girl who's educated herself.'

'As opposed to waiting for someone like you to do it, you mean?'

'Now, now, Norah,' he said and raised his hands in surrender. 'I never laid a hand on you.' He laughed again and she saw red.

'You know, Hugh, these days you could be had up for what you did,' she said.

'For warning you off Dan Gildea? I was doing you a corporal work of mercy there.'

'Not Dan Gildea. I'm not talking about him.'

107

'What so?'

'You know,' she said.

'What?' he said playfully but she could hear irritation in it. 'What am I being blamed for now?'

We sound like a married couple, she thought, bickering over drinks. She wished she hadn't said anything. This was an old grievance that had long ago lost its potency. But it was too late now.

'The magazine, Hugh, that's what I'm talking about.'

'Oh that,' he said and looked at her bashfully. His eyes in this light seemed wounded and murky. There was a thin brown line of porter residue on his lips. 'How did you know it was me?'

'Who else?'

'You never let on.'

A third brandy and port materialised in front of her. She had no memory of Hugh ordering and it registered dimly with her that it was her round.

'I wasn't a complete greenhorn,' she said, 'despite what you thought.'

'Oh come on, Norah, you were as pure as the driven snow; that's what made you so attractive.'

'Look, Hugh, you made my life a misery, isn't that enough for you?'

'I didn't do anything to you. If you were bloody miserable I can't help it . . .'

'Let me tell you a story, Hugh . . .'

He grimaced and reached for his pint.

'God, Norah, I think I preferred you when you were giving me the silent treatment.'

'When I was a kid, I was probably eleven, maybe twelve, I was coming home from school and passed this man on the street. He looked quite normal coming towards me, he had a shirt and an overcoat but as he drew closer I could see that his flies were open, baring all . . . and I wasn't shocked, not

108

really, I was fascinated, though I knew I shouldn't be. I'd never seen, you know, an adult . . .'

'Prick?' Hugh interjected.

'. . . yes, and I was mesmerised by all the hair. I'd never thought there'd be so much hair. So anyway, he passes me by and I'm determined I'm not going to look at him, look at his face, I mean.'

Hugh laughed uproariously, which degenerated into a coughing fit.

'And after he passed, I knew, I don't know how I knew because at that age I knew nothing, but I knew I mustn't look back at him, that I mustn't give him the satisfaction . . .'

'So you're equating me with a flasher?'

'If the cap fits,' she said. How was she going to get home? She was really sloshed now.

'I often think of those photos. Couldn't get them out of my head. To tell you the truth, I was as fascinated by them as by my friend on the street. I kept the magazine. Still have it, in fact.'

'Jesus!'

She didn't tell him that the images often came to her mind unbidden when Louis made his careful advances and she felt the familiar heave of dread that accompanied his well-meaning tenderness.

'Truth is, Hugh, I had a terrible crush on you then, which just goes to prove there's no accounting for taste.'

It seemed a paltry thing once said, not the great admission she'd often rehearsed. How much easier it would be if we could simply say things, she thought, when they needed to be said. Hugh looked at her blankly.

'You didn't know?' she asked.

'No,' he said, 'it's not that. It's just that night, the night of the party, I had a room booked in the Parliament.'

'With my name on it?'

'Yep, but, you know in the end, I couldn't do it.'

'What – deflower me?'

'Yes,' he said sighing.

'What stopped you?'

'You were just too . . . innocent.'

'I thought that's the way you liked them,' she said. She couldn't stop it now, this parrying tone.

'But . . . and I know this is going to sound corny, you were different.'

'Oh please, Hugh, don't . . .'

'Norah,' he said and grasped for her hand. 'I mean it.'

'Then I might have believed it, but not now. The irony is that if you'd made a move then, I would have said yes.'

This time both of them laughed.

The pub began to fill up with after-work drinkers. At six, the barman turned the lights on and the mood changed with it. There was a crush at the bar now, bodies pressing up against them, orders being shouted out, money changing hands over their heads. A lounge girl came on duty, a small dark creature, hair scraped into a fierce-looking ponytail, concealer on her cheeks vainly applied to hide teenage acne. Her nails, Norah noticed when she sidled up beside them with her loaded tray, were bitten down to the quick. She and the barman had something going, or at least he thought they had, he kept on calling her 'Michelle love' and Norah noticed the girl bravely trying to hide her steely contempt. Norah smiled at her, trying in some way to reassure her, but she felt grotesque with drink now as if all her gestures were huge and exaggerated and crude. Their conversation had run out of steam but Norah wasn't capable of winding up the evening. When Hugh went off to the lavatory, she contemplated gathering her things and making off into the night. But there was no dignified way to end this. Hugh returned and before he could settle back on to his perch, she said, 'Why don't we do it now?'

'Do what?'

'The room in the Parliament,' she said. 'Why don't we do it now?'

'Aren't you married?'

'What's this, Hugh, an attack of scruples?'

'Seriously, though . . .'

'This has nothing to do with Louis . . . this belongs to a time before him. This is something I wanted all those years ago and couldn't have. Now, I can. There seems a justice in that, a sweetness . . .' The sweetness sprang from revenge, she thought, but she didn't say that. 'It'll be a kind of reprise, an encore.'

'It can't be an encore,' he said. 'It never happened the first time.'

The crowd surged behind them. In the mirrors she could see hands raised with notes crumpled in them.

'What do you say, Hugh Grove?'

She felt a kind of power now as if she'd got the upper hand.

'What would be the point, after all this time?' he asked.

It hadn't occurred to her that she might be the one doing the persuading.

'Oh, Norah dear, the world has done its job on you, alright,' he said, bleary-eyed.

'Well, then,' she said, touching his arm, feeling suddenly sorry for him, '*you* don't have to feel responsible for it.'

'Oh God, Norah, I don't know . . .'

'Is that a yes, then?'

He smiled wearily but he agreed, as she knew he would.

*   *   *

The night of the Christmas party Elaine was still up when he got home. She'd dressed the Christmas tree and was sitting in the darkened sitting room, the fairy lights flickering on and off among the silvered baubles. She'd had a bath and was sitting on the sofa with the TV on but the sound low so as not to wake Hugh Junior who was just after his night feed and asleep in the Moses basket at her feet. She smelled of bath salts – almond blossom, was it, or passion flower – and there was a dampness in her cleavage just visible beneath the folds of her white towelling dressing gown. It parted at the knees and he could see the tiny reddened tributaries of veins around her knees. The rewards of childbirth, she'd said ruefully more than once. She looked up when he came in but said nothing, merely opened her arms and Hugh fell upon her gratefully like a man saved.

THE GREAT WALL

'Get in!' he ordered.

Owen stood, damp, on the cobbled quay, hands on hips. Below him the ornate prow of the black gondola and the upturned face of the gondolier, beaming. A professional rictus. The choppy water glinted. Her stomach heaved.

'Murph,' Owen warned. 'I'll go without you.'

In that moment, she despised him. His doughy face and his squinty glasses and his sandy hair standing on end. His little paunch and his embarrassed-looking legs in crumpled shorts. There was no end to her catalogue of contempt.

'Venice,' he had said that morning, towelling his damp hair and looking out of the high casement window overlooking the canal. 'City of lovers . . .'

She had expected a roll call of masterpieces; Giorgione's *La Tempesta*, Bellini's Madonnas, Titian's *Presentation of the Virgin*.

'Canals, gondolas,' he went on.

'Gondolas?' *Wingbeat of alarm. Wingbeat of memory.*

'Well, it *is* what Venice is famous for. We'll have to take a spin in one at some stage.'

Rock and lurch of water. A pair of splintered glasses.

When Owen went down to breakfast ahead of her, she rang her mother.

'Is all well in the bedchamber?' her mother had asked.

* * *

It was Owen who had insisted they wait; part of his deference to her culture. He often spoke about her culture – it made her think of the laboratory – though she had grown up in the same suburb, albeit that the Devoys owned a semi-detached, half red-brick on Prosperity Drive and she lived in a flat over Uncle's takeaway in the village. Her notion of village was the dim memory of her grandmother's house, part of a rickety huddle, drenched and rotten. In time, Uncle had graduated from the modest quarters over the shop, leaving the place to Kim's mother.

Despite their proximity, Kim hadn't met Owen until college though he'd ordered food many times from the Great Wall, he'd told her. The No. 24, he'd said, Chow Mein. With chips, he'd added sheepishly. Typical, she thought, remembering her time serving behind the counter as a schoolgirl and taking orders on the phone. It was chips with everything.

He'd been right about the waiting, though. For two whole days, they hadn't ventured out of their cool, tiled room. The heavy double doors remained closed to the world, the eyelids of the slatted window shutters turned demurely down. They made love hungrily, repeatedly. The sheets were musky with the days-old scent of their sex. Exhausted, they drowsed deeply, lethargic with ravishment and the clenched release of orgasm. They did not shower or wash; they bathed instead in the pungent secretions of lust. They barely ate – they snacked on nuts and chocolate from the minibar. They slurped beer and spilt spumes of it over one another and watched as it seethed in ferment on their heated skin. In the afternoons they coupled on the marble floor and slept afterwards resplendently naked, waking in twilight, gathering the sheets from the tiles to swathe around them as they journeyed to the bed and started again. They emerged on the third day to barbed sunshine and a sky fat with dark cloud. She could sense rain in the air. The clouds spoke to her. *It was what she looked at when the others were defecating so as not to shame them.*

* * *

114

Owen was itching to get started though Kim had lounged in bed late, lazily reluctant to quit their pungent nest. It was an indolence that alarmed him. He watched her body curled like a cat in the crushed sheets at noon. *Stink and sweat of daytime, bone-cold nights. Seventeen bodies huddled together to sleep, fetid clothes, salt larded in the creases.*

'Come on, Murph,' he'd said, fingering her silky hair which fell in a fan on her back-turned shoulder. He ran his hand over her delicate haunch, marvelling at its perfection and his own unworthiness. She seemed to him in that moment the most perfect creature he had ever seen. That was when he remembered Quinny. Out of nowhere the memory of her kneeling as if in adoration in front of the oven, her head to one side, her hair falling about her shoulders.

'Come back to bed, Doctor,' Kim purred and gripped him blindly. He pulled his hand away sharply. Suddenly the foul airlessness of the room, the rank sheets, Kim's sour unwashed smell revolted him and he wanted out.

Once out, she had seemed happy to walk across the pigeon-scattered expanse of San Marco or to follow him along the narrow alleyways of the Giudecca which plunged into darkness or unexpectedly led back to a shy piece of waterway. There was water all afternoon, glimpsed between stone and arch and pooled between flagstones in sad, unexpected corners, wet pockets of secrecy. Late in the day, a misty rain began to fall. Owen had brought a transparent plastic rain cloak, one he used for cycling to college, and they shared it, wandering until twilight when the air, moist with intermittent drizzle, cooled to a lavender chill. Perhaps it was the weather, or the unpeopled melancholy of off-season Venice, but by dusk he felt invaded by a bleak sense of bereavement. He blamed it on the intrusive memory of Quinny. She hadn't crossed his mind in years. She was a maid who'd looked after him when he was a child, to whom he'd been very attached, or so his mother told him.

He remembered her hair mostly; auburn, unruly, so long she could sit on it. You were her pet, his mother would say, with an odd emphasis. His treasured pink bunny had come from Quinny. There was a postcard of the beach in Courtown where they used to go on holidays, in which Quinny had featured, straw-hatted and solitary, minding his baby brother Fergal, and shielded from the sea by a striped windbreak. He'd kept the card for years, a childish treasure, until it, like Quinny, had vanished. All he is left with are these fragments of memory as if all of it had happened to someone else.

Just like now. The ordinary tramping about was so at odds with their first days of erotic intimacy that it rendered them strangers, and strange to one another in the glare of the world. Or was it the ghostly impersonators who were out here on the street? The watery movement of Venice made him doubt everything. He could see now that he had been afraid of their wantonness, afraid he would never be able to satisfy her. What kind of a fool was he to trade sexual pleasuring for *this* ridiculous sightseeing? Which was why he'd struck on the idea of the gondola to take them swiftly back to the scene of their delicious crimes.

'I mean, it, Kim,' Owen threatened.

No more matey Murph. He must really be angry now. She'd never really seen him angry. Not her mild-mannered Owen who had wooed her so tactfully, who had, right from the start, bided his time. For several years he had been Dr Devoy from Art History who came into the Campus Café to order the lunch special and an Americano; he seemed to survive on a diet of spag bol and caffeine. She made a beeline for him because he always left silver under the saucer. And he always talked to her in a way which suggested that she wasn't just the little immigrant waitress, or a refugee from the sciences. (She was studying Pharmacy.) He'd asked her her name – always a trick question. Nobody in Ireland could get their tongue around Phuong; she'd wanted to be Margaret or Elizabeth but her mother had decreed otherwise. We must, she said, hold on to as much as possible.

'Kim,' she'd said. 'Kim Nguyen.'

'Noo-en,' Owen tried it out. 'Noo-en. Sounds strange.'

'It's a very common name,' she'd said, 'like . . .'

'Murphy?' he prompted.

That's where his nickname for her had come from. She liked it; it made her feel neutral.

On graduation day just as the group photograph was being taken on the steps of the Aula Maxima, Kim peering from under her mortar board, trying to pick out her mother in the crowd, saw Dr Devoy make his way across the quad and step into the picture. In that moment he was transformed into her tousled, slightly shambling Owen. She called him doctor now only to poke fun at him and draw attention to the eight years between them.

He had been so keen to avoid cultural faux pas that he ended up drawing attention to insults she'd missed.

'Murph, have you seen my address book? You know, the little red book. Oh God, I didn't mean that!'

Don't mention the war.

It was just this deference that had won her over, so used was she to chronic, low-grade cruelty and casually intended slights. (At school she had been the Yellow Pack, the Flied Lice, her family lumped together as Boat People.) But Owen would never knowingly hurt her and she clung to that knowledge.

'Would it not be more suitable if you did not marry out,' her mother had said when, after their short and utterly proper courtship, Owen had proposed.

'But it was you who wanted us to assimilate,' she countered, bristling.

Wasn't that what all the education was for? she wanted to say. What her mother had slaved over deep-fat fryers for all these years? To marry well?

'Still, you should not marry before your sister,' her mother replied.

'That,' Kim had said, 'is the old way.'

Her sister Mai, brow knitted, looked up from the jigsaw she was doing with Lu. He had spread out the thousand pieces that made up the mythical scene – Sinbad the Sailor on the High Seas – on the dining-room table. Perplexed at the air of disapproval, he shifted his gaze from one face to another; he was seven and a lone boy among women. Mai was still wearing her paper hat and the blue nylon housecoat with the Great Wall logo on the breast pocket. Kim fought off the familiar undertow of guilt at being the younger sister. While she shared a flat with three girls from the lab, Mai still lived at home.

'I'm twenty-three, practically an old maid,' Kim went on, sensing the resistance. 'You wouldn't want to scupper my chances, would you, Mai?'

Mai said nothing.

'Look,' Lu cried, holding up a jagged piece, 'here is the lady's face from Sinbad's ship!'

The boy stood as a rebuke between them.

'The figurehead,' Mai said to him, 'it's called the figurehead.'

'Would you, Mai?' Kim persisted.

'It is not a question of personal wishes, Kim,' her mother said. 'It is a matter of form.'

'No,' Kim told Owen decisively, 'let's walk back.'

Smell of diesel – until the engine broke down. She gets that whiff passing a petrol station forecourt and she has to cover her mouth to stem her rising gorge. Then the sickening tilt as they drifted. She wakes up sometimes in a cold sweat imagining the bed is the junk and the room is the sea, refusing to settle. Her stomach remembers the hunger pangs. Nothing would stay down.

'Ah, Murph, we've been walking for ever,' he complained, though he prided himself on his tourist stoicism.

118

She shrugged.

'Look, I'm not even sure I could find my way back.' This was a lie; he knew exactly where he was. Unlike her, he'd been here before.

'Anyway, it'll cost too much,' she said. 'They're a tourist trap, you said so yourself.'

She remembered everything.

Thirst – in the midst of all that water – a terrible thirst.

Everything he said, banal, throwaway remarks, his most pompous assertions.

'Oh, come on,' he wheedled. 'It'll be romantic.'

She looked away, arms across the breasts he had so recently fondled, her neck taut, something in her temple throbbing.

'*You* go, then,' she almost spat.

She was wearing that cute little denim jacket over a polka-dot sundress. Like a Saigon streetwalker, he thought savagely.

This was meant to be a treat. He wanted them to drift into the sunset – muted, though it was, by the rain – steeped in the rose-water light. She would lounge on the red velvet cushions as the gondolier plashed lazily. His bride. He was secretly proud of the possessive. But she would never be all his. Just this morning she had been on the phone to her mother. In the middle of their honeymoon! Over something *he'd* said, no doubt. He'd eavesdropped on the nasal tones which always sounded peeved to him. He knew the intonation was crucial. A tiny inflection could transform mood and meaning. But he'd never learned her language – even the college language lab didn't run to Vietnamese – so he didn't understand those shifts; he only knew when they had happened.

Wake of the big ships, mountains of swell. Huge tankers, their armoured flanks like impenetrable fortresses would loom up in the night and bear down on them. She would arch her neck back, her gaze clambering up the sheer slopes of those vast riveted surfaces and see no end to them. When the ships passed that close, they were transfixed with terror and delight. Could they be seen? Would they be swallowed up? Or picked up? But by whom?

'I'm not getting into that thing.'

'But why?'

'I don't want to,' she said.

Simply that: I don't want to. Well, my girl, we can't always do what we want.

'Please yourself.' He marched over to talk terms with the gondolier. He was the one with the Italian, he thought victoriously. Kim, reluctantly bilingual, did not want to learn another language.

'It makes you . . .' She always wrinkled her nose when trying to explain.

'Bifurcated?' he ventured. He liked to finish her sentences.

Two choices, Father said. Drowning or drought. He wasted away; some old weakness of his chest. He spent days gasping for air, cracked lips turned beseechingly to a glistering sun. He saw things in the sky, in the shadows of the sea. The sun seemed to drive him mad. Too late, too late, he kept on saying, over and over again. What did he mean? That they were all doomed, or that they should have left sooner, as her mother had pleaded. But Father was a professor, he knew better . . .

Owen knew she would follow; he was the navigator, she was lost. They had to sit close; that was the nature of the gondola, but he could sense her anger in the tense way she held herself, taking trouble not to allow the thin stuff of her dress to rub against his bare knee. The gondolier poled away silently. Thank God, Owen thought, he's not one of those singing ones. They passed illuminated facades of palazzos, windows fat with umber light, the gay barbershop poles on the dark skeletons of the jetties, and against the skyline the dusty pink outlines of spires and cupolas. He noticed how she clutched her knees with her hands, the knuckles showing white. Her jaw was similarly clamped and her eyes were shut precisely so she wouldn't see what he had wanted to show her.

They buried him at sea. It sounded regal, but it wasn't. They had nothing to wrap him in; the captain and his son picked him up and slung him overboard like a bag of meal. He barely made a splash. She saved his glasses; he had lost everything else. He had lost her already. The captain's son used to stick his penis into her from the back . . .

How adolescent, Owen thought.

She'd told him, she'd told him all of it. How could he not remember? It wasn't even 24 hours ago. Haltingly . . . after they had made love. She thought of them as cigarette words. He had reached over her and fished out a cigarette and lit up. Was it because they were lying down together? Was it the incense of the smoke? But the words after love were like the love itself, a safe harbour. She'd hesitated but he'd said tell me, tell me all about it, I want to understand.

'Jesus, Murph,' he breathed when she had picked her way through the story. It was the first time she had told anyone. 'It's like *The Raft of the Medusa*.'

'The what?'

'Painting,' he said. 'By Géricault. Terrible thing – a hundred and fifty people piled on to a raft that drifted for twelve days. The occupants turned on one another, well, they were desperate. Even resorted to cannibalism. Géricault painted it all, the degradation, the despair . . .'

Kim felt a tide of fury. She had squandered this intimacy on him. He couldn't understand, how could he? Or he could only understand like this, in brushstrokes, impasto, the oiled representation of life on canvas.

'. . . but also the hope,' Owen went on, 'the hope of rescue. On the horizon you can see the tiny little silhouette of the *Argus* that picked up the few who survived.'

She turned away from him and lay on her back. Owen had been her hope of rescue. When she looked up at the ceiling, it was a map of shadows.

At Camp Three in Galang, there was privacy, at least, some-where to hide even if it was only the dank corner of a tent and the emblazoned protection of the Red Cross, though Mai had fallen pregnant there. One of the Thai clerks. Afterwards Mai told her she thought it might help their application. They all expect it, she said. It didn't help; by the time their Irish papers came through, Lu was nearly two. Their little brother, her mother decreed, so that Mai's honour could be kept intact.

'We were saved, too,' Kim said, 'if you could call it that.'

As soon as they docked in front of the railway station she clambered out on to the quay like a fugitive. She stood there for a moment with a look of what Owen took to be sheer spite, turned on her heel and stormed towards the hotel, her damp, ill-chosen sundress sticking to the back of her legs. He is left to pay off the gondolier – a scandalous amount, which he's glad Kim doesn't witness him handing over. Two things soften him as he follows her: the memory of their first days in Venice which makes him secretly blush, and the dim real-isation that maybe she's seasick. The canals can be rough and when the *vaporettos* pass they leave a swell which has made even Owen's cast-iron innards lurch a little. I've been an insensitive boor, he thinks, as he hurries down the quilted corridors of the hotel. By the time he opens the bedroom door, he is not only ready to conciliate, he is quickened by desire and the memory of it sewn into the fabric of the room, full now with the spilt gold of artificial light. But she is on the phone again. His goodwill evaporates.

What has passed between them is not irrevocable. Heedlessly Owen will trample on the sensitivities of his oriental wife many times. (It's how his mother with her bourgeois candour describes her daughter-in-law at the golf club, as if she were some exotic brand of tea or spice.) Despite the fact that to Kim she'd said, 'Call me Irene, we don't want any of that old mother-in-law business.' But Owen knows Kim's formality will not allow that. You can be the daughter my mother never had, he tells her, and then wonders if that's what Quinny, the maid, was. Perhaps that's what his mother has always wanted? Instead of the four sons she got?

After the honeymoon Owen stops thinking of Kim as his bride, his anything. He comes to regard her, as his mother does, as someone just beyond the radar of understanding. And Kim, as she did the first time, will seal her lips and say nothing. She keeps her silence on principle because once should be enough to talk of these things. Owen will persist in his misapprehension because she *has* talked of it only once; in his mind it is tied up with lust and desire and the tender aftermath of love.

In time, for Kim, the journey and the feelings of shame and repulsion associated with it recede, return to secrecy. It becomes like a deception, something she has withheld. As if Owen had never known. And in a strange way that pleases her.

LOVE CHILD

'Misfortune?'

The desk clerk smirked. Julia sighed; her name was a joke every stranger thought he was the first to get. But as the clerk scrawled her name on the registration card, Julia realised this would be the last time the joke would be on her. The clerk was a paunchy man with oily black hair and a neat moustache. He peered over a pair of half-glasses. Despite his spotless white shirt, dicky-bow and braces he had a vaguely dissolute air, like the MC of a Weimar cabaret. Or perhaps it was because Valentin – for such his name badge declared him as – was the sole representative of manhood on the premises; the Hotel Nathaniel (formerly the Alhambra) was a women-only hotel. As he riffled through her passport, seeking out the title page, Julia had a chance to take in the foyer.

It was a dim ill-lit cavernous place with a gallery visible in the higher reaches. There were mosaic panels set into the walls and tiles in the risers of the stairwell that turned a corner sharply out of sight to the left of reception. The Eastern echoes of its former existence were repeated in the crazy-paving floor and the fountain which played idly in the centre of the lobby. A battered-looking leather sofa and scarred coffee table were set against the wall opposite the elevators. Stranded in the vast distance of the place they looked like museum pieces or priceless *objets* to be marvelled at but not used.

The foyer was not designed to entertain loiterers. Only a devoted narcissist would sit there, Julia thought, caught between Valentin's sardonic gaze and the glassy reflection of the plate-glass windows that gave on to East 53rd Street. The set of revolving doors at the entrance seemed frozen into disuse and she had had to pick up the semen-coloured plastic phone on the wall outside to get in. Valentin had done the honours, bowing slightly as she hauled her suitcase inside and he made his stately way back to his post. Moving in from the street was like travelling back in time, Julia realised, for whatever renovations had been made to the Nathaniel, formerly the Alhambra, over the years, seemed only to extend to the frontage – the aluminium windows, the tinted glass. The further you travelled into the Nathaniel the more old-fashioned – or decrepit – it became.

There were admonitory notices everywhere. On a silver pod inside the door – ALL VISITORS MUST REPORT TO THE FRONT DESK. A noticeboard beside the reception warned guests not to bring male visitors to their rooms, not to ask for quarters, not to play loud music, not to cook after 10 p.m., not to drink alcohol in the corridors, not to hog the public phone in the foyer and never to ask for credit. The only positive sign was pasted over the lift buttons and scrawled in red marker. PRESS ONCE, it said as if the denizens of the Nathaniel needed directions for even the most basic tasks. But even in that Julia felt there was warning. What would happen if you were so bold as to press twice, she wondered.

Between the lifts, a Christmas tree stood. It was the only concession the Nathaniel had made to the season. It was an artificial tree, spindly, white, three-legged and it looked as if it had fallen victim to some terrible wasting disease. The silver baubles on it were frosted with white, bits of which shed like flaky skin on the worn maroon carpet which was placed underneath as if expressly to catch the dandruff.

'I'll need to keep your passport, Miss Fortune,' Valentin said. A smile hovered on his lips, but he suppressed it. 'For registration purposes, you understand. I can have it back to you later this evening.' He eyed her speculatively. 'I'm on all night.'

'Okay,' she replied, though usually she did not like to be parted from her passport.

That time on the package holiday in Portugal had taught her a lesson. She had left it, just like this, at the hotel desk and had forgotten to pick it up the next morning. She and Eric had travelled over a hundred miles before she realised she didn't have it. Eric had been furious.

'Jesus, Jules,' he swore as he did a dangerously daredevil U-turn in the hired car, a rackety Fiat. The car had seen better days. The passenger door was arthritically stiff and there were several scrapes and dents on the bodywork as if it had been used as a getaway in a previous existence. Eric took his rage out on the gearstick, and for a moment Julia had a cartoonish vision of it coming away in his hand. 'You'd forget your head if it wasn't tied on to you.'

Eric had the happy knack of getting everything about Julia wrong. If only she *could* have lost her head . . . But now there was no Eric and what difference did it make if she had no passport?

'And you'll be staying how many nights, Miss?' Valentin had stopped using her full name, she noticed.

'Three,' Julia replied, 'I've booked for three.'

In case she lost her nerve.

Julia gingerly pressed the lift button. While she had been at the desk, the two lifts had stood with their doors eerily agape though there was no one inside and no one had emerged from them. The doors kept making nervous forays as if they ached for closure but some neurotic hesitancy prevented them. Then suddenly, as she approached, both doors clamped shut as if they had drawn courage from one another, and both lifts whirred into action in answer to some higher calling. After a wait of several minutes – during which she contemplated pressing again for fear she had not pressed hard enough, except that the notice made her think better of it – Lift No. 1 opened, empty of course, and Julia stepped in, dragging her case behind her. Her reflection in the mirrored walls looked grey and emaciated. Her hair was flat and greasy, though she had washed it only that morning, half a world away. Under the glare of the lift's fluorescence, she felt twitchy as if she were giving off static. After all the contraptions she had gone through at the airport she firmly believed that as soon as she jabbed one of the buttons inside the lift an alarm would go off or a red light would flash over her head and give her away. But after several false starts, the lift lumbered into action. The doors opened clamorously several times on the ascent, unbidden, it would seem, and Julia would brace herself for a new arrival, but there were no signs of life in the Nathaniel. She could have been in a ghost hotel. When she finally alighted and wandered through the dingy corridors on the 12th floor, she could hear from other rooms the tinny babble of televisions and the mournful clatter of plates. She got the impression of caged, solitary lives and behind each door she imagined used rooms smelling of stale dinners and tart body spray.

Room 1210 felt very used. The motif of Middle Eastern splendour had not made it this far and the room was a junk shop of dowdy styles. Yellowing walls, a brown carpet. When she switched on the bedside light it gave off a low-wattage tobacco hue. The bronze radiator growled when she put her gloved hand on it but it was warm, very warm, and she was glad of that. The bed was cloaked in an evil pink nylon bedspread; a rug at its foot was the colour of sick; a wastebasket with a plastic inset was embroidered with a small tangle of hair. She wandered into the bathroom. Where the white tiling halted, the walls were painted in a mouthwash green, speckled here and there with traces of mould. To match the walls there was an acidy eau-de-Nil drip scored into the hand basin and the mirror sported the tributary of a crack. The perfect place, she thought, to end it all.

Behind the moss-coloured drapes in the bedroom she discovered a full-length glass door. After a lot of tugging she worked the handle free. She stepped out on to a balcony and into the glorious thrum of the bitterly cold night. It was her first taste of fresh air – if such the air over Manhattan could be called – and the cold felt different too. Brisker, cleaner. She leaned over the parapet and far below – well, twelve floors – a lighted centipede of traffic snailed towards a vanishing point between the glow-worm skyscrapers. The melancholy toot of car horns played a symphony; the diva sirens wailed. On the building opposite, an electronic tickertape mouthed a silent red greeting: Season's Greetings 1987. She inhaled deeply – this would be Julia Fortune's last Christmas.

From the moment she had stepped on the plane, she had felt hunted. Firstly, the form-filling. Reason for trip? Business or pleasure? Pleasure, she had written. And it was true, in part. She was surrendering to an illicit intoxication, a longed-for cessation of hostilities, and there was relief in it, if not pleasure. The form demanded where she'd be staying and Julia found herself looking furtively at what her neighbour was writing, an old schoolroom insecurity coming into play. He was a rough-looking fellow, from the country she guessed, with drills of red hair and raw hands and she knew that he would be bedding down at some ready-made address in Queens with half a dozen other illegal Paddies. Thaddeus Gavin, she saw his name was; Thaddeus, how biblical, she thought.

'Bit of handle, isn't it?' he said to her, grinning when he caught her staring.

'What?'

'Thaddeus,' he said, tapping the form with his chewed biro. 'Ted, for short.'

She didn't know if this was a chummy attempt at an introduction.

'This is the best time of the year to go. They think you're going over to visit relations.' He winked broadly. By next week he'd be a hod-carrier on a construction site run by the Irish mafia. Julia wasn't trying to fool anyone – not yet, anyway – but she felt implicated in his chummy freemasonry. Everything about her visit so far was above board. In fact, it was the boldest gesture of her entire twenty-seven years.

Hers was almost the last case to emerge on the baggage carousel at JFK and it travelled forlornly on its circular journey towards her. When she went to heave it off the belt, it almost sucked her on, and but for the intervention of brawny Ted she might have toppled over and been carried off on an endless loop.

'Want to meet up?' he asked, blushing to his roots as he righted her case on the floor.

'Meet up?'

'Ah you know, like, for a pint maybe?'

Oh, she thought.

'I'll only be here a few days,' she said, which sounded so terminal it made her want to gasp.

'Ah right so,' he said and he was so easily defeated that she almost felt like changing her mind. 'Sure, it was just an idea.'

If she was in a Hollywood film, she thought, this would be the start of a romance. But this was the Irish version – two inarticulate people angling to be the first to give the other the brush-off.

The cab journey from the airport had only intensified her feeling of being on the run. The taximan drove like a lunatic, swinging from one lane to the other, as they hurtled towards the city. Her heart lifted at the familiar skyline – there was the Empire State, the Chrysler. She smiled to herself. Wouldn't

Hetty have loved this! It was from here, after all, that she had sprung. Then they had nose-dived underground into an acid-lit tunnel full of numbed traffic roar, before emerging into the heart of the frosted silhouette they had seen minutes before, towers looming up all about her in shining sentinels.

Now it was she who was looming over it. For the first time since she had left home, Julia felt, there on the balcony of the Nathaniel, a moment of unadulterated victory. She had made it! Nobody could stop her now. She was reluctant to go inside again for fear the brief bout of euphoria might fizzle out in the musty confines of the room but she could feel the cold air solidifying in her lungs and she thought she might die of frostbite if she stood out there any longer.

Shivering, she retreated into the fusty warmth of Room 1210. Unzipping her case she fished out her toilet bag and deposited it in the bathroom. The mirror with its jagged seam, she discovered, was actually the door of a cabinet with glass shelves. She lined up her toiletries, adding her tweezers, face cream and the orange tube of capsules. Sleeping tablets. Since the break-up with Eric she hadn't been able to sleep and the doctor had prescribed the tablets to get her over the hump, as he called it. Eric had been Julia's last chance and she had thrown herself into the relationship. That was her downfall – mistaking willed abandon for love. But she had managed to fool him and herself for three years. When he had broken up with her, he had said sadly (though it had sounded as if he had been calculating the odds for months) something is just not right. The something, though he didn't know it, was Hetty. She shut the door of the cabinet. It made a disapproving click.

She wandered back into the room and turned on the television, a large, old-fashioned black-and-white model encased in mock mahogany. She kept the sound low. There was a quiz show on one of the channels and every so often as she unfurled her dressing gown and pyjamas, her underwear, her squashed

shoes, she caught glimpses of people in frozen poses of consti-
pated glee. She remembered Hetty's mother telling her once
that the contestants were auditioned, not for their general
knowledge but for their ability to 'do' hysteria. She spoke of
America fondly, or so Julia had thought. It was only in retrospect she realised that Jenny Gardner was being ironic. Julia
wondered how much of her existence had been built on the
foundations of someone else's throwaway lines. Someone who
literally could not bear her. But, however indirectly, she was
here because of Jenny Gardner.

She had told her mother she was visiting an old college friend
for the holidays. A lie, the only one in this whole escapade.
Christmas at the Fortunes' was raucous and extended; her
absence would barely be noticed.

'But I was counting you in,' was her mother's only protest.

Julia had expected more resistance. In some odd way she
was disappointed how quietly her mother had acquiesced in
what could only be perceived as a whim – haring off to New
York the day before Christmas with next to no notice, though
in fact she'd been planning the trip secretly for weeks. The
break-up with Eric – a month before – had made it more
understandable. Like her, he was in Loss Adjustment at
Hibernian Life and Julia had been going out with him long
enough for her mother to be sure that she was about to follow
the well-worn path of her sisters down the aisle. Even Greta,
her mother had said with more than a hint of blame when
Julia had announced the split. Even Greta who was considered
a lost cause is what she meant. But her mother's baffled disappointment meant that Julia was granted a brief reprieve;
allowed, as her mother said, to be out of sorts.

Julia was the only one living at home. The last of five, the
final disappointment, the last gasp to rescue the unfortunate
family name. Five evenly spaced daughters – Greta, Rose, the
twins Kitty and Liv, and finally Julia – had exhausted her

father's hopes of an heir. Her mother ineffectually tried to curb their spirits as if the communal force of five girls in the house was the ultimate insult to her father's manhood. A gaggle of geese, he called them. Despite the hectic display of feminine chaos, the prevailing mood of the house was depression, though the word itself was considered too pretentious for the Fortunes. In the dumps was the closest they got. Her mother put any shift into the melancholy register in herself or her girls down to the Monthly Visitor; her father filed all unpredictable behaviour under Evil Moods. All that female energy had exhausted him into submission.

Julia's memories of him as a child were always of activity. Under the car endlessly tinkering, pushing the hand-mower around their abused garden. Theirs was the most unruly patch on Prosperity Drive, which ached so much after prim respectability that the Fortunes with their indiscreetly large brood were considered only a step above tinkers. The garden did nothing to dispel the reputation. The lawn – Julia would have hesitated to use the word – was a patchwork of scutch grass and clover, the fuchsia bushes had gone feral, the roses arched stalkily and proclaimed neglect in their badges of disease, their swarms of whitefly and stains of black spot. Added to that, her father liked to fix things. But not before he had taken them apart. So their driveway was marred by oil blotches from engine parts that had bled and behind the gate there were several old tyres stacked. The family car, a fifteen-year-old Ford Anglia – another totem of the Fortunes' poor standing on the Drive – was left outside year round to rust and grow moss in its window ledges. Julia felt this mangy piece of concrete was truly her father's domain, the only place he was safe from female surfeit. Poor Dad, Julia thought, poor beleaguered Dad.

Her mother, on the other hand, was easy-going to the point of slothfulness. She was dumpy with it, her girth expanding with the disappointed expectation of each birth. She was much smaller than Julia's father so that when Julia got to the age of speculating about such things, she wondered how it had worked between them; physically, that is. Did her mother have to stand on a chair? Was that why there had never been a brother? But mostly she wondered what on earth had possessed them to fetch up together. To think that love or passion or desire might have moved them seemed inconceivable. Or maybe it was the fact that a boy was inconceivable . . .

Whatever it was, by the time Julia came along they seemed animated by a kind of lazy contempt for one another. Decisions sank between them in a lather of low-grade recrimination.

'Dad, can I go to the tennis hop?'

'What does your mother say?'

'She said to ask you.'

'That's your mother for you!'

'Well, can I?'

'Am I expected to make all the hard decisions around here?'

'Is that yes or no?'

'If your mother says it's alright . . . she's the boss, after all.'

Which meant nobody was the boss. Julia's friends envied this laissez-faire approach but she felt cheated, the runt of the litter, not worthy of even a marital spat. She remembered her sisters exciting rows of operatic dimensions between her parents.

There was a knock on the door. Julia froze. Who could it be? Who knew she was here? Cautiously, she inched the door open. A very tall black woman stood outside. Her hair had been viciously straightened but there was one lock of silver amidst the black which stood out like the tail of a skunk. She wore glasses with elaborate wings that swept upwards like encrusted extensions of her eyebrows. She bent forward deferentially, as if by folding herself up she could negate her great height. She must be six foot tall, Julia estimated. She wore a white cardigan over a navy polka-dot dress made of some filmy stuff. Her large feet were carelessly pushed into fur-lined carpet slippers.

'Hi, hon,' she said, smiling broadly. 'Gloria, 1209.' She pointed regally at the next room. Her door was ajar. Julia caught sight of a miniature winking Christmas tree and heard waves of TV laughter from an unseen set. 'I thought I'd be neighbourly.'

Julia smiled tightly.

'You just shipped in, then?' Gloria asked, peering beyond Julia at her disembowelled case spilling its contents on the floor.

Julia nodded.

'You like to join me for a little celebration?'

Julia looked at her blankly.

'It's Christmas, honey, or hadn't you noticed?'

Inwardly, Julia groaned. Christmas Eve in the big city and it was not possible to be left alone. And just now Julia wanted to be very anonymous.

'Thank you,' Julia said, 'but I have plans for tomorrow.'

The sleep of the just, she thought.

'We all got plans for tomorrow, honey.'

Julia felt reprimanded.

'I'm talking about tonight. My place, 7.30.'

Gloria smiled munificently.

'Where y'all from, then?'

'Dublin,' Julia said mulishly. 'Dublin, Ireland.'

'My, my, aren't you a long way from home! Well, honey, you get back to your settling in,' Gloria said, waving a lavish hand in Julia's direction. She backed away a few paces. 'You're going to just love it here – we're all just one big old happy family at the Nathaniel.'

Julia shut the door briskly. She collapsed on the bed, her heart pounding from fright, and lay there, fully clothed. Even though her throat was tight with anxiety, she felt numb with tiredness. Sleep was the only escape . . .

Hetty appeared in her troubled slumber. Her dreams of Hetty were always steeped in grainy family album hues, each scene preserved in envelope corners over a handwritten caption – 11 June 1972. The first time she saw Hetty. The Gardners had moved in two doors up about a week before – moved into the Vances' house, which her mother to this day persisted in calling it, even though the Vances had left in '71. Julia had been kneeling on the bed, her elbows propped on the windowsill, looking out at the Fortunes' rumpled back garden – Kitty sunbathing on a deckchair pretending to study, Liv in her vest and undies painting pots, her latest craze. Then she saw something she wasn't expecting – signs of life in the garden second next door. A girl of about her own age had appeared, stepping gingerly down the cracked path which led to the hedged-off bit of the garden. She was a plump creature in a white smocked dress with puff sleeves and bare tawny legs shod in pink plastic sandals. She climbed aboard the swing set which had been left by the Vances. Once garden-shed green, the paint had flaked off in places and hadn't been touched up so its predominant colour now was rust. There was a wooden slatted seat and a pleasingly dried scooped-out hollow of ground underfoot where the Vance kids had left their signature with their heels many years before. The Vances were a generation older than the Fortunes so Julia had known them only as young adults – Lilian in her nurse's whites coming off duty from night shift at St Jude's, Gay – amazingly – returning in priest's clothes from the seminary. It was hard to imagine either of them ever being children.

She watched as the girl climbed on the swing and tentatively got momentum going. She called out, something that Julia couldn't catch – Pop, was it? – and a man appeared and ambled down the garden. She called to him again and he came in behind the swing and started to push. With his hand on her back, the girl was propelled forward almost as high as the swing's crossbar and when she swung back it was as if she were flying through the air. She was crying out from fright or glee, Julia could not tell which, but she could sense the girl's exhilaration. Then a woman appeared – her mother, Julia supposed – and she joined in, clapping her hands as the girl flew higher and higher, as if this were some kind of daring performance. It was a performance alright, Julia thought, of a kind she had never witnessed. As if the very fact of their connection were being celebrated, the parents on the ground, the child airborne. Some spiteful part of her wanted it to end badly . . .

'Hi, I'm Henrietta Gardner, but my friends call me Hetty.'

Julia was sitting on the wall of the front garden swinging her legs and chewing on a toffee when the little American girl approached. Up close, she was round and very pleased with herself, despite the silly name that sounded like a character in a prissy children's book. Julia, in mid-chew, felt in the presence of a commanding adult.

'Wanna come and play?' Hetty persisted.

Julia shrugged and slid down from the wall; she found such directness unnerving but compelling. She followed Hetty, several paces behind.

'Mawm!' Hetty yelled when they entered the Vances' house by the back door.

The house remained much as the Vances had left it. The red-and-white kitchen cabinets with the corrugated glass, the faded striped wallpaper scattered with illustrations of kettles and bread bins and tea canisters, the same mud-coloured lino. The kitchen table was new – glaring yellow Formica on tubular legs with matching chairs. Hetty went directly to the fridge when there was no response from her mother and lifted out a bottle of orange squash. This added to her precocious air of command. In the bluish glare of the open door, Julia caught a glimpse of cities. Cartons and bottles, tubs teetering on the shelf edges, an impression of largesse.

Hetty climbed on a stool and fetched down two plastic beakers, setting them on the counter and filling them noisily. She popped a straw into both. Solemnly, she handed Julia one.

'Candy?' Hetty asked.

'No, Julia,' Julia replied, 'my name is Julia.'

'I mean would you like a candy, Julia?' Hetty repeated very slowly making Julia feel utterly stupid. She burrowed into one of the kitchen cupboards and fished out a tin, opening it with a flourish to reveal a stash of chocolate bars. Julia snaffled one quickly, fully expecting the arrival of an ogre mother who would insist on her putting it back. She slurped noisily on the straw, thinking how exotic this was. The only time she'd used one was in Cafolla's when they'd gone there for ice-cream sundaes on the twins' Confirmation day; she didn't think of them as domestic accoutrements.

Hetty's mother appeared then.

'Who's this little citizen?' she asked – not what are you doing eating me out of house and home?

She was a slight woman, her heavy blond hair tied back in a bouncing ponytail, a leafy freckling on her cheeks; she wore a T-shirt and a pair of jeans. Her features were sharp; her candour interrogative.

'Mom, this is my new friend.'

Julia felt thoroughly appropriated by this declaration. Hetty hadn't gone through the ritual Julia was used to, in which you slunk into a loose kind of alliance and if you didn't fall out you supposed it was a friendship. But it wasn't an altogether unpleasant sensation to be taken in hand like this.

'Name, rank and serial number?' Mrs Gardner asked.

Julia looked to Hetty for translation.

'Don't mind Mom,' Hetty said in an aside. 'She's a bit kooky.'

'You're spending a lot of time around there,' her mother would say, as if there was something suspect about her new friendship. 'Are you hoping some of their Yankiness will rub off on you?'

Yes, Julia wanted to say fiercely, yes.

But no, it was more than that. She wanted both to own the Gardners and be possessed by them. In their company she felt singular, but what she longed for was to be indispensable.

Information was one way. She scavenged for biographical detail. Bob was from Faithful, Arkansas, Jenny from New York, New York. That's the way she said it. So good they named it twice, Hetty would add. Secrets were another. They had met at a monument in Paris, Hetty said, and love blossomed. *Love blossomed.* Julia puzzled over such phrases of Hetty's. She was full of declarations which sounded adult to Julia and too emphatic to be queried.

'I'm a love child,' Hetty informed her gravely. (Julia could not shift the image of the Gardners delivering Hetty in front of some grand equestrian statue.) 'What about you?'

Julia had no idea. As far as she was concerned she had sprung from some dark mood of her father's and a blind eye turned by her mother.

Hetty and her parents presented a united front; they were part of her play as if they were enjoying a second childhood. They went to the Stella Cinema together for the double-bill Saturday afternoon matinées; they made their own popcorn and shouted out answers in unison when *Quicksilver* came on the TV.

'We're making memories,' Hetty said, 'that's what Mom says.'

Julia was so casually included in their lives that it made her feel, at times, that she was more witness than participant. She would watch all three of them cavorting around the living room in a cushion fight and feel a creeping wariness she could not explain. She could not entirely trust this gaiety. In the midst of the laughter she got the whiff of loss.

'I don't know why they're such a great hit,' her father would complain mildly. 'Sure, isn't he on the run?' Her father's theory was that Bob Gardner was a draft dodger. 'Although, he doesn't

138

look like a yobbo.' (Yobbos had long hair and wore – ironically enough – army surplus.)

Mr Gardner – no, Bob, she corrected herself, for such Mr Gardner liked to be called even by children – had a sharp haircut and wore a smart suit to work. The shiny kind that Mormons wore. She imagined him going door to door peddling religion although she knew he worked in the airport. But her father's speculations made her anxious and prone to drawing up inventories of impermanence. Well, they were renters, weren't they? They used Bakelite dishes instead of delft as if they were on an extended camping trip. She noticed, too, that instead of loose covers Mrs Gardner – Jenny – used tie-dyed throws on the sofa and chairs. They were like conjuring props as if with one swift movement Jenny could make the furniture disappear. And her father was on a contract, Hetty told her, and could at any time be called home, a phrase Julia had only seen on gravestones. It was this air of contingency that made the Gardners' tenure so imperilled. One day she might knock on *their* door and be greeted by silence. She would peer in through the letterbox and see only a shaft of hazy light falling in an abandoned hallway. These things happened, she knew; she and Hetty watched *The Fugitive*. The soundtrack boomed in her head.

Julia awoke, startled. She pressed her temples to rid herself of the ghostly echoes and realised that the rat-a-tat was at her door. Rumpled, she rose from the bed and opened the door. It was Gloria again. She looked at her watch – half past midnight. Still on Irish time.

'You ready then?'

Gloria was wearing a crown-shaped party hat. She sipped from a pale green cocktail with a cherry floating on the top.

'You don't want to miss my Japanese slippers!' she said, gesturing to the glass.

Julia allowed herself to be led into Gloria's room. If Julia's room was merely used, Gloria's was possessed. Every available space had been filled. There were bookshelves and a display cabinet, a table under the window. In the corner near the bathroom Gloria had set up a breakfast cooker. As well as the Christmas tree there were streamers and balloons and golden paper chains hanging from the light fittings and draped over the picture frames. She raised a jug and poured Julia a large cocktail. She handed her a paper hat. Inasmuch as she had thought about it, Julia had somehow expected that this would be a party but now she realised that she was the only guest. Was this woman trying to pick her up? Or adopt her?

'Come on, come on, it's Christmas. Don't they celebrate Christmas where you come from?' Gloria chided, sensing her reluctance. She invited Julia to sit and don the papery headgear. Then she went to a corner of the room and dropped a stylus noisily on a record. Frank Sinatra eased his way into the room.

'The anthem of New York,' Gloria said, mouthing the words.

In response Julia thought: I want to sleep in a city that never wakes.

The Gardners used to listen to music like this and smooch around the sitting room while she and Hetty played upstairs. They would hear giggling and sometimes whoops of laughter followed by strange silences. Hetty would put her finger to her lips. The secretive gesture made Julia feel thrillingly included.

'They're making a sister for me,' she would say, nudging Julia as they sat at Hetty's white melamine dressing table brushing each other's hair. The trick of the triptych mirror made Julia believe that there was already a third presence in the room. When she got excited, Hetty would often grab her hand or clutch her arm. Her touch made Julia agitated. She would feel a terrible seizing at her throat that could have been tears or fright. She remembered once lying next to Hetty on her bed. Hetty was chattering as usual but instead of listening, Julia found herself contemplating the plump satin pile of her instep and inexplicably wanting to kiss it. It had made her blush all over.

The bed had a canopy of white netting over it and she had stared intently at its tiny honeycomb pattern until the shameful desire passed.

'This is like a four-poster bed,' she said, trying to change the potent mood.

'Mosquito net,' Hetty explained, wrinkling her nose. 'Mom thought there'd be mosquitoes here.'

For the first time Julia considered that Prosperity Drive might be an exotic destination for the Gardners, a far-flung, wild place with who knows what hidden dangers.

How they spent those seemingly endless hours of childhood, Julia couldn't catalogue afterwards, hard as she tried to piece them together. The activities seemed too banal to bear the weight of charged memory: Ludo and cards, the disrobing of dolls. Hetty had three Barbies – air hostess, party girl and nurse – while Julia had only a battered Sindy, a hand-me-down from Rose. The plastic pellet that was her right breast had been chewed by the dog (a bitch, of course) that the Fortunes had briefly owned before it was run down on the avenue by an ambulance on its way to St Jude's. The clothes that Sindy had come with were long vanished, compensated only slightly by a host of rough-looking replicas that Greta had run up on the sewing machine. (Thanks to Greta, the Fortunes' pants and jackets sported pale patches where the pockets had been removed to tart up Sindy's wardrobe.)

Once or twice, Julia was allowed to stay the night. A sleepover, Jenny Gardner called it. Julia would wake in the small hours, the light from the landing creeping in under the lip of the door, the steady rise and fall of Hetty's breath in the bed beside her, the wispy canopy overhead and she would feel, however briefly, a certainty about her place in this world. Emboldened she would reach out and stroke the little dark hairs on Hetty's forearm. But it was a feeling that could only flourish while the household slept.

'You look done in,' Gloria said after the third Japanese slipper.

'Jet lag.'

'You flew in from Ireland today?'

Julia nodded.

'Say, hon, I don't even know your name,' Gloria said.

Julia took a deep breath. Now was as good a time as any.

'Henrietta,' she said. 'Henrietta Gardner. But most people call me Hetty.'

She took a large gulp of Japanese slipper to damp down the wail she could feel rising in her throat. As if Hetty had just died, as if she had just killed her. She stood up, dropping her glass. Gloria rushed to the bathroom and came back with a cloth. She righted Julia's glass and began to mop up the seething stain which was spreading on her pale rug. Julia in her silly paper hat watched and sobbed.

'Hetty, honey, what is it? What's troubling you?'

Gloria was on her knees gazing up at her. In all these years no one had asked her so directly.

'My friend,' she started. Gloria's extravagant eyebrows were arched in compassionate query.

'My friend died.' There, it was said.

Gloria stretched up her hand and grasped Julia's.

'Why don't you sit back down and tell me all about it, hon.'

On Christmas Eve, fifteen years before, Hetty had cycled to the shops on an errand for her mother. Crackers, Jenny Gardner kept on repeating at the funeral, a box of Christmas crackers. Julia was at home. The Fortunes had one house rule: after nightfall on Christmas Eve was family time. So even before Hetty's death, Christmas had felt to Julia like a day of bereavement, a zone of female disappointment. It was a cold, wet night and Hetty had pedalled down Classon's Hill near the old dye works which every child in the neighbourhood had been told to dismount for. Conditions were bad, greasy underfoot with poor visibility. Hetty must have been travelling at some speed, hurtling down the forbidden hill. A pebble must have struck the spokes, or maybe she had hit a pothole. She applied the brakes. The cable snapped. She went over the handlebars and hit her head against the stone balustrade of the bridge. Stone dead, they said as if a gravestone had been instantly erected. Stone dead.

Julia came to a full stop. How could she explain that in her adult life she had met no one who could match the captivating passion – wasn't that what it was, passion? – that a dead twelve-year-old playmate had inspired. Not even Eric; especially not Eric. If it had just been Hetty, she might have recovered. Hetty at least was safe in her memory, a constant companion, the wise child who would never enter the treacherous gangland of adolescence or know the guile and wrangles of adulthood. She remained embalmed for Julia, like a child martyr of the Church. No, it was the loss of Jenny Gardner that had really stung. Jenny had simply cut her out. She couldn't bear to see Julia. She would cross the street if she saw her coming. Even at the funeral she refused to make eye contact; it made Julia feel invisible, as if *she* were the one who had died. Weren't mothers supposed to cleave to the companions of their dead children, treat them as substitutes, invest them with the souls of their lost angels? Not Jenny Gardner. Julia was like an insult to her. A smack in the face. She was as antagonistic as if Julia had pushed Hetty over the parapet. Or as if she had intuited, somehow, Julia's first spiteful thoughts that summer's day she saw Hetty on the swing.

'It's nothing personal,' Bob Gardner explained to Julia's mother, 'it's just too painful for her. Maybe after a while . . .'

But time only solidified Jenny's dark resolve. The milestones in Julia's life – leaving school, her first boyfriend, going to college (the first of the Fortunes to do so because she was the last) – these exaggerated the chasm between her and the Gardners. There were times in her teenage years when Julia would pray for them to disappear. Why don't they move back to America, she would wonder, vehemently wishing for the very thing that had haunted her childhood. Why don't they move on? But for all their seeming transience, they were as rooted (or stranded?) in Prosperity Drive as the Fortunes were. She'd heard – but never saw since she was never permitted to enter their house again – that Jenny Gardner had preserved Hetty's bedroom exactly the way she had left it, her unopened Christmas presents still intact in their shiny wrapping. (She had asked for a surprise that year, Julia remembered; only Jenny knew what was wrapped up inside.) So Julia's last image of Hetty was at the moment of flight, her body in mid-air, still intact, still joyous and alive, her head laced and tinselled with Christmas . . .

'Hush now, hon,' Gloria was saying, rubbing her back as if she were winding a child. 'Your friend Julia wouldn't want you to be grieving like this, now would she? She'd want you to be getting on with your life, making a fresh start.'

Julia nodded dumbly. Of all the dislocating experiences of the past 24 hours, this was the strangest, hearing herself being described posthumously in the third person. It was like someone walking over her grave. She shivered.

'Maybe, hon, you should get some sleep?'

Gloria steered her to her door as if she were feeble. She had trouble with the key – everything in this country turned the wrong way – and Gloria took it from her and opened the door of 1210. Her passport was lying on the floor where Valentin must have slipped it under the door when he got no reply. She picked it up and put it on the bedside locker.

'Alright now, honey?' Gloria asked.

Julia nodded. Thank you seemed such a paltry thing to say to this woman to whom she had blurted out her entire life so she said nothing. She took her clothes off, letting them drop where they fell, and crept into bed. There was a dull thudding in her head, a drumbeat of drink and grief. She looked at her watch. It was almost 2 a.m. She closed her eyes but the room spun about making her feel sick. Sleep seemed out of the question. Maybe now was the time to do it, sick and sore and purged.

She rose and went into the bathroom. She opened the cabinet – she was cut in two by the gashed mirror – and fished out her nail scissors. She went back into the room and picked up her passport. She opened it to the halfway point and began to hack through its pages until only the covers remained. She gathered up the shredded remains, put them in the wastebasket and stepped out once more on to the balcony. Sheltering the flame with her hand, she struck a match and set fire to the contents. Her past flared briefly, singed and then shrivelled into charred blackness. Smudges of it escaped and danced briefly in the frosty air, mingling with the hot clouds of her breath. If anyone could see her, they would think her crazy – or a jumper. A naked woman on a balcony going up in flames. She didn't care.

'Happy Christmas,' she whispered into the darkness. 'Happy Christmas, Hetty Gardner.'

TWELVE STEPS

After a month in Faithful, Arkansas, Ted Gavin met Paula Spears in the only bar in town where he could get away from work. Skipper's was the sort of place his students would never frequent. There were no happy-hour specials, no imported beers, and no bloated big screen tuned to sport. The only soundtrack was the low murmur of conversation and the thwock and rumble of balls from the pool tables in the back room. The other patrons were ageing, down at heel, occasionally raucous and seriously intent on quiet oblivion. They approached drinking with a steady diligence, as if it were a vocation. Joy and inebriation were intermittent by-products of the process but for a lot of the time it was work, something to be got through. As he settled in at the bar, Ted noticed the lone woman perched precariously on the next stool and said hello. It was an old impulse – from home – though he was careful to say it as neutrally as possible, so it could be ignored or taken for an unattributed grunt if unwelcome.

'Howdy,' she said cheerfully and that's how it started.

Ted was relieved to have met Paula, to have met anyone. Even he realised that drinking alone in a place like Skipper's would have been too despairing, too lonely, too effing sad.

They met at Skipper's every Thursday – as if by chance. It had never become a fixed arrangement. Neither of them owned a mobile phone. They were pals, drinking partners, mates – he did not have the exact word for what Paula was to him. Female friend? Too cold and tame. Fuck-buddy? Hardly. He had never slept with Paula, never felt even the merest twinge of lust, and for Ted that was a blessing. (He had a history of miscalculation with women – with a few drinks he could come over all gamey but he couldn't sustain the bravado.) Sex had never come into the equation with Paula; for starters, she must have a decade on him. She was a small, wiry woman with stick-thin legs and pragmatically chopped blondish hair. Her face was the only fleshy part of her – smooth, moon-like, with unaccountably merry eyes. Ted couldn't have described what she wore – some nondescript uniform of faded denim and pallid cotton. He could not even say she dressed carelessly; that would seem too deliberate, too much of a statement. Paula's clothes seemed immaterial, even to her. She didn't excite strong feelings in him; in her company, Ted found himself slowing, mellowing. They pondered on trivia – why are suitcases in films always empty, where does the Midwest end?

'The Midwest doesn't end,' Paula used to say, 'it just goes on and on.'

Ted had only the vaguest idea where Paula lived and he had never invited her back to his hangar-like flat in a student block by the railway tracks. It was one large, high-ceilinged room, sparsely furnished, with a bathroom attached. The place was clad in aluminium siding and the acoustics were terrible. There was a heavy-footed football player living over him, whose progress across the floor above sounded like rolls of thunder and made the light fittings epileptic. He had never invited anyone there. Three nights a week, at 3 a.m., a goods train would roll by, thunderous but slow. The trains were so long – once he counted sixty-two cars – that it could take a half-hour for them to pass, by which time their ponderous trundling would have lodged deep inside his brain. Afterwards, he couldn't sleep in the surging silence. Silence didn't bother him, but this busy emptiness did. It had become part of his routine never to be home on the nights the trains rolled.

He and Paula would sit companionably and drink until Paula's money ran out. Usually before his. She worked on a checkout in a supermarket. But what either of them did, didn't seem to matter much. That was a relief for Ted. Usually when he mentioned he was a writer it aroused the kind of curiosity he couldn't bear, given the state of his novel – sprawling, amorphous, impossible to explain away in a quick sentence. He would start: it's about a woman in recovery from a disastrous marriage – as if you could recover from a disastrous marriage – who escapes by solitary drinking, well, not just drinking . . . All his explanations ran into qualifying clauses. What he didn't say was that it was about his mother, with the names changed to protect the guilty.

Of course, they shared stories. It's what people do over drinks in a bar with no laid-on entertainment. Paula's story was unremarkable in its soap opera misery. She was a doomed statistic come to life. Her first marriage, a teen wedding – shotgun, of course – was to Donny who did a flit when the baby was six months old. He picked up his coat one evening, she said, and just walked. It was a detail so deliberate that Ted immediately made a mental note of it. He imagined the coat – a lumberjack's large check, lime-dusted at the cuffs (Donny was a bricklayer) and saw a sandy-haired youth with a belligerent mouth, hooking a thick finger through the collar loop, maybe swinging it over his shoulder as he sauntered out to his car. Sauntered was how he'd do it, Ted decided. Or maybe he hadn't even planned it beforehand so his casualness was genuine. A single tumbleweed would brush by the steel toe of his boot as he opened the

148

car door. No, it would be a truck, wouldn't it? . . . Ted shook himself; these writerly riffs were too self-indulgent by far.

Paula moved in with her sister who was shacked up with Larry Spears. And, well, Larry was unemployed and Paula and baby Mikey were around the apartment all day while Jen was out at the plant and, well . . . Paula inhaled so deeply on her cigarette, her cheeks sucked into cadaverous hollows . . . well, things happened.

'He had two of us pregnant at the same time,' she said. 'I was further along. So I made him pick. And I won! The big door prize.' Her laugh turned into a tubercular hacking.

Marriage number two lasted five years by which time Paula had had Debra, several miscarriages, and had taken to drinking to dull the pain of bruised cheekbones and black eyes inflicted by Larry Spears. She stayed – for the kids – and to prove herself right.

'I'd lost my sister over this guy,' she said, stubbing out her cigarette and making a sour face. When she finally came to her senses and left Larry, she was so far gone on alcohol she couldn't look after the kids. That was six years ago.

'The funny thing is I didn't drink at all until I met him,' Paula said.

Well, if you can't beat them, join them, Ted thought.

'I never beat them if that's what you're thinking . . . just couldn't handle them and the drink . . .' she said hotly and downed her vodka in one go.

Except for such flashes of feeling, she told Ted her sorry tale matter-of-factly, dry-eyed. It had the tone of a well-rehearsed and strangely impersonal monologue, the sort of thing he imagined you'd hear at an AA meeting. Everything about her seemed to have already passed into a kind of dirty realism, Ted thought. But although her life sounded fictional, he never doubted that Paula was telling the truth.

His own story, in comparison, seemed almost well adjusted.

'Well,' he began, 'I'm Irish, as if you hadn't guessed.' He gestured to his flame-coloured buzz-cut flecked with grey. 'And the accent.'

He had won a green card lottery in the Nineties; his sister Joan had entered his name. Before getting legal he'd worked on construction sites in New York.

'I was the joker, the storyteller, the Paddy with the gift of the gab. The fellas on the buildings with me were always telling me to write it down. So I did.'

He didn't tell Paula that he'd kept the writing a secret. (She was getting the official version.) The scribbling wasn't something that would have gone down well with the blokes he worked with by day and went drinking with by night. For all their loud exhortation, they'd have thought a writer in their company suspect. But the idea they had so casually planted was surprisingly tenacious. Ted's writing ambitions grew in the dark he had consigned them to. Sometimes he thought it a curse – this 'idea' of writing – but the urge was the strongest he'd felt in years. Strong enough to make him apply for and get through a writing programme in Syracuse and get him this, his first teaching job.

'That's how I ended up in Faithful,' he told Paula.

There had been a girl in Syracuse. Sandy. Rangy, intense, she looked like a throwback to the Seventies (before Ted's time but he recalled her type from films his sisters watched – *The Graduate, Play Misty for Me*) with a toffee-coloured mane of hair which she swung about like an extra arm – as much a part of her emphatic expression as her voice. She was like his very own cheerleader, as if he were a personal project. She enthused about the raw energy of his prose, his untutored way with words, his Irish syntax. But still, he doubted her. Was she trying to butter him up? Had she fixed on him only for the curiosity of his accent, the whiff of the working class from him, the otherness of his experience? He remembered a trip they had taken towards the end, when, in his mind, their destinies had irretrievably forked. The trip had been Sandy's idea; she had a car. A mystery tour, she said.

'You're going to love it,' she told him as they drove towards the coast.

She brought him to Breezy Point, a gated community of Irish-Americans who had clustered together on the far tip of the Rockaway Peninsula.

'It'll be like going home,' Sandy had said in her relentlessly confident way. Immediately he felt his truculence rising. Why did people presume you were homesick, he wondered, and that all you wanted was to go home? And if home wasn't on offer, that you'd be charmed by a miniature version of it, transplanted to Queens and set behind gates? They arrived at a checkpoint. Yes, a checkpoint with a mechanical arm and a lockhard with a cap!

'Not to worry, with your accent I'm sure we'll pass,' Sandy said gaily. She was right. The bloke in the uniform waved them through. Oblivious to his irritation, Sandy pointed out the store names – Deirdre Maeve's, the supermarket, the pub called the Blarney Stone. Ted seethed; she had brought him to theme park hell. The shore was the only place that seemed authentic. It could have been somewhere on the coast of Donegal. At home, he had always loved the sensation of being on the edge of land, of being able to look out and see nothing ahead but the tantalising horizon. But now he was on the other side and he knew what he was looking back on.

When he and Sandy stepped out on to the beach, they were almost blown away. The wind whipped the words out of their mouths. Sand swirled about them as they trod down a narrow passageway in the dunes between a high fence strung with netting. Notices were pinned on the wire.

'Plovers nesting. Please do not disturb the birds.'

It was while they were considering this that they were attacked. The birds seemed to come from nowhere. Flocks of them, clamouring and hostile, swooping low and aiming straight for their faces. Ted could hear their beaks clacking rustily at his ears as they squawked and screeched and constantly regrouped. This was no murmuration of starlings like you might see at home, where the sky would be sooted with waltzing swathes of birds, scattering and re-forming in an aerial show. No, these birds were killer squadrons. The racket was terrible, louder even than the howling gale.

'Duck,' he roared at Sandy as the plovers drilled towards them.

'Mother birds,' Sandy shouted back. Instead of keeping low, she stood and waved her arms about. 'Shush there, now, we're not going to touch your babies,' she roared at them. 'We wouldn't harm a hair on their little heads, would we, Ted?'

Feathers, he wanted to say, they have feathers on their heads; he didn't want to be implicated in this coochy-coo baby talk. Sandy smooched up her lips and made clucking sounds herself.

'Oh, mommies . . .' she went on, pursing her lips and pouting like a child, 'there, there, don't fret' as the demented birds nose-dived about her, pecking at the tails of her hair whipped into a frenzy by the wind. Even as she shielded her face, she continued her high-octane crooning. The tendernesses screamed at such decibels made Ted want to turn on her, just as the birds were doing. In the midst of the screeching flurry, he could hear only how loud and insistent Sandy's love would become. He threw his coat over her (her hair in a rage around her head seemed to particularly aggravate the birds) and steered her jaggedly back towards the car.

'Jesus,' he said once they were safely inside. 'That was like something out of Hitchcock.'

But far from being upset, Sandy seemed exhilarated by the encounter, her face speckled with sea spray, her hair damply aflame.

'That was motherhood,' she said. 'Fierce motherhood.'

'Time for a drink,' he said and they repaired to the Blarney Stone.

Nothing personal, he told Sandy when they broke up. It was straight after they'd graduated. She was going back to Cleveland, he to a summer on the buildings in New York. Why, she kept on asking him, tenderly but persistently. How could he say it? It was the way you talked to those effing birds.

When he had arrived in Faithful, Ted had been invited to several faculty dinners. He was always on his best behaviour. He just didn't feel he could let his hair down among people who watered their wine or drank Dr Pepper. Delia Myerson, the chair of the department, was a middle-aged medievalist who threw vegetarian dinners for her staff with missionary zeal. She was new to the job.

'You'd imagine given her speciality she should be serving huge sides of ham and great big drumsticks,' Ted said to Miles Sandoval, one of the faculty poets. They were out on Delia's deck where the smokers were banished.

'She's desperate to be liked,' said Miles. 'Tries too hard.'

Miles steered Ted to the edge of the decking.

'You've got to find a circle here,' he said confidentially. 'Something outside the university, preferably. Else you'll be stuck with this bunch all the time.' They both surveyed the scene – the littered remains of a dinner party, a heated discussion of the masculinism of Ernest Hemingway.

'Like what?'

'Well, there's the Church,' Miles started.

'I don't think so – can't see a lapsed Catholic making it as a born-again Baptist, can you?'

'There's always hunting . . .'

Ted didn't want to admit that he'd never seen a gun, let alone picked one up to shoot small furry animals.

'Or the gentlemen's clubs,' Miles went on, using the euphemism Faithful employed for its strip joints.

'I'm not that sad, Miles, thanks.'

'What about a writing group? Great way of getting chicks.'
Thrice-married Miles inhaled his considerable paunch and ran
a large paw through his luxuriant mane of bottle-black hair.

'God, no. Sounds like a busman's holiday.'

'Really, Ted, they're so grateful to have a guy in these groups
they'll offer all sorts of favours. I love those serious artistic
types. So intense.'

Oily fucker, Ted thought.

'Two workshops and an Irish lit. class a week is intense
enough for me, thanks.'

'Or find some of your compatriots. There's an Irish dame . . .'
he paused, frowning. 'Say,' he roared, sliding back the glass
doors that led into the dining room. 'What's the name of that
Irish gal who works for Hillbilly Realty?'

My God, Ted thought, is this for real? Property and irony
lying down together.

'Hetty, you mean,' Delia called back. 'Hetty Gardner.'

Delia rose from the table and came out on to the deck.

'Yes,' she agreed. 'You Irish should stick together.'

Delia gave him Hetty's card at the end of the evening.
Realtor, it read, with the Hillbilly logo. He imagined Delia
thinking with an efficient and good-natured sigh of relief –
well, that's Ted Gavin sorted. But he knew the last thing he
would do was to ring Hetty Gardner. Moving in these circles
he already felt like an impostor. He could scarcely believe
himself that only five years ago he was a hod carrier, working
away on scraps of short stories. The same stories that had
been published by a university press with a tiny print run.
But this Hetty Gardner wouldn't necessarily be impressed by
the slim volume entitled *Diaspora*, sparsely and grudgingly
reviewed ('A tough new voice from the land of the Celtic
mists,' said one. 'But where are the women?' another
complained.) He told himself he might look her up when he
had the novel finished. He was used to putting things off;
wasn't his whole life in hock to this effing book? How else to

explain his monk-like existence in Faithful, the long solitary hours spent in his dreary flat, poring over the derelict manuscript when he could have been out chasing women? Time enough for that, he kept on telling himself, when the book was done. If he felt momentarily tempted to contact Hetty Gardner, he soon argued himself out of it. She probably wouldn't be his type; her name alone made him think she was Anglo and a Prod. Anyway, she was probably here to get away from tribal associations. What other reason would there be for winding up in Faithful, Arkansas?

His was shame. The baby of the family, sent to college while his sisters Brenda and Joan worked in a hairdressing salon to supplement his fees. Ted, who had gone to the US on a J–1 visa in the final year of his arts degree and had never gone home.

'Is this what we educated you for?' his mother wrote. It was the strangest sensation receiving a letter from his mother – the first time ever. 'Your sisters scrubbing their fingers to the bone, so that you could hightail off to America? (Amerikay, he could hear her say it, like in some poor-mouth emigrant song.) To work on the buildings?'

He couldn't tell her that the reason he wouldn't go home was her. That he couldn't face the claustrophobic disappointment that was their two-up, two-down house in Main Street, Mellick. Couldn't face another day with his mother sitting in the good room with the blinds drinking whiskey miniatures from a teacup and melting into grandiose tears. Couldn't bear his sisters, all hair lacquer and nail polish, dancing attendance on her, trying to make up for the shortcomings of the man of the house. And latterly that meant Ted, not his unlamented father.

His poor da was straight from Irish father central casting. A pigeon fancier, the only time he was at peace with the world was when he was whispering to his cooing birds locked in barracks in the back yard. Otherwise, he was an emotional caveman. He was given to volcanic rages in which he would slice and joust with anything at close quarters. Dinners were upended if the portions weren't large enough; furniture broken and knick-knacks smashed if he were thwarted. What saved his father from caricature was that he didn't drink – he wore a pioneer pin – but that made his moods even more unpredictable. Nowadays some underlying mental condition would probably be diagnosed – bipolar disorder, schizophrenia – but what difference did it make having a name for it? His father had made their lives a misery. But at least he'd had the grace to exit early, keeling over in the midst of one of his choleric outbursts when Ted was twelve. For Ted's mother, though, that was his father's greatest crime. That he'd had the cheek to die, leaving her with three dependent children. His sisters were promptly apprenticed out, while his mother's life became a pooled and rancid stillness. The only thing that animated her was her punishing ambition for Ted.

'You're going to be a doctor,' she would say, 'or an engineer . . . that'll show him.' As if Ted's whole purpose in life was to spite the memory of his father.

It was his mother who took to drinking. Messily. Alcohol made her cravenly sentimental and affectionate; queasily so. She'd take Ted's hand and caress it, fingering the lines of his palm like a foolish astrologer.

'Oh Ted, Ted,' she would say, 'what would I do without you?'

Sometimes he wondered whom she was seeing when she planted a sloppy kiss on his fourteen-year-old lips.

'I never touched a drop until I was thirty,' his mother used to say, 'it was your father drove me to it.'

Ted knew what was coming next.

'Do you know that when I got married to your father, my boss offered us a case of whiskey for the reception and I was disappointed.' His mother had been a barmaid in The

Thirsty Scholar. 'I had no value for it. I'd have preferred a canteen of cutlery.'

This was what Ted wanted to retrieve in his novel, the girl his mother had been, the one who would have chosen a case of knives.

Ted thought of himself as a social drinker; well, he liked to have other people to drink with. Days would go by and he wouldn't even think of alcohol, but once he stepped into Skipper's on a Thursday evening it was the beginning of a roll that would finish up as a dull ache and a thick head on Monday morning. (Luckily, he didn't teach on Mondays.) He didn't have blackouts, he didn't have bruises and scrapes he wasn't quite sure how he'd acquired, he'd never arrived at school drunk. He cleaned up well, and usually he had prepared his classes. Usually.

One Tuesday in February he was saddled with a giant hangover and a workshop devoted – as he'd decreed the week previously – to the study of character. Snow had started to fall that morning in lazy swirls; by the time workshop was over it would be slick underfoot. Bypassing the present was a favourite trick of his when he wasn't in the mood for teaching. He turned to face the students sitting in boardroom formation waiting for him to start. Paula was on his mind. She hadn't shown up at Skipper's on Thursday; she'd obviously had a better offer. He had camped out at the bar for the rest of the night expecting her to arrive at any moment and feeling both anxious and peeved that she had left him in the lurch. He brooded on her absence over the weekend, drinking steadily as he did. It was still rankling with him as he stood before his workshop. Three hours of unprepared class time yawned ahead of him. He improvised.

'Take a woman,' he began.

Someone snickered.

'Early forties, victim of a violent marriage, who finally leaves her husband and then has her kids taken away from her because she drinks too much. A woman who lives in the vain hope she can get them back . . .'

Was it vain? He felt the first stab of misgiving.

'Delusional, in other words.' That was Valerie Kleber. A professed Christian (her email tag was JCdiedforme), she was a severe beauty, with long black glossy hair, serious glasses and the kind of mouth which was pert now, and later, Ted suspected, would grow thin and judgemental. Her father was some class of a minister.

'Let's not reach for labels, Valerie,' he said, riled at her diagnostic certainties. 'This is a study of character, not a case history.'

There was a sharp rustling of papers and searching for pens.

'What does she do?' Valerie asked.

'Does it matter?' He was playing for time. Already, he felt seedlings of betrayal sprouting.

'What's her name?' Taylor Payne demanded.

'Let's call her Paula,' he said. How pathetic was he that he couldn't even think up an alias for her? 'She works in a store, on the register.'

'This sounds like a total cliché.' That was Taylor again shaking his shoulder-length blond locks, emanating a glassy boredom. A poet by aspiration, forced to dirty his hands with fiction. When he wrote in class a smirk played on his features as if he were contemptuously amused by his own trifles.

'Some clichés are true,' Ted said.

'You mean this is a real person?' Sonia Matheson was either incredulous or sceptical; Ted couldn't work out the difference. He thought of her as large, sweet-natured and dim, but sometimes there was a gleam in her fat eye that could have been sarcasm.

'What I want you to do is to get inside the biography, so to speak. Find something authentic in the seemingly banal. See beyond the cliché.'

'But is she real?' Sonia persisted.

'Let's go,' Ted directed, anxious for the soothing silence that is fifteen students scribbling furiously, one eye on the clock, and would be a blessed balm for his hangover. The next best thing to the hair of the dog. But the class sat there, pens poised, waiting for something else, something more from him. At the corner of his eye, snow danced.

'Is she?' Sonia asked again.

'Okay,' he relented. 'She's a character in my novel.'

Jesus! Ted had a few golden rules, one of which was never to be confessional with his students. *Talk about their work, never your own.* So why had he just blurted that out? Because he thought it would divert attention from the truth: that he was using his best friend as writing fodder. It was Paula's biography that had been creeping into his novel, or, as he had taken to calling it euphemistically, his work-in-progress. He'd spent the last couple of months not writing but taking notes. Little nuggets Paula had given him – the way Larry's voice would go all soft before he struck her, how for months she had spied on him emerging naked from the shower and felt the scalding burn of desire, how once she'd sucked him off with the baby watching. Ted listened avidly. Paula's experiences were so far removed from his mother's that they would give his book the burning frisson of fiction. And that was okay, he told himself. Divorced from their origins, even the most intimate details could be used, once you disguised them enough.

To the toll of her confessions, he had added his own observations about Paula. His protagonist had developed her hairstyle, her furious way of smoking, her vulnerable optimism. Was that why he didn't fancy Paula? Because she was more value to him as raw material? No wonder he hadn't been troubled by inconvenient lust; he'd been trying to get inside Paula's head, not her knickers. She was the only one who could give the kiss of life to his 40,000 words of false beginnings.

Ted rose and walked to the window of the classroom. He pressed his forehead against the glass, glad of the cool clasp of it on his temples. Outside the snow was having a tantrum. Angry trees made semaphore warnings. He felt like a character in a bad workshop story – overloaded with epiphany. *Jesus!*

'This Paula,' Valerie said, cocking her head quizzically.

He wasn't in the mood. Two hours of student versions of Paulas – foxy lap dancer, bisexual trucker, Baptist preacher's wife – had exhausted him more than his thudding head. He felt dispirited – and chastened for using Paula as a quick fix for his class.

'This Paula,' Valerie repeated. She looked like a scrubbed virgin but he had seen her at student parties – the girl had a sassy mouth and a taste for dirty martinis. But it was her sexual frankness that intimidated Ted. Though he would never admit it, he was afraid of her voraciousness. Afraid of her.

'Yes, what about her?'

'She's not just a character, is she? She's a real person.'

Ted raised his hands in surrender.

'People are more than their biographies, Valerie. That's what today's exercise was all about.'

'She needs help, you realise that, don't you?'

Valerie laid a polished fingertip on Ted's arm.

'She needs an intervention.'

'A what?'

'You know,' she said with a sweet fanged smile. 'She needs to stop drinking, she needs a twelve-step programme. She needs to be confronted. You know, tough love.'

Ted was in no mood for tough love.

'Let's just stick to fiction, Valerie, there's a good girl.'

'Don't patronise me,' she snapped.

'Look, Valerie, there's a difference between writing and real life. The sooner you realise the difference between the two, the better.'

She changed tack.

160

'Are you trying to tell me something, Ted? I can call you Ted, can't I?' He got a whiff of musky scent as she flicked her hair back over her shoulder.

'Look, Valerie, if you want to talk about your writing, I'm happy to accommodate you. Otherwise . . .'

'You don't like my work, that's it, really, isn't it?'

He was tempted to be honest with her: it's not your work I don't like, it's you.

'Your character study of Paula was flashy, Valerie, amusing in its way, but there was no depth in it, no pain, no real pain. You failed to imagine her fully.'

She grimaced sourly.

'It wasn't a character study, it was caricature. Whereas *my* Paula . . .'

'Your Paula?' she queried. 'Who's confusing fiction and reality now?'

And she turned on her sharp heels and left.

An hour later, Ted was in Skipper's. He usually didn't go in on Tuesdays but he was parched and after the encounter with Valerie he felt in need of a stiff drink. He sat at the bar, slung his change on the counter.

'The usual?' Skipper, holding a glass aloft, asked.

The beauty of Skipper's was its monosyllabic honour code. 'Howdy!'

He looked up to see Paula just arriving. What was she doing here? He associated her with Thursdays and the well-oiled trajectory of the weekend. Somehow, he thought she only came in when he was here. Maybe she had a Ted for every night of the week? Get a grip, he told himself. You sound like a bloody jealous husband.

'Paula! There you are!' he said, aiming for hearty, sounding feeble. He felt a twinge of irritation at her for not showing up last week. Then a pang of guilt as he remembered what his students had been doing for the past couple of hours.

'What brings you in here on a Tuesday night?'

'I drink here every night, Ted.'

It was his turn to feel betrayed.

'What happened last Thursday then?'

'Who are you?' she snapped. 'My parole officer?'

'Steady on, Paula,' he said. 'What'll you have?'

Paula granted him a forgiving smile. What an unlikely couple we are, Ted thought.

'Got a letter today,' Paula was saying, 'from Debra.'

Debra was Paula's eight-year-old daughter; she was fostered out. She wrote dutiful letters to her mother every so often on notepaper dotted with pink hearts. Usually they were catalogues of her little doings – school, sleepovers, her sister Amy (Paula always bristled at the mention of Amy; foster sister, she would spit) and finished with a flourish of smiley faces and florid endearments. *Lots and lots of love, Debra. Big kisses, Debra. I love you, Mommy.* Paula always latched on to these.

'See,' she would say, 'she hasn't forgotten me.'

'Great,' Ted said.

He was annoyed suddenly by Paula's awful faith that everything would work out.

'What the hell's bugging you?' she said.

'Nothing, nothing. Bad day, that's all.'

'Tell me about it!' Paula started one of her long litanies. 'Brian, you know the day manager, comes in today, he's in a foul mood. And I'm stacking, see, in detergents and he says Paula – hey Paula, you gone deaf or something? I've been calling you to the register for the last five minutes. We got a line stretching out to the parking lot. Get your fat ass up there! Little shit! He's not much older than my Mikey. I could put him across my knee and spank him . . .'

'Did you?'

'Did I what?'

'Did you ever hit Mikey?'

Mikey was her son by Donny, the bricklayer. Being older and more troublesome he was still in care and had refused to have any contact with her.

'What's gotten into you?' Paula's eyes blazed.

Ted was thinking of when he was a boy. How he'd longed for his mother to strike him. He wanted the badge of a bruise, some physical proof of damage. His father's anger was aimed at things, not people – small portions of food, lost pigeons, recalcitrant plumbing. Lately, Ted, too, felt like just breaking things. He took a gulp of beer.

'Nothing,' he said miserably. 'Want another?'

On the following Thursday he didn't go to Skipper's. He walked as far as the door but something stopped him. He had the sensation that there was someone right behind him, someone about to tap him on his shoulder. But when he looked back there was no one on Gibson Street; just the overhead traffic light turning from red to green. Another weekend in Faithful. He bought a slab of beer in the liquor store and went home to a TV dinner. The weekend felt all askew without the anchor of Thursday with Paula. His self-imposed exile didn't last. Damn it, he missed her, and his guilt about using her as biography fodder for his students had abated by Monday. Several days without drink had cleared his mind and cured him of the watchful paranoia he had fallen prey to. So it was with a light step that he pushed the swing doors open into Skipper's after a week's absence. His heart lifted at the sight of Paula perched at the bar swathed in cigarette smoke. It felt like a homecoming as she hallooed to him and tapped the stool beside her in that welcoming gesture that made him feel unquestioningly accepted.

'Hi, Ted,' she said.

He settled into his familiar seat – whoosh of torn leatherette – and gave her a comradely squeeze around the shoulders.

'Guess what?' she said. 'I've had a letter from Mikey's case worker. Wanna see?'

'Sure,' he said. He was determined not to yield to scepticism. He wanted to wind back to a time when his motives towards Paula were pure. If they had ever been. Paula rummaged in the large canvas sack that served as her handbag.

'Here it is,' she said, fishing out a crumpled-looking piece of paper. 'Dear Mrs Spears,' she began, 'Your son Mikey has been the subject of a special case conference . . .' she began haltingly. Paula was quick with her own words, but she stumbled over bureaucratic prose. Ted found his attention wandering despite his best intentions. There was a scuffle at the door. Well, there often was at Skipper's – usually someone being thrown out. He turned towards the source of commotion. Three faces detached themselves from the blur of the crowd, for there was a crowd. And Ted recognised every single one of them. Eight of his graduate students from workshop, led by a determined, leather-jacketed Valerie. She marched up to the counter and clamped her hand on Paula's shoulder.

'Are you Paula?' she demanded.

'What the hell?' Paula started.

Ted swung down off the stool.

'Now look here, Valerie. I don't know what you're doing. But leave Paula out of this,' he muttered to her.

'So,' Valerie said, sidestepping him, 'there really is a Paula.'

'What's it to you, lady?' Paula said.

'Um,' Valerie mused, 'Ted here was rather unkind in his characterisation of you.'

Paula recoiled as the rangy Valerie looked her up and down. Beside her vividness, Ted thought, Paula looked like cardboard. Pale, depleted.

'We're here to save you, Paula.'

'Save me, from what?'

'From yourself.' She jerked her head towards Ted standing with his hands hanging. 'And from him.'

'Look, lady, I don't know what religion you're selling but I'm not buying.'

'What we have here is a standard co-dependency situation. He needs you to drink so he can. You're enabling each other.'

'Who the hell is this, Ted?'

'She's one of my students. Take no notice.'

'You're never going to get your kids back, Paula. You've got to face that fact. Look at yourself! Why did you lose them in the first place? Because.' Valerie paused here and advanced, wagging a crimson-nailed finger. 'Because your first loyalty is to this.' She picked up Paula's vodka and slammed it down on the counter spilling its contents.

'Hey!' Paula said, affronted by the waste, and clambered down unsteadily from her stool to square up to Valerie. 'What's it to you, anyway?' Then she fixed on Ted. 'How does she know all this about me?'

'Because dear old Ted's been getting off on your story.'

'Ted?'

'Only last week we were all doing a character study of you which he tried to pass off as a person in his novel. This from the guy who's allergic to the confessional in *our* writing!'

'Valerie, that's enough!'

'You're not in the classroom now, Ted.'

Ted turned to Paula beseechingly but Valerie persisted.

'What you need, Paula, is to get away from people who are sucking the lifeblood out of you.' She shot a steely glance at Ted.

'What the fuck!' Paula exhaled. 'Is this, is this your idea of a joke?'

She was pacing up and down now, but there was nowhere to run to – no back entrance and Valerie's army stood four-square blocking the front door. Skipper's regulars gaped dully.

'You need a real friend,' Valerie went on, 'the kind of friend who will be totally straight with you. With no bullshit.'

Paula stared at Ted.

'You been writing about me, Ted?'

'It wasn't like that, Paula, honest.'

'You been spilling my secrets? Talking about me in class?'

He shook his head vehemently.

'You sad motherfucker!' she spat.

'Anger is good,' Valerie interrupted.

'Know why I drank with you? Because I felt sorry for you. Living alone with the ghost of a fucking book, how sad is that.'

'Paula, please . . .' Ted started.

'And all this time you've been sniffing around me like some perv going through my undies.'

There was a ripple of gnarled laughter from the curious crowd of onlookers. Valerie placed her talons on Paula's shoulder.

'C'mon, Paula,' she declared, 'let's get you sober, girl!'

She linked Paula's arm and to the applause of the bar's patrons (even the pool games had halted) she frogmarched her towards the exit, surrounded by a phalanx of Ted's students.

Ted slumped back on to his stool. The rest of the bar returned to their drinks, feeling let down in the wash of anticlimax. Ted signalled to Skipper for a double whiskey, which Skipper wordlessly pushed towards him. He drank greedily from the golden glass.

'Have I just lost a regular?' Skipper asked.

'She'll be back,' Ted said. 'Can you see Paula on a twelve-step programme? I don't think so!'

That was three months ago. He had tried to track her down, desperately at first. He found out where she worked – Melvin's Superstore on Sycamore – but she wasn't there. Brian, the day manager, who looked about twelve, said she'd simply disappeared.

'Heard she went to one of those Christian rehab places, out Conway direction,' he added as the pair of them stood in the dog food aisle.

'You don't have an address, do you?' Ted could hear the jilted panic in his voice.

Brian shrugged.

'Sorry, dude.'

He's avoiding Skipper's these days. One public scene in a town this size is quite enough, thank you. But it comforts him to imagine Paula still there, sitting at the bar happily, blamelessly sozzled, easing into blissful unwind. Climbing carefully down from the stool to go the Ladies' Room, rubber-limbed, wavering – or was that only how she looked to him because he was often in a similar state, dreamily drunk and blearily semi-detached?

He's still showing up for workshop. Well, life goes on; that's the trouble with it. Valerie Kleber smirks at him with a bitter lemon twist, while the others treat him with mutinous contempt. Well, why wouldn't they? He'd been unmasked as a sad old fuck. Wasn't that Paula's verdict? He felt bereft. Paula hadn't just walked out of his life – she'd walked out of his novel too. Now both of them were gone. There was a bleak sense of relief in acknowledging the novel had defeated him; but the loss of Paula, that was another thing entirely. That's the lesson, he wanted to shout at Valerie, smug with victory, that's the difference between fiction and reality. Reality breathes and hurts and drinks too much; it lets you down, it leaves things unfinished, up in the air, high and dry. Whereas fiction, fiction is just still life. Still fucking life.

He goes to the fridge – big as a starkly illuminated spare room – and reaches for a beer. He releases the ring pull – it seethes – and he raises the can in a silent toast. To Paula. Saved and lost.

DRAG

Clothes maketh the man, Mother used to say. Her words stay with you as you riffle through the hanging ghosts in your wardrobe. It's a moment of infinite anticipation. What to wear? The evening's expectations are secreted among the limp fall of fabrics, the yielding crush of shoulder pads, the sly whispers of silk. You whisk two or three recruits from the comradely army in the closet and set them up around the room – over the mirror, on the twin mother-of-pearl inlaid handles of the wardrobe, or fainting on the bed. It makes it seem more like play; makes more of a ritual of it. Often the bedroom will end up strewn with discarded clothes, denuded hangers, fleets of shoes poised in the second position and still you won't have made a choice. You find such disarray intoxicatingly seedy, though nothing could be further from the truth. You're a careful dresser, in fact discreet, but unambiguously feminine. You don't go overboard, of course. No polka dots, no stilettos in pre-school colours. But you don't like sober either – otherwise, what would be the point? It is called dressing up, after all. You can't stand calculated understatement, that eunuch look the younger ones go for. Those pinstriped trousers or sober little black suits with a white T-shirt peeking underneath and a bit of underwire cleavage just to tantalise. That really *is* drag. You're doing impersonation, not caricature. You'd love to totter around in platforms or heels but there's your feet to consider. And your height.

You can't afford to magnify flaws. It's all about disguise, as any 'girl' will tell you. The opaque tights are your biggest compromise. With a different anatomy you'd go for broke and wear fishnets. But if you're big-boned you can't play the vamp with any kind of grace. Anyway, you want to look like a woman, not a tart.

The bridge club variety, you mean, the blue rinse brigade, George sneers. Bitchy! But according to George, you have slender hips – this said with some envy – and a real waist. You appreciate George's fitting-room verdicts, admiration professed if only to the mirror. Makes you feel real. Your biggest weakness is floral. Not loud, but more the summer garden variety. Mother used to have swing dresses with pink coins of colour like lily pads dimpling a Monet lake. You used to love those. Maybe you're operating out of sentiment, or nostalgia. Though even you would baulk at admitting that your fashion sense is down to Mother's frocks. But, look, you loved your mother. It's not a crime, is it? Though these days any extravagant expression of affection, particularly for your mother, seems to arouse suspicion. Suspicion of what, you'd like to know. You're not afraid to admit that you idolised Mother – God rest her. You keep her alive this way too, with those blessings of hers. You use them sincerely though sometimes people, including George, presume irony. (You open your mouth and your mother comes out, George says.) Maybe you cling to Mother's memory simply because for so long there was just the two of you.

Father disappeared when you were two – he did one of those magic tricks. Put his hand in the till and went up in a puff of smoke. Left you both in the lurch, Mother would say. In your mind's eye you saw a drunk on a deserted street, lewd smile, evil laughter, rotten teeth. Something to do with that word lurch, as if he had reeled off and blundered into another dimension. Of course, he wasn't like that at all. The family

169

photograph (yes, just the one; this was a time when fathers took the photos rather than appearing in them) shows him in a rumpled suit, hair in corn drills, shirt collar askew. He looks like an overgrown schoolboy, his worthy clothes over-tended, unloved. He was a solicitor's clerk. He worked in a chamber of brown linoleum, bentwood chairs, a hatless coat-stand, a mahogany desk inlaid with green leather. There was a hatch to keep the public at bay. He stayed in the inner office, trapped behind towers of thick-lipped manila folders. Keeper of the chequebook.

'He couldn't even get cheating right,' Mother would lament.

It was the first out-of-character thing he had ever done. For years he had plodded off to work every morning, peck on the cheek for Mother, and the promise of promotion. Before you came along, a late child, unexpected. Of course, you don't remember him. Useless, was Mother's verdict. And she made him so over the years. What use could he possibly have been? Mother was your world. Authority, breadwinner, confidante. If that screwed you up, as George would put it, then so be it.

The dressing up started at home. Mother did it, and you copied her. She had a wardrobe that housed a future that never came. A ball gown in turquoise taffeta whose skirts seemed tainted with water marks when you looked at it in a certain light. A couple of cocktail dresses, one in black silk, backless, another in plum velvet with a sequinned bodice, heavy as a suit of tears. Some of her clothes you can only remember fragments of now – pink netting here, the fringes of a scarf there. The greatest treasures were hidden away. A fur stole, all watchful eyes and snakish tails, pungent with mothballs, wrapped carefully in tissue paper in a hat box on top of the wardrobe. The wedding dress the light had turned to ivory still rustling superstitiously under a clear plastic shroud from the dry cleaner's. And below in the shadows of frothy hems,

Mother's shoes. You remember pushing plump five-year-old feet into a pair of her white patent slingbacks. Cold in there. They bowed in the middle like a sagging bridge and the heels threw you forward into the mousehole of the toe. And the lovely clatter they made, the slap and clack! It was a trade-off with Mother. If you agreed to have your hair washed and not to scream when the shampoo got in your eyes, Mother would allow you to wear her shoes for a treat after bath-time. Forget satin corsets and suspenders, you say. The memory of being naked in heels seems to you the ultimate in erotic.

Then you moved on to her evening gloves. She had several pairs – cream, pearl grey and black. Your little fingers burrowed to the tips – it was like climbing inside her – the scalloped ends bunching around your bare bony shoulder. You liked to rummage in the drawer where she stored her headscarves. Horses and anchors and nosegays of daffodils. You'd toss them in the air and in their fluttering descent, her bouquet was released – *Blue Grass*. You fingered her floral polyester blouses – cross-your-heart, fabric-coated buttons, sleek to touch but toothily static. Skirts billowed round your head. No slacks here – Mother didn't hold with them though she acknowledged they were handy if you were a working woman. Which, somehow, implied that she was not. The final frontier was her underwear. Flesh-coloured brassieres, lace-hemmed bloomers, the shivering agony of slips. You turned her roll-on into a straitjacket, your arms and torso encased like an Egyptian mummy; then you lay on the floor and played dead.

Mother was on a fixed income. She managed a nursing home and you lived in. You spent your childhood among old ladies, querulous or melancholy, sagging folds of skin merging with crumpled clothes. Their bony fingers with rings they wouldn't, or couldn't, part with, twitched on counterpanes or feverishly counted off the decades on beads. There was the accompanying smell – though Mother was scrupulous about hygiene – which is not urine, as people like to think, but the sour odour of organs slowing down. Vapours of decay, in other words. Not the ideal environment to grow up in but it was home. You felt singular among all that fading female energy, a buoyant child, beloved.

'Baby,' they would call after you as you dodged past the asparagus ferns in mock-brass urns in the hallway. They always had their doors ajar.

'Baby!' Sometimes it sounded menacing, envious. You were baby to all of them. Some other baby, some lost baby. In her turn, Mother lavished endearments on her patients – sweetheart, pet lamb, even love – and they would invariably soften and wilt and bend to her will. For a moment they would shed their pruney carapaces and smile beatifically at her. But for you she reserved a special term. Darling, come and help Mother out of her dress. Darling, run and get the bedpan for Mrs Proctor. Darling, tell Mother that you love her.

Maybe that's why you were slow to make friends. How could the world outside ever replicate Mother's love and that of all those senile surrogates? You didn't feel the lack, not when you were a child. And, afterwards, you had George. Mother and George never met. Well, you kept them apart, didn't you? Mother would not have taken to George's vulgar candour. Is George the kind of friend we'd like to cultivate, darling? No, would have been the answer. No one would be good enough. You feel a stab of resentment when you think of it now, when you stand here faced with a wardrobe full of clothes that echo hers. It makes you wonder. Have you somehow turned into Mother? All dressed up and nowhere to go?

No, not true. Tonight you have somewhere to go. On the bed you lay out a jade velvet skirt, a black sateen jacket, a white blouse with an extravagant ruffle to hide the crêpey skin around your neck. They lie there playing dead, as if you were dressing a corpse. You wanted to do this for Mother, to choose

172

a costume for her final journey. The thought excited you even in the midst of grief. The turquoise taffeta, the fur stole? You liked the thought that the fox with its hunter's eye and the long drip of its tails might be buried, and once below ground might reassemble itself and emerge into the night to prowl again. But no, Mother had left detailed instructions. She wanted a shroud, plain brown from the Poor Clares. But you did help with her make-up; that undertaker had no idea! Now you sit in front of the triptych dressing-table mirror doing your own. Like most of the furniture, it's Mother's. All wrong here. Too big and overpowering for the rooms of a semi-d on Prosperity Drive, a place Mother would have looked down her nose at. Scruffy children playing on the street and next door attached, darling! True, on summer evenings you are plagued by boys ringing the bell wanting their football back, and when you look out on your pocket-sized lawn you find your Calla lilies trampled and broken. But despite that you've grown to like it here. You stop and chat to that nice Mrs Devoy and have a nodding acquaintance with Mrs Elworthy, a working woman like Mother, with two little girls and no sign of a husband. You don't belong here exactly but you can't be put out. You own it, something Mother never did. You have something to leave. But to whom? You shake away the mournful thought and examine your pores in the mirror. You used to watch Mother doing her face. If Father had stayed around you might have been as fascinated by his shaving rituals. As it was, Mother didn't have anyone to watch admiringly as she powdered her face, sending clouds of motes reeling into the air, or applying lipstick – *Coral Island* – to pouted lips. No one, that is, but you. It was the ceremony that compelled you. The mask behind which Mother's face disappeared, the glossy lips, the brooding eyeshadow – *Deadly Nightshade*. You were fascinated by the tweezers, the eye pencils, the emery boards. The mystery of all the little brushes – what were they for? – the powder puffs, the pale squares of make-up in a box like your water paints, the tiny bottles of gilded nail polish. Even then you were learning how to be a woman.

Mother used to bring you with her when she went to the cosmetic counters at Switzers. You used to love that. Picking up the phials of perfume, lifting the heavy glass stoppers and inhaling the scents – tea rose, verbena, musk – while Mother tested lipstick on her hand, or had her cuticles done. What a pair you must have made! Mother in her starched whites from work – she wasn't a nurse but she said people had more faith when they saw a uniform – and you in your shorts and sandals, a crop-haired urchin. You were going through your tomboy period then. The assistants were charmed that you were so taken with the products.

'Lovely to see a sensitive boy,' one crooned. She had alarming black hair in a Cleopatra cut and an ochre complexion.

'The world will soon beat it out of him,' the other said tartly as she redid her fearsome lashes. And they both laughed knowingly.

You blushed defiantly. Mother was too discreet to point out their mistake. Afterwards, years afterwards, she said. 'But, darling, that would have spoiled it for you. You wanted to be a boy then. I knew it was just a phase you were going through.'

You're all done now. Ready for the performance. Roar of the crowd, smell of the greasepaint! Despite the numerous times you've made yourself up – how many times in a woman's lifetime, who could calculate? – you've never quite got used to the dusty, caked feel of foundation. And the look, despite your best efforts, seems fake. If Mother were alive today – a preposterous thought; she'd be 108 – she'd say pityingly, 'Look at you, darling.'

Tonight is a special occasion. It's a work thing. A party to launch the new consultants' clinic. Fancy place, atrium preening with plants, a coffee dock, and lifts – a far cry from the old dingy surgeries and tatty waiting rooms. You work for a foot surgeon. Mr Stafford. He's portly, self-important. But he's got a right, you suppose. He wears three-piece suits like a lawyer and a handkerchief in his breast pocket, his only concession to flamboyance. He keeps his distance – from you, from his patients. He's like an old-fashioned headmaster. You think he would secretly like to be called Sir. You wouldn't mind, but in this day and age you're not sure if that's not a crime too. So he relies on his bearing and his obvious wealth to command respect. With his fees, that's not hard. He's married, of course, and years older than you, but he depends on you for all sorts of things. His Girl Friday he calls you, which shows his age and yours, because you get the reference. George says you're like the 'other woman' for him. Nothing could be further from your mind but George has always revelled in being outrageous.

You met her at secretarial school. She started off as your pal, at least that's what Mother called her. The one with the strange name, Mother would add, as if you were besieged with friends. Short for Georgina.

'What a handle,' she would say, 'I don't know what possessed my parents!'

'Why didn't you shorten it to Georgie?' you asked.

'George makes more of a statement,' she said.

George was always brighter than you. Her brisk, brunette manner was a cover for ambitions a well-read girl from her background couldn't afford. You and she started out working in the typing pool at the gas company together. Clackety-clack, ding! A synchronised orchestra like Esther Williams and her troupe on dry land. You went for lunch every day at the Parliament Hotel, and to dances on Saturday nights at the Arcadia, long since demolished. Your first holiday abroad – when you were thirty-two, imagine! – was with George.

175

You went to Rome on an organised tour. It was only after you arrived that you realised it was for honeymooners, eloping or fleeing their families, or wanting to get a blessing direct from the Holy Father. You and George were the only singletons. That's the word they use now, a production-line term as if you were cartons of milk or an easy cheese serving. George flirted madly with anything in pants, but you were too embarrassed. A pair of the hotel's breakfast waiters, brothers, took a fancy to you. There was a particular night on the Piazza Navona – the boys took you to see the Neptune fountain. Ridiculous to call them boys, but now you can't see them as men. George was walking ahead, draped around Nando – how lightly she distributed her favours, you thought; what a prude you were then – and you were leaning against the curved lip of the fountain desperately holding off his brother. You remember the hardness of Licio's body grinding up against yours, how insistent his ardour was, and how little it meant.

'*Cara*,' he breathed.

And suddenly you thought of Mother. No, not suddenly. You were always wondering what she would think. Perhaps if you had succumbed then. What? Perhaps you could have banished Mother altogether. But you couldn't. And then you dissolved. Not discreet ladylike weeping, but something more akin to the fountain beside you, as if some inner hydrant had been opened and was spraying everywhere, drenching the bystanders. Licio backed away, hands aloft in defence, then thumping his breast in Latin exasperation, saying 'I do nothing.' Mother was dead only six months then.

'What on earth's the matter?' George asked after the brothers had sloped off fearing your hysteria was contagious. You shook your head. You felt ashamed, as if you had acceded to some squalid backstreet encounter and miserable because you knew you had queered George's chances.

*   *   *

176

Despite that, she stayed. Despite her beautiful kissable mouth (she has always known how to make the most of her best features) and her sauciness and her proud, uncompromising name. You felt sure she would marry but she never did. Here the two of you are – twenty-five years on – still girls together, though others might snidely call you companions. She will be at the party too – for backup. Nothing worse than wandering around these drinks and finger-food functions without an anchor, without someone to go back to. That's what George has become. The woman you go back to. Like Mother, really.

There, ready. Except for the jewellery. Mother's locket, with that picture of Father cut down to size. You thread her wedding band around the chain. It wouldn't be right to wear it on your finger. On your breast a costume brooch – also hers – like a spray of baby's breath.

Exploitation, George calls it. 'I wouldn't do it for my fella,' she says hotly. Hers is the president of a bank. George plays golf with hers; she dresses down for casual Friday.

But you don't see it that way. The surgeon's wife is sickly and can't often attend these things. Nothing Mr Stafford can do about it. (Her feet are perfect, apparently.) So you're roped in. You're happy to do it. You see it as part of your job. You collect his dry-cleaning, you make him tea, you arrange his appointments, you order flowers for his wife. Soon you'll be doing the rounds of nursing homes recommending the best one for her particular needs. Well, you do have expertise in that area. So what's the big deal about swanning around in your finery for an evening, playing the role of hostess? Although you'd never admit it to George, you actually enjoy it. You enjoy being mistaken for his wife. You like the way he steers you about the room with his hand lightly at your elbow and introduces you as merely Pauline (though in his rooms it's always Miss Larchet) as if you two are intimate. That's why you have to look the part.

That's why the impersonation has to be perfect. You are not playing yourself.

Perfume – always the last thing before you leave. A quick spray at the ears and the wrists. It buoys you to the door like the splash of holy water the ladies at the home used to spray you with. A good luck charm, a way of warding off evil. *Blue Grass*. Mother is with you.

ASSISTED PASSAGE

It was not a glamorous ocean liner. Not like the *Oriana* or the *Castel Felice* she'd seen in the brochures. No, the *Australis* was a peeling monster, a colossus of weeping rust and complaining steel; the gangways smelled of sea rot. When they'd pulled out of Southampton, the passengers had unspooled thousands of streamers, the frail satin-coated ribbons of candyfloss pink and bridal white strained and then snapped, amidst a tremendous symphony of triumph and grief. Names were flung into the air, arcing flimsily like trailing cobwebs across the narrow strip of roiling water that separated ship from shore, as the streamers sank dejectedly into the fermenting foam and the crowd on the quay was reduced to a frantic, fleshy blur.

Anita imagined the *Australis* as the little ship, swollen-sailed, in the bottom right-hand corner of the schoolroom map at the Tranquila convent. She heard the ports of call in a teacher's droning rote. Port Said, Aden, Colombo, Fremantle, Melbourne, Sydney. The momentousness of the journey only became real when they were gathered all together for safety drill on A deck, a ragbag of refugees and migrants, families like steps of stairs, gangs of lanky young men and tight bunches of girls with brassy laughter and high-built hair.

Anita had shared her first night at sea with just such girls in Cabin C12, a tight coffiny space, overseen by a glassy grey monocle.

'Would you look at this? No better than steerage,' Stasia Kearns muttered. 'Sure, the convicts would have better than this.' Stasia was from Tipperary, plain and plain-speaking. Anita was assigned the bottom bunk, sleeping under Stasia – the Irish side of the cabin, the other girls joked. Muriel Kendall from Glasgow (call me Mew) and Lil Fuller, a Londoner, made up the group, whose rituals were to become so familiar – Stasia undressing like a nun on a strand, struggling out of her clothes under cover of her dressing gown, Mew and Lil gaily stripping off. Both of them boasted exotic underwear – lace-topped slips and coloured knickers – peach and peppermint. Mew backcombed her hair and sprayed her beehive into a sticky helmet; Lil had a miniature city of cold creams and compacts and an elaborate bedtime routine of blemish-hunting.

'Oh Gawd,' she would moan, 'a nose hair!' Tweezers were brandished with operatic brio.

In their company, armed with only hairbrush and toothpaste, Anita felt like a scrubbed and indolent child.

They were barely out of port when the feverish round of on-board romances started. Mew took her feline nickname, her beehive hair and her tight shift dresses to the Brisbane bar where beer came cheap at five cents a glass and flirted with a series of young men. But her constant companion was Viktor Varga, a Hungarian music teacher who practised on the bar-room piano all day. He must have been forty, a sombre man with professor spectacles and a russet beard, and miles too old for Mew – Lil said she was making a fool of him – but he was invaluable as a source of gossip, a constant witness to the shenanigans that were supposedly going on right under their noses.

'Vic says there's two fellas who've already swapped their wives,' Mew reported. 'So they'll be setting up house with strangers when they get to Sydney.'

Stasia tut-tutted; Lil paid little attention. She was single-minded in her devotion. She lusted after the assistant bursar, Bob Penney, a clean-cut fellow with pinched-thin features and a dapper air, who sat in a timbered kiosk on B deck dispensing cash or transcribing pencilled messages of love and regret and transforming them into the rat-tat urgency of telegrams. Lil loved the uniform, the seamed trousers, the gold epaulettes, the peaked cap.

'As good as getting an officer,' she said as she invented excuses to parade past his little box with the three clocks overhead, an owlish chorus line of London, Sydney and New York time.

'They're not allowed to fraternise, you know,' Stasia said.

'What?'

'Not allowed to mix with the passengers,' Stasia explained.

She was the only one spoken for. Promised to Frank W. McKinney, the manager of a sheep station in Western Australia.

'What's the W stand for, darling?' Lil asked.

'I never asked,' Stasia said miserably.

She had ribboned bundles of his letters, which she spread out on her bunk and leafed through like a perplexed bookkeeper. They'd been corresponding for two years – Stasia had answered his ad in a lonely hearts column. *Wanted*, it had read, *Irish colleen to make an exile very happy. Build a little bit of home in a far-off land. Must be able to cook.* Stasia had a photograph of him, ruddy and corpulent, standing, arms folded, on a belt of red earth bisected by a slash of blue horizon.

'So he's really only a pen pal,' Lil said.

'Oh no,' Stasia said, 'he's popped the question.'

Lil's silent oh mirrored the porthole.

'We're engaged,' she said as she wrung her naked ring finger. 'On paper.'

'What about you?' Lil, narrow-eyed, demanded of Anita.

*   *   *

What about her? She was travelling on assisted passage to a new life in Sydney. Her Uncle Ambrose was sponsoring her. He'd visited the summer before, arriving unannounced with a great welcome for himself. Her father was the superintendent in St Jude's Hospital (janitor, fixer of beds, jack of all trades) and they lived in a small cottage just inside the gates. Anita had never met her uncle before and he was most unexpected. A big beery man who towered over her neat father in his mustard work coat. Uncle Ambrose came bearing a wallet full of photographs of toothy boys and a blonde woman with sunglasses and a polka-dot dress.

'Meet Peggy,' Ambrose said, 'the wife.'

'Not the wife he went out with,' Mam muttered.

'So what are your girls up to, Mossie?' Ambrose asked.

Mam inhaled deeply. Viv had just announced she wanted to enter; by September she would be a postulant. She had incubated her piety in the draughty classrooms of the Tranquila convent, thriving on the penitential discipline, the ringing of bells, the droning of prayers and the robust Christianity the nuns offered. At home, *The Word* came sailing through the letterbox but seemed destined directly for Viv; she would snaffle it quickly and take it into the bathroom, reading it behind the locked door. It was a glossy magazine – well, by their standards – boasting full-colour plates of the accomplishments of the Foreign Missions. White-robed Fathers posed in the doorways of adobe mission churches, or stood surrounded by beaming parishioners. Viv pinned one of these pictures over the bed. It showed a barefoot, umber-skinned boy climbing among the high branches of an orange tree with a large wicker basket strapped around his waist. Behind him there was a searing blue sky. The caption read: *Moses, our houseboy, gathers in the harvest.* Anita often gazed up at Moses and thought, if there is a heaven, this must be it. The acid sky. A tree that bore oranges – imagine! And a beautiful boy with a dazzling smile to fetch them down.

Up till then, Anita had thought she and Viv shared everything. A room crushed under the eaves, a sagging double bed. She'd known Viv's perilous menstruation, slept in the copper snaggle of her hair. But with Viv's announcement, she'd realised how little she knew. When she wasn't looking, God had come between her and Viv.

'One of them wants to be a nun and the other one might as well be,' Mam said.

'Lenore,' Anita's father said warningly.

Sensing the discord, Ambrose eyed Anita.

'And what about you, Neet?' Ambrose was the first to call her that, making her name sound like an anagram.

She shrugged. She was eighteen, just finished school and hadn't thought about the future, her own or anybody else's. She hadn't been much of a scholar. She struggled with the big picture of History, Mathematics defeated her, she scorched and burned in Home Economics. The only reprieve came in Geography. The ritual naming of things. Principal towns and their industries; rivers and their tributaries, the mapping of boundaries. Her heart lifted whenever the laminated map was pulled down over the blackboard. She loved to trace the jagged outlines of countries and the intricate fieldwork of continents. She would run her hand along the grid-lined oceans. When she placed her finger on the black spot that was home, high up and almost out of reach, she felt the tiny pulse of connection. What she longed for, though, was a kind of telescopic vision so that she could see all the other worlds that were contained in there – St Jude's, the cramped rooms of home, but mostly, the insides of other people's heads.

'What plans does she have, Mossie?' Ambrose demanded, all business.

Her poor gentle da looked at her quizzically. There'd been talk of a secretarial course and afterwards the typing pool at the Gas Board. Girls like her didn't have plans; life took its course; things happened.

'She should come out our way. Trip of a lifetime. We'd sponsor her, see her right. Great life out there, Moss. We'd fix her up with a nice Aussie bloke.'

That was the clincher for Mam. She had often regaled Anita and Viv with tales of her own ancient flirtations. Racy episodes with young men that dissolved into hilarity in the retelling or petered out with the same line. 'And then I met your father.'

Anita wasn't sure if it was a happy ending.

'Soon,' her mother would go on, as if she couldn't wait, 'your titties will grow like this.' She grabbed one of her capacious breasts and placed Anita's hand on it. 'Then your monthly bleed. Ready to be a woman.' The word had a fat, obscene sound. Anita could hear the womb in the middle of it. Her titties, as if in sympathy, barely grew. Now with Viv out of the picture, all of her mother's romantic energy would be trained on her.

'She'd love that, Ambrose, wouldn't you, Nita?' Mam had said.

It was a done deal, as far as her mother was concerned, as good as an arranged marriage.

Nothing could have prepared her for the terrible vertigo of seafaring. The heft and sway of the waves formed a sickening horizon at the portholes, the decks seemed always at a dizzying tilt. When storms came, they churned not only her innards, but the digestion of the ship. It became sick in a gale, coughing up its fixtures. In the dining room the cutlery would fall in a silvery faint, the soup bowls drooled.

Port Said was their first stop, though they were not allowed to disembark. All the same, Mew urged them to don their best dresses, in which they promenaded along B deck. Below them hawkers held up cages of screeching birds. There were goats on tethers and chickens in crates.

'A gunny gunny man,' Bursar Bob said cheerily, 'look girls! He's going to do a trick.'

They crowded around the rails, Lil moving in to his side, Mew winking at Anita in companionable conspiracy.

At the foot of the gangway, a large robed man with an extravagant moustache held a little chick in his palm and lifted it up to them, as if for inspection. He stroked its beak and made purring sounds at the golden furry ball. Anita expected a swish of handkerchief and for the peeping chick to disappear. The conjuror smiled, a silvery flash, popped the chicken into his mouth and swallowed it whole. He beat his chest and roared triumphantly. Coins rained down on him from the *Australis*. He scrabbled desperately on the ground amid the hail of copper, then plucked a fresh chick from a crate by his feet. Anita thought she was going to be sick.

The *Australis* moved on. They approached the Canal. The Suez, a puckered seam Anita remembered from the schoolroom map. After so much open space they were suddenly enclosed; after so much solitude on the high seas, they were suffocated by land, miles of it, ochre and tinder dry, flat and arid, sentries of palm trees the only relief from the cloudless skies. And after weeks as a solitary ship on a singular journey, there were other craft, liners and tankers and launches, as if this narrow tumult of water were spawning craft. It was a welcome break from the vastness of ocean, the monotony of an empty sea. They travelled through the Canal at night. As darkness fell, the *Australis* sprouted illuminated wings; the crested insignia on her prow opened up and on its nether side was a huge searchlight by which they navigated their way. It was like a giant mothcatcher, or a portable moon that kept just ahead of them. Halfway down they halted in the Great Bitter Lake to let the north-bound convoy through. Our sister ship, Bursar Bob declared, as the *Sydney* passed by and recognised the *Australis* with an ill-tempered belch of her klaxon. Lining her decks, leaning over the rails, their doppelgängers waved at

185

them. Anita stared at the familiar silhouette, the same geometry of funnel and porthole; even their signature smoke scrawl in the sky was replicated. The *Sydney* drew level and for a moment they were twinned. And then, with an impatient belch, she was gone. Anita, standing on deck, felt her old life receding.

Aden was dry land. By then they were clamouring to get off, to still the incessant tossing of the sea, which had filled their heads like the fluid in a barometer. The first impression they encountered on terra firma was its oddness, the awful solidity of the fixed viewpoint. And the noise of humanity crammed into a small space. They tripped gaily down the gangplank of the *Australis*, four girls in summer prints clutching their day passes, and melted into the crushed stench of the marketplace. Men and animals jostled on the quay; stallholders ululated as if trading were a form of penance. Their smells intertwined, sweat and spice and shit. In his professional capacity, Bursar Bob had furnished Lil with a set of rules. Don't drink the water, don't reveal too much flesh, don't talk to the natives. The natives moved in droves, haughty and disparaging, or crouched like raptors on the ground throwing dice and hissing.

'Your Arab,' Bursar Bob had said, 'should not be encouraged, particularly by such flowers of Empire.'

'I love it,' Lil had whispered, 'when he talks flowery.'

I am not a flower of anybody's empire, Anita thought savagely.

They trod daintily through the narrow, arcaded streets and dark alleyways in their floral frocks and strappy sandals in search of civilisation, which Bursar Bob had assured them existed. A troop of soldiers on camels and bearing flagstaffs passed them by; there was a constant traffic of skinny boys on overburdened donkeys, but they ended up dusty, tired and disappointed. Bursar Bob had failed to materialise so Lil had an excuse to be downcast. Anita, Mew and Stasia had less reason, but as happened constantly during their voyage they infected one another with their moods.

They had planned to buy trinkets but there weren't shops as they knew them; there were small dingy stores, but they sold only household goods and provisions. There were rickety stalls set up on street corners stacked with strange fruit but, schooled as they were in Bursar Bob's precautionary fear, they didn't linger long enough anywhere to get engaged. If a stall-holder addressed them, they imagined they were being mocked or cursed.

Eventually they found the Crescent Hotel recommended by Bursar Bob ('The Queen stayed there!'). They flopped gracelessly in the tea rooms, perspiring heavily in their soiled finery. It was a high-ceilinged establishment with tiled floors and cane furniture. Terracotta urns housed spidery ferns, which whispered in the deliciously cool air generated by the snappish whirr of ceiling fans working away like trapped winged creatures. They ordered iced tea and petits fours, fanning themselves with the menu cards while a slippered boy waiter, wearing a fez and starched whites, padded from table to table bearing decorated trays of shivering china. It was a reprieve from the onslaught of sensation – and heat – outside, and they wallowed in it.

Lil was distracted – as ever – by the prospect that Bursar Bob, having recommended the Crescent, might actually turn up there himself, so she kept a beady eye on the revolving doors while Mew and Stasia bickered over the tepid tea and the tots when the bill came. Anita excused herself and went in search of the Ladies' Room. She hoped it wasn't going to be one of those holes in the floor that Bursar Bob had warned them about.

A sign with an elaborate curlicued finger pointed downstairs and Anita followed it down one flight of steps and then another, finding herself in a dark brown corridor lined with louvred doors. Like the saloon bars in a Western, she thought. It was warm down here, warm and airless, and she found her forehead beading and her underarms dampening again. She ploughed on to the end of the corridor but it was a dead end. She must have made a wrong turning, or gone too far. She was about to retrace her steps when one of the doors opened and a man stood there, guarding the door with his arm. He wore a high turban-like thing on his head, flecked with black and white, and what looked like a white nightshirt with a pair of pyjamas underneath. His skin was the colour of treacle. He smiled at her quizzically, as if *he* had lost his way and was about to ask for directions. Instead he made a small, chuckling sound. She noticed the large gap between his front teeth that made his otherwise placid face – steady brown gaze, a flared nose – look comical.

'I was just . . .' she began. But he probably had no English.

She did not want to be rude and simply turn her back on him in case he'd think her haughty. He dropped his arm and pushed the louvred door back. Was he inviting her in, she wondered. Or daring her? She should not go in, she told herself, but out of politeness she found herself stepping into a tiny room more constricted than Cabin C12, even with four girls in it. There were two cots; the bottom one where the man had been lying – sleeping? – showed signs of disarray. It was spitefully hot inside. Hanging from the window frame was a blue uniform like the shadow of another man quenching the white block of light. It had brass buttons and gold epaulettes and a name tag over the breast pocket; she saw he was Mohammed. He closed the door behind her silently and shot a rickety bolt across to lock it. Now she should be panicking, she told herself. Now she should be crying out, screaming *Help, Help!* – This was exactly the kind of thing the bursar had warned them against. But she didn't do any of these things. She noticed he was barefoot and this, somehow, made him seem less threatening. Slowly he began to unwind his headgear as if he were unfurling a plait of hair and let it slither to the floor. He gestured to her. She unbuttoned her cardigan and peeled it off. It was like a game of forfeits where the moves had already been decided. He caught the hem of his tunic and whipped it off over his head; she inched down the zip of her dress working blindly behind her back. She lifted it away from her – the bodice of it was stiff and when she dropped it on the floor it stood for a minute or two before surrendering and falling. Standing in her vest and pants, she faced him in his loose pantaloons swathed around his loins. Soon, she thought, he will speak and then I will return to my senses, but he didn't. He put his hand to her face and crushed her mouth into a buckled rose so that even if she had wanted to speak, his mouth on hers would have prevented it. He led her by that kiss to the crumpled bed and they fell on it together. She thought of the crudest, most knowing thing she could do. She thought of her mother. She opened her legs.

Afterwards, she gathered up her spilled clothes and swiftly dressed. She slid the lock back and looked behind her before she stepped outside. He lay there, spent, but watching her intently. Although he showed no signs of moving, she made a fugitive dash for the stairway and started the climb up into the light, her thighs throbbing, her heart agape. Stasia was standing at the head of the stairs in the lobby of the hotel.

'Where on earth have you been?' she asked. 'We've been looking all over for you. Lil and Mew had to go on ahead.'

'I got lost,' Anita said.

At Colombo, the *Australis* moored some way off from the port. Squat white buildings quivered on the horizon; rowing boats jostled in the swell the ship brought. Men stood on the buffeting boats and called up to the towering decks, beads and trinkets threaded through their fingers, while their empty nets trailed disconsolately in the choppy waters. *Sahib!* From this distance, Anita wasn't sure if they were even selling anything; they might, with their glossy hair and squinting smiles, have been simply pleading for mercy. *Sahib!*

A tender ferried passengers ashore but only Mew took up the offer. Lil was having a pig of a period, and Stasia was penning a letter to Frank W. Anita lay out on one of the timbered deckchairs strewn around the pool, like a giant watery eye on A deck, deserted. She felt bereft of curiosity. The floating world of the *Australis* was her only interest now and, when she allowed herself to remember it, the scalding memory of submitting to the golden man in Aden. It wasn't that it had been unpleasant; even when he had borne down on her he had not been rough. There was something athletic about the way he had moved whereas she had felt like a burden – a white flour sack – that must be manoeuvred into place. When he'd done – *that* – an unbearable spear of pleasure ran through her, a piercing sensation followed by a hollow falling. But in the girls' company, she was smugly silent. She had gone beyond them, left them behind with their useless and florid romantic speculations. When she thought about Aden, the secrecy of the encounter gave her more pleasure than the memory.

The entire ship celebrated when the Equator crossed the international dateline. Anita wondered why. These were imaginary lines on a map, but, by that stage of the journey, what had once absorbed their interest – the moody changes of the ocean, the flowery foam of the ship's wake, even the heartbreaking sweep of alien sunsets – had dimmed. All that could rouse them now was noisy diversion. It was a calm evening, a starry night. On went the summer frocks they had not worn since Aden, though they had to throw on their northern hemisphere coats and woolly cardigans to ward off the chilly southerlies. Lil wore a pair of evening gloves. This was the night she intended to bag Bursar Bob and, sure enough, at some time in the small hours the pair of them slipped away. Mew danced showily with Viktor Varga. He was courtly with her; she was tipsy and broke her heel. At midnight, the ship's hooter was blown three times, echoing eerily over the night wash of waves, a puny reminder to the elements that they had had been there, a nautical graffito. Later the stewards blacked up and slung grass skirts over their whites and did a high-kicking dance on A deck, as the passengers clapped and hollered, and snaked around the pool, conga-style.

'C'mon,' Mew urged her, having abandoned Viktor, but she couldn't join the raucous carnival; it seemed disloyal.

After the Equator it was all downhill. The blanched decks, even the Brisbane bar, lost their appeal. Their hygiene took a knocking; they took to bathing less; their bars of sugar soap lay unused for days on end. They started to skip meals because they were too lazy to rise and dress. Their lethargy had found its natural home – an ocean-going liner adrift in an endless sea. They dozed on their distressed bunks, abandoned by dreams, sinking deeper into a comradely lassitude, as if even their sleep had become bored with them. In the privacy of the cabin they could no longer face one another; they turned towards the wall and escaped into sleep. When Anita did venture up on deck there were fewer and fewer passengers around. It seemed as if they were losing people overboard.

When they entered Fremantle, they did lose half their number. Mew said goodbye noisily in the cabin. She wept and had to blow her nose a lot. Even her swept-up hair had a distressed look. It looked in danger of imminent collapse as she backed out the door with her beauty bag in tow.

'I'd sooner stay,' she said, 'and go with you girls to Sydney.'

Stasia was disembarking too, though Mr Sheep Farmer was still another day's journey away.

They waved Mew and Stasia off, then Lil retreated to Bursar Bob's office on B deck. With the *Australis* on Antipodean time, the clock was ticking loudly. Where once their association had been impossible, now it was doomed and required a great deal of mournful attention. Anita stayed on deck, looking down at the speck that was Stasia standing on the quay with her two cardboard suitcases, waiting for her trunk to be unloaded. She seemed forlorn standing there, fingering her ringless hand. The sight of Stasia, so tiny and singular, made Anita afraid. She was suddenly overcome with a mesmeric weakness, her breath coming sharp and shallow. The sea sparkled maliciously; the sky sick with cloud. She felt all at once her own invisibility and the terrible asthma of distance as if the world might at any moment inhale and swallow her whole. Viktor Varga came upon her like this.

'Your Scottish friend? She is gone?' he asked, meaning Mew.

She made to speak, but when she opened her mouth the wind rushed in and choked her. Viktor fished in his capacious jacket pocket and produced a brown paper bag.

'Here,' he commanded gruffly, 'breathe into this.'

He placed a grounding hand on her shoulder. The crinkled brown paper inflated and crumpled before her eyes, eclipsing all else. Viktor kept time. When her breathing subsided he took the bag away. Then he wrapped his big arms around her.

'Lento,' he said, rubbing her back, 'lento.'

She was glad Mew couldn't see this; she'd have accused her of moving in on Viktor.

After Fremantle she and Viktor seemed to gravitate towards each other. With the girls gone – and Lil fully occupied – Anita couldn't bear the silence of the cabin. Viktor, too, came up out of the Brisbane bar. He'd lost much of his audience and the ship itself seemed intent on throwing them together. She would come across him on deck, not gazing out over the water or raising his face to the spitting sun, but bent over, sunk in contemplation, his hands linked prayerfully. Sometimes she thought of telling Viktor about what had happened in Aden. But it would have been too much like confession, appealing to an older man with a benedictory hand. She was done with that; particularly now. So they just stood together, two figures linked by silence, and that other unlikely association – that he had clamped a paper bag over her mouth to save her.

If their departure had been a blizzard of noise, their disembarkation on Circular Quay was stealthy and unmarked by ceremony. The *Australis*, having embraced a crowd, seemed to want to exhale its passengers one by one. When the time came, Lil was nowhere to be seen, probably off with Bursar Bob, so Anita left Uncle Ambrose's address scrawled with Lil's lipstick on the mirror in the cabin.

She was shepherded with the crowd into a large arrivals shed through which they had to be processed. It was there she found Uncle Ambrose, ducking and weaving through the crowd at the far, dim end of the shed, trying to find a free place at the barrier. She felt suddenly shy at the sight of him. But when she finally made it to the barrier he opened wide his arms.

'There you are!' he said. 'Didn't think I'd recognise you. But sure you haven't changed a bit.'

Haven't I? she wanted to ask.

Over Ambrose's shoulder, Viktor Varga came into view, suitcase in hand. He was in shirtsleeves, his tie askew, damp patches of sweat under his arms. The heat seemed to make a fool of him. She disengaged and Ambrose wheeled around.

'You must be the uncle,' Viktor said, stretching out his hand to shake Ambrose's. Ambrose eyed him warily. 'Your niece speaks of you.'

'This is Viktor,' Anita offered. 'Viktor Varga.'

'Good man,' Ambrose said and began to move away.

Viktor put a restraining hand on his arm.

'Maybe your boys like to learn the rudiments of music, yes?'

He set down his case and took a battered-looking notebook out of his pocket. Uncle Ambrose grudgingly obliged with his address, then snatched the book from Viktor halfway through because he was having trouble with the dictation.

'Good man,' he repeated with a forced heartiness as he scrawled out his phone number. Then, irritated, he tugged on Anita's arm and bustled her away.

'Rudiments of music, me arse,' he muttered as they made their way through the crowds. 'Has his eye on you, more like. Bloody foreigners!'

Anita stole a glance over her shoulder. The bloody foreigner was standing forlornly between two large hatches of forbidding sun-glare, the entrance where they'd come in from the quay and the exit towards which Ambrose was steering her. Steeped in swampy shadow, Viktor was looking directly at her, appealing, but for what she didn't know. She considered waving to acknowledge their closeness. Yet what exactly was it but silence, an unspoken complicity? Instead, she turned away, not wanting to acknowledge the small stab of betrayal she felt. Ambrose took her hand and led her towards the light. They stepped into glorious sun-drench.

The great expanse of the harbour opened up before her. The white-capped water shimmered, playful like an ocean on a buried treasure map. The bridge arched in a pocket of blue.

'Here it is,' Ambrose declared, pointing towards the scene as if he had painted it himself. 'The beginning of a new life!'

But despite the rinsed sky and the bracing blueness, Anita didn't believe it. Her new life had already started. It wasn't out there; it was growing inside her.

CLODS

Clods hit the coffin lid. It was a country funeral. They didn't go in for covering up the grave with what looked like a carefully cut sod of golf course.

'Thanks,' Louis said.

'For what?' Norah tugged at his sleeve playfully as they turned away from the graveside. It was an unruly day of spring, blustery and grey, the new-leaved trees tossed as if by grief. The wind shivered as they led the mourners down the ragged path between the furred gravestones. She wasn't sure if she should link him. It seemed too proprietorial; he no longer belonged to her, after all. Neither had she been sure of whether to wear black. Would that be laying claim to a grief that didn't belong to her either? (In the end she chose a Lenten purple.) Norah had not cared much for Louis's mother but only because she sensed his mother did not care much for her. It had been the first time she had encountered hostility for its own sake. The mere fact of her had been enough. And, of course, she was spiriting away Mrs Plunkett's only son.

The noonday pub smelled of damp coats and the night before. There was a further round of condolences as neighbours came up and pumped his hand, saying simply 'Louis' as if his name were an incantation of mourning. Norah went to sit in a corner under the dartboard. He caught her eye above the knot of people gathered at the bar and cocked an eyebrow, part query, part apology.

'A hot whiskey,' she called.

He clapped his thighs in search of his wallet, then hitched up the tails of his overcoat and rummaged in his pockets. If Norah missed anything from her former marriage it was the knowledge of those trademark gestures, so familiar, so typical, so male. These too had once been hers.

Nobody approached her, though Cora behind the bar had waved a vague greeting to her as she came in. The intervening years had reduced Norah to a once-familiar face that could not be instantly placed. But then, her memory of those who had peopled her young marriage had also dimmed. She recognised the postmistress (what was her name?) who used to beam at Norah as if she were visiting royalty. And there was Louis's Uncle Pat, haphazardly shaved and bow-legged, leaning against a stool, his chest softly growling as he tried to draw breath.

Ray, Louis's boyhood friend whose approval had once been so important, was handing out fistfuls of shorts, a cigarette clamped in the fork of his thick, scored fingers. He had smiled shyly as he passed Norah earlier in the church. She was sitting several pews down on the groom's side while he had stood beside Louis at the front, a brotherly arm around his shoulders. She had watched the back of Louis's head, his hair curling over his collar, his ears large and defenceless, the soft hulk of his back, and felt a choking sort of sadness. Not for him, but for the ancient loss of him.

'It's Louis,' he had said when he rang with the news.

From his new life in America. She still regarded it as his new life though it was hardly apt. He had been away five years now. She had considered it running away. That was not her way. Hers had been to dig in deeper, to disappear into the debris of their marriage, to live among the ruins.

'Louis Plunkett,' he added hastily as if there were a danger she would confuse him with some other Louis.

When he had first gone away he had rung regularly at odd hours of the morning because he couldn't get the hang of the time difference. She remembered those conversations and the poignant intimacy they achieved over the transatlantic hiss, the stalwart solidarity of two people who had survived a calamity as if their broken marriage were an external event, a natural disaster like a hurricane or an earthquake. Then the phone calls had petered out and she knew he had found someone else. He had settled in Ann Arbor, a place that sounded to Norah like the name of another woman. Safe in the arms of Ann Arbor.

'It's my mother,' he had said. In the background she could hear the disappointed cadence of airport announcements. 'I was wondering . . .'

'The funeral?' she prompted.

There was an audible sigh from the other end.

'Would you?'

She had agreed heartily; it was only now, sitting in the albuminous wash of a lounge bar afternoon, that she wondered what she was doing here.

Louis finally broke away and brought her the by now tepid whiskey. He took off his coat and slung it on a stool beside him. She resisted the temptation to lift the sleeve that was trailing in the sawdust and to fold it carefully. Even when they were married she wouldn't have done so; it would have been too wifey. They had prided themselves on not being conventional even as she marched down the aisle in white. To check one another they had used pet names. 'Now who's being Agatha?' he would taunt when she complained about having to pick up his dirty socks from the bedroom floor. 'Bangers and mash, George,' she would bark when he would ask what was for dinner. She smiled now at the bragging childishness and saw the fierce denial at the centre of it – George and Agatha. As if they had never played themselves. Louis had boasted to friends that he wouldn't have a rolling pin in the house because theirs wasn't that kind of marriage.

Which meant that Norah had to use a milk bottle; for baking, that is. All her piecrusts had the letters MBL imprinted on them. Sometimes, faint vestiges of the warning on the bottles would also appear before the tart went into the oven: Must Not Be Used Without Permission.

'Well,' he said, 'this place hasn't changed.'

She wasn't sure if he meant the pub or the country.

'You look well,' she offered.

And he did. The years of hot summers had given him a glossy, cosmetic air. His clothes – the neat jacket, the tastefully sombre tie, the stiff white shirt – bore the hand of another woman. She tried to imagine the woman at the other end of his life, roused in the graveyard hours by the death of someone she had never known, standing in her slip at the ironing board pressing his good clothes while he called Reservations.

'I'm knackered, to tell you the truth. Haven't slept in days.'

The pub was clearing slowly. The postmistress (Mrs Baines! – the bane of our lives, Louis used to say) came over to shake his hand. She was a stout, raddle-faced woman with small, pert lips.

'Your poor mother, Louis,' she said, peering at him with an inquisitive sympathy. 'All alone at the end.'

Louis shifted uncomfortably.

'And with no family here, but Pat and . . .' she paused and turned to Norah, 'your good self, of course.'

Norah did not know whether to feel complimented by this, her first official inclusion, or to be offended by the obvious reproach.

'If she were at home itself. They go downhill once they go into those homes.'

There was a moment's silence.

'You'll be selling the place, I suppose. Nothing to keep you here now.'

Norah felt oddly, bleakly disowned.

*   *   *

198

She had visited Mrs Plunkett once at the nursing home after Louis had gone away. She felt she owed it to her; it was a last-ditch attempt to be liked, she realised now, though with Louis gone it was less likely than it had ever been. It was an old manor house set in half an acre of rutted parkland. A modern annexe had been built on, with floor to ceiling windows which gave on to seeping foggy fields. Matron directed her to the Rec Room; in her mind's eye Norah saw a dry dock full of rusting hulks.

Mrs Plunkett was sitting in a large circle of plastic chairs as if a group therapy session were about to start, or an afternoon tea dance. Only one other chair was occupied by an old man in a cap with a leathery face and chipped teeth. He had no legs; he sat there like a lewd version of a nodding children's toy, his stumps swaddled in a tartan rug, grinning broadly and winking at Norah.

'Mrs Plunkett?' Norah whispered.

Her mother-in-law was sitting upright with her hands firmly planted on a walking frame, but in fact she was fast asleep.

'Mrs Plunkett?'

Startled she awoke and seemed ashamed, as if Norah had come upon her having a secret tipple.

'It's me,' Norah said. 'Norah.'

Her mother-in-law's eyesight was failing.

Norah drew up a chair beside her.

Mrs Plunkett registered no surprise at her former daughter-in-law being there. Just as she had barely reacted when Louis told her they were separating. It was as if their lives were inauthentic in some way, Norah had thought, as foreign and as passively regarded as a television soap opera.

'Did you come down today?'

'Yes, on the train,' Norah replied, wanting to elaborate but finding nothing more to say. There had never been much small talk between them.

'I find the days very long here,' Mrs Plunkett said after a while. 'I can't get round, do you see. I can't get round like I used to.'

'Have you heard from Louis?' Norah asked. She was still hungry for news of him then, or even to talk about him in a kindly and abstracted way.

'In the summer you can walk in the garden but with my pins I've seen the last of the garden, I'd say.'

'Does he write?' Norah asked gingerly.

'Timmy there,' Mrs Plunkett gestured conspiratorially to the man with the amputated legs. 'Timmy there's always asking how much land I have. I think he's after me.'

Norah abhorred this flirty gaiety. She preferred the patients who sat sunk in primeval gloom. A restive silence fell between them.

'It's night-time there now,' Mrs Plunkett said suddenly.

'Night-time where?'

'Where Louis is,' she said quietly. 'I count the hours . . .'

As did Norah, frequently. It was a kind of mental house-keeping. Before going to sleep she would do a quick calculation and think, without rancour or envy, he's probably leaving work now, or going to the cinema, maybe. It was a way of placing him, of rendering him fixed.

'And neither of us have him,' his mother said.

The key turned stiffly in the lock and Louis stepped into the small hallway, which smelled of damp disuse. It was icy as if the cold fingers of death had edged their way into the place. The kitchen of the small cottage had been 'improved' since Norah had been there last. There was a fridge now in place of the bucket of water Mrs Plunkett had once used to store milk. The fireplace had been bricked up and in its place a two-bar electric fire with mock coals had been installed. Louis stooped and plugged it in. It cast a phosphorescent glow on the parquet-look lino which had been laid over the old flagstones. The only sign of life in the place was Louis's two bags opened and spilling out their contents on to the floor. He fished out a woollen sweater and put it on. (It was true, Norah thought, exile makes people soft.) Then rummaging further he retrieved a bottle of duty-free whiskey. He hunted around for glasses, sliding back one door and then another of the kitchen cabinets, which released musty little bouquets of neglect. He found two dusty tumblers with bees painted on them, free offers with a honey promotion.

'So,' Louis said, setting the bottle and beakers down on the kitchen table. It could have been an interrogation scene: two near strangers sitting on hard chairs in a darkening room lit only by the sickly hue from the fireplace.

'So,' he repeated, 'how have you been?'

She felt she had so little to offer. Years of recuperation, a steady but mean renewal of her life. She spoke about her job; she was head of her department now with her own office and a car. She did not talk about men. It was an unwritten rule between them, a kind of deference. He enquired about Patricia, the baby sis, he always called her. And her mother, of course, who was slipping slowly into senility.

'The poor old bird,' Louis said, refilling their glasses. 'Who's looking after her?'

'I am,' she said.

'Oh, I see, the dutiful daughter.'

'I couldn't just abandon her.'

'Like I did, you mean.'

The accusation sat between them in the gathering dusk. Louis narrowed his eyes over the plume of spirits in his glass. Norah watched him covertly. She could barely see him in the deepening shadows so she had to imagine his bog-coloured eyes, those big soft hands of his, the fluttering nerve in his cheek. As she had done for five years.

She remembered once, shortly after they separated, finding a note from Louis in the kitchen. He still had a key to the house. She had never got round to asking for it back. The kettle had been broken and he had scribbled a message to her on the back of an envelope.

'What you need,' it read, 'is a new element.'

For a moment she thought he was being philosophical and she remembered standing there contemplating this proposition, basking in his new wisdom about her, as if he were offering one last remedy in a gnomic code. Then, stung by her own foolishness, she crushed the note into a tight ball and set fire to it in the sink.

Darkness fell. The reproachful silence between them blossomed into a mournful but easy complicity. Too easy, Norah thought.

'I really should be going,' she said.

'You can't drive with all that drink in you,' he said.

She'd learned to drive since they'd split up; it seemed apt, as if she were finally taking control of her life. A blue Micra sat outside, a nifty compact, a perfect ladies' drive, as the salesman described it. Louis put a restraining hand on her wrist. It was the first time he had touched her since they'd met.

'I can't, Louis.'

'Why not?'

'Not here.'

'You mean people will talk? Hell, let them. I mean, technically, we're still man and wife.' He cupped his hands over hers. They sat like that for several minutes like children making a solemn pact. She could feel goose pimples rise on her forearm. She attributed the stirrings within her to the artificial heat and the whiskey.

'Don't, Louis, please.'

She disentangled her fingers.

'The Big No,' he said in mock basso.

She rose and shrugged on her coat.

'Is this it, then?' he asked.

*   *   *

It was she who had asked that question when they had parted. After the break-up (she favoured the term break-up; it suggested a dramatic shipwreck as opposed to breakdown, which was like an engine running out of steam) she felt obliged to remove the framed photograph of their wedding from the mantel. But she still kept a holiday snap of him stuck into the corner of the dressing-table mirror. There had been no final ritual – no death, no divorce – so he remained there like some lost figure, a hostage or a pilot missing in action. They were still, after all these years, just separated, as if only time and circumstance were keeping them apart. The Ex, she would say jokingly, if anyone asked who it was. The ultimate abbreviation. The Ex. Shedding the ring had taken longer. It took until Louis stopped wearing his. She had met him by chance on the street. It was the first thing she had noticed, the naked finger. He had rubbed at it self-consciously.

'I didn't see the point,' he had said.

She had felt betrayed. Somehow she had always thought that this was something they would do together. She had imagined a grand gesture, the pair of them standing on a bridge and flinging the gold tokens high into the air and watching them dazzle briefly before falling into the waters below.

They made love desperately on his mother's bed. She had thought it would be like a gentle stroll through a childhood haunt; a marvelling at the orchard's windfalls, an easy climb to the dark aperture of the old barn, a cushioned fall in the springy hay. Instead they clawed at one another, all fingernails and spittle. They wrestled greedily, their sweaty flanks slapping against one another, both of them bellowing and braying, joyously aghast at this suddenly unleashed appetite. They lay afterwards on the candlewick bedspread, smelling of semen, their good clothes crumpled and gaping. If they had been naked it would have seemed less illicit, Norah thought. And yet as they lay there, fingers barely touching, eyes locked in the questioning embrace of aftermath, she realised that this was the first time she had desired Louis. It had not been a matter of comfort. Her own, or his. An hour passed in a grave, sprouting silence.

'I'm an orphan now,' Louis said finally.

He had broken the spell. She had forgotten his weakness for lofty self-pity. She pulled herself up and wedged several pillows behind her. His hand rested lazily against her thigh. She listened as his breathing grew quieter, steadier, and he drifted into sleep. She wanted to reach out and stroke his hair or touch the blue-veined skin around his temples but she was afraid of her own tenderness now. And, anyway, she would only wake him and what was the point in that?

It was the early hours of the morning before she slid from the bed. She wrapped her coat around her and stepped into her abandoned shoes. She stood for a moment in the doorway before picking her way through the dark kitchen.

'Bye-bye,' she called out softly as she pulled the front door to. There was no reply. As she drove through the moonlit countryside she thought of him lying on the littered remains of the conjugal bed, like an undiscovered corpse.

BOOM

'Dee-da.'

'Did you hear that?' Frank Shaw has just come into the kitchen. It is a late summer's evening after rain, drenched and lambent. He is in shirtsleeves, tie loosened, elasticated braces like forked leather tongues. 'He said Daddy!'

Rosemary, rubber-gloved in suds, turns around to look down at her toddler son. Little Timmy is sitting in the playpen on an upholstered bottom, clenched fist aloft in salute.

'Dee-da.'

The child seems rapt at something going on at calf level – the tanned denier of his mother's stockings, her pert kitten-heeled slippers, the pink feathery rosette on her instep that he always wants to eat.

'He said Daddy!'

'No, he didn't!' Rosemary lifts a glass in her muffled paw and holds it up to the golden light.

'I tell you, he said Daddy.'

Timmy's father stoops down, a big urgent face leering through the bars. 'Say it, Tim, say it again.'

Dee-da.

'Oh, Frank, you're hearing things.' Rosemary tamps down something on her eyelid with the back of her pink gauntlet.

'Say it, Tim, Da-dee. Da-dee.'

'Dee-da!' the child brays. 'Dee-da!'

Today you have been to see the Man with the Quiet Voice who smells of tobacco and wet tweed and isn't called the Doctor. The Doctor has an office full of sneezes, a torch with a blazing light and a finger made of sandpaper that he puts on your tongue. Not like the Man with the Quiet Voice who sits on a wet park bench with his hands hiding in his pockets while the rain drips from the hood of the go-car down on to your knees. Mum sits beside him in her clear plastic raincoat so that you can see her dress and her cardy and everything underneath. How's my little man, the Man with the Quiet Voice says, gripping your nose in a fleshy vice between his big fingers. Say hello, your mother says, sweet and secretful. Say hello to the nice man, Tim.

'Tim! Ti . . . m?'

His name has always sounded emaciated to him. Timid, timorous, a thin-lipped emaciated hum. When the strangeness of waking up calling out his own name passes, he thinks it might have been Reggie calling him. Maybe she's left a message and it's her subliminal voice that has woken him. But no, when he checks, the red light is steadfast.

'You still have a machine!' Reggie marvelled.

Voicemail and texts and disembodiment, that is Reggie. Now, there's a name! He loves the two-syllable strength of it, the juicy rich double consonant of the diminutive.

'Yeah, well, you can imagine what convent girls made of Regina,' she'd said. 'They pronounced it with an I!'

Tim was lost.

'Rhymes with?' She'd cocked a saucy eyebrow. Tim had to think hard. Sometimes Reggie made him feel quite maidenly.

Now that he's up he goes to the window and stares out over the water. His is a docklands flat. Regenerated. The water below is a hemmed-in canal basin. At the other side is a large flour mill. A pair of monolithic towers of bleached concrete rise up looking like they've been lightly dusted with confectionery sugar, a six-storey warehouse of blistered stone with cataracted windows stares back at him. As Tim watches, a door opens in the lowest floor at water level and a man steps out on to a metal platform. He lights up. His cigarette tip glows against the inky water and the glower of a wakening sky. In his white baker's coat and paper hat he looks like a clownish doctor, a refugee from a Marx Brothers fancy-dress party, stepping out of a portal of the last century. Tim inches the sash window open a fraction. The rattle of a candy-coloured commuter train leaving the depot at the far end of the basin animates the silent scene. Its empty windows are ablaze, a glow-worm on the move, its clatter at a distance like industrial knitting. There it is, Tim thinks, the world is officially awake now.

Paris is an hour ahead but even so Tim does not dare to ring Reggie at this hour. She would be livid. Their life is like this – careful calculation and fearful discretion. One weekend in three they spend together. Here, there or somewhere in between. The rest of the time airline schedules keep them apart. To anyone looking in from the outside, they are a boom-time couple. What is the sound of boom? The rush and seethe of cappuccino-makers, Tim would say, the bloated heartbeat of car stereos. But these were only signature tunes of prosperity. What of the boom itself? Was it the low, threatening rumble of thunder, the zip and whistle of fireworks or the flat thud of explosion? The abstract sound of boom.

'Oh God, Tim,' Reggie would say when he would speculate like this, 'get a life!'

But Tim is old enough to remember what everyone calls the bad old days. Dole queues and hunger strikes, explosions on the streets, when everything seemed in short supply, except chronic damage.

The first time the Man with the Quiet Voice comes to your house he brings a comic. You sprawl on the kitchen floor as the colours leap out at you in great muscled arms – Zap! – and fiery explosions. Boom! *He and Mum sit at the kitchen table. There is silence between them just like when you and Mum are together, Mum doing the ironing, the smooth swaying motion of her hand, the small slap of the iron's flex hitting against the legs of the board. It creaks when she puts her weight behind something tricky – the collars and cuffs of Dad's shirts. She hums along to a tune playing on the radio, catching a word here and there. Except today she's not ironing; she's saying small soft things to the Man with the Quiet Voice and then laughing in a silvery way. You can see the Man is holding her hand, examining her fingers like the Doctor checking for warts. You know what's going to happen next. She's going to open her mouth and say Aaaaah.*

'Aw, Rosemary!'

It's Dad, voice vivid with complaint.

'What?' Mum turns around, hand on hip.

'How many times have I told you – I don't want Timmy reading comics.'

Dad stands, arms crossed, bulging biceps, cape flying.

'Sure he can't read yet, isn't he just looking at the pictures?' Mum says.

'I just don't want this kind of rubbish in the house.' Dad leans down and whips the comic away. *Whoosh!*

He rips it in two.

Wa-a-h! Hot tears of injustice.

'Perfect!' Mum bangs the iron down. 'Just perfect!'

He likes the disruption that is Reggie Mundy. Her flights away, her lavish returns. He's in love, or at least in thrall, and he has never felt so helpless. He is dazzled by her and dazed by the distance between them. When he turned seventeen, she was going into High Babies. Then there's her job. A trolley dolly with Plein Air, that's how she described herself.

'We're the cheap and nasty airline,' she explained. 'Our on-board snacks are called Plane Cheesy. Says it all.'

He finds Reggie's sardonic tone, this light contempt, disconcerting.

'Our safety instructions are to stop screaming and lower your mask. And if you're travelling with children, it's time to pick your favourite.'

Tim loves his work; it's a calling. If he ever got to the point of regarding it as lightly as Reggie does hers, he'd have to jack it in. He took her on a tour of the studio one night when P45 was recording. She was coolly impressed.

'P45,' she breathed. 'That makes you a legend!'

Or did she mean a has-been, Tim wondered.

When other teenagers were buying rock albums, he was buying LPs of sound effects. Most people could detect that boy in him, until, that is, he saved some coked-up boy band from mediocre oblivion. *Then*, he was a wizard.

'My God, Tim, it's dark down here,' Reggie had said. 'Don't you feel buried alive?'

In comparison to her harsh, over-lit world, the studio must have seemed sunk in a pre-modern gloom but Tim did his best work in the graveyard hours. There was a sanctity about the studio then as if it were a cathedral of sound, though sometimes that idea was hard to sustain, watching wasted musicians sitting around smoking their brains out. He was the organist: the sound channelled through his hands and became transformed. He wanted to mix music so that each constituent part – the woozy reverb of a bass, the crystalline ting of a hi hat, even the grating dry rub of a palp along a guitar string – would detach itself and cry out, so that the listener might think he was stoned. He loved the absolute clarity of those moments himself, the certainty of singular sensations. That's what he wanted to reproduce, *that* purity. But he couldn't possibly explain that to Reggie. Purity? Reggie?

Once you meet the Man with the Quiet Voice in the church. You have to sit at the end of the last pew on the aisle that leads to brazen glory. He and Mum go off to light candles. What'll I do, you ask. You say your prayers, Timmy, there's a good boy, Mum says. What'll I pray for? Mum seems flustered. She storms up the aisle. She seems always to be running away. Pray for your mother's intentions, sonny, the Man with the Quiet Voice says as he follows her, coat-tails flying. Their voices came back to you, solemn and jilted, from the side aisle where the shrine to the Blue Our Lady is. What's that man's name, you ask when Mum comes back. What man, she replies crossly.

They had met in Paris. It sounded romantic in the telling. What they neglected to say was that it was not in the Luxembourg Gardens or Montmartre, but in a launderette on Rue Pascal on a Sunday afternoon. Tim was enduring the desolate idleness of a foreign city; the band was sleeping it off at the hotel. There were museums he could have gone to but Tim was not up to the solemn, wearying silences of art. He was drawn into the launderette by the sound of it.

'How sad is that!' Reggie said.

No sadder than doing your laundry amidst the splendours of Paris, Tim thought. It was one of those automated places. A voice from a tall headstone of stainless steel barked the machine number, the programme required, the length of the wash. It was a flat voice, daleky, robotic. Tim liked the effect of it and the absurdity of the disembodied voice like a muezzin calling for prayer, issuing instructions to the unwashed.

When he stepped inside the small glassy shop he was met with the bland owlish glare of stacked washers and dryers. Reggie was standing in front of the talking plinth, coins in one palm, the other hand raised in expansive helplessness while she barked at the flinty dial. 'But how much do I put in?'

'Can I help?'

She turned swiftly. He got an impression of blond exasperation.

The Man with the Quiet Voice appears out of the bathroom wearing Dad's dressing gown. You are lying in wait outside for the game you and Dad play. You would hide in the well of the stairs and when you heard the bathroom door open, you would leap out with a tiger growl – Grrr! – and Dad would grab you and tickle you until you cried for mercy. You pounce. Jesus Christ, the Man swears. Denis, Mum cries and puts her hand over her mouth. Then she yanks you up roughly by the arm from the top step and propels you down the landing. Go to your room, this instant, and not another word!

Dee-da, Dee-da, dee-da, dee-da . . .

Of course, he compared her to Ruth – Ruth whom he probably should have ended up with. See, Tim argued with himself, I'm thinking of ending up with someone while Reggie is only starting out. Tender and pliant Ruth Denieffe who'd exuded an easy empathy, while being vehement on his behalf. Ruth who *got* the music thing – I'm a failed singer, she would say tartly, I know about vocation. She was a teacher, a zealot for instruction, a fierce and unlikely authority figure who stood at only five foot two and scared her pupils half to death, or so Tim suspected. Ruth had been mournful, half-finished songs in the bathroom and eerily silent when they made love. Reggie was operatic, all noise and protest. Ruth crept around him with her cloud of feline hair, her childlike limbs, her soft velour wardrobe. Reggie was a fusty mess of smudged cotton balls on the bedside table, her eyes in little dishes in the soap hollow of the bathroom basin, her clothes and heels all sharp angles. Reggie felt like danger, flashy and menacing as gold fillings; Ruth had been soothing balm.

His relationship with Ruth had seemed like a premature rehearsal for what Tim thought real life would eventually be. They'd had five years that were as good as marriage. He'd met her parents, spent Christmas with them once on Prosperity Drive. Her footballer brother was home from England and drank too much and there had been a bit of a scene, Ruth's mother dissolving into tears, her father maintaining an honourable silence as Barry harangued them about how they'd always favoured Ruth and John over him, despite the fact that he had made something of himself. Tim had never met John who had gone into a monastery straight after school. He was talked about with a reverence that Tim associated with the long-dead. Tim was fascinated – weren't other people's families so much easier to read, he thought. None of it had put him off Ruth. It was just he couldn't quite believe that he had got it right with her; couldn't trust to it. And when he had suggested to her that they take a break – just a break, that was all he meant so he could chastise himself into conviction – Ruth had given up without a whimper. He had expected resistance, a fight, but she had seemed primed for defeat as if *she* had never quite trusted him.

'Phee-ew,' she said. 'I've been expecting this.'

Was it relief or brave regret he heard? He never could work it out.

He turns on the TV and slumps in front of it with the sound down. The breakfast news comes on. The newscaster, dressed like a sober schoolboy, sits casually on the side of the desk, feigning informality. Suddenly there is live coverage. Footage of panic, a fluorescent street strewn with wrecked cars, the glare and din of fire engines. Stretchers bearing shrouded forms being humped inexpertly along; the walking wounded lean and limp. Northern Ireland, Tim thinks dully, an old response, but no, he corrects himself, aren't we living in a time of peace? The Middle East, then. He catches a glimpse of the wrought intaglio of an art deco Metro sign. Jesus, this is Paris! Where Reggie is. She might be lying under debris, mangled, mutilated. Her fiery head crushed, her hair smeared with blood. He imagines phoning her and her mobile ringing out. Before he can locate the remote, the carnage has disappeared and it's back to the newscaster with a tickertape of shares running along the bottom of the screen. Has he dreamt it up?

Bleary-eyed, he makes for the kitchen, checking the clock over the cooker hood before starting to make coffee. It is 7 a.m. The clock makes a silent digital calculation. He still expects it to declare itself. He remembers the magnified announcements of the wall clock in his grandmother's parlour, which measured the hours with a grinding wheeze and the minutes with a disapproving tick, as if every moment mattered. And every moment did. In Mellick there was a time for the kettle to be boiled, for the cake of bread to be taken out of the oven, for the incantation of the Angelus.

The Angel of the Lord declared unto Mary . . .

'You'll love it,' his father had said in that tone of false encouragement. Like when he wanted Tim to play football. *Thwack!*

'Will Denis be there?'

'Who?' Dad barked.

Mum glared at him and left without saying goodbye.

The two weeks they were away – a package holiday to the sun; well, they'd sent men to the moon, hadn't they? – seemed endless. He listened to the mournful bellowing of cows, the slap of their full fat udders swinging rudely from side to side, the splattery skeetering of hooves in the mud, the hup-hup of the boy who drove them. To the racket of the tractor and the baler passing by the gate. To the melancholy ripple of birdsong when he was put to bed even though it was still light outside.

'Time for bye-byes,' Gran would say. She still used baby talk though he was nearly seven.

But mostly he was listening out for the scrunch of wheels on gravel and for Mum to come home.

To his shame he is persistently and sickeningly jealous. He has fantasies of throttling anybody who looks crooked at

213

Reggie. He would use his bare hands, blacken eyes if need be. *Ker-pow!* He has logged away all of the stray names she mentions – Jason, the steward who's emphatically not gay, Ted, the divorced pilot, Marco, the great guy on the ground at Fiumicino – so that when she's delayed he visualises her being with one of them simply because he knows their names. He has pressed her gently for details.

'This guy, Jason, have I met him?'

Reggie would shake her glorious hair. 'No, he lives in Paris with Kate,' she would say evenly.

'And Ted?'

'We met him at check-in once, remember? Tall guy with epaulettes? Drives a plane.'

'I'm only asking,' he would say.

'You're not only asking, Tim, you're checking up on me – there's a big difference. Don't you trust me?'

No, no, no. He could see how clichéd it was, the jealous older man making inventories of possible betrayal. Even after a year with Reggie, he still felt like he was handling unstable explosives, except he was the one ready to go off at any moment.

The last time you see the Man with the Quiet Voice is in Bradleys. You remember the cold clammy feel of the gauge as the shop lady measures your bare feet for sandals and your mother kneading her fingers on the top of the clover pattern in the leather to make sure you have enough room to grow. Suddenly, he is upon you. This fella's going to be big as a house, eh, Timmy, me boy, he says loudly. He grips you on the shoulder and does a trick with his hand so that a florin suddenly appears at his fingertips. Denis, Mum hisses. Jesus, Rosemary . . . The two of them go off and huddle in a corner of the shop. And Mum says please, please. And the shop lady says 'Would Sir like to . . . ?' You flex your feet in the new sandals with the blond soles. You don't want him here. You want it to be just you and Mum and the shop lady marvelling at what a big boy you are as she puts your old shoes in the cardboard box that is like a coffin for a hamster. And when the shop lady attaches the balloon that comes free with each purchase to your finger, you want that moment just for yourself too. And you want to wave to the lady and to reach up for Mum's cool hand. You don't want her saying don't and please and not in front of the child or the shop lady saying 'Is everything alright, Madam?' or the man saying Jesus Christ and you can't and please, please. Or Mum suddenly catching you and dragging you out of the shop with the Man coming after and it's such a squeeze in the doorway that . . . Bang! It is all over. He burst my balloon! you yell. You are out on the street and Mum is crying. And the Man with the Quiet Voice is standing in the doorway. No, no, it was just an accident, Mum says, we'll get you another one. Her tears keep coming. The string is still attached to your forefinger. It trails on the pavement behind you with the torn red scrap that was your balloon. That man . . . you begin again. And she turns, your mother, and strikes you – Wham! – across the face. There is no man, she says. Do you hear me? There is no man.

To this day he cannot bear to be in a room full of balloons; too much imminence.

'A sound man?' Dad is incredulous.

His mother presses START. It is his sister Maeve's birthday and she is baking a cake so their conversation is punctuated by the aggravated whirr of the Magimix.

'He'd be an engineer, though,' Mum counters, 'a sound engineer. That's what they call it.'

'He'll be gofer in a studio, more like. Making the tea.'

'We all had to begin somewhere, Frank.'

Frank Shaw, self-made man, scrap-metal merchant, bristles. He is clutching his son's exam results; Tim is sixteen and wants to leave school. He's eavesdropping at the kitchen door, egging his mother on silently.

'No son of mine,' his father starts. STOP.

215

The no son of mine speech is well rehearsed. Tim can recite it by heart.

'Your son has always answered the call of a different drum.'

Mum is scraping the bottom of the bowl. Tim can hear the impatient slap of the rubber spatula.

'You've always been a fool about that boy, Rosemary. Needs a good kick up the arse, if you ask me. Look at this – an F even in Geography!'

'What does any of it matter, once he's happy?'

'Oh well, excuse me, pardon! Once he's happy! There's a recession on out there, in case you hadn't noticed.'

Rush of the tap as his mother fills the mixing bowl and sets it aside to steep.

'He'll be turning his back on everything I've built up.'

'For God's sake, Frank, isn't it obvious he's never going to follow you into the business?'

'Not to me,' Dad says and for the first time Tim feels sorry for him.

Dad used to take him along to the scrapyard on Saturday mornings. It was a hellish place even though his father sat in an elevated Portakabin high above it, doing business over the phone, looking down on the hillocks of twisted metal, the mountains of toothed machine parts, the crushed fangs of cars. Dad didn't seem to register the sudden, calamitous vomiting of scrap from the buckets of the diggers, the hollow volcanic thud of empty skips being hoisted and dropped, the shattering waterfall of shards rushing down the chutes into huge containers. How could he bear all that deafening medieval clangour, and still have appetite for battle when he got home?

When he was little, Tim would put his hands to his ears to shut out their rows; his mother's shrill defiance, his father's querulous misapprehensions. Later, he used headphones. Heavy metal was the best.

Mum opens the oven door. The hinges protest.

216

'Ah, Frank, can you really see it?' his mother says, all tempered reason. 'Our Tim!'

Our Tim. He can't work out her tone.

His father harrumphs.

'Anyway, if it doesn't work out, sure doesn't he have the business to fall back on?'

'Oh yes, good old dependable Frank, always good to fall back on.'

'Don't be like that,' he hears Mum say.

There is silence then. Is that a prelude to agreement? Tim wonders. His mother makes some move. Tim imagines her stroking his father's temple with a floury hand.

'Do it for me,' Mum wheedles, 'for my sake.'

Tim can hear her desperation now; not for him but for herself and for fear of the memory he holds of the Man with the Quiet Voice whose name cannot be spoken. His father is silent; somehow, she has bought his acquiescence.

'Reggie?'

'Tim,' she says.

Oh relief. Thank God! He imagines her corpse reassembling itself into just-woken Reggie, like a roll of film rewound. As if his call has brought her back from the dead. There is a sound in the background. Like the movement of sheets, like a companion disengaging. His heart tightens. Dread giving way to something meaner and entirely more personal. Gone now the images of carnage, the blood-spattered pavement, the public catastrophe.

'Are you alright?'

'Yeah . . .' she says uncertainly. He imagines her blurred by sleep, hair comically askew leaning on a plump elbow. Post-coital.

'I just saw it on the TV, the bomb.'

'Bomb – what bomb?'

'You didn't hear it? Nightclub – petrol bomb, they think.'

217

'I was fast asleep. What time is it?' She is waking now, coming into focus.

'I was worried – I thought you might have been caught up in it.'

She rises, he can hear her. He imagines her, mobile in hand, with the sheets draped around her stumbling towards the window, parting the nets and looking out on to a Parisian street, narrow, cobbled, slimed with rain. He hears her opening a window. He imagines her sticking her blowsy head and goose-pimpled shoulders out over the sill.

'Ugh, wet!'

A siren wails.

'What's that?' he asks as he hears the latch closing.

'Nothing,' she says.

'There's someone else there, isn't there?'

'Oh, Tim, don't start . . .'

An ambulance, Tim guesses, listening to the Doppler effect, the off-tune coming and going of it. Maybe one he has seen earlier on the TV? Maybe on its way back from the scene? The immediacy of connection startles him – images he has just seen translated to a bowl of sound at his ear.

Dah, dee-da-da-dah, dee-da-da-dah, Dah, dee-da-da-dah, dee-da-da-dah.

Each city had its own tonic sol-fa and Tim recognised them all. He'd never told Reggie; it seemed too anoraky even for him, or maybe it was something he was keeping in reserve. For a moment just like this . . .

Dah, dee-da-da-dah, dee-da-da-dah . . .

That wasn't Paris, that was Rome.

'You're lying, Reggie,' he says simply.

There is silence at the other end of the phone.

'How do you know?' Her voice has lost its penny-bright insistence.

Pooof! All over.

Like someone letting the air out of a balloon.

218

You'd had to walk all the way home, your feet hurting in the new sandals. You'd reached the Green when you heard the first explosion. All you remember is the funny smell, a strange silence as Mum halts and listens as if to some soft aftershock. Then the banshee wails begin as fire engines pass blaring importantly, ambulances cluck and pock. It is a symphony of distress as if the world has been agitated by your private tempest. That day of all days, no one takes any notice of a pregnant woman streeling along the street weeping silently and a boy still smarting with hurt, holding on to his fury by a string and blaming the Man with the Quiet Voice for all of it. Dad is frantic. Jesus, Ro, where have you been, I've rung every hospital in the city. Haven't you heard? Three bombs, all at the same time, I was out of my mind with worry. In your condition! He catches you by the lapels and examines you like the doctor in a temper. He pauses at your reddened cheek. What were you doing in town, anyway? Shoes, Mum says dully. You often think of him afterwards, Denis, imagine him blundering down Nassau Street straight into the fiery red maw of it . . .

He goes to his parents' for Sunday lunch, roast beef with all the trimmings. Something else Reggie sneered at. Tied to your parents' apron strings, she would say. But she was at an age where she was still rebelling against hers; he has gone beyond that. Age has chastened his mother or is it the longevity of her deception? His father has mellowed, too; a bad hip has softened his cough. His sister Maeve – conceived on that holiday in Majorca, Tim suspects, which his mother bashfully referred to afterwards as their second honeymoon – has taken over the family business, rebranding Dad's scrap metal as architectural salvage.

'Where's Reggie?' Mum asks as she clatters round the kitchen tidying up after lunch.

'In Paris,' he says.

No, he corrects himself silently, Rome. In Rome with bloody Marco.

219

'How do you keep up with her?' Mum says as she scrapes the gravied remains of the plates into the bin. 'All that gadding about! Wasn't like that in our day. You put up and shut up.'

This is for his father's benefit, like much of what she says these days.

Over coffee, they fall into musing about the past. His parents often retreat into reminiscence now. For Reggie's amusement they retold all of Tim's baby stories. But they don't need an audience.

'Remember when Tim said his first word?' his father starts.

'He was slow to talk,' Mum chips in with that old reflex of contradiction.

'I was absolutely convinced you'd said Daddy,' his father goes on. 'I heard you say it. Clear as a bell. But would your mother believe me? And would you say it again? On demand?'

'Curse of the firstborn. Poor Tim wasn't allowed childish babble,' Mum says ruefully. 'Every sound had to have a meaning.'

Tim enjoys these archival squabbles. It gives his parents a chance to be softer with one another, which they weren't in the original versions of these stories. And he hasn't the heart to correct them. His first word was not for either of them. Even then it was the song of the sirens he heard.

CHINESE BURNS

The seductive power of the bruise, once discovered, cannot be unlearned. She had been trying to stem the fidgeting, that was all. Her mother's fingers worked constantly at the seamed hem of the turned-down sheet as if she were trying to undo it, stitch by stitch. Norah had been sitting by the bedside doing the crossword, speaking the clues aloud. In compensation, she supposed.

'Seven Across: Discomfort one gets in the face, four letters, third letter i.'

It was something her mother used to do when she was in her health, roping Norah and her sister Trish in, often unwillingly, to finish it off. Norah has persisted with the ritual despite the fact that her mother can hardly be said to be participating any more. These days her mother is sequestered in a self-imposed silence. The loss of I, Dr Somers calls it. Though, occasionally, an answer will come from the dim, clouded caverns of her mother's brain. *Pain.*

Norah had got annoyed at the frenetic scrabbling of fingers on counterpane. Simply that. It was a sudden flare of anger, a pinkening rage, and, reaching out, she pressed down on the soft fleshy underbelly of her mother's arm. (There are still, surprisingly, seemingly untouched parts of her mother's anatomy that are youthful almost.) It was an admonitory gesture, not a slap, not anything even remotely rough. It was pressure, gentle pressure. Just to make her stop. But even to herself, Norah's justifications sound courtroom false.

By the time she'd got as far as Twenty Across – *Scorn to see girl's father at home* – there was a bruise. A blue blush on the skin, just above the veiny tributaries of her mother's wrist. It is the only quickening impulse in her mother's pathology, this seeming rush to ruin. It reminds Norah of the fast-forward sequences in TV nature programmes showing pert blooms turning to slatternly rot in the crisp blink of a camera shutter. *Disdain.*

By morning, as if in affront, the bruise has turned livid, blood-angry. She fully expects Tena to confront her about it. Tena is one of the 'new Irish', or a 'non-national,' depending on the terminology you favour. The latter, Norah thought, made her sound like a minus quantity, as if by coming to Ireland she had lost all rights not just to her original identity but to any identity at all. Tena is still in her twenties, younger than Norah by at least a decade, yet Norah, who is her boss, is slightly afraid of her. When she looks at her she sees in Tena's clear eyes the shrewd appraisal of someone much older. A grandmother peers out, the grandmother Tena often speaks of, who raised her. A woman who couldn't read or write, who'd learned to sign her name by practising in six-year-old Tena's lined copybook. Now Tena with her impeccable unaccented English, her pragmatic efficiency, is a world away from her grandmother's life of pickling and thrift. But it is her native skills of care-giving rather than her arts degree with business communication that she is using in Norah's employ. She brings to the work something both alert and demanding.

At the interview, Tena had insisted on showing Norah exactly where she came from on the globe that sat on the bookshelves in the good room. Zadar, Croatia. A walled city, she explained, pointing to the Dalmatian coast. She'd mentioned Roman ruins as if a familiarity with the antique was a prerequisite for the job. Provenance, it seemed, mattered. When Norah was showing her out that first day, Tena looked around the hall curiously.

'And this is where you grew up?'

Norah nodded and pulled a self-deprecating face. Tena ran her blunt, capable fingers appraisingly along the high sheen of the half-moon table. For a moment Norah thought she was trying to put a price on it.

'Aren't you lucky!' she had said with neither envy nor rancour.

It is not how Norah feels. She is thirty-seven, divorced, living with her ailing mother in her childhood home on Prosperity Drive.

Explain this! Norah imagines Tena's sharp interrogative, as she lifts her mother's bony hand up for inspection. But even after three days, when the bruise is a sullen nacreous yellow, Tena seems not to have noticed it. Norah feels relieved but also vaguely dissatisfied. If Tena has missed this, what else is she missing?

Norah contemplates calling her sister. She doesn't know why; Trish, away for years, is not the person she would naturally confide in. The distance militates against it. Trish is in Italy so could know nothing of the local conditions that have produced her mother's bruise. How could Norah explain to Trish the creeping sense of victory she feels because her crime has remained undiscovered? And if Norah did ring her, Trish would only ask those horribly concrete questions she has always asked. How does Mum feel, inside, I mean? Is she dead already, do you think? Does she know what's going on? Trish had always wanted answers from Norah whereas with their mother she had wanted love untainted by fact or history. And yet, just now, it is Trish Norah wants to talk to.

There has always been a gap between the sisters; five years, and now a couple of thousand miles. Norah used to believe the reason was Patrick, their almost-brother. She remembered the pregnancy, her mother growing menacingly big, the globe of her belly hardening while she became softer, abstracted. Norah was too young to realise that this sturdy cargo might turn into a rival. She'd never even thought of it as a baby-to-be, just a burden her mother had to get her arms around. Which is how it turned out. Patrick was stillborn. Because Norah had been a witness to her mother returning from the hospital with neither burden nor heralded baby, it had to be explained to her. Daddy, weeping, said the child had gone to heaven, that Mam had had a little angel whom God had called home. (It was the first time Norah had seen her father cry, though not the last; when he was ill towards the end, his eyes would fill every time he looked at her.) Norah was worried Patrick might be in limbo. No, no, her mother had insisted, Patrick had been baptised in the hospital so there was nothing to worry about. But Patrick lived in a domestic limbo, belonging to the golden time before Trish. Just one more thing she was excluded from. Until Norah broke the silence.

How the argument with Trish had started Norah couldn't remember, but once ignited it followed the same trajectory so that it was always the same argument, essentially. It was late at night close to Christmas and Norah had come in from a party.

'Well . . . ?' Trish demanded when Norah threw herself on the sofa and kicked off her shoes; they were pinching her. Trish, fourteen and extravagantly bored, got up and turned the sound down on the TV. Their mother was on night shift at the telephone exchange.

'Well what?'

'How did it go?'

The party had been a washout. The boss had asked her up to dance and she'd made a fool of herself. Mr Grove, years older than her, had always made her feel uncomfortable. He had a lascivious manner, a viperish laugh. In his company,

Norah felt lumpish and raw as if the joke was always on her. And yet, and yet when he took her in his arms, she had felt a swell of helpless weakness. Not like a swoon, it couldn't have been that, she argued with herself. No, it was a strange tenderness that overcame her but seemed to emanate from him. It was unaccountable. This was Hugh Grove! (Huge Rove, the girls in the office called him on account of his wandering eye.) It had made her cry. She'd wept on his shoulder during a slow set.

'Oh, Trish,' she said, 'it was the office party. What do you think happened?'

'I dunno,' she said, shrugging. 'Did you get off with anyone?'

Trish purported to have a jaded and mechanistic view of romance.

'As if I'm going to tell you that.' Norah remembered her embarrassed exit from the dance floor, escorted by her friend Dan, who'd intervened as Mr Grove stood, hands hanging, staring after her and everyone smirking, thinking he'd tried to feel her up.

'You never tell me anything,' Trish said.

Norah knew this trope by heart: her shortcomings as an elder sister. After their father had died, Trish had often pestered her about him – what was he like, what did his voice sound like, why did he die? – impossible questions that irritated Norah as if she were the repository of all grown-up information.

'Ah, go on,' Trish had said, 'tell me.' She was standing in front of the TV, a hectic car chase playing out silently behind her.

'Tell you what?'

'Anything . . . you're the one who acts like you know everything. Miss Know-all!'

Something about Trish's tone, the peeved assertion of both Norah's superior knowledge and her withholding, rankled. Some hot little bubble of anger popped and it was out before she could stop herself.

'Okay, okay, here's something you don't know. We had a brother.'

'What?'

'Before you were born,' Norah said.

'And why did nobody tell me?' Trish said, grabbing Norah by the wrist. For a minute she thought Trish was going to give her a Chinese burn. In their childhood tussles, it was Trish's trademark torture; she would manacle Norah and screw the skin into a handcuff of pain. Even if she had, Norah couldn't have answered. She didn't know how Patrick had come to be hidden in the first place. Her mother and she had never spoken of it, not even to decide that Trish shouldn't be told. But once it was said, Norah felt a sickening turnover of betrayal – as if she'd exhumed some grubby secret of her mother's – and a lurch of shame that was all hers.

'Is that why I'm called Patricia – to make up for him?'

That had never struck Norah before and she shook her head but Trish was disbelieving.

'You and Mum,' she said, letting Norah go and pushing her away, 'you and your secrets.'

Norah potters around the kitchen cleaning the grill and watching a bad soap on the little portable TV she bought when she moved back home. She picks up the crossword where she left off. Working her way methodically through the black-and-white grid on her own, Norah sees the neat satisfaction of filling in all those blanks. Certain things remained cryptic, of course. Like what had made things between her and her mother so difficult. Not just now; always. Her father's death had bound them, but in a covert way. It had forced them to become a team, joined them in the freemasonry of grief. Norah was eleven, old enough to understand, her mother decreed, thus granting her pre-eminence. She had taken Norah into the dim cramped space under the stairs to break the news. (Well, it was the place of punishment in the house, where she and Trish were sent when they misbehaved.) Her mother said they wouldn't be disturbed in there, meaning by Trish. She, being only six, had to be spared, but Norah was privy – that was the word.

'You know the way your daddy's been sick?' her mother began. She was sitting on an upturned orange box (where Norah, the punished child, usually sat). The highest point of the space under the stairs was piled with cardboard boxes of old and broken things. Norah was able to stand upright but only just and the sloping ceiling with its peeling timber boards made her want to duck. Her mother had not turned on the light – a naked bulb over the door – but she had left the door open a crack, letting in the sickened light of the house.

'Well,' her mother went on matter-of-factly, 'you know the way his hair's fallen out and he hasn't been able to keep things down . . .'

Her father's illness had infected all of them. Norah could barely remember a time when he hadn't been sick.

'It's just that Daddy's not going to get better.' Her mother's lips trembled a little when she said this.

Norah waited. She felt sure by the rising pitch of her mother's sentence that there was worse to come.

'Did you hear me?' her mother asked, crossly, or so Norah thought, as if her attention had been wandering.

'He's going to die, Norah, your precious daddy's going to die,' she said all in a rush as if Norah's silence had forced the admission out of her.

Since that day, Norah felt there had always been a spiteful undertow at work between herself and her mother, as if, despite their apparent closeness, something bitter and illicit was at work. Whatever governed the surges of the relationship – the volatile moon, who knew? – it had reached its lowest point when Louis came on the scene. Louis, her husband. Or ex, she should say. X marks the wound. It was not that her mother disapproved of him; in fact, she professed to like

Louis. She thought him presentable, husband material, as if he were a bolt of cloth at a knockdown price. He got on with people. That was Louis's gift. His affability. But her mother imbued Norah with a terrible uncertainty about him.

'Are you sure?' she kept on asking as if there was something unstable, not about Louis but about Norah. As if she couldn't depend on Norah's feelings about anything, least of all about her beloved. That's what her mother used to call Louis. Your beloved. And Norah couldn't work out if it was sarcasm or envy.

'I wonder,' her mother would muse, 'what your father would have made of him.'

Trish takes up several pages in Norah's address book, each old address scored out to make way for the new. Even on paper she seems elusive as if, in reversal of their childhood pattern, she is intent on wriggling out of Norah's grasp. When she finds the number, she hesitates. Ringing Trish always involves effort – effort to sound upbeat, generous, which in the circumstances is difficult to sustain. She lifts the phone and listens to the soft burr of the dial tone. She rehearses openings. *I've done something terrible. You won't believe this. I didn't mean to. Now I'm afraid I might do it again. It's just that her helplessness provoked me. How dare she be so weak, so frail that my impatience could actually wound her? My mere impatience!* She dials the long number.

'*Pronto!*'

It wasn't Trish; it never was. A seemingly endless parade of voices answered for her. This was Claudia, who had next to no English.

'Can I speak to Trish?'

'*Patreezia non c'è.*' Whatever it meant, Norah recognised the no in it.

'This is her sister.'

'Norah?' Claudia queried. She might not speak English but she could put two and two together. Norah almost blurts it

228

all out to Claudia but no, that would be a false confession, cataloguing her crime to someone who doesn't understand her. Her panic ebbs and another sensation replaces it, seething, vengeful.

'Can you pass on a message?'

'*Messaggio, sì*,' Claudia says after a few seconds of cogitation.

'It's about my mother,' Norah begins before remembering to keep it simple. 'Please tell my sister her mother is dead.'

'Dead?' Claudia repeats. '*Morta? Madre?*' Her husky smoker's voice reaches an incredulous pitch.

'*Sì*,' Norah says obligingly and puts the phone down. *That* would get Trish's attention.

There are things about her situation that Trish has never understood. It is not the mortifications of being a carer; Norah can handle those. It is being back on home territory, joining the roll call of the damaged and the lost, as if her adult life had simply and silently unspooled. She sometimes meets the other adult children of Prosperity Drive when she is out on her errands. There is Barry Denieffe, who got a trial with an English soccer club and went off as a teenager to some dismal mill town across the water. It wasn't that he hadn't made it, exactly; he had just never made it to the First Division. He was back now living with his ageing parents, idle mostly; what, she wondered, did a retired footballer do with his life? Barry had been a frighteningly good-looking boy (Norah had nursed a painful crush on him for a while) with a mop of unruly jet-black hair, dark brown eyes and a lithe, loose arrangement of his limbs as if his body owned him. When they had played football on the street, Barry counted as three on the team he played for. Now if you passed him, you'd nearly give him a penny. His muscle had turned to sag and, it was rumoured, there was a broken marriage behind him. It was, Norah thought as she passed him, as if he had been sheltering this beaten, lonely personage for years inside the burnished armour of a cocky athlete.

Then there was Mary Elizabeth Noone. Her parents had insisted on this full handle even when they were kids, and would berate anyone who dared to shorten it. She was a fat, middle-aged envoy from a skinny and delicate childhood. She'd had scarlet fever and that weakens the heart. But the weakness, it transpired, had actually been of the mental variety. She lived alone in her parents' home (she was a late and only child) and failed to keep herself clean. Ballooned by medication she talked loudly to herself on the avenue. (As a child this was considered charming and fey; even the adults played along with the notion of Mary Elizabeth's imaginary friend.) Now her voice boomed out in hostile interrogatives shouted across the street at all comers. 'Are you still my friend?'

Even the dead companions of childhood come back to haunt Norah. She remembers Julia Fortune who overdosed in a hotel room – in New York, was it? Some love affair gone wrong, apparently. And Hetty Gardner, that little American kid who was killed falling off her bike going down Classon's Hill. Or Finn Motherwell, the asthmatic. Finn had been deemed Norah's special friend. When he was poorly, Mrs Motherwell would send for Norah so that she could read to him in bed.

'Here's our little Florence Nightingale,' she used to say, looking at Norah doe-eyed even though Norah hadn't volunteered for the position: she'd been summoned. It wasn't that she didn't like being with Finn. His frailty made him like an honorary girl and he seemed to like, and be grateful for, Norah's attention. But he would often fall asleep before Norah had finished even a chapter. She would sit in his room, book in hand but unlistened to, and feel miserably duped.

Armed with the baton of the newspaper, Norah climbs upstairs and resumes her position of vigilance. If Patrick were here now, she thinks, he'd be thirty-four. She imagines a personable, jokey man (she imagines Louis) with a blond wife and three small children, their father's face (from the bank of photographs on the sitting-room mantelpiece) transposed on to a slender frame – and with a more trendy haircut. He would have called her Sis, breezed into the house all cheery and have been able to cajole their mother out of every sour and wrinkled mood. A capacity of which Norah would be jealous, of course. God, even her fantasies disown her!

On the off-chance that her mother is listening, she calls out the next clue aloud: 'Pined quietly in misery feeling the pinch, six letters, last one d.'

But it is no good. She cannot distract herself. The black squares of the grid are like holes torn in the sky. Compulsion, like the urge for nicotine, overtakes her. She picks up her mother's thin wrist, the scraggy chicken part at the back of her hand where she is just bone. Gathering the slack skin between her fingers, Norah squeezes. Hard. Her mother's eyes flicker open. She looks at Norah wordlessly but there is no shock, or even surprise. It is as if she expected it.

Then the telephone rings.

'Norah?' It's Trish. 'She's gone?'

Norah can hear the disbelieving wobble in Trish's voice.

'Yes,' she can hear herself saying, evenly, steadily.

'Nipped,' her mother interjects suddenly.

'What was that?'

'That was Tena. Tena's here with me.'

'Oh, Norah,' Trish says and there is a snotty sound, emotion clogging in her nose. Then there are noisy tears. She can imagine Trish's face reddening up, the fishy pout of her lips, her ugly wail. That's the trouble with caring, Norah thinks, it makes you care less.

'I should be there,' Trish says. 'Are you alright?'

Finally. Norah is about to answer but the lump in her throat won't allow it.

'Just come home,' she says. It sounds like a confession, as if she had told Trish about the bruise.

'Norah,' Trish rushes in, ruining the cadence. 'I have to tell you something . . . the reason I couldn't . . .'

There is a smothering sound; Trish wiping her face with her sleeve.

'Louis,' she says simply.

'What do you mean, Louis?'

'Nothing happened, Norah, I swear it.'

For some reason the group photograph at her wedding comes to Norah's mind. The guests scattered artfully on the lawn in front of the hotel and the photographer calling out designations – 'Bridal party, the bridesmaid, best man and the groom's parents, please.' There is Trish, swathed in the full-length plum taffeta with the spaghetti straps Norah had chosen, and Louis in his penguin suit, nuzzling his nose into her corsage. And Norah, foolish and deluded bride, thinking how lovely they get on so well. Like a brother and sister.

'It was me,' Trish is wailing now, 'all me, all in *my* head.'

And what about Louis's head, Norah wants to scream.

'He never knew . . . I swear to God. How could I tell him something like that? But I couldn't stay, that's why I went away. I couldn't be near the pair of you, feeling what I did . . .'

Norah puts her hand up to stop Trish though it's a useless gesture; she can't be seen. She doesn't want to be party to this, some secret Morse of her marriage being tapped out in front of her after the fact.

'I was trying to do the right thing . . .' Trish has moved on now to self-justification; Norah has to stem that.

'Do you want to say hello to Mother?' She hears Trish's intake of breath.

Norah places the receiver in the crook of her mother's neck. Her mother beams – a special smile for the prodigal. She leaves them to it. She rushes down the stairs, out the front door and into the street. It's early summer and Prosperity

Drive looks at its most benign. A phantom moon graces the still-bright sky. Windblown blossoms from the cherry trees nestle at the kerbsides; laburnums weep over the pebble-dash walls. The first street games would be starting about now – hopscotch, skipping and football. Standing outside the garden gate, she sees Finn Motherwell in his Aertex shirt, his ragged V-neck jumper, a pair of crumpled shorts and those spindly legs, knees like doorknobs. He's standing in goal, between two sweaters acting as goalposts, and he's sucking on his inhaler. When he fell over, all the boys thought he was fooling. When they couldn't rouse him, someone went for his mother. Norah remembered Mrs Motherwell in her flour-daubed pinny, hurrying up the street, then dropping to her knees at this spot. (One of the older girls had thoughtfully made a pillow of one of the goalpost sweaters.) Mrs Motherwell, a squat homely woman with prominent teeth, keened and moaned, while all the kids watched, aghast at this demonstration of passion. She crushed Finn's head to her breast like the marble Pietà in the Servants' Church. This must have been what it was like for Our Lady, Norah had thought; only begotten son took on a whole new meaning.

What she'd done or failed to do hadn't made any difference to Finn. As it wouldn't with her mother. Only the secrets and lies would persist, leaving their indelible marks.

BODY LANGUAGE

Suddenly, miles inland, Trish can hear the sea. It's in the middle of Beginners' English in an upstairs room at the Eureka Language School on the Corso Vannucci, the wooden casements thrown open to a lilac dusk and the lazy, muted purr of the *passeggiata* drifting up from the street. Seven eager Italians gaze up at her as, mid-sentence, her hearing ebbs away and the ocean rushes in. They are doing The Body. She is pointing to her calves – *polpaccii* – when the hissing starts. By the time she's got to *orecchio*, her ear is a seashell seething with tide. She dismisses the class early; it is too disorientating to hear their plaintive chorus of body parts coming at her in waves, as if on a staticky radio. She tries worrying at her ear to clear the sibilant fog. She remembers the sensation from childhood, the chlorine-clogged hum of the swimming pool. The trick then was to tilt her head sideways and wait for a trickle to emerge. She leans over but it only intensifies the underwater boom. She feels she's drowning in waves of home . . .

For as long as she could remember Trish had wanted to be elsewhere. When she was eight a new estate had been built at the end of Prosperity Drive. There were a half a dozen bungalows, detached, all of them different. These houses had lush open spaces in front in place of hemmed-in gardens and some of them had names emblazoned on timber signs or engraved on small boulders in the grass like the tombstones of deceased pets. For Trish it was like straying into a small patch of TV America. Here a boy in jeans and a baseball cap might appear out of one of the doorways and drive off in his father's Buick. Her best friend might live in Number 4 and be a cheerleader rather than Connie Long, fat, loyal and haunted by the Third Secret of Fatima, who lived over a newsagent's shop in the village. Trish pestered her mother to move.

'Don't be ridiculous, Patricia, they're way beyond our means.'

Means were often mentioned by her mother. It infuriated Trish; everything about her mother's candid widowhood infuriated her. Even the gritty courage of her mother's loneness made her mad. She remembered camping trips where her mother played the dad, collecting the kindling, lighting the fire, or outings to the countryside in an unreliable Volkswagen that she had belatedly learned to drive. Not many mothers drove then, and the necessity that had prompted her mother to take up driving (several years after her father's death) seemed to make it a heroic undertaking. She worked nights at the telephone exchange so she could be with her girls when they got home from school. Leaving Trish's sister Norah in charge, she would rush out of the house at eight in the evening oozing crisp scent and a daytime efficiency. She would ring from work on the hour to check that everything was okay. In the mornings Norah prepared breakfast and packed their lunches, while their mother slept. The house seemed hungover; she and Norah tiptoed about and talked in whispers while the golden glow from the bedside lamp leaking under the door of their mother's room gave off hints of bordello. Although there were only five years between them, Norah had always seemed much older. It was she who had been mother's little helper, witness to their father's death, a grave and stubborn child schooled in the intricacies of adult grief, a vigilant reader of moods. Because she remembered their father (Trish would practise calling him Dad but it seemed as slangy as referring to Christ's father as Joe) Norah had always seemed as weighty and grounded as a parent. For her the word had been made flesh. But for Trish her father hovered, incorporeal, like a notion of Christian perfection. Dead and revered he belonged to a time before the world had fallen. Or was it before Trish had fallen?

Trish liked to hear her mother talk about work – the flirty conversations she had with men while connecting them to far-off places, the gossip about the 'girls' at the exchange, their doomed romances, their broken engagements. When they rang up they would simply ask for Edel, and Trish would have to do a double take to remember that it was her mother they were talking about. This night-time place that her mother escaped to bristled with a youthful, dangerous energy, a far cry from Prosperity Drive where she and Norah were stranded among mothers and fathers. Trish despised all couples – those walking arm in arm on the street, or even the ones clearly at odds, hurling insults at each other like Connie Long's parents. The taunting confidence of even badly working families, the rectangular rectitude of them, made the world their mother had built seem rickety and frail as an isosceles triangle. All that work, all her mother's labours, only emphasised what they could never have: the seamless symmetry of family.

Trish does not remember her father; any knowledge of him comes through Norah. She conjures up Fifties films, a man with a hat and pipe and flecked tweed overcoat, the brilliance of hair oil, the complicated mysteries of shaving. She was six – and absent – when he died. A neighbour, Mrs Devoy, had taken her away for a few days to give her mother a break so that her father's death, for Trish, has become a time of lazy blur and unexpected reward. A seaside chalet, the crash of waves, the rough gaiety of the Devoy boys. This is as far back as her memory goes – to that china-blue timber hut, Mrs Devoy in a black bathing suit, her skin glistening with tiny specks of sand, lifting her high into the air against a shimmer of sea. When Trish thinks of her birth it is that moment on the beach as if Mrs Devoy had delivered her there on the sand. As if she had just popped out, shiny and new. It doesn't matter that it doesn't fit; wrong mother, for one. It is a milestone for Trish, the first conscious memory she is sure is hers.

As a teenager, Trish imagined her life as a film, as if every moment of her day was being recorded by an electronic eye. It buoyed her up to imagine the drum of a soundtrack in her ear, the glide of a camera in her wake, a voiceover more knowing than she was. It was the only way she could transform the stifling landscape of Prosperity Drive into the vast meanwhile of movies. (That and taking two European languages at school, shunning History for Italian.) Even when she went further afield, Trish could not shake off the sensation that they were living in an abandoned outpost. In the summer she and Norah would pedal for miles along the coast road to the public baths. They were open-air sea baths, penned in by whitewashed walls but with the wide open horizon clearly visible. The windswept esplanade pushed out into a thin, dirty sea with the lofty leftover bustle of Empire; the dingy seafront houses peeled. The Irish Sea sucked and slapped and retreated so far it seemed to disappear, leaving the strand puddled and bereft. When Trish thought of it now, she felt sorry for it, if it was possible to feel sorry for a place. From this distance she realised that her vision of home was coloured with a good deal of self-righteous, adolescent gloom. She had to concede that there had been moments when, in a sudden burst of winter sunshine, the cobalt-blue sea and the seagull-chequered beach could have been an exotic and undiscovered Arctic shore. But these transformations had always been fleeting, and as an adult, Trish could only achieve them when she was stoned.

In Italy she is emphatically elsewhere. In the ten years she's been in Perugia, her mother's mild eccentricities have given way to the bottomless pit of regression that is Alzheimer's. Early onset. She has to be spoon-fed – infant food, egg in a cup, milky tea from a beaker with a teat. When she drifts off in mid-chew, Norah has to bark to retrieve her attention. 'Mother, Mother!' (Both of them have stopped calling her Mam; it is too soft, too companionable.)

'They get stuck in a certain time,' the doctor has explained to Norah. 'Often the richest time of their lives, courtship say, or early marriage.'

'Which must be why she keeps on telling me to be quiet or I'll wake the baby,' Norah remarks when Trish rings home. 'She'll use the commode for the day nurse, but not for me, oh no! I have to take her to the loo . . .'

Norah's reports of their mother are marked by a cruel frankness, and although her talk disturbs Trish, she lets Norah continue. It's a trade-off for not being there.

'It's like potty training in reverse . . .'

Trish switches off, preferring to remember holidays years ago when her mother would gaily pee in the middle of a field in full view. There was no skulking in the bushes for her.

'In our day,' she would tell the girls, 'we just went in the orchard and buried it.'

Trish, a fastidious child, would avert her eyes as her mother lifted her skirts with flirtatious abandon. The only thing that would stop her was the witness of cows. Whenever her mother saw the black-and-white plaid of a herd she would turn and run. The cows would stare complacently, intent on their placid, lugubrious chewing, but for her mother they were somehow a threat: it was the only dark spot in her gaiety. Now she seems all dark spots, a querulous patient, reduced to the soiled intimate whiff of an invalid.

Trish steps out on to the Corso. There are things she should pick up – bread from the bakery, vegetables for dinner, some fresh pasta. But how can she function, half deaf, in the interrogative clamour of the marketplace? Besides, it is soothing to walk like this, melding with the drifting crowd, her jilted ear unable to tune into the sharp fragments of conversations all around her. It reminds her of her early days in Italy, surrounded by the babble of a language she didn't understand. It was a kind of newborn sensation to sit in a café or a bus assaulted by the racket of conversation whose meaning she couldn't hope to decipher. For several glorious months she was like a mute infant, wordless and uncomprehending, feasting on strange beauties, depending on exaggerated gesticulation. Innocent. But, like babyhood, it was a passing phase. She couldn't pinpoint the day when she didn't have to look out the windows of the train to check on the names of the stations, when she had ceased to remark on the nutmeg hills, or register the sentried cypresses and the umber church towers, when the landscape had retreated to a homely distance. It took several years but she had certainly reached that stage when Norah announced that she was coming to visit.

Even with Louis out of the picture, Trish dreaded the prospect. Norah would probably want to talk about her marriage break-up even though almost a year had passed since it had happened. If it were anyone else, Trish might have relished a post-mortem. Her early twenties were spent in such tortuous inquisitions with her pals. Long winey nights in perpetual dusk picking through the entrails of broken love with inferior men. But she'd never done that sort of thing with Norah. Norah didn't confide; she was too elder for that. And if she did bring the marriage up, Trish was afraid Norah would detect her guilt and mistake it for the fatal lack of empathy that had always dogged their relationship. Would she be able to last a week in Norah's company without succumbing and mentioning Louis's name?

When Norah arrived, Trish showed off shamelessly. The balmy nights, the lavender hue of Perugia's medieval streets co-operated in the ruse. Away from home where she was so rootedly righteous, Norah had seemed at sea, ponderous and heavy-limbed. She'd got sunburnt on her first day, which Trish saw as a ridiculous failing; she was bamboozled by the noughts in the currency. While Trish was out teaching during the day, Gianni showed Norah the sights. They zoomed around on Gianni's scooter with Norah riding pillion, clinging perilously to his slender frame. He was a Classics scholar but doing hours at the Università per Stranieri to pay the rent. Gianni's training meant he was the perfect tour guide. He spoke of the ancients as if they were immediate relatives; he read the architecture as if it were as obvious as motorway signage. For him history was not something separate, whereas for Trish the charm of Italy was its lack of associations. She did not want to have it all explained away, by Gianni or anyone else. But she was delighted that he was around for Norah's visit (though they had broken up shortly afterwards). He looked good with his dark shoulder-length hair and his unexpected green eyes and he had impressed Norah as thoughtful and steady. He had been a vital part of her armour; he had helped to throw Norah off the scent. But, she kept on reassuring herself, there was no need to worry. Norah had no idea, no idea at all.

The evening before Norah was due to leave they sat outdoors at a pavement table on the Corso at sundown drinking beers and watching the evening crowds stroll by. Norah had not mentioned Louis once, which unnerved Trish more than if she'd spent the week bad-mouthing him. At least that way he would have been a presence; this way it was as if he was dead.

'How long more do you think you'll do this?' Norah had asked.

Trish bristled, as if being in Italy were some trinkety experiment.

'What do you mean? This happens to be my life, in case you hadn't noticed.'

'But you can't be a penniless foreign language teacher for ever, Trish.' She couldn't work out if Norah's expression was pitying or stricken. 'It's just that Mother often asks . . .'

'Mother probably doesn't know who I am any more.'

'That's not true . . . she has moments when she's perfectly lucid.'

'She thinks I'm still a baby – you said so yourself.'

'Come home, Trish, before she forgets everything.'

But Trish did not want to see the shambling mother replica that Norah described; perversely, she wanted the tomboy mother of her teens, the woman who had embarrassed her by trying to make up to her what could not be made up for. Or the mother at the airport, biting back tears, repeating the only two Italian words she knew – spaghetti and Caruso. Or was that the beginning of the illness? She couldn't say to Norah – I *want* to forget everything and can't. And out of a kind of panic about Norah's naked entreaty, she asked, 'How's Louis?' Anything to distract from the coming-home business.

'What do you mean, how is he?'

'I mean, how are you two? Now, I mean.'

'I don't want to talk about this.'

'Do you ever see him?' Trish asked. She could hear the longing in her voice, but Norah was too irritated with her to notice. Could it be that . . .

'He's gone to America,' Norah said miserably. 'And he has someone else.'

Even further away than before, Trish thought.

Now she lets herself into the gnarled front door of the flat on Via Alessi, and climbs the stairs wearily, still worrying at her ear.

'Pat-ree-z-iah!' Claudia shrieks from the other room. '*Telefono!*'

It still irritates Trish, this strange elongation of her name with the squeal inserted in the middle of it and the long yawn at the end. She struggles with *their* names – the Fabrizios, the Giuseppinas – why can't they do the same?

'*La tua sorella*,' Claudia says as she retreats to her bedroom, half shod in slovenly bedroom slippers, cigarette in hand. Claudia smokes in a sullen sexy sort of way, drawing fiercely but exhaling slowly, leaving lazy queries of smoke overhead. Nursing her ear, Trish goes to the phone. She lifts the receiver. The hum in her ear adds to the echoey sense of distance.

'Trish?' Norah says tentatively.

Who else would it be, Trish thinks.

'It's Mother.'

'What about her?' Trish asks, panicky.

Three months ago, Norah had rung with the same tone of voice and told Trish that her mother was dead. She'd never understood why. Shock tactics? Some macabre carer's joke? Or an unconscious desire to punish Trish for a crime she didn't even know about? Every time she rings now, Trish braces herself. (After all, even in the story, the wolf finally came.) And Norah's lie about her mother being dead had another consequence. It had made Trish confess. About Louis. She'd felt a compunction to explain her absence. Thinking there was nothing to lose, she'd blurted it out. Not all the details, no; Norah wouldn't have wanted to hear that. But the scene replaying in Trish's head as she confessed was the engagement party when it had all started.

When Louis and Norah had got engaged, they'd had a party on a boat in the harbour. It was quite a showy thing for Norah but Louis was a party animal, a showman, jokey in a brotherly sort of way. He and Trish laughed at the same things; he was playful with her and she sort of flirted with him. But only because it was utterly safe – he was her sister's boyfriend and not her type at all. Buffet food was served below deck and Louis's musician friends (he played in a trad band at the weekends) were providing the music down there. Trish had come up on deck for a smoke. It was a Saturday afternoon, windy, a blue sky with racing cloud, and the air as zingy as

242

toothpaste. Dan Gildea, Norah's gay friend from work, was taking snaps of the happy couple.

'Come on, baby sis,' Louis called out to Trish and gestured to her to join them where they stood leaning against the guard rail. 'Hold it a minute, Dan.'

Trish sidled over and stood beside Norah.

'Don't want to be muscling in,' she said to Norah.

'Don't be silly,' Louis said, leaning out and winking at her.

'Ready?' Dan shouted.

There was a sudden turbulence behind them, a roaring swell and a fevered agitation of the water.

Next thing Trish felt Louis touch her on her bare arm. The one that was stretched along the rail behind Norah's back. Louis clasped it at the elbow and stroked it once. She felt a charge from it. Was it intended or did she just imagine that part of it? Something was changed by that touch, that's all she knew. Something in her. She leaned out to check but Louis's profile beyond Norah remained set. Just at that moment, Dan took the photo so Trish's face was obscured by a windswept nest of hair. But Norah kept the snap; she even had it framed, although Louis was a squinting parody of himself in it and Trish was reduced to a tangled blur. Only Norah was looking at the camera.

'Oh it's not for us I'm keeping it,' she told Trish. 'Look at me, I look like I'm about to be taken to the gallows.'

No, Norah had kept it because the commotion they'd sensed as the picture was being taken was a huge cruise ship that had glided into the frame as Dan pressed the button. The ship filled the entire background – a giant white wall of glinting windows, a riveted fortress on the move. There must have been six floors of decks and the passengers were crowded at the rails, a sea of indecipherable faces, some waving, others sending out semaphore flashes with their cameras, others just standing there, forlorn with farewell. The whale-ish ship dwarfed the three of them and blotted out everything else – the jaunty sky, the choppy waters, the landmark beacon at the mouth of the harbour.

'Surreal,' Norah would marvel. 'It's all about what's going on in the background.'

Trish had stayed for the wedding and then bolted. That touch had driven her to Italy and given her the elsewhere she'd always longed for. She'd told herself it was honour or renunciation, virtues she associated with Norah, but she suspects now it was simply cowardice.

The phone gives off a cackle.

'They've moved her, to the hospital,' Norah is saying. That's the way it is with Norah: no preliminaries.

'Oh.' Trish switches the receiver to her good ear.

'I think you'd better come.'

'I can't just drop all my classes . . .'

'Patricia!' Norah interjects sharply, the command of the sickroom. Several seconds tick by. Trish can hear a faint chipmunk babble in the background, a dozen other conversations jamming up the airwaves.

'If it's a question of money,' Norah offers.

'No, no, it's just . . .'

Superstition? That if she stays away she can ward it off. The truth is, she hadn't expected a warning. She'd expected a fait accompli, a swift and retributive absence as it had been with her father.

'I thought you'd want to be here . . . for the end. It's very close.'

Too close, Trish thinks.

'I'll see what I can do.'

She's angry with Norah – this is her territory; she knows how to do it. She was there when their father died. Mostly Trish doesn't want to face Norah, with the confession about Louis lying there between them.

'Hurry,' Norah says, 'please hurry.'

244

The note of pleading in Norah's voice scares her. She gets off the phone and promptly throws up.

When Trish wakes the next morning the room appears sluggish, but as soon as she tries to lift her legs over the side of the bed it becomes animated, and tossed by some unseen storm it begins a sickly rotation that makes her retch. She finds herself clutching the bedside table in a vain attempt to hold everything down, to slow the movement, to induce stillness. But even that slight exertion brings her out in a prickling sweat. The world seems to have shifted on its axis. It is slipping away from her like the deck of a sinking ship.

'Madonna!' Claudia exclaims. '*Che cosa?*'

'A brain tumour, probably,' Trish says, 'that's what got my father.'

Claudia lights up in the doorway of Trish's room. She blows her smoke rings out into the hall in deference to Trish's condition. Trish watches her intently, hoping that if she latches on to something fixed she will feel less queasy. But Claudia appears to be miles away, trapped in a vertiginous distance, like a slothful Virgin in a seashell grotto, reduced to a speck by an artist demented by the rules of perspective. It makes Trish's stomach heave to look at her. Meanwhile, booming in her ears, she can hear Norah's voice as if her temples house the breathy bowl of the telephone. She spends the day in a fever but by evening the room has stopped lurching around her and the nausea has abated. She feels well enough to go to the doctor – the English doctor. Trish has never fully trusted the Italian lexicon of illness; after all, they didn't have a distinct word for hangover.

'It's an inner ear infection,' the doctor tells her. 'Quite common. A simple course of antibiotics should clear it.'

'Will I get my hearing back?'

'Oh yes,' he says lightly. 'Any loss is temporary.'

While he is scribbling out the script in his illegible hand, Trish enquires about air travel.

'Well, as they used to say, is your journey really necessary?'

Trish hesitates. She feels a strange panicky rush, the prelude to denial.

'No . . .' she answers doubtfully, afraid that the doctor can see right through her, as if her deafness has made her transparent.

'Well, then,' the doctor says, rising. 'You can afford to wait.'

Out on the flinty blue piazza Trish feels curiously bereft. In the distance a church bell bleats. Or is that a cock crowing? A huddle of pigeons at her feet takes fright, flapping fiercely as they scatter skyward. The shuttered architecture averts its gaze. A cold wind whips about her as she stands on the deserted cobbles. The puddles shiver. Her clogged head throbs; in her belly she feels the umbilical dread of reconnection.

Flying back, the oceanic rage in her ear is replaced by an entombed silence. In the twilight capsule of the aircraft, she remembers her journey out. The cosmetic ease of Duty Free: the bleak rush of getting off the island; the anticipation of being in the heart of Europe and not secreted away on a tiny speck in the Continent's armpit; and trying not to think about Louis. She finds herself dissolving into tears. She's crying, but without sound it isn't like grief, it is like something simulated and shallow. She is in a different kind of elsewhere, tramping through a sonic snow, muffled and woolly. She thumps her ear with her fist, desperate to get it to work. But she is deaf to all appeals, even her own.

The light in the hospital room is warm and dim, the blinds tilted downwards. Trish and Norah sit, one on each side of the bed. The silence – apart from their mother's shallow breathing – and the crepuscular light make it impossible to tell what time of the day it is. The air is rank with the creamy, erotic smell of lilies. Trish bought them at the airport, not wanting to arrive empty-handed.

'Funeral flowers,' Norah said as she arranged them in a vase.

Trish resented the implied reproach. As if she'd got her timing wrong. Not late, but too early. The etiquette of death would always defeat her.

When she had arrived, Trish had approached her mother's bed cautiously. The chestnut rinse her mother had used in her hair had drained away leaving a delicate sheen of silver. Someone – probably Norah – had combed it and it lay fanned out on the pillow. Trish had bent over her mother in the bed. She was barely conscious, her eyes closed, her brow creased with the effort of drawing breath. All Trish could do was to lift her limp hand and hold it momentarily before letting it fall again. It had seemed inappropriate to kiss her – even on the forehead. (That was what you did to a corpse.) There was not a flicker of recognition. It was true what Norah had said, her mother had forgotten everything, including Trish.

Being close at hand has made no difference. There has been no absolving of grief, just a banal mood of solemnity. Her hearing has clarified but there is still a feeling of remove, as if she's thousands of miles away. She feels cheated. After so much evasion there is nothing to fear except this, an embarrassed anxiety, the secret wish for it to be over. She rises and paces up and down. She and Norah have been by their mother's bedside for almost a week. There is all the time in the world but they don't talk about Louis. Their days are punctuated instead by the routine sounds of the hospital which reach them in their shuttered room but lay no claim to them – the dull thud of footsteps in the corridors, the officious swish of doctors on their rounds, the squeal of trolleys. At mealtimes there is the metallic din of soup urns and the dolorous toll of aluminium domes clamped on dinner plates.

'The troops,' Mother mutters, 'the American soldiers. They're making too much noise. Every night, every night . . .' Her voice trails away.

Trish looks at Norah. For direction, explanation.

'She's wandering,' Norah says.

Mother stirs and opens her eyes, startled. She is not as frightening to look at as Trish had feared. In fact, she looks strangely innocent as if her mental regression has smoothed away the creases of age, as if she has undergone a purifying process.

'Victor,' she says feebly.

'Daddy isn't here,' Norah says evenly, 'it's just me and Trish.'

'Victor,' she repeats, 'I've done something terrible.'

Trish and Norah stand up, each holding one of their mother's hands, primed for a confession.

'Victor,' she says, 'I've killed a cow.'

Trish catches Norah's eye. They are both seized by a terrible giddiness. Norah is the first to titter, then Trish takes it up and soon they are laughing uproariously, spluttering behind their hands, unable to stop. Trish has images of her mother in a bullring, flourishing a red cloak, while a hapless cow veers and staggers towards her. The sacred cow, the fatted calf, the images come thick and fast. Norah is bent over double in the chair, tears streaming down her cheeks, groaning with mirth. A nurse comes to the doorway.

'Ladies!'

Trish and Norah look up at her, then at one another and a fresh volley of laughter explodes between them.

'Out!' the nurse commands.

They obey, still unable to stifle the laughter.

'I hope you realise,' she says sternly, 'that hearing is the last of the patient's senses to go.'

They only sober up when they are left outside in the corridor and the nurse closes the door of the room on them. They do not look at each other for fear of setting each other off again. They loiter in the hallway. The stairwell of the building is glass-covered, an atrium filled with the blush of a spring

248

sunset. After the darkness of the room it is almost as if it is they who have passed into another dimension – celestial and luminous. It soothes them. After a few minutes, the nurse opens the door of their mother's room and beckons them in, standing sentry by the door, her arms folded like a sceptical constable. She shakes her head gravely. Norah moves towards the bed. She stops. Trish hears a strangled sound, animal, primitive. It seems to emanate not from Norah's mouth but from somewhere deep in her belly. Trish is shocked; Norah is sobbing messily. She clutches at Trish's shoulder and burrows into her. There is a painful lump in Trish's throat where all her own feelings seem to have lodged. Here it is; she takes a deep breath. Mother is dead. And we laughed. Did our mocking gaiety kill her, she wants to ask. Were Mother's last words a final lucid gift or another of her florid meanderings? But there is no one to ask. She can feel the knobs of Norah's spine through the thin fabric of her blouse. Her body, huddled against Trish's heart, feels broken. Absurdity and grief, that's what they are left with, and between Norah and herself a kind of equality. In the face of death they are equally at a loss. She strokes Norah's hair. It smells of Mam and nettle shampoo. *Capelli.*

SICK, DYING, DEAD AND BURIED

Audrey Challoner has a glass-topped coffee table in her living room. Underneath is a removable tray divided into compartments of different sizes like the cubbyholes in an old-fashioned haberdashery counter for spools and pins and bobbins. The compartments house a series of whimsical objects – six marbles in a dish with tongues of blue and yellow like fossilised snails, a tiny tri-wing model aeroplane with Nazi insignia, a brooch depicting a spray of fuchsia and a sprig of green, an ornament of a swan with ruffled china feathers and a gaping chasm in its back (for flowers, a pincushion?), a small doll with a rag body and a plastic head crowned with a mop of blue hair, and a high-tinted, scallop-edged postcard from the Sixties, it must be, showing a beach scene in County Wexford. The items, seemingly random but so deliberately displayed, mystify because they are at odds with their surroundings.

Audrey's place, her friends say, pristine! You'd think it would be cluttered and homey; you're expecting a candy-coloured crochet throw over the sofa, some bold patterned curtains, a Turkish kilim on varnished floorboards, framed group snaps from adventure holidays abroad. Not *this*. Unadorned magnolia walls, beige carpet, a sofa the colour and texture of oatmeal. The blandness unnerves. It is not what they imagine of *their* Audrey, who is capable and cheerful and a bit of a bohemian. She is single and coming up for fifty.

Her bedroom, not often seen by visitors, gives a glimpse into Audrey's inner life although it's more library than boudoir. White bookshelves climb from floor to ceiling; there are teetering piles of paperbacks beside the bed – the in tray – and another scattering of volumes in smaller towers on the bureau in front of the window. Just now, for example, spine up, face down on the counterpane, is a slim volume of short stories, entitled *Diaspora* by an Irish writer, Ted Gavin, from a small university press in the US. Audrey is a demon on the Internet. At her book club – first Saturday of the month, a group of women of a certain age – she riles as often as she entertains. The others find her reading choices odd and pretentious because they are so determinedly not mainstream. She eschews the bestseller lists. She favours short stories over novels, because, she tells them, her concentration is fatally flawed.

'I'm plunged so deep into other people's lives at work that when I come home, I want something I can escape from easily.'

Perhaps that's why her flat seems like somewhere Audrey is perched, rather than inhabits. Her friends will tell you that Audrey resides here, but she 'lives' elsewhere, the children's ward at St Jude's Hospital, they mean. *That* is her world. Children with cancer. So when new acquaintances see Audrey's coffee table collection, they wonder if the items belong to child patients Audrey has cared for at St Jude's. Dead children. But they would be wrong. Audrey's treasures belong to the living. That is, living, as far as she knows.

It was the day her first child died, nearly thirty years ago now. His name was Phillip. Phillip Prince; it's a name she will never forget. Summer as if in insult crowned at the window, shimmering trees rustling on blue when he breathed his last. She feels motherly about Mr and Mrs Prince now but then they seemed no more than careworn shadows. Phillip was their first child. They can't have been much older than Andrey was, but then she was a young nineteen. His parents sat by his bedside, a hand apiece manacling his five-year-old wrists, as if that might hold him down, keep him here. His bald head and translucent skin made him seem like an ancient sage. Soon he would be. Soon he would know more than the three adults in the room about the darkness that falls after death.

Audrey knew it had happened before the parents. She'd never seen anyone die before but she had heard about the death rattle and she recognised it when she heard it because she was youthfully proficient and, unlike Mr and Mrs Prince, she was not saddled with hope. But she wasn't brave enough to make the pronouncement. She could do the cheery optimism, which mostly meant telling barefaced lies to the child, but not this awful verdict. She got up busily as if she had somewhere to go, someone to see, and made blindly for the door. Then she was ploughing down the sunlit corridor like a sluggish swimmer. She needed air, she told herself. She could see the sliding doors ahead of her, opening and closing like a pair of lungs but she knew she could not inhale until she got outside. The air came in leafy gasps, the rose garden a blur of peach and lemon. The hospital kiosk, like a doll's house, stood in the midst of the furred bloom, its ice-cream machine humming whitely. A child – a healthy child – in a smocked dress was being handed a cone by an unseen adult hand, a flake plunged into its creamy whirls, the tip curled like an elegant question mark. Audrey did not want to see one jot of childish pleasure; it wasn't enough to be outside, she realised, she needed to get away completely. Away from this sick place.

The avenue beyond the gates to the hospital was lined with houses. There were aprons of communal green in front of them where a crowd of the neighbourhood children played. Audrey had come to know them through their games. Hunched over jacks on the cracked pavement near the gates of St Jude's, intent as ancient seed-throwers. They would scatter the jacks – like tiny metal models of atoms – then throw the spongy black rubber ball high in the air. Before the ball bounced they had to harvest all the strewn jacks, cupped in their palms or balanced on the front of their hands. The rhythm of the game always fascinated Audrey; the scattering so insouciant, the attempts at retrieval frantic.

Out on the street the children played sprawling games of soccer, Cops and Robbers with clothes-peg guns, German jumps, hopscotch. Though they weren't supposed to, they often infiltrated the grounds of St Jude's, which gave them plenty of cover for games that involved hiding. Like Sick, Dying, Dead and Buried. This was a new one for Audrey. Here's how it worked. One child was on the den and counted to ten. The others splayed out and hid. At the end of the count they had to emerge and find another refuge. The child who was 'on' was armed with a ball and tried to target the others as they darted about. The aim was to kill by degrees. One strike of the ball and you were sick, two and you're dying, and so on. Did other kids have such morbid games in their repertoire, Audrey wondered, or was it a response to their proximity to St Jude's and the omnipresence of painful death?

But the day Audrey was trying to escape, the children were not involved in play. They were collecting for charity. They had set up a row of stalls along the avenue, five or six upturned orange boxes with planks set across them. Someone had made a banner, strung between a pair of bamboo sticks. It was made of an old sheet with a message scrawled inexpertly on it in black magic marker – HELP BIAFRA! The letters spelling help were large and capacious but the word Biafra was crushed together and downward falling where the childish hand had run out of space. Against her will, Audrey halted.

*   *   *

'We're going to have a bring-and-buy sale,' Norah Elworthy announces, 'for the starving children of Biafra.'

Norah is going through her religious phase. Soon she will lose her vehement faith. The death of her father will shake her belief not only in God but in the goodwill of the universe. But for now it is intact and she is emboldened by this opportunity afforded by a civil war thousands of miles away on the continent of Africa. It is not hard to convince her young companions. They are Irish, after all – famine is lodged in their DNA. The dread of the workhouse and the stench of the coffin ships lurk in their collective memory. They have read about the Great Hunger in their history primers, heard their parents argue about it with rebellious relations who bang the table after too much drink and talk darkly of blight, yellow cornmeal and Empire. But, more immediately, they are responding to beetle-browed Norah Elworthy, who, even at ten and a half, has a commanding presence. She is their moral compass and a bossy-boots. She it was who told them there were child patients in St Jude's Hospital at the end of the avenue, and who, when they disbelieved, led them in single file around the back of the ward buildings to prove it. She pointed to the bald kids tied to drips in the upper windows and mouthed the words of the Gospel: 'Suffer the little children . . .'

For the charity sale Norah divided the kids into pairs and ordered them to call to every house on Prosperity Drive, Barry Denieffe remembers. She was like a general, or a political canvasser. She dragooned adults as well as children into her plan. She was the kind of kid adults liked, or liked to think they resembled when they were young. Which is why even Miss Larchet, who was pretty stuck-up most of the time, contributed, giving them jewellery – a garish red and pink brooch, a string of beads, a swan ornament thing. If it had been Barry she'd probably not have answered the door; he had rung the bell too often asking for his ball back when it sailed over the high creviced wall of her back garden, which ran along the stretch of road where they played their makeshift games. If she did give it back, it was accompanied by a peeved complaint about her Calla lilies being snapped and broken by his uncouth games. Uncouth – it was the first time he'd heard the word.

'We need good stuff,' Norah had told them. 'Proper things that we can sell.'

If the adults demurred, she told her troops to say: 'Jesus says we must give until it hurts.'

Although Barry couldn't remember Jesus ever saying such a thing.

'Enabling' is how he will describe Norah at his AA meetings thirty years later, surprised that she figures in his addiction confessional.

'But in a good way,' he will add hurriedly. Some words in this parlance of redemption have been traduced.

He had never thought much about Norah in the intervening years; well, you don't, do you, unless there's call for it? Childhood companions get lost, some of them literally. He remembers Finn Motherwell, claimed by asthma when he was eleven. Died on the street during a game of soccer. Barry has cause to remember. He was lining up for a shot at goal when it happened. Finn was standing guard in the goalmouth marked by two woollen cowpats on the concrete. Barry dummied at the last minute, knowing that Finn would go the wrong way. Even at that age, his instinct was never wrong. (The killer instinct; that's how his last manager in Colchester described it when he put Barry on the transfer list. The killer instinct he no longer had.) Finn dived away from the swerving ball – GOAL! – and fell awkwardly. He never got up. What would have happened if Barry had missed? Or if he'd lost the ball in a tackle with one of those Devoy boys a minute before he took aim? Would Finn still be alive? Barry has spent years brooding on this, although Finn's name never comes up at AA.

Maybe because Finn is dead. Norah Elworthy, on the other hand, is very much alive. Barry sees her on Prosperity Drive almost every day. He is back at home living with his parents, on the dole, doing odd jobs; she is looking after her mother. But when he spots her, he cannot bear to meet her gaze, let alone talk to her. Ridiculously, he feels Norah Elworthy is disappointed in him.

Dying. Victor Elworthy is all at sea with the word. Yesterday he was living; or at least, he didn't know he was dying. Now he has moved into the waiting room. Edel is being stoic about it. So stoic that Victor doesn't know what she's thinking. Over the years, his wife has become a mystery to him and even this – diagnosis, verdict – has failed to break her secretive carapace. Where once he thought he knew her, now he's totally at a loss. When they met, Edel had made a play for him; came up to him bold as brass and asked him out. She seemed brazen and direct. Uncomplicated. That's what he had liked about her. But she had fooled him. Now that they have shared twelve years together, a house, a bed, and two little girls, Edel seems to be the very opposite. She is hidden and helpless, yet full of a shrill kind of resistance to him, particularly where the girls are concerned. As if it was she who had a thing growing in her head.

When the doctor made his pronouncement, Edel drew her breath in sharply then sighed as if someone had taken a burden from her. The consultant, dressed in a white coat like a posh grocer, said the word.

'How long?' Victor asked. Isn't that what you're supposed to ask?

The consultant pulled a face like a boy found out in a lie. Victor doesn't even remember what he said; he only knows it sounded like a job estimate – in single figures.

The day before yesterday he was on shift; now he's ordered to be idle. Because of what the doctor knows. He's lying on the couch in the back room because it's darker in here and light disturbs him. He's always worked nights so he's got used to being sunk in a kind of twilight. Now he's been thrust into the daylight and it seems too bright, too busy for him. It's two in the afternoon and he can hear the girls scampering in and out of the house; Edel has the front door open to save her having to let them in all the time. They're involved in organising some kind of a bazaar – at least Norah is, and Trish is doing her bidding. Norah's been back and forth several times with a swag-bag of goodies she's begged from the neighbours. Tomorrow they're going to set up stalls on the avenue and sell the donations for a good cause.

'For the dying children of Biafra,' Norah says when he asks. She seems to stress the word dying. Or is that just him?

The children don't know, of course. Not yet. How could he and Edel tell them when he cannot believe it himself? He can't believe that this blustery day of early summer, with a little hint of rain on the wind, is his last. He's alive still, of course, but every day is his last now. He can't believe that this is how it's going to end – so soon, so bloody unfinished. He is panicky and calm in equal measure. In the calm moments he lapses into a post-mortem view of himself and his life – like what went wrong with him and Edel. He can admit now that things between them have not been right for years. He thinks it was Patrick – the baby son they lost between Norah and Trish. He'd been dead for some time in the womb, they told Edel, but she hadn't noticed. That's when things started to sour, Victor believes. Edel seemed to think that all he'd ever wanted was a son and heir, and that she had failed to deliver. She pre-empted his disappointment by presuming he already blamed her. To tell the truth, he hadn't cared that much then about his name carrying on. There was time, after all. Now there isn't and he's furious.

When they came out of the consultant's office, he even thought of saying to Edel why don't we climb into the back of the car and do it there and then, like I'm a kerb crawler and you're on the game. But he didn't. Edel would have been repulsed. As if the only thing the news had made him feel was that he wanted to give her one. When that's not it at all. Being in the waiting room has made him greedy. Greedy to have and to hold. He wants to grab hold of the girls, Norah in particular. He doesn't know why. He shouldn't have favourites but damn it, man, he's dying, and she's his firstborn and it's Norah he wants. To touch her and hang on to her for dear life.

'Norah,' he calls, weakly. 'Norah?'

The stalls were laden with battered treasures. An armless doll with eerily closed eyes, any number of cheap gawdy ornaments, a box of marbles, several Dinky cars, a set of dominoes, stacks of comics and women's magazines, some *Reader's Digest*s, a couple of furry toys, jigsaws, moth-eaten paperbacks . . . The children crowded together behind the stalls – there must have been a dozen of them – as Audrey fingered their lovelorn merchandise.

When she looked up, there was Mo Dark. He was the only child she knew by name because he lived in the porter's lodge with his mother, Nita, who worked in Accounts Payable. He would stand out, anyway, what with the colour of his skin. The fat girl, who seemed to be the ringleader, prodded Mo forward.

'He's a Biafran orphan,' she said. 'He was smuggled out in the last airlift by an Irish missionary.' Despite herself, Audrey smiled. Mo looked sheepish. He knew she knew it was a lie. But a lie in a good cause. And Mo was skinny and dark enough to fit the bill.

'These are his Airfix models,' the girl went on, 'he's donated three of them.' The spindly planes sat on the counter – beautiful and intricate.

The blue-rinse doll was the next to catch Audrey's eye.

'It's had a hair transplant,' the smallest of the girls told her, a dark, sprite-like creature. 'See!' She parted the doll's middle-aged perm to demonstrate. A bald doll with a new head of hair. Audrey wanted to laugh out loud. Has God done this, she wondered. Has God got a sense of humour?

'Lemonade?' another girl demanded, perilously holding up a large jug filled to the brim. 'Only thruppence!'

'Hetty's mother made it,' the ringleader informed her. Hetty poured it gingerly into a paper cup. Audrey grimaced as she swallowed; it was eye-wateringly bitter.

'Fairy cake?' Hetty urged.

'Julia baked them,' the ringleader said, pointing at a tall girl with a grey gaze and a brown fringe that kept catching in her eyelids.

'Or these glossy magazines?' prompted a gangly boy, holding up copies of *Vogue*.

'Woo-hoo!' another boy jeered. 'Barry likes ladies' maga-zines!!!' He had the knotty look of a scrapper but then he broke into a terrifying wheeze, smothered by a deep draw on an inhaler.

Surrounded, Audrey scoured her uniform pockets for small change. Soon, she would have to go back, explain herself. She'd probably be fired; a dereliction of her duty of care. If you can't deal with grief, you're in the wrong job, she could hear Matron say. What about the parents? How do you think they feel? Audrey peeled back the paper casing around the fairy cake and bit into the sawdusty taste of desiccated coconut.

Irene Devoy was doing the ironing on a midsummer's Friday afternoon in an empty house. Rory and Owen in Irish college for a glorious three weeks; Fergal over at his Nana's, Liam at work. Six months pregnant, she found the silence of the house oppressive with the children away and had to have the tran-sistor radio on, even if it was turned down low, so as not to feel completely alone. When the boys were about, there was no respite; they brought the flurry of the street with them. They were always grappling with one another, pushing and wrestling and no matter how many times Irene sent them back upstairs to come down properly, they thumped about the house as if they were intent on bringing the very walls down. But without them, it seemed too solid, too enclosing, and seethed with absence.

When the doorbell rang – a set of chimes that rang once when the bell was pushed and sounded a lower note with a disappointed cadence when the finger of the caller was lifted off – Irene knew by the length of the exhale that it was a child. One of the neighbourhood kids looking for the boys, she supposed. When she answered she found Norah Elworthy on the threshold with her younger sister Trish in tow.

'Rory and Owen are not here, girls,' she said brightly. A bright tone could be deflective, especially with children, and often worked to dispel her own gloom.

Irene always had difficulty placing Norah in terms of age – was she older or younger than her Rory? She could never remember. But she knew Trish was nearly six. She was born the same day as Fergal, she and Edel Elworthy like twin barges on the street, eyeing each other's bumps competitively. Norah was uncertainly plump, hair tied wispily in two limp plaits with a severe middle parting. Despite Edel's best efforts, Irene noticed that she always looks slightly dishevelled as if keeping her hair pert and her clothing straight was all too much for the girl. Trish, on the other hand, was scampish-looking, much darker and prettier than her sister. Her hair was cropped short – not the way Irene would do it if she had a girl, too tomboyish – but her clothes, a navy pinny over a white T-shirt, were just so. Hard to believe those two came out of the same house.

'We're looking for donations,' Norah said, 'for the starving children of Biafra.'

Irene had seen the photographs. The flyblown faces, the distended stomachs, ribcages like bared teeth.

'Money?' Irene asked, sighing. They were plagued during the summer by children with their hands out – bob-a-job, selling lines for charity.

'No, we don't want money,' Norah said, 'we want things. We're having a sale. A bring and buy sale. You bring something and then you buy something else.'

The girl might find it hard to keep her hair and clothes straight but Norah could be a haughty miss. Still, it was a good cause.

'I might have some cast-offs from the boys. In the garage. Follow me.'

The Elworthy girls trailed after her as she heaved the up-and-over garage door. She rummaged first in the shelves on the dim back wall of the garage. More Liam's domain. Nothing much there – some neglected-looking tools (Liam was not what you would call a handyman), the blade of a hacksaw, some fishing line on a spool. On the floor there were a number of cardboard boxes filled with miscellaneous items, old toys, things that no longer worked. The first items of her own she came across were a stack of her magazines. *Women's Weekly*, *Women's Own*, *Women's Realm*. At the bottom of the pile she found years-old issues of *Vogue*. She didn't know why she kept these. The fashions displayed inside – the floral shirtwaist dresses, the Chanel suits – which used to give her so much pleasure, were now very dated. They belonged to a world that was as impossibly glossy as the paper they were printed on. But Irene had belonged to such a world once, if only in a minor key. In her early twenties she had been a beauty queen. Now she was rummaging through boxes in her suburban garage, the mother of three sons with another on the way, a mound of ironing to get done and no help in the house. She threw the *Vogue*s after the other magazines, into Norah's large plastic bag.

In one of the wooden crates there were some old soft toys belonging to the boys, too grubby to be passed on to the new baby, a couple of jigsaw boxes with thousands of pieces, half of them missing, probably – in they went. This was handy, she thought, a way to control the rising tide of stuff that three boys and a grown man generate. In another of the boxes marked in Liam's hand DO NOT THROW AWAY she found some *Reader's Digest*s. She looked at the dates – some of them went back to before they were married. They were clutter, pure and simple, taking up space that could be used more productively. If she could clear away these boxes on the floor, then Liam could park the car in here again. Wouldn't he thank her for that? He was always saying they were turning into the Fortunes, whose car had moss growing in the window frames from being left out in all weathers. There were a couple of Ed McBain paperbacks – Liam liked those tough guy kind of books; private dicks, wasn't that what they were called? And he liked war. Here were some Nevil Shutes. Holiday reading, he said, but she felt sure he wouldn't read these again. Maybe it was his work that made Liam hang on to everything. He was in the Department of Public Works. He was forever talking about restoring and renovating, cleaning monuments, resurrecting the past. Remembrance. That's when she thought of the postcard. Afterwards, she would wonder if the idea had been there all along, because the thing Irene really wanted rid of was tiny. A needle in a haystack.

'Hold on there,' she ordered Norah and Trish and hurried back into the house. She climbed the stairs and went into Rory and Owen's room. She reached in under Owen's bed, her fingers finding dust-bunnies until they hit something solid, a rectangular tin box that once contained a selection of Turkish Delight, a Christmas present from one of Liam's maiden aunts. It was Owen's treasure box. Irene rummaged through a set of football cards, a shiny conker, two small marbles (or were they the eyes of a blinded teddy?), a pencil sharpener, a sticky badge from the Horse Show, until she found the card lying face down on the floor of the tin like a groundsheet. She considered for a moment getting rid of the entire box. That would be easier to explain. But none of these other things were offensive to her. Just this, the card. Irene lifted it out and looked for one last time at the girl in the picture from five summers ago. The girl who'd been their maid. The girl who was dead now. Who had killed herself in this house. Who was dead and mourned, not by Irene, but by her nine-year-old son who kept this as a memorial to her. Irene slid the card into the patch pocket of her apron. She closed the lid of the box and pushed it back under the bed, sending it as far as she could into the cobwebby darkness. Maybe Owen would forget there ever was a tin box. She went downstairs, out the front door and back into the garage where Norah was still patiently waiting. She heaved a set of *Reader's Digests* from Liam's box and slipped the card into one of them before tossing them into the gaping mouth of Norah Elworthy's bag.

The doll's name was Flossie, and it was given specifically to her by Auntie Babs – not like most of her other toys, which were hand-me-downs from Norah. Auntie Babs, who was her godmother, sometimes stayed over in their spare room when Daddy was at work and Mam wanted to have some fun. Flossie had a plastic head, arms and legs but her body was soft and pillow-like. She had shoulder-length blond hair and a fringe. She was Trish's favourite doll. She'd had Flossie since she was three. Which was ages ago. Flossie went everywhere. To bed, on holidays, to school. She had been chewed on, been sick over, trampled on, driven over by Daddy in the car, even put through the washing machine and the wringer, but as Mam always said – Flossie was indestructible. But that wasn't true, was it? Flossie had got sick. Her gorgeous blond hair began to come away in handfuls.

There were bald patches all over the top of her head; her fringe disintegrated. Trish was inconsolable. When she took Flossie out on the street, Mary Elizabeth Noone said the doll must have picked up nits at school and that's why her hair was falling out.

'Your doll is as stupid-looking as you,' Mary Elizabeth said.

Trish ran home, patting Flossie's thinning head.

'Well,' said Mam, 'we'll have to send her to the doll's hospital, the place where sick dolls are made better. If her hair is falling out then she must be very sick.'

Flossie had to be kept in the hospital for seven days and Daddy collected her when it was time. When he produced Flossie from behind his back, Trish couldn't believe it. He'd brought the wrong doll home. This Flossie no longer had long blond hair; she had a perm and it was blue! Trish examined Flossie closely; everything was the same – the pink dress with netting that she'd worn into the hospital, her cloth shoes, her long-lashed eyes – all except for the new hair.

'It's a blue rinse,' Mam said and she and Daddy seemed to be smiling. 'Just like Granny Elworthy!' Mam added, and Daddy didn't smile any more.

'She's had a hair transplant, see,' Mam said, parting Flossie's curls to show Trish a new skullcap of plastic that Flossie had acquired from which the blue hair grew. But Trish didn't want to see it. This wasn't Flossie but some skullcapped impostor, a changeling doll the hospital had sent back in Flossie's place thinking Trish wouldn't notice. It wasn't just the Granny Elworthy hair; everything about Flossie had changed.

She could never love her in the same way; how could she? She wasn't the same doll any more; not the doll to whom Trish had whispered all her secrets. Where were those secrets now? Buried under Flossie's sewn-on scalp, that's where. And lost to both of them.

When she heard Norah telling Barry Denieffe that they should give until it hurt, Trish knew what she would do.

'You're going to donate Flossie?' Mam asks. Disbelieving.

'For the starving children of Biafra,' Trish tells her seriously.

'Aren't you the best girl, for giving away your favourite dolly?' And she gives Trish a hug and smothers her with kisses.

For the first time Trish feels the cool thrill of deception. By saying nothing she has fooled her mam. It's a lie without words. She feels a hard pellet in her heart where before she knew only softness. She can't wait now to be rid of the doll with the strange thing growing on her head.

They cannot know it but those children saved her. If they hadn't been there, Audrey might well have kept on going, become known as the probationary nurse who walked off the job just weeks from getting her badges. They stopped her in her tracks, pushed their way into her drama, the living asserting their precedence over the dead. The living with all their little trinkets. How poignant and pointless the things we leave behind, she will think often over the years as she gathers up the belongings of her little patients who've passed on. Often the parents can't bear it, don't want to be reminded of the gay balloons, the spangled optimistic get-well cards, the stick drawings by small invalids. Audrey never keeps these; she gathers them in cardboard boxes, tags them and puts them in an office in the basement that Nita Dark found for her. (Nita knows every nook and cranny of this place.) In case the parents should ever come back. They never do; never want to set foot in St Jude's again.

Audrey has never kept a memento of a sick child. But the treasures of the healthy children on Prosperity Drive are something else. These she keeps as talismans: the lucky objects that kept her loyal to her vocation and taught her this. Distraction is what we seek; like children in the midst of a tantrum, we can be diverted by shiny inconsequential things, a change of tone. When she looks at them, Audrey considers these her real badges of honour.

Of all of them, the postcard is the thing Audrey treasures most. Blank on the back, she had found it stuck between the pages of a *Reader's Digest* in the job lot she bought from the children that day. She thought the magazines would be handy for the waiting room in St Jude's. Short, distracting and not too demanding; that's what you need when you're waiting for bad news and you've exhausted your store of small talk. At the very least, there's the cartoons and the little teasers and jokes. When the card fluttered out, Audrey kept it. She didn't know why. The randomness of it, she supposed, as if it was meant for her.

It is, she thinks, like a child's eye view of heaven. China-blue sky, albino sand, lime green and red buckets and spades. Stalks of tough seagrass frame the view as if the photographer, like a peeping Tom, had parted the stalks to steal the image. There is a young woman in the mid-ground wearing a dark dress, her legs folded beneath her, her profile shaded by a straw sun hat. A striped canvas windbreak shelters her and a baby, who's lying on its back on a turquoise beach towel, curled hands aloft. You can just about make out the plump folds of the child's thighs and the pale globe of its hairless head. The mother has her hand on the baby's stomach which is clothed in something white. Maybe she's tickling the child; you can imagine it gurgling with glee. Or maybe as a new mother she can't bear not to touch the child, the umbilical connection made flesh. Either way, mother and baby are absorbed in each other, their gaze ruling out the rest of the scene. There are some swimmers in the sea, a couple of children thrashing in the shallows. In the far distance, the beach sweeps away into the white litter of a seaside town and the blue hills.

The image evokes the burnished contentment of a childhood day at the seaside with all its gay accessories – the sun hats, the windbreak, the buckets and spades. Or perhaps it is simply the memory of heat that the postcard captures. Whatever it is, Audrey knows that in her dark days – and she has had them – how could you not? – she imagines that this is where all the lost children have gone. To a day littered with colour and a sickle-curved beach that seems to go on for ever.

WHILE YOU WAIT

Edel had never told anyone how she and Victor had met. She was ashamed of it because it had not been a lucky accident. She had seen him and wanted him; the direct line between wanting and having had never been so clear to her. He had been sitting at the heel bar. It was the latest innovation at Roches Stores, an American idea. There was a high counter like a saloon bar and a row of tubular stools with red leatherette cushions, fixed to the floor with bolts. A neon light that read 'While U Wait' flashed on and off overhead. It was a Monday, mid-morning, quiet. Edel had already twice tidied all the little compartments on the electrical counter where she worked, sorting the miniature bulbs and the fairy lights, standing the squat white fuses upright, marrying the two-pronged plugs, male and female. She was loading coins into the till when she saw him halt at the counter opposite. She busied herself – Roches' biggest boast was 'our staff are never idle'. She stacked batteries while she watched him heave himself up on to one of the high stools at the heel bar and unlace his shoes. He deposited them on the countertop and she heard him say 'Heels and soles'. He had a newspaper folded into his jacket pocket and he fished it out and began to read.

There was something absurd and defenceless about him sitting there in his stockinged feet. The heels of his socks were worn thin and she could see the dull rose of skin through them. There was a hole in the big toe. It put him at a

268

disadvantage, she thought, as she eyed him surreptitiously. His dark hair was cut jauntily and slicked down with hair oil which gleamed under the store lights. He had a fleshy face, scrubbed and babied-looking. He wore heavy-framed spectacles. Oh dear, she thought, they'll have to go. He was smartly dressed, a tweed sports jacket (no elbow patches, thank God) and a shirt and tie. There was a noticeable crease in his dark pants – a mother's touch, she hoped. A clerk, she guessed, taking his elevenses out of the office. The shoemaker set to on the shoes. It was a noisy machine with a belt drive that whined like a dentist's drill. The heel bar seemed to Edel like a pocket of heavy industry in the midst of household linens, electricals and cosmetics. It had the fumy smell of a factory and the clattery serious air of male business. The regular customers were nearly all men; the women who came to the heel bar were usually limping and in distress, bearing a stricken stiletto or a single shoe with an amputated heel.

Heels and soles took less than ten minutes, Edel knew. She would have to move quickly. She was alone at the counter and shouldn't leave. Vi (no, she corrected herself, Miss Hunter – Roches' policy forbade staff using one another's Christian names, too familiar) would not be back from her break for another fifteen minutes and the shoemaker was already on to the left shoe. The neon sign tantalised. The shoes were being handed over now. Money was changing hands. There was the sharp ring of the till. Edel watched as he bent over to tie his laces. Then he eased himself down from his high perch. He flexed his feet in his newly minted shoes, turned on his fresh rubber heels and walked away. And then she noticed that he had left his newspaper behind. She darted out from behind the counter across the aisle, whipped the paper and ran after him. She caught up with him at the main entrance. Cold blasts of air came in through the revolving door, meeting the dry heat of the store. She tugged gently at his sleeve. He wheeled around.

269

'Your newspaper,' she said, 'Sir.' (More of Roches' policy.)

He smiled, at first surprised, then gratified.

'Why, thank you, Ma'am,' he said.

She saw a flicker of appraisal. Her move.

'Why don't you ask me out?' Edel asked boldly.

The revolving doors gasped hot, then cold.

'Why don't I?' He smiled cheekily, then stashing the paper under his arm was swept away in the cool carousel of the glassy doors.

A week later, Victor Elworthy came back and bought a two-pronged plug at the electrical counter and asked Edel Forristal to a matinée at the Savoy.

Edel felt she had come a long way. She felt it particularly when she went home to Mellick. And contrary to her expectations it was not a pleasant sensation. She had been so homesick in the city at first, staying in a damp bedsitter on the North Circular Road where the bulbs were always blowing and the public phone in the hallway was always ringing – but not for her. She spent weeks waiting for someone to shout up into the well of the landing – 'Call for Number 4'. She felt rebuked by the gay chatter of the girls in Number 3, their stifled laughter on the landing on their way back from a late night, their sleepy early morning conversation. She lived near the cattle mart then. She remembered the loneliness of those drear November mornings, watching the cattle being shipped in, their wild eyes visible through the slats of the trucks, their caked tails waving feebly, their plaintive protests audible over the hissing of tyres, the jangle of bicycle bells, the drone of buses. It made her feel doubly desolate. The bellowing cattle reminded her not only of home, but of the loneliness of home, the suffocating sadness of a place that felt already abandoned even before she had left it.

Then she met Babs who worked in Hosiery. They moved into a cheerier flat. Granted there was still green mould growing in the shared bathroom down the hall and the electricity meter was greedy as an infant. Suddenly in the midst of cooking dinner the last coin would drop down and the bubbling of potatoes, or the chops hissing on the pan, would quietly subside like the stealthy withdrawal of affection. The hothouse glow of the two-bar fire would fade slowly to black while plumes of steam from their damp washing, straddling the backs of the kitchen chairs, gloomily exhaled. When Edel looked back on it, everything in this world seemed metered, monitored, rationed. Oranges were a luxury; war a live memory. But after six lonely months Edel felt she had arrived.

The city became, thanks to Babs, a place of possibility. Babs knew where to go – picnics in the Botanic Gardens, afternoon tea at the Metropole where you could easily snaffle a second iced fancy from the cake tray if you took the precaution of sharing a table. Edel would remember this time as a kind of courtship. A courtship with the city itself in which the crowded tram rides to the sea and the smogged rough and tumble of the municipal baths were like shyly offered gifts. She liked the city's mix of serious grandeur – the pot-bellied former parliament, the flint-faced university, the declamatory statues of patriots – and the slatternly charm of the streets with their fruit sellers, their littered pavements, the garish fluorescence of ice-cream parlours. It was just such a mixture of gravity and contingency that she wanted in a man.

Victor worked nights. He was a Linotype operator on the *Press*. Later in their courtship he had taken her on a tour of the works one Sunday morning when the case room was idle. He proudly showed her his keyboard, which to Edel looked for all the world like her mother's treadle sewing machine. Bigger certainly, more masculine, the heavy ingots of lead hanging on pulleys hinting at a more weighty purpose. But what was he, really, only an industrial typist, Edel thought, refusing to be visibly impressed. Another evening he took her to see the presses run. They stood in the loading bay, a smell of ink in the air as the press thundered and rattled. Only then could Edel begin to understand Victor's urgent pride in his work – the hugeness of the press, the pulse and noise like the roar of war. Oil-begrimed men clambered on the platforms of the vast machine beneath the feathery wave of the newspapers as they reared and dipped overhead with the crazy motion of a rollercoaster. Other men sorted and bundled the copies as deftly as if they were large decks of cards. Then, packed and smacked, the papers juddered down rollered chutes into the black gape of the delivery vans. All in the dead of night, as if secretly. Saturday was the only evening they could meet, and even then Victor was wide awake and buoyant at midnight when Edel was ready for bed. She tried not to dwell on this mismatching too much; it brought her back to the manner of their meeting. By rights, she should have waited. Waited for the right man to come along. Trusted to chance.

Edel had no real desire to learn to drive. She had been quite happy to sit back and be a passenger. But Victor was insistent.

'Come on,' he said, 'there's nothing to it.'

But when she sat behind the wheel she felt it was intrinsically wrong. She should not be in charge of something so large and powerful. And she wasn't in charge of it. Even turning the key in the ignition made her fear the car would suddenly leap into life.

'Not until you put her into gear,' Victor said, snorting with laughter.

They inched around the back haggard in Mellick, Edel nosing the car tentatively around the perimeter, past the black doorways of the outhouses, circling the water pump on its altar of concrete, the rusting mangle in its bed of nettles. These things seemed grounded and necessary, while she sat in a candyfloss car, playing. She did not feel so bleakly inauthentic in the city with Victor. In fact, he was considered quite a catch, a man with a job and a car, good-looking in a neat, presentable way, smart, keen. Keen at first, Edel thought. Lately she had noticed a certain creeping reserve and she wasn't sure if it was her own nervousness about losing him, or a cooling on his part. Some reserve of her own prevented her from asking. The nerve she had used to attract him deserted her at close quarters. She had begun to brood about what a young man with a car and a salesman's good looks could get up to on sunny afternoons when he was free to wander the city alone. She felt acutely the need for something definitive to happen. Perhaps that was why she had asked him to come home with her for the summer holidays.

'Well,' Victor said finally, laughing. 'We can't just sit here. Let's try again. And remember . . . the clutch.'

Damn him, she thought. Teaching her to drive had been all his idea, anyway. Edel suspected that it was boredom; they were into their second week at Mellick and in this setting Victor had seemed ill at ease, his jocular manner a handicap in the face of the busy disapproval of the Forristal household. It was the haymaking season so the house was empty for the long hot afternoons and Victor was at a loose end. He had offered to help but Ned, Edel's brother, had considered this preposterous. As he did Victor's presence. He was a city boy; what would he know about such things? He might as well have been a woman, as far as Ned was concerned.

The Zodiac was Victor's only trump card. It conferred on him a status he would not have otherwise enjoyed. He ran Edel's mother into town to do the shopping; he drove Ned to the creamery. Ridiculous and all as they thought the large sugared lozenge of a car was, the Forristal family found it – and Victor – useful.

After a few days Victor took her out on the open road. Strangely, it was easier away from familiar sights and Ned's reproachful looks when he returned to the house in the evening to find Edel stranded in the yard with Victor, helpless with laughter, as the car juddered and stalled. Her mother considered the whole driving business unseemly. She just about tolerated being driven about by her daughter's young man. She suffered Victor's eager offers of transport with a mute embarrassment. But seeing Edel behind the wheel was another thing altogether. It just wasn't proper. That's what she thought, Edel knew. Away from the sceptical eyes of home, and out on the empty tarred road, Edel could build up some speed. She wanted to succeed at driving, not for her own sake, but for Victor's. Particularly if he was having doubts about her.

Edel had never been as conscious of her background before. But seeing the way her mother and Ned lived through Victor's eyes made her feel anxious. Ned's spattered wellingtons standing splay-footed on the brush mat inside the back door, the crude washboards and tin bath they used for the laundry, the chipped crockery, even the scummy top on the milk carried in an enamel jug straight from the dairy, spoke of a dour futility. The constant feeding of the range, the endless hauling and carrying, the grinding impoverished repetition of their routine began to oppress her. Ned had made his peace with Victor in the way that men did. They had found their common ground and traded information about cars and tractor parts, engines and horsepower. But her mother had been more resistant. Victor was the first man Edel had ever talked about, let alone brought home.

'You're getting to be a bit of a speed merchant,' Victor said, interrupting her thoughts: '50 mph, no less!'

She braked immediately.

'No, no,' he said, 'don't do that. You're really getting the hang of it now.'

Gliding through the dappled countryside in the glinting sunlight with Victor, she convinced herself he was right. She *was* getting the hang of it. She rounded a bend and almost collided with a herd of cows.

'Whoa,' Victor said as if it were he who was driving the animals.

Edel geared down and applied the brakes gently. All she could see ahead were the black-and-white rumps of a dozen beasts lazily swaying while a young lad with a stick hollered at them.

'Great,' Victor muttered under his breath, 'we could be behind this lot for hours.'

'They won't have far to go,' Edel said, 'probably to the next gate.'

She was happy to chug along behind the chequered cows, watching their flaky flanks and skeetering hooves on the tar and keeping a safe distance. They were in no hurry, after all.

'Come on, come on,' Victor urged.

The slow patience of the countryside irritated him.

After about half a mile, the young boy swung open a gate on their right and urged the cattle in off the road, threatening and cajoling by turns. He stopped as Edel eased the car by, and stood almost in salute as they passed. He had heavy straw-coloured hair, a knotted little face, small contemptuous eyes. He stood for several minutes looking after them. Edel watched him in the rear-view mirror, a small, defiant figure standing at a gate.

The sun was very low now and they were driving due west. A mile further on, they veered around another bend in the road into the full glare of the setting sun. Victor leaned over to pull down the visor to shield Edel's eyes. As he did, something solid and heavy blundered across her vision. Everything seemed to go dark as if a large rain cloud had plunged the sky into stormy relief. But this thing, a corpulent shadow, kept moving. Edel braked, the car slewed dangerously and she came face to face with the petrified eye of a Friesian just as the bonnet of the car ploughed into its mud-caked flank. There was a soft, cushioned thud as the car glanced off the animal and spun wildly, skidding headlong towards the ditch.

'Jesus!' Victor yelled as they came to a jolting halt on the rough camber, and the engine cut out.

He peered out the passenger window at the felled cow lying on its side and thrashing ineffectually. Blood wept from a jagged gash in its belly that showed its livid innards and streamed on to the tar road in a sticky pool. Edel, lifting her head from between her hands which were still gripping the steering wheel, saw only the cow's eye watching her with mute, terrified appeal. Then the animal moaned.

'Let's get out of here,' Victor said.

'What?'

'I said, let's get out of here.'

Edel hesitated. She knew exactly what should be done. She should get out of the car, run back to the youngster who had been driving the cattle, and get him to summon his father. He would come with a knife and cut the animal's throat to put it out of its misery. Edel had seen it done several times. But going back would mean owning up.

'Shouldn't we . . . ?' she began.

'Ignition,' Victor commanded and for the first time behind the wheel she was swift and decisive, as if all the hours of instruction had been for this moment. She did as she was bid, turning the key, feeling the power surge up through the accelerator as the car righted itself and moved confidently forward. But by the time the power had reached her fingertips it had been reduced to a faint but pervasive trembling.

A couple of miles further on, she pulled in at a shady crossroads. The sun had gone down. Victor got out slowly and went to examine the front of the car. There was a large dent in the radiator and a blood-flecked hollow in the left wing where metal had met flesh.

'Thirty quid's worth at least,' he said, coming round to her side and opening the driver's door.

She dragged herself over to the passenger side. Her limbs felt like lead.

On Edel's instructions, they hid the car in the outhouse of the abandoned house with the oak tree. The large shed was out of sight of the boreen and no one would have any business going in there, she told Victor. They told the Forristals they'd run out of petrol.

'Typical,' Ned said, 'that's women for you!'

And so the ill-advised expedition became all Edel's doing.

Victor left first thing in the morning to take the car back to the city and get it fixed. Edel invented excuses for his departure. Egypt taking control of the Suez Canal, she said, they'll be needing him at the paper.

'Took fright, didn't he?' her mother said.

She and Victor would never talk of it again; not then, nor after they were married. It was only a dead cow, Edel would tell herself. Or a dying cow, dead now one way or another. But in her nightmares it would resurface, Victor shouting, 'Clutch, clutch!' and she wailing, 'No, no, I can't. I can't do this!' She would awake aghast in the dawn hours (Victor beside her, still on nights, newly asleep) with a windscreen image of the scene vivid in her head. The beast's bewildered eye, its baffled pain, the bloodied haunch of the sugarplum car and Victor hissing at her to put her foot down.

ACKNOWLEDGEMENTS

Some of these stories have previously appeared in the following publications:

Arrows in Flight (Scribner/Townhouse), *Bridges: A Global Anthology of Short Stories* (Temenos), *The Chattahoochee Review*, *The Faber Book of Best New Irish Short Stories*, *Glimmer Train*, *The Honest Ulsterman*, *If Only* (Poolbeg), *Irish Short Stories* (Phoenix), *New Irish Short Stories* (Faber), and *The Threepenny Review*

I have a loyal band of first readers who saw this work at various stages and offered insight and advice – Rosemary Boran, Joanne Carroll, Orla Murphy and Terri Scullen. To them, a heartfelt thanks. Thanks are also due to the Arts Council of Ireland for a literature bursary awarded in the course of writing the collection.

Mary Morrissy, October 2015